THE BESTSELLING NOVELS OF
Tom Clancy

THE BEAR AND THE DRAGON

President Jack Ryan faces a world crisis unlike any he has ever known. . . .

"INTOXICATING . . . A JUGGERNAUT."

—*Publishers Weekly* (starred review)

RAINBOW SIX

Clancy's shocking story of international terrorism—closer to reality than any government would care to admit . . .

"GRIPPING . . . BOLT-ACTION MAYHEM."

—*People*

EXECUTIVE ORDERS

Jack Ryan has always been a soldier. Now he's giving the orders.

"AN ENORMOUS, ACTION-PACKED, HEAT-SEEKING MISSILE OF A TOM CLANCY NOVEL."

—*The Seattle Times*

DEBT OF HONOR

It begins with the murder of an American woman in the back streets of Tokyo. It ends in war. . . .

"A SHOCKER CLIMAX SO PLAUSIBLE YOU'LL WONDER WHY IT HASN'T YET HAPPENED!"

—*Entertainment Weekly*

continued . . .

THE HUNT FOR RED OCTOBER

The smash bestseller that launched Clancy's career—the incredible search for a Soviet defector and the nuclear submarine he commands . . .

"BREATHLESSLY EXCITING!"   —*The Washington Post*

RED STORM RISING

The ultimate scenario for World War III—the final battle for global control . . .

"THE ULTIMATE WAR GAME . . . BRILLIANT!"
                                                    —*Newsweek*

PATRIOT GAMES

CIA analyst Jack Ryan stops an assassination—and incurs the wrath of Irish terrorists. . . .

"A HIGH PITCH OF EXCITEMENT!"
                                        —*The Wall Street Journal*

THE CARDINAL OF THE KREMLIN

The superpowers race for the ultimate Star Wars missile defense system. . . .

"*CARDINAL* EXCITES, ILLUMINATES . . . A REAL PAGE-TURNER!"   —*Los Angeles Daily News*

CLEAR AND PRESENT DANGER

The killing of three U.S. officials in Colombia ignites the American government's explosive, and top secret, response. . . .

"A CRACKLING GOOD YARN!" —*The Washington Post*

THE SUM OF ALL FEARS

The disappearance of an Israeli nuclear weapon threatens the balance of power in the Middle East—and around the world. . . .

"CLANCY AT HIS BEST . . . NOT TO BE MISSED!"
—*The Dallas Morning News*

WITHOUT REMORSE

The Clancy epic fans have been waiting for. His code name is Mr. Clark. And his work for the CIA is brilliant, cold-blooded, and efficient . . . but who is he really?

"HIGHLY ENTERTAINING!" —*The Wall Street Journal*

Tom Clancy's
Op-Center

MISSION
OF
HONOR

Created by
Tom Clancy and Steve Pieczenik

written by
Jeff Rovin

BERKLEY BOOKS, NEW YORK

TOM CLANCY'S OP-CENTER: MISSION OF HONOR

A Berkley Book / published by arrangement with
Jack Ryan Limited Partnership and S & R Literary, Inc.

PRINTING HISTORY
Berkley edition / June 2002

Copyright © 2002 by Jack Ryan Limited Partnership and
S & R Literary, Inc.
Cover art and design by Complete Artworks Ltd.

Visit our website at
www.penguinputnam.com

ISBN: 0-425-18670-9

BERKLEY®
Berkley Books are published by The Berkley Publishing Group,
a division of Penguin Putnam Inc.,
375 Hudson Street, New York, New York 10014.
BERKLEY and the "B" design
are trademarks belonging to Penguin Putnam Inc.

PRINTED IN THE UNITED STATES OF AMERICA

10 9 8 7 6 5 4 3 2 1

Acknowledgments

We would like to acknowledge the valuable assistance of Martin H. Greenberg, Larry Segriff, and Robert Youdelman, Esq.; Joel Gotler and Alan Nevins at Artists Management Group; and Tom Colgan, our editor at Berkley Books. But most important, it is for you, our readers, to determine how successful our collective endeavor has been.
                                                 —Tom Clancy and Steve Pieczenik

ONE

Maun, Botswana
Monday, 4:53 A.M.

The sun rose swiftly over the flat, seemingly endless plain.

The landmarks had changed in the decades since "Prince" Leon Seronga had first come here. Behind them, the Khwai River was not as deep as it had been. The grasses of the plain were shorter but more plentiful, covering familiar boulders and ravines. But the former army officer had no trouble recognizing the place or reconnecting with the transformations that had started here.

One was his personal growth.

The second was a result of that growth, the birth of a new nation.

And the third? He hoped that his visit today would begin the greatest change yet.

Walking into the new dawn, the six-foot-three Seronga watched as the deep black sky seemed to catch fire. It started at a point and spilled all along the horizon, like liquid flame. Stars that had been so bright just moments before quickly dimmed and faded like the last of fireworks. Within seconds, the sharp, crescent moon dimmed from sickle-edged brilliance to cloudlike. All around him, the sleeping earth became active. The wind began to move. High-flying hawks and tiny kinglets took flight. Fleas started to creep along Leon's army boots. Field mice dashed through the grasses to the north.

That is power, thought the lean, dreadlocked man.

Simply by waking, by opening a blind eye, the sun caused heaven's other lights to flee and the earth itself to stir. The retired Democratic Army soldier wondered if Dhamballa felt a hint of that same prepotency when he woke each morning.

It was still too early in his ministry. Yet if a leader is a leader born, he must feel something of that flame, that heat, that strength.

The temperature climbed rapidly as daybreak spread along the plain and into the sky. The red softened to orange, then yellow, and the deep blue of dawn became the soft blue of day. Perspiration began to run down Leon's sides, down the small of his back, and along his lower legs. It collected on his high cheekbones, under his nose, and along his hairline. Leon welcomed the slick moisture. It kept his flesh from burning under the sun's merciless glare. It also prevented his jeans and high boots from chafing his thighs and ankles. It was amazing. The body knew how to take care of itself.

While nature unfolded as it always did, with both grandeur and detail, there was also something special about this morning. It was more than what Leon was about to do, though that was extraordinary enough. Without realizing it, he had been waiting over forty years for this moment. There were fifty-two men marching behind the former Botswana army colonel in two tight columns. He had trained them himself in secret, and he was confident of their abilities. They had parked their trucks by the river, over a quarter mile from the distribution compound, so they would not be seen or heard.

But for a brief time, the sights and sensations took the fifty-six-year-old Botswana native back to when he had first witnessed dawn on the majestic floodplain.

It was on a savagely muggy August morning in 1958. Leon was eleven years old, the age of passage for men of the small Batawana tribe. But while Leon was told he was a man, he did not yet feel like one.

He clearly remembered walking between his father and his uncle, both of whom were big and powerful. They were followed by two other village men who were equally strong of back and stamina. In Leon's mind, they were what a man was supposed to be: tall and upright. He did not yet understand the concepts of confidence and pride, loyalty and love, bravery and patriotism. Those qualities came later, the qualities that made the inner man.

Back then, he found that he had the will and ability to slaughter animals for food, but he did not yet understand that it was a man's prerogative—and often his responsibility—to kill other men for honor or country.

Leon's father and his uncle were both seasoned hunters and trackers. Until that morning, Leon had never caught anything more ferocious than hares and field mice. While Leon walked alongside the men, he knew that he did not truly walk among them.

Not yet.

On that morning nearly a half century before, the five men had gathered outside the Serongas' thatched hut. It was well before sunrise, when only the newborns and chickens were awake. Before leaving, the men ate a breakfast of sliced apples and mint leaves in warm honey, unleavened bread, and fresh goat's milk. Even though her son was going on his first hunt, Leon's mother did not see them off. This was a man's day. A day, as his father had said, for men who were among the oldest hunters in the human race.

That morning, the men were not armed with anything like the Fusil Automatique assault rifle Leon Seronga carried now. They were armed with nine-inch knives tucked in giraffe-skin sheaths, iron-tipped spears, and a coil of rope carried around the left shoulder. That left the right arm unencumbered. Barechested, dressed only in sandals and loincloths, the men made their way unhurriedly along the eastern edge of the flat Khwai River floodplain. Eleven miles to the north and thirteen miles to the south were the villages of Calasara and Tamindar. Straight ahead, to the east, was game.

The men walked slowly to conserve their energy. Leon had never been so far from the village. The farthest he had ever gone was the Khwai River, and they had crossed that after an hour. They stayed wide of the grass, which stood nearly as tall as his lanky shoulders. It hid burrowing adders and brush vipers. Both snakes were poisonous and active in the early morning hours. But to this day, Leon still vividly remembered the sound of the grass bending gently in the early morning breeze. It reminded him of the way rain sounded when it slashed through the trees on its way to the village. It was not a sound that came from a single place. It seemed to come from everywhere.

Leon also vividly remembered the faint musky scent that rode the early morning breeze from the southeast. His father Maurice told him that was the smell of sleeping zebras. The men would not be hunting zebras because they had very sensitive ears. They would hear the men coming, and they would panic. Their hoofbeats and braying brought lions.

"And lions bring fleas," the older man had added quickly. Even then, Leon knew that his father was trying to take some of the scare from what he was about to say.

The elder Seronga told him that as kings of the plain, lions were privileged to sleep late every morning. When the cats woke, when they had yawned and preened, they would hunt zebra or antelope. Those were animals with meat on them, enough food to make a difficult chase worthwhile. Maurice assured Leon that lions ignored men unless they got in their way. Then the great cats would not hesitate to attack.

"For a snack," Leon's father had said with a grin. "Something to give to the cubs."

Leon took the warning very, very seriously. The boy had once dangled a piece of hemp over the head of a small dog. It jumped up and bit Leon instead. The bite had hurt him terribly, burning and stinging at the same time. Even Leon's toes had tingled with pain. He could not imagine the agony of being dragged down by lions and bitten all over. But he had faith that would not happen. His father or the other men would protect him. That was what adults and leaders did. They protected the smaller members of the family or tribe.

Even the smaller men, like Leon.

On that great and majestic morning, the hunters from Moremi were after giant forest hogs. The brown-and-black bristled herbivores inhabited the intermediate zones between forest and grassland. That was where hog ponds and the reeds they liked could be found. A family of the animals had been spotted the day before by one of the men. The pigs moved in small groups and tended to become active not long after dawn, be-

fore predators were up and about. Leon's father had told him
that it was important to catch the hogs when they were just
beginning to forage. They knew the lions were not awake yet.
That was when their attention was primarily on food and not
on potential predators.

The men were successful that morning. They killed a fat old
hog that had wandered from the group. Or maybe the group
had wandered from the hog. Perhaps they had left it out there
as sacrificial prey. The knee-high pig was speared by Leon's
uncle, who had crept close from behind and then launched
himself at the beast. Leon could still hear the animal's squeals
of pain and confusion. He could still see that initial jet of blood
from behind the pig's shoulder. It was the most exciting thing
he had ever experienced.

Leon's father had rushed forward. The dying animal was
flipped onto its side before the other hogs were even aware
that anything had happened. The beasts did not scatter until
Maurice had already knelt on the beast's shoulder, pinning it,
and slashed its throat. The animal was quickly noosed with
one of the ropes. That would prevent it from bleeding and
attracting carrion feeders like silverbacked jackals. The blood
would also keep the meat moist as they transported the heavy
carcass under the searing sun.

While Maurice and his brother stanched the bleeding, the
young boy and the other men found two long branches. These
were quickly stripped with the knives and used as carrying
poles. Before the pig was trussed, Maurice paused to slip a
bloody finger between his son's lips. Then he bent very close
to his son. He wanted the boy to see the conviction in his eyes.

"Remember this moment, my son," the elder man said
softly. "Remember this taste. Our people cannot survive without shedding blood. We cannot exist without risk."

Less than four hours after the men had set out, the animal
had been slung loosely between the poles and was being carried home on the shoulders of the men. Leon walked to the
side. His job was to hold the end of the noose and keep it
tight. Leon was never so proud as when they walked into the
village with his kill on the end of a leash.

The hog was a good-sized animal that fed the village for two days. After the meat was finished, its bones already carved into trinkets for sale to occasional tourists, another group of men went out to hunt. Leon was sorry not to be going with them. He was already thinking of tackling a zebra or gazelle and maybe even a lion. Leon even told his mother of his dream to kill a great cat. That was when he got his nickname. Bertrice Seronga told her son that only a prince could get close enough to kill a king.

"Are you a prince?" she asked.

Leon said that maybe he was. The woman smiled and began calling him Prince Leon.

Leon went on nearly 300 hunts during the next five years. By the time he was thirteen years old, Prince Leon was already leading his own parties. Since a son could not command his father, Maurice proudly withdrew from those hunts so that his son could learn about leadership. During that time, most of the kills were also his, though Leon never did slay a lion. But that was not his fault, he decided. It was the lions' doing. The king of beasts was much too smart to come within range of his spear.

Seronga wondered, then, if the lion is so powerful and so clever, who could kill it? The answer, of course, was death. Death killed the lion just as death must kill the most powerful of men. Leon wondered, though, if the lion was strong enough to hold death back. He had once watched a lioness die after making a rare solo kill of an antelope. He wondered if the lioness had expended herself in the chase. Or, knowing that she was soon to die, had she held off death long enough to enjoy this one, last chase.

In 1963, the world changed. Leon's thoughts turned from the habits of animals to the habits of men.

Hunting became more difficult as the men of the Batawana tribe had to go farther and farther to find game. At first, they thought the ranging habits of the animals had changed. Seasonal lightning strikes had caused fires that changed the landscape. Herbivores had to follow the grasses, and meat eaters had to follow their prey. But in 1962, men from the capital city of Gaborone and from London arrived in the small village by airplane.

At the time, Botswana was known as Bechuanaland. It was a British protectorate and had been so since 1885. It was being protected, Leon had been taught, from South African Boers and other aggressors. The white men from Gaborone and London told the Batawanans that the animals were being hunted out of existence. The men said that the tribespeople had to change the way they lived or eventually they would perish.

The men from Gaborone and London had a plan.

With the blessings of the elders of all the local tribes, the government transformed the entire floodplain and vast, surrounding areas into the Moremi Wildlife Reserve. Tourism rather than hunting would become the mainstay of the people of the region.

A good deal of money was paid to every family. Construction teams arrived by truck and airplane three weeks later. They razed the old village and built houses of wood and tin. Farther out, where there were no signs of civilization, they also built the Khwai River Lodge. They made that of stone and tile. Each week, the trucks that brought food to the lodge also brought food that the villagers could buy. Schools were established. Missions that had been responsible for education and medical care took a more active role in the running of the local villages. The old gods, gods of the hunt and of thunder, were displaced and forgotten. Radios and then television replaced storytelling. European-style clothes and jewelry and housing were coveted. Life became less arduous.

Less exciting.

The animals of the floodplain were saved. So too, the Batawanans were told, were their lives and their immortal souls.

Leon had never been convinced of that. What his people had gained in security they had lost in independence. They had been given knowledge at the expense of wisdom; faith had taken the place of religion. They had secured life and surrendered living.

When he was eighteen, Leon left the village. He had read about a man in Gaborone, Sir Seretse Khama, whose Democratic Party was working to free his nation from British control. Leon enlisted in Khama's Democratic Army. It was a peaceful group of nearly three thousand men. Their job was to hand out leaflets and ensure the security of their leader. Leon did not enjoy that work. He was a hunter. Together with five men who felt the same way he did, Leon formed the Brush Vipers. They worked in secret to collect intelligence on key British officials. Among their discoveries was a plot to frame Sir Khama for embezzling funds from his Democratic Party.

Within days, the chief plotter vanished. Sir Khama never learned of the plan against him or of the counterstrike. But the English knew. Leon had made very certain of that. Despite the quiet demands of the foreign office, the Englishman was never located. Few outsiders who went into the Okavango Swamp alive were ever seen again. Men who went into the swamp and had their throats slashed from ear to ear were never found. Leon did, however, give the chief foreign officer the man's watch. The Batawanan told him he had no desire to start a collection of British timepieces.

The CFO got the message.

A year later, the British ceded control of the country. Bechuanaland became the Republic of Botswana, with Khama as its first president. The changes that had started were not undone. People liked the goods from Europe and America. But President Khama made it difficult for other groups to enter his country with new distractions and foreign ideas.

It was only then that Leon and his young colleagues realized what a huge responsibility they had won for themselves. They were no longer protecting one man.

Like Khama himself, they were looking after a nation. In a continent buffeted by ancient tribal rivalries and wars of land, water, and precious minerals, they were suddenly responsible for the security of nearly half a million people. Their own families depended upon their vigilance.

Leon was given a commission as second lieutenant and joined the Botswana Defense Forces. He served in the army's elite Northern Division. Among other regions, Batawana and the floodplains of Maun were under their jurisdiction. Seronga helped to organize security along the border with war-ravaged Angola. He also instructed native Angolans on intelligence-gathering techniques to use against the Portuguese. Like his brothers in Botswana and South Africa, he wanted to see the Europeans driven from Africa.

Despite the efforts of Leon and the president, the nation continued to change. Leon watched as his people became fat and eviscerated. Like the hogs Seronga and his father had hunted so long ago, the Botswanans were prey for hunters: men from Europe who came back with money. Botswanans sold the hard-won coal mines, the copper mines, the diamond mines. They had thrown off political control only to surrender to economic control. The revolution had been for nothing.

During this time, his greatest comfort was his own family. Lieutenant Seronga married when he returned to the north. He and his wife had four sons. In time, they began bearing him grandchildren.

It was for their sake, finally, that he left the Defense Forces. He retired on a pension for a time. But then something happened. He found a new cause, a new army to lead.

Leon and his men rounded a clump of high grasses. Some of his old soldiers had returned. They had done the legwork for this crusade. They had found and watched the deacon missionaries. They were supported by new and idealistic fighters such as Donald Pavant, his right-hand officer. Pavant was a little extreme, but that was all right. His youth and impulsiveness were balanced by Leon Seronga's age and wisdom. Other men had joined them, including a handful of white warriors Gaborone, men who believed in their cause. Or perhaps in the money to be made by driving the foreigners out. Regardless, they were here.

Seronga and his unit came upon a familiar pond. The watering hole was smaller than it used to be. Irrigation had changed the floodplains, and the pigs had been relocated. Only the field mice and a few flightless birds came here to drink. But it was still unmistakably the pond where he had begun his road to manhood. In the rising sun, Leon imagined he could still see the long shadows of his father and the other men. He could still taste the blood of the pig on his lips.

And one thing more. Leon could still see his father's dark eyes, hear his father's words: *"Our people cannot survive without shedding blood. We cannot exist without risk."*

Fortunately, the other members of Leon's old Brush Viper unit felt the same as their former leader did. The men had remained in contact over the years. When one of the Brush Vipers heard Dhamballa speak, an opportunity presented itself to undo the mistakes that had been made. Leon went to hear the man in Machaneng, a village to the east. He was captivated by what he heard. He was even more impressed with what he saw: a leader.

They had to work with Europeans again, only this time they would do it right. They would take back what had been lost.

Distant structures appeared on the horizon, beyond the waving grasses. There were six of them built of logs with ceramic tile roofs. The sun glinted on the white satellite dish in a clearing. It played on the chrome of the cars and vans parked in the dirt lot.

Leon motioned for his men to stay low behind the grass. He knew that they should have come here in the dark, but it was important that he see the sun rise. Besides, the tourists inside the compound would not be up yet. Scouts had reported that the shutters remained closed until nearly eight A.M. The foreigners liked their sleep.

Saving the nation would not be easy. And it would not be bloodless. But that was to be expected.

Revolutions seldom were.

TWO

Maun, Botswana
Monday, 5:19 A.M.

Father Powys Bradbury opened his eyes a moment before the sun peeked over the windowsill. He smiled as he watched the white walls and ceiling brighten. It was good to be back.

The South African native usually rose at first light. Throughout his forty-three years as a priest, Bradbury had made it a habit of saying his morning offering at the break of day. The prayer was about dedicating one's day to the Sacred Heart of Jesus. It seemed only right to do that when the day began, not when it was convenient.

The short, wispy man continued to smile as he lay in his small twin bed. The bed was tucked in a corner of the white-walled room. The only other pieces of furniture were a night table, a wardrobe at the foot of the bed, and a desk across the room. There was a simple laptop computer on the desk. Father Bradbury used that primarily for E-mail. The computer was surrounded by stacks of books and periodicals, which were also piled on the floor of the small room. The priest subscribed to newspapers from across the continent. He enjoyed finding out what other Africans were thinking.

The wardrobe contained two sets of his priestly vestments, a white bathrobe, a windbreaker for cool winter nights, and one pair of jeans and a Cape Town sweatshirt. Father Bradbury wore the jeans and sweatshirt whenever he played soccer with his more sports-minded congregants. Apart from the short pajamas he had on now, these were the only clothes the priest owned. He believed wholeheartedly in Psalm 119:37 which said, "Turn away mine eyes from beholding vanity; by Your way give me life."

Father Bradbury's only indulgence was a compact disc player that he kept on a shelf above the desk. He enjoyed listening to Gregorian chants while he wrote or read.

Father Bradbury stretched soundlessly. There was no one in the adjoining room. The seven deacon missionaries who were attached to the Church of the Holy Cross were in the field. But silence was a way of life for Father Bradbury. He had first developed a fondness for it at the Seminary of Saint Ignatius in Cape Town, where silence was mandatory for all but prayer. He felt there was something civilized about quiet. It was something that separated humans from the braying, roaring animals of Africa. He had never agreed with the notion that noisy, crowded cities were the hubs of civilization. To him, civilization was a place where sophistication was not as important as loving cooperation.

In just a few moments, the energies of the white-haired priest would be turned to the service of God. His attention would go to the people of the surrounding villages. Father Bradbury took a minute to enjoy one of the few times of the day that were truly his.

The night before, Father Bradbury had returned from a five-day visit to the archdiocese in Cape Town. He always enjoyed his meetings with Archbishop Patrick and other mission priests. The cathedral itself was made of shining white stone, an inspiration to see and to work in. There were two bell towers framing the main portal, each of them five stories high. Their ringing could be heard all over the city. Archbishop Patrick himself was also an inspiration. He always had stimulating ideas about how to bring the word of Christ to people who had little familiarity with the Church and its teachings. The seven men actually had a great deal of fun as they went to the Veritas Production House to make audiotapes. Using simple readings and commentary, the clergymen outlined gospel values. These audiotapes would help the deacon missionaries of southern Africa bring new believers to the fold. Unlike Father Bradbury, who remained in his own parish, the deacon missionaries were the men who worked in the field, who went to the isolated villages and regions shaken by poverty, disease, and hunger.

Father Bradbury drew a deep breath of the dry, hot air. He exhaled slowly, then listened to the wonderful silence. Once in a while it was broken by chacma baboons that approached the compound in search of a handout. Though the grasses, insects, and fruits they ate were plentiful, the dog-nosed primates were among God's laziest creations.

There were no apes today. Nothing stirred but the wind. And it was absolutely delicious.

The air in Father Bradbury's native city was dusty and humid, and the streets were loud, even at night. The clergyman had been in Botswana for eleven years. He had spent seven of those years as a deacon missionary. He still had the rough feet and sunburned face to prove it. He had spent the last four years as parish priest at the forty-seven-year-old Church of the Holy Cross, which ministered to the neighboring villages of Maun and Moremi. Bradbury missed the church terribly whenever he was away. He missed the calm, he missed his ministry, and most of all, he missed the individual congregants. So many of them had given their time and their energy to make the church an extended family. The priest loved being a daily part of their lives, their thoughts, their faith.

Whenever Father Bradbury was gone, he also missed the tourists. For purely proselytical reasons, Archbishop Patrick had supported the construction of the tourist center adjoining the church. Each week, over four dozen tourists came from Europe, North America, the Middle East, and Asia. They enjoyed great comfort. Porcelain bathtubs, teak floors, mahogany sleigh beds, wicker chairs with thick cushions, and sumptuous native rugs. They ate from bone-handled silveware and copper plates. There were unfinished oak beams all around them. Guests had rich cotton sheets on the beds and elegant damask tablecloths in the dining area. Tourists used the walled compound as a staging area for tours and photo safaris. Many of the visitors were young. Religion did not play a large part in their lives. Archbishop Patrick thought that an inspirational place like the reserve might bring them nearer the creator. For

Father Bradbury, the tourists also brought something, something more secular but no less important. Their wide-eyed awe at the countryside reaffirmed his own sense of wonder and pride in the region.

The priest threw off the lightweight top sheet. Even this far from the river, Father Bradbury needed a mosquito net. He was grateful for it. The priest had what his mother used to call "candy-sweet veins." Mosquitoes loved him. In addition to sore feet, he did not miss the mosquitoes, gnats, and parasitic warble flies that were part of his years of carrying the word of God from village to village. There were fleas here, but at least they could not fly. A shower a day with medicated soap, and they showed no interest in him.

Father Bradbury rose. He knelt briefly beside the cross that hung above the bed. Then he headed for the tiny washroom built between his room and the deacons' quarters. Along with the tourists, plumbing had come to the compound. It was a welcome addition to the rectory.

After showering in the tiny washroom, Father Bradbury dressed. Then he stepped outside into the warm morning. A small flagstone walk led from the rectory to the small church. Beyond that, only partly visible behind the sanctuary, was the tourist center. The government-licensed enterprise consisted of an office, bungalows, the lobby and dining room, and a parking area. Father Bradbury took a moment to look across the six-foot-high wall at the rising sun. The wall had been built to keep out animals that strayed from their usual terrain. That usually occurred twice each year during a period of drought or flood. When that happened, wildlife officials always came to take the animals to a safe haven closer to Maun. They did so quickly, since lost herbivores tended to draw predators. And hungry predators drew tourists with cameras.

The sky was shading from deep blue to cerulean. There were no clouds, just the fair, faint crescent moon high on the northern horizon. It was a good morning and a good life.

A few seconds later, both the morning and Father Bradbury's life were changed.

There were a series of loud pops from inside the compound.

At first, the priest thought some of the hanging ceramic flowerpots had dropped from the tile eaves of the tourist center. Then he heard shouting. It was not shattering pots that had disrupted the peaceful morning.

The priest ran around the church. His sandals clopped on the stones of the walk. At the front of the church was a rose garden that he had planted himself. He had put them there so they would have the early morning sun. The church protected them from the late morning on. Father Bradbury reached the courtyard that fronted the tourist center.

The sixty-three-year-old director of the center was already standing outside. Native Maunan Tswana Ndebele was still dressed in his underwear. He was also wearing a look of tempered rage. His bare arms were raised ear high. About ten feet behind him, one of the tour guides and several tourists were grouped together just outside the door of the main office. They were all facing the open gate. Their hands were also lifted. None of them moved.

The priest noticed several bullet holes in the oak door frame. He turned toward the gate.

The gate was made of iron bars that resembled Batawana spears. The door had been swung inside, and over four dozen men were assuming positions along the inside wall of the courtyard. They were dressed in camouflage uniforms with black berets. Each man carried a firearm. They did not wear insignias or chevrons of rank. They were not government soldiers.

"No," Father Bradbury muttered. "Not here."

The group looked like any of the small, organized militias he had read about in his newspapers. During the past decade, they had caused revolutions in Somalia, Nigeria, Ethiopia, the Sudan, and other African nations. But there had been no rebels in this land since the 1960s. There was no need. The government was democratically elected, and people were generally content.

The soldiers were approximately two hundred feet away. The priest walked toward them.

"Father, don't!" Ndebele warned.

The priest ignored him. This was an outrage. The nation was run by a lawfully elected government. And this reserve was holy ground, not just the home of a church but a place of peace.

The militiamen finished filing into the courtyard. They stretched from the parked vehicles on the west side of the entranceway to the satellite dish on the east. One of the men walked forward. He was a tall, lean man with long dreadlocks and a resolute expression. His rifle was slung over his right shoulder. He wore a belt with extra rounds, a hunting knife, and a radio. He was obviously the leader of the unit. Not because of what he carried but because of how he carried himself. His dark eyes glistened even brighter than the sunlit sweat that covered his forehead and cheeks. He walked on the balls of his feet with his knees slightly bent. He did not make a sound as he crossed the coarse dirt of the parking area.

"I am Father Powys Bradbury," the priest said. His voice was soft but firm. The two men continued to approach one another. "Why have armed men come to our compound?"

"To take you with us," the leader replied.

"Me?" Bradbury demanded. The priest stopped just a few feet from the taller man. "Why? What have I done?"

"You are an invader," the man told him. "You and your kind will be driven out."

"My kind?" Father Bradbury said. "I am no invader. I have been living here for eleven years—"

The leader interrupted with a sharp gesture to the men behind him. Three of the soldiers jogged forward. Two of them seized Father Bradbury by his forearms. Tswana Ndebele made a move as if to protest. The motion was met by the distinctive click of a rifle bolt.

Ndebele stopped.

"Everyone stay where you are, and there will be no casualties," the leader declared.

"Do what he says," Father Bradbury shouted. He did not struggle, but he did look toward the leader. "I tell you, you have the wrong man."

The leader did not respond. The two men continued to hold the priest in his place.

"At least tell me where you're taking me," the white-haired clergyman implored.

The third militiaman went behind the priest. He pulled a black hood over Father Bradbury's head. He tied it tightly around the clergyman's throat. Father Bradbury gagged.

"Please don't hurt him!" Ndebele cried.

Father Bradbury wanted to reassure the director that he would be all right, but he could neither turn nor yell. It was all he could do to breathe in the tight, stifling mask.

"You don't have to do this!" the priest gasped. "I'll go peaceably."

Hands pushed roughly against Father Bradbury's shoulder blades. He stumbled forward. Only the men holding his arms kept him from falling. They tugged him up and ahead. The priest went with them.

Father Bradbury said nothing more. It was all he could do to breathe. The heat was terrible, and the darkness was unnerving. He also did not want to show fear to these men.

But Father Powys Bradbury could not hide his fear from God. And it was to God whom he spoke silently as the militiamen led him from the compound. The priest silently recited his morning prayers and then prayed for himself. He did not ask God for salvation but for strength. He also prayed for the safety of the friends he left behind and for the souls of those who had abducted him. Then he prayed for one thing more.

He prayed for the future of the land he had come to love.

THREE

Washington, D.C.
Tuesday, 7:54 A.M.

It was a dark, rainy morning and DiMaggio's Joe was not as jammed as usual. That was fine with General Mike Rodgers. He had been able to find a parking spot directly outside the coffee bar. And he spotted a small, clean corner table on the inside. He walked to the back of the room, slapped his damp cap and his copy of the *Washington Post* on the empty table, then got in line.

The line at the counter moved quickly, and to Rodgers's amazement, the display case actually had what he wanted. He paid for his oversized corn muffin and an ultratall cup of coffee. Then he returned to the table and sat on the stool, facing the back wall. He gazed into the past. He had to remind himself why he had become a soldier in the first place. And this was certainly the place to do it.

The legendary DiMaggio's Joe was located in Georgetown on the corner of M Street and Wisconsin Avenue. The coffee shop had been established in 1966 by a transplanted New Yorker named Bronx Taylor. Taylor was a New York Yankees fan back when the Washington Senators were their rivals and people could still smoke in coffee shops. The widower had retired and moved to Washington to be close to his daughter and son-in-law. He needed something to do, and he decided to be provocative. Taylor succeeded. Fans of the baseball Senators used to come in to yell at Taylor. They were all blue-collar workers back then. Janitors from Georgetown University, bus drivers, barbers, and butlers and gardeners from the tony old houses. The men would come in and deride the Yankees over juice, sausage, and watery eggs. And pie.

And coffee. And a smoke or two. And more coffee. Taylor made a fortune at this little place.

When Bronx died four years ago, his daughter Alexandra took over. The diner was gentrified. The woman replaced the catsup-stained white tile walls with wood paneling. Instead of a counter and booths with large, solid Formica tables, there were now wood stools with stands that had wobbly metal lattice tops. And Alexandra no longer served just one kind of coffee. For that matter, she no longer served just coffee. There were flavors and fragrances and blends that ended in an *é*. Rodgers still ordered plain and black coffee, even though it tasted as if it were brewed with potpourri.

Apart from the name of the place, Alexandra had left one thing more or less intact. Taylor had covered all four walls with framed photographs and faded newspaper front pages. The pictures were of Yankee Stadium and the star players of the 1940s and 1950s. The yellowing headlines in coffee-stained frames boasted of winning plays, pennants, and world championships. Alexandra had collected them all on the back wall, and they were the only reason Rodgers still came. The mementos took him back to the summers of his youth.

Rodgers grew up in Hartford, Connecticut, which was closer to Boston than to New York. But he was still a Yankees fan. The Bronx Bombers had flash, confidence, and poise. They were also largely responsible for his becoming a soldier. Mike Rodgers could not hit a baseball worth a damn, as his lifelong friend and former Little League teammate Colonel Brett August often reminded him. Rodgers had the eye, but he did not have the power in his arms. Rodgers sure could shoot, though. He started by building orange-crate pistols. They used tightly stretched rubber bands to fire squares of cardboard with surprising accuracy and force. Then he graduated to Daisy BB guns. The sleek Model 26 Spittin' Image was his first. Then his father bought him a Remington Fieldmaster .22 caliber pump to hunt small game. Rodgers shot the squirrels, birds, and rabbits that fellow students used for dissection in biology class. What he did would not be fashionable today. But in the early 1960s, it earned Rodgers a commendation from the school principal. The teenager's interest in firearms led him to study history. To this day, weapons and history remained his greatest passions.

Those and the New York Yankees, he thought as he looked up at a sun-browned photograph of Mickey Mantle and Roger Maris with their bats slung casually across their shoulders.

Thanks to the Yankees, Rodgers associated the idea of wearing a uniform with belonging to an elite team. Since the Yankees did not need a sharpshooter—except when Boston fans came to town—Rodgers turned his sights on that other great team with uniforms, the United States military. Rodgers's extended tours of Vietnam and his devotion to the service had kept him from having any long-term relationships. Except for that, the forty-seven-year-old general never regretted a day of the life he had chosen.

Until four months ago.

Rodgers finished his coffee. He looked at his watch. There was plenty of time before he had to be at Op-Center. He went to the counter to order another ultratall cup.

As Rodgers waited patiently in the short line, he looked around at the young faces. They were mostly college faces with journalists and members of Congress here and there. He could tell them all at a glance. The politicians were the ones lost in newspapers, looking for their names. The reporters were the ones watching the politicians to see who they sat with or who they ignored. The students were the ones who were actually discussing world events.

Rodgers did not see any future soldiers among the many students. Their eyes were too lively, too full of questions or answers. A soldier needed to be committed to just one thing: following orders. The way Striker had done.

Striker was the elite rapid response military arm of the National Crisis Management Center. Rodgers was the deputy director of the NCMC, familiarly known as Op-Center. Upon joining Op-Center shortly after its inception, Rodgers had formed and trained the unit.

A little over four months ago, while parachuting into the Himalayan mountains, General Rodgers and Colonel August had watched as all but one other member of Striker was shot from the sky. In Vietnam, Rodgers had lost close friends and fellow soldiers. On Striker's first foreign mission, he had helped them through the death of Private Bass Moore. Shortly after that, he had seen them through the loss of their original field commander, Lieutenant Colonel Charlie Squires. But Rodgers had never experienced anything like this.

Even worse than the scope of the slaughter was the helplessness Rodgers felt watching it happen. These young soldiers had trusted his judgment and his leadership. They had followed him without hesitation out the hatch of the Indian Air Force AN-12. And he had led them into an ambush. Rodgers was seasoned enough to know that nothing was guaranteed in life and war. But that did not stop him from feeling as if he had let the Strikers down.

Op-Center's staff psychologist Liz Gordon told Rodgers that he was suffering from trauma survivors' syndrome, a form of post-traumatic stress disorder. The condition manifested itself as lethargy and depression resulting from escaping death that took others.

Clinically, that might be true. What Rodgers really suffered from was a crisis of faith. He had screwed up. Being a soldier was about risking your life. But Rodgers had gone into a situation without being aware of an obvious potential danger. In so doing, he had disgraced the qualities his uniform meant to him.

But Liz Gordon had told him one thing that was certainly true. If Rodgers continued to dwell on what had gone wrong, he would be no good to Op-Center or its director, Paul Hood. And both needed him now. Striker had to be rebuilt, and Hood had to deal with ongoing budget cuts.

Enough, thought the general. It was time to get out of the past.

Mike Rodgers turned from the back wall. He sat down, unfolded the newspaper, and scanned the front page. Rodgers was one of the few people at Op-Center who still read a printed newspaper. Paul Hood, intelligence chief Bob Herbert, FBI liaison Darrell McCaskey, and attorney Lowell Coffey III all got their news on-line. To Rodgers, that was like engaging in cybersex. It was a result without an interactive process. He would rather have the real thing.

Ironically, the New York Yankees were mentioned in an article below the fold. The piece described some megatrade with the Baltimore Orioles. It sounded to Rodgers as if the Birds were getting the better end of the deal. Even the Yankees were not as sharp as they used to be.

Of course, no one dies when the Yankees make a bad call, Rodgers reflected. He looked at the other headlines.

The one that caught his attention was beside the baseball article. It was about an apparent paramilitary action in Botswana. The nation rarely showed up on the morning intelligence reports. The government in Gaborone was stable, and the people were relatively content.

What was most surprising were the eyewitness accounts of the action. At least four dozen armed men entered a tourist compound. After firing a few warning shots, they abducted a Catholic priest who ministered at the adjoining church. The priest was well liked and had no known enemies. The kidnappers had not demanded a ransom.

Rodgers's immediate thought was that the priest had heard someone's confession, and the men wanted the information. But why send a small army to grab a single individual? And why attack in daylight instead of at night? To make sure the army was seen?

Rodgers would have to see if Bob Herbert had any information about the kidnapping. Even when he was down on his abilities, Mike Rodgers could not help but ruminate about military issues. The army was not just his profession but his avocation.

He read the rest of the front page while he finished his coffee. Then he refolded the newspaper and slid it protectively under his arm. Rodgers made his way through the pinball array of tables to the front door. He pulled on his hat and stepped onto the slick pavement.

The rain was heavy, but Rodgers did not mind. The gray tones of the morning suited his mood. And though the dampness did not feel comfortable, he was surprised to find that it made him feel good. The pictures reminded him of what he had dreamed. Each droplet reminded him of what he had. Something that his former teammates did not possess: life.

As long as Mike Rodgers had that, he would continue to do the one thing that had ever really mattered.

He would strive to be worthy of his uniform.

FOUR

Washington, D.C.
Tuesday, 8:33 A.M.

The National Crisis Management Center was housed in a two-story building at Andrews Air Force Base. During the Cold War, this nondescript, ivory-colored structure was one of two staging areas for flight crews known as NuRRDs—Nuclear Rapid-Response Divisions. In the event of a nuclear attack on the nation's capital, their job would have been to evacuate key officials. Ranking members of Congress, the entire cabinet, and both officers and logistics experts from the Pentagon would have been flown to secret bunkers built deep in Maryland's Blue Ridge Mountains. Their task would be to keep food and supplies flowing to soldiers, police officers, and civilians, in that order. They would also have worked to keep open as many routes of communication as possible. Other leaders, including the president, vice-president, their top military advisers, and medical personnel, would have been kept aloft aboard Air Force One and Air Force Two. Both planes would have flown at least five hundred miles apart. They would have been refueled in-flight and protected by an escort of NuRRD fighter jets. This would have allowed the commander in chief and his successor to remain separate moving targets.

With the fall of the Soviet Union and the downsizing of the Air Force's NuRRDs, evacuation operations were consolidated at Langley Air Force Base in Virginia. The newly vacated building at Andrews was given over to the newly chartered National Crisis Management Center.

The two floors of upstairs offices were for nonclassified operations such as finance, human resources, and monitoring the mainstream press for possible hot buttons. These were seemingly innocent events that could trigger potential crises. They included the failure of Third World governments to pay their troops, accidents such as a U.S. submarine ramming a foreign fishing vessel or yacht, the seizure of a large cache of drugs, and other seemingly isolated activities. But nothing was ever isolated. A disgruntled military could stage a coup. A sunken ship may have been an attack on intelligence-gathering capabilities. And the drug bust might lead to violent clashes as other dealers moved in to fill a void. All of these were events that fell within Op-Center's sphere of activity.

The basement of the former NuRRD building had been entirely refurbished. It no longer housed living quarters for flight crews. It was where the tactical decisions and intelligence crunching of Op-Center took place. The executive level was accessible by a single elevator that was guarded on top 24/7. Paul Hood, Mike Rodgers, Bob Herbert, and the rest of the executives had their offices down here. The small offices were arranged in a ring along the outer wall of the basement. Inside the circle were cubicles that housed the executive assistants as well as Op-Center's intelligence gathering and processing personnel. On the opposite side of the room from the elevator was a conference room known as the Tank. The conference room was surrounded by walls of electronic waves that generated static to anyone trying to listen in with bugs or external dishes.

Bob Herbert pushed his wheelchair down the oval corridor. His coat was damp, and his ears were cold, but he was glad to be here. This was an important day.

Herbert had nicknamed this hallway the Indy 600. According to his wheelchair odometer, it was exactly 600 yards around. There were no windows down here, and the rooms were not spacious. The facility reminded Herbert more of a submarine than the headquarters of an agency. But the building was secure. Anyway, Herbert never believed all that crap about people needing sunshine to brighten their mood. The thirty-nine-year-old intelligence head only needed two things to make him happy. One was his motorized wheelchair. The balding intelligence expert had lost the use of his legs in the Beirut embassy bombing in 1983. Only the quick work of physician Dr. Alison Carter, a visiting foreign service officer, had prevented him from losing his life. The wheelchair did not just keep Herbert mobile. It had a foldaway arm, like an airplane seat, that housed his computer with a wireless modem. Everything Herbert needed, including E-mail addresses to order pizza, were literally in his lap. Op-Center's technical expert, Matt Stoll, had even installed a jack for a satellite dish. At times, Herbert felt like the Bionic Man.

The other thing that made Herbert happy was when outsiders left him and his coworkers alone to do their jobs. When Op-Center first began operations, no one paid them much attention. Whether they were saving the space shuttle from saboteurs or Japan from nuclear annihilation, everything they did was covert. It passed under the radar of the press and most foreign intelligence services. The relationships they established were ones they chose to establish. They did so quietly with Interpol, the Russian Op-Center, and other groups.

Unfortunately, the dynamics changed drastically after Paul Hood personally resolved a highly public hostage standoff at the United Nations. Foreign governments complained to the White House about Hood's unsanctioned military activity on international territory. The Central Intelligence Agency, the National Security Agency, and even the State Department complained to the Congressional Intelligence Oversight Committee. They accused Paul Hood of usurping personnel and chartered responsibilities from both agencies. The Pentagon said that Op-Center had monopolized the spy satellite capabilities of the National Reconnaissance Office.

All of that was true. But the truth did not always tell the whole story. None of these activities were done for the aggrandizement of Paul Hood or the NCMC. Under Hood, Op-Center functioned without the bureaucracy, infighting, and egos that undermined the effectiveness of those other agencies. That helped Op-Center to achieve its chartered goal: to save lives and protect American interests.

Because of politics, not effectiveness or cost-efficiency, the CIOC had ordered Paul Hood to cut his operating budget. He had done so. This morning, Hood was supposed to learn the results of the quarterly follow-up conducted by the CIOC finance subcommittee. Hood, Rodgers, and Herbert hoped that tempers had cooled somewhat in four months. The previous day, the men had submitted their written petition to get some of the cuts rescinded. Among other things, training a new Striker team was going to take additional funds. Hood had been optimistic. Rodgers had been pessimistic. Herbert had declared himself neutral.

"Neutral like Sweden," Alison Carter had joked. The night before, Dr. Carter and her former patient had gone to dinner. Carter had just completed a secret assignment for the State Department. Though she did not say so, Herbert took that to mean she had participated in an assassination. Officially, the United States government did not sanction such killings. Unofficially, with the help of medical specialists, they executed them brilliantly.

During the course of the mission, Carter had exposed extensive collaboration between supposedly neutral Sweden and Nazi Germany during World War II. She was proud of that fact. She said that she had never believed any nation or individual could be completely impartial about anything.

Herbert disagreed. He insisted he had to be neutral. As he pointed out to Dr. Carter after one glass of wine too many, *"It takes an Optimist, Pessimist, and Centrist to spell Op-Center."*

She had groaned and made him pay for dinner. Then she left him with this thought: *"Tell me,"* Carter asked. *"Do you ever use the neutral gear on your wheelchair?"*

Herbert informed her that there was no neutral gear on his chair. Just forward and backward.

"Exactly," she replied.

Herbert passed Paul Hood's office. The door was open. Since Hood's separation from his wife Sharon, he had been getting to the office earlier and earlier. For all Herbert knew, his boss had slept here instead of going back to his new apartment.

Not that it mattered. Staying busy had helped keep Hood's spirits from sinking. The intelligence chief certainly understood that. His own wife was killed in the blast that had cost him the use of his legs. After her death, all Herbert wanted to do was work. He needed to keep his mind moving forward, engaged in something constructive. If he had dwelt on the loss, his mind would have stayed in place, idling angrily, digging downward.

That was probably why psychologists called the result the pits of depression, now that Herbert thought about it.

Hood was gazing at his computer monitor. Herbert rapped lightly on the doorjamb.

"Good morning," Herbert said.

Hood glanced toward the door. He looked tired. "Good morning, Bob," Hood replied.

The director's voice was low and flat. The day had just begun, and already something was not right.

"Is Mike in yet?" Hood asked.

"I haven't seen him," Herbert replied. He swung into the doorway. "What's up?"

Hood hesitated. "The usual," he said quietly.

That told Herbert a lot.

"Well, let me know if there's anything I can do," Herbert said.

"There will be," Hood assured him. He did not elaborate.

Herbert smiled tightly. He lingered a moment. He thought about trying to get Hood to talk but decided against it.

Herbert backed his wheelchair from the doorway and continued down the hallway. Psychologist Liz Gordon was already at work. So was Director of Electronic Communications Kevin Custer. Herbert waved good morning to each of them as he passed. They waved back. It was a welcome touch of normalcy.

He did not bother trying to guess what Hood had to say to Rodgers. Herbert was an intelligence man. And right now, he had very little intelligence to go on.

But he did know two things. One was that the news was grave.

Paul Hood had been mayor of Los Angeles before coming to Op-Center. He was a politician. Hood's silence a moment ago was not about keeping secrets. It was about protocol. His tone had told Herbert that the news was bad. The fact that Hood did not want to tell Herbert, his trusted number-three man, meant that Mike Rodgers was entitled to hear it first. That told Herbert it was personal.

The other thing Herbert knew was that Alison Carter was right: Neutrality was a myth.

Herbert was an optimist. Whatever this was and whatever it took, he would help his teammates beat it.

FIVE

Okavango Swamp, Botswana
Tuesday, 4:35 P.M.

The Okavango River is the fourth longest river system in southern Africa. The wide river runs southeasterly for over 1,000 miles, from central Angola to northern Botswana. There, it ends in a vast delta known as the Okavango Swamp. In 1849, the Scottish explorer David Livingstone was the first European to visit the region. He described the swamp as "vast, humid, and unpleasant with all manner of biting insects."

"Vast" is an understatement.

The great, triangular delta covers an area of some 6,500 miles. Much of the region is under three feet of water during the rainy season. For the rest of the year, just over half the swamp is as dry as the surrounding plains. Amphibians such as frogs and salamanders breed in cycles that produce offspring who are air breathers by the time the rains stop. Other animals, such as lungfish and tortoises, burrow into the mud and estivate to survive.

The Moremi Wildlife Reserve is located beyond the northeastern corner of the Okavango Swamp. The reserve's 1,500 square miles are a strikingly different world from the marshland, a self-sustaining ecosystem of lions and cheetahs, wild pigs and wildebeests, hippopotamuses and crocodiles, storks and egrets, geese and quail, and rivers filled with pike and tiger fish.

There is only one animal that dwells in both regions. And right now, a force of them was making its way from one area to the other.

After leaving the Maun tourist center, Leon Seronga had led his four-vehicle caravan north through the reserve. The unit was riding Mercedes Sprinters that had been given to them by the Belgian. "The Necessary Evil," as Seronga referred to him in private, among his men. Each van held fourteen passengers. The vehicles had been flown to the Belgian's private airfield in Lehutu in the Kalahari. That was where they had been painted the green and khaki of Moremi Ranger Patrol vans. Before crossing the reserve with their prisoner, the men had all donned the olive-green uniforms of rangers. If any real rangers or army patrols stopped the RPVs, or if they were spotted by tour groups or Botswana field forces, they would claim to be searching for the paramilitary unit that had kidnapped the priest. Depending upon who approached, Leon's team was equipped with the proper documentation. The Belgian had provided that as well.

Dhamballa saw to the spirits, but the Necessary Evil and his people saw to everything else. They said they supported the cause and hoped to benefit by having the mines returned to Botswana ownership. Leon Seronga did not trust the Europeans. But if anything went wrong, he could always kill them. And that made him a little more comfortable.

Leon was sitting in the rearmost seat of the second van. His prisoner lay on his side in the small storage section of the van. The men had tied his hands behind him and bound his feet before laying him inside. He was still wearing the hood and was wheezing audibly. The van was hot. Inside the mask, it was even hotter. Leon had kept the mask on for two reasons. First, to dehydrate the priest and keep him weak. Second, to force him to draw some of his own exhaled carbon dioxide with each breath. That would keep the priest lightheaded. Both would make Father Bradbury more cooperative when they reached their destination.

The priest was nestled among stacks of thigh-high wading boots and several cans of petrol. The other vans were packed with food, water, weapons, blankets, and the nine-by-nine-foot cotton canvas military tents the group would be using when they stopped for the night.

After more than twelve hours driving through the reserve, the group reached the southernmost edge of the Okavango

Swamp. Their arrival was marked by a dramatic increase in humidity. The climate was one of the reasons the swamp had been selected. It was hospitable to insects. In particular, the mosquitoes at the perimeter of the water provided more security than a battery of soldiers. And those sentries did not have to be provisioned.

The drivers parked the vans on the south side of a grove of high, thick date palms. The vehicles would be needed for a mission three days from now. Leon and his team would be driving to the Church of Loyola in Shakawe, which was to the north. That would begin the second phase of the program.

The thick trunks and long leaves of the trees would keep the vans from being baked by the sun. Six- and seven-foot-tall batches of feathery papyrus plants would provide cover from any passersby.

Because it was well after dark, the militiamen made camp. Four guards were posted around the perimeter. They would serve shifts of one hour each. The trip would resume at daybreak.

The night was noisier at the water's edge than it was in the reserve the evening before. Insects, birds, and toads hummed, barked, clicked, and wailed continuously. Because of the thick foliage, the sounds did not penetrate into the swamp. Even the breathing of the sleeping militiamen seemed loud and very, very close to Leon. They remained trapped in the immediate vicinity, as if the noise were coming from headphones. But it was like white noise. Within minutes after curling up on his blanket, the exhausted but satisfied Leon Seronga was asleep.

The symphony ended shortly before dawn. When the men woke, Leon selected six men to continue the journey with him. He left Donald Pavant in charge of the bivouac.

It was just after the rainy season, and the dark waters still stretched to the outer boundaries of the swamp. While the other six men pulled on their hip boots, Leon untied the priest's hands and legs. Father Bradbury was cautioned not to remove his hood, or he would be dragged through the water. He was also warned not to speak. Leon did not want his men or himself distracted by chatter or prayer. Then the priest was hefted onto the back of one of the men. He was weak, and Leon did not have time to walk him through the swamp.

The militiamen set out, wading through the sloshy waters. They had tied a pair of motorboats to a tree on a small island 400 yards offshore. The boats were hidden among high reeds where they would not be seen. Seronga had not been worried about rangers spotting them as much as poachers. The islands of the swamp were an ideal hiding place.

The men moved as they had on land, in two tight, parallel columns. Seronga liked to keep his men organized and disciplined at all times.

The mosquitoes were relentless for about 250 yards from the shore. After that, the only real threat the men faced were burrowing asps. The snakes typically stretched their yard-long bodies on the silty marsh bottom. Meanwhile, their flat heads rested on the shore, on raised roots, or on floating branches. Though they could not bite through the vinyl of a boot, the snakes could be stirred up and washed over the top in deep water.

The militiamen continued to walk toward the northeast. They made their way slowly through thickets of high cattails and around stocky bald cypress trees. The bald cypresses literally sat on the soft marsh bottom like bowling pins. They passed mounds of dry land as well as swamp knots. These were raised masses of tangled tree roots. Small lizards actually made permanent homes on the swamp knots. Countless generations of amphibians were born, fed on insects and rainwater, mated, and died without ever leaving the knot.

Upon reaching the two boats, the men were divided. Seronga and the priest got into one with two guards. The remainder of the men climbed into the second boat. They fired up the engines and sped into the brightening morning.

The journey northward lasted nearly ten hours. Seronga and Dhamballa had selected a base that was close to the northeastern edge of the swamp. If it became necessary for Dhamballa to escape, the Barani salt pan and the rugged Tsodilo Hills lay to the west. The relatively unguarded border with Namibia was just a short, fifty-five-mile trip to the north.

By the time the men reached their destination, the sun was low on the horizon. It shone in long, tawny red streaks beyond the rich green of the plants and trees. The swamp itself was already dark, its surface like an oily mirror. But there was something different about this section from anything the men had encountered before. A low, symmetrical, treeless hill rose from the water. It was approximately twelve acres of black earth, soil topped with a layer of fertile, gray brown humus. Built on the low-lying hill were five thatched huts. The walls were made of thick, slab-cut pieces of baobab tree. The rooftops were interwoven roots sealed with mud. Battery-powered lights were visible through the thatching of the central residence, which was also the largest of the huts. The other, smaller huts contained cots for the soldiers that were stationed here, supplies, additional weapons, communication and video gear, and other equipment that had been brought in by the Belgian.

Only one structure was radically different from the others on the island. It was an oblong shack about the size of two coffins set back-to-back. Except for the floor, which was made of wood, it was built entirely from corrugated tin. There were iron bars in front and a tin door behind them. The door was open. There was nothing and no one inside.

The waters to the north and east of the small island had been completely cleared of trees, plants, underwater roots and logs, and other debris. The roof thatching used to complete the huts had come from this effort. The work had been necessary in order to create a 150-foot flight strip for the Belgian's Aventura II 912 ultralight. The small, white, two-seat amphibious aircraft could set down on water or on land. Right now, the needle-nosed airplane sat perfectly still in the lengthening blackness. Beside the plane was the seventeen-and-a-half-foot red cedar canoe that Dhamballa used to leave the swamp. It was covered with a fiberglass tarpaulin to protect it from animals looking for a home. Like the airplane, it sat motionless on the flat surface of the swamp. The sixty-pound vessel was tied to a post that had been driven into the shore of the island. The pole was actually a small totem of a loa or god. The three-

foot-high mooring was made of bald cypress that had been
carved in the shape of a tornado. The image personified the
mighty loa Agwe, the divine force of the sea.

Two armed guards patroled the island at all times. As Seronga and his team neared the southern shore, the sentries
turned bright flashlights on them. Seronga and his men
stopped.

"*Bon Dieu,*" Seronga said.

"Pass," said a voice as one of the flashlights snapped off.

Seronga had uttered their password, the name of their guardian deity. One of the guards left to inform Dhamballa that the
team had returned.

The men walked ashore. Seronga quickly removed his
boots, watching as the soldier carrying Father Bradbury set
him on the shore. The priest fell back, wheezing through the
mask, unable to move. The militiaman stood over the prisoner,
while another soldier bound his hands. When they were finished, Seronga walked over. He grabbed Father Bradbury under an arm and hoisted him to his feet. The priest's robes were
thick with sweat.

"Let's go," Seronga said.

"I know your voice," the priest gasped.

Seronga tugged on the priest's slender arm.

"You are the leader," the priest continued.

"I said let's go," Seronga replied.

Father Bradbury stumbled forward, and Seronga had to hold
him up. When the clergyman regained his footing, the men
started walking slowly through the warm, soft soil. Seronga
directed the priest toward the main hut.

"I still do not understand," Father Bradbury went on. "Why
are you doing this?"

Seronga did not answer.

"The mask," Father Bradbury implored. His voice was
breathy and weak. "At least won't you remove it?"

"When I have been instructed to do so," Seronga replied.

"Instructed by whom?" the priest persisted. "I thought you
were the leader."

"Of these men," Seronga said. He should never have answered the man. Additional information gave him new avenues to poke and prod.

"Then who are we going to see?" Father Bradbury asked.

Seronga was too tired to tell the priest to stop talking. They were almost at the hut. Though the Batawana native was leg weary, seeing the hut gave him strength. It was more than just the soft, welcoming glow through the wood slats. He was renewed by the knowledge of who was inside.

"Forget about me," the priest said. "Have you no fear of God's judgment? At least let me save your soul."

His soul. What did this man know? Only what he had been taught. Seronga had seen life and death. He had seen Vodun power. He had no doubt about what he was doing.

"Look to your own soul and your own life," Seronga advised.

"I have done that tonight," Father Bradbury replied. "I am saved."

"Good," Seronga told him as they reached the hut. "Now you will have a chance to save the lives of others."

SIX

Washington, D.C.
Tuesday, 10:18 A.M.

For most of his career, Mike Rodgers had gotten up with the sun. There were soldiers to drill, battles to fight, crises to settle. Lately, however, Rodgers's world had been quiet. There were reports to file about the mission to Kashmir, dossiers to review for possible new Strikers, and endless sessions with Liz Gordon. There was no reason to be in early.

Also, it was difficult to sleep. That made it damned difficult to get up as early as he once had. Fortunately, the decor and the caffeine at DiMaggio's Joe brought him up to something resembling full speed.

Rodgers parked and walked toward the building. The rain had stopped. He carried his rolled-up newspaper, whacking it in his open hand. The blows smarted. The general was reminded of basic training, when he was taught how to roll newspaper tightly to form a knife. Another time, the DI showed them how to use a crumpled piece of newspaper or napkin to disable someone. If hand-to-hand combat were inevitable, all a soldier had to do was toss the scrap to one side. An opponent would always be distracted. During that moment—and a moment was all it took—the soldier could punch, stab, or shoot an adversary.

Rodgers entered the small, brightly lit reception area. A young female guard stood in a bulletproof glass booth just inside the door. She saluted smartly as Rodgers entered.

"Good morning, General," the sentry said.

"Good morning," Rodgers replied. He stopped. "Valentine," he said.

"Go right in, sir," the guard replied. She pressed a button that opened the elevator door.

Valentine was Rodgers's personal password for the day. It was left on his secure GovNet E-mail pager the night before. Even if the guard had recognized Rodgers, he would not have been allowed to enter if his password did not match what was on her computer.

Rodgers rode the elevator to the basement. As he stepped out, he bumped into Bob Herbert.

"Robert!" Rodgers said.

"Morning, Mike," Herbert said quietly.

"I was just coming to see you," Rodgers said.

"To return some of the DVDs you borrowed?" Herbert asked.

"No. I haven't been in the mood for Frank Capra," Rodgers said. He handed Herbert the *Washington Post*. "Did you see the article about the kidnapping in Botswana?"

"Yes. They caught that item upstairs," Herbert told him, refolding the newspaper.

"What do you make of it?" Rodgers asked.

"Too early to say," Herbert answered truthfully.

"The uniforms don't sound like the men were Botswana army regulars," Rodgers went on.

"No," Herbert agreed. "We haven't had any reports of paramilitary activity in Botswana, but it could be a new group. Some idiot warlord who's going to turn Botswana into the next Somalia. Or the soldiers could be expatriates from Angola, Namibia, any of the countries in the region."

"Then why take a priest?" Rodgers asked. He was uncharacteristically anxious, tapping a foot and toying with a button on his uniform.

"Maybe they needed a chaplain," Herbert said. "Or maybe the priest heard someone's confession, and they want to know what was said. Why are you all over this, Mike?"

"There's something about the size of the group and the timing of the attack that bothers me," Rodgers said. "Why send so many soldiers to kidnap a single, unarmed man? And in daylight, no less. A small squad could have picked him up in the middle of the night."

"That's true," Herbert agreed. "But you still haven't told me why this is important. Do you know anyone over there? Do you recognize something about the abduction scenario?"

"No," Rodgers admitted. "There's just something about it—" He did not finish the thought.

Herbert's eyes were on the general. Rodgers was restless. His eyes were searching, not steady as they usually were. There was an unhappy turn to his mouth. He looked like a man who had put something down and couldn't remember where.

Herbert flipped over the newspaper and glanced at it. "You know, now you've got me thinking," the intelligence chief said. "If this is a paramilitary unit that's been dormant somewhere, maybe they chose this target as a way of announcing themselves without having to face a firefight. If it's a new group, maybe they wanted to give their people some field experience. Or maybe they just miscalculated how long it would take to get to the church. Didn't that happen to George Washington during the Revolution?"

"Yes," Rodgers said. "It took him longer to cross the Delaware River than he had expected. Fortunately, the Brits were all asleep."

"That was it," Herbert said. "So there could be trouble percolating somewhere in southern Africa," Herbert said. He slid the newspaper into the leather pocket on the side of his wheelchair. "I'll make calls to our embassies, see if this smells dangerous to anyone. Find out if there's any additional intel. Meanwhile, Paul was asking if you were in yet."

Rodgers's expression perked. "Did he hear from the CIOC?" the general asked.

"I don't know," Herbert said.

"He would have told you if he had," Rodgers said.

"Not necessarily," Herbert said. "He's supposed to brief his number-two man first."

"That's according to the Good Book," Rodgers said. The Good Book was what they called the National Crisis Management Center Operations Book of Codes, Conduct, and Procedure. The CCP was as thick as the Bible and almost as idealized. It explained how life should be lived in a perfect world.

"Maybe Pope Paul's found religion after all these years," Herbert said.

"There's one way to find out," Rodgers said.

"Go get 'em," Herbert said.

"I will." The general stepped around the wheelchair. "And thanks for checking out that priest for me."

"My pleasure," Herbert replied.

Rodgers threw him a casual salute and started down the hall. It was strange to hear Hood's old nickname after all these years. Press liaison Ann Farris had given it to Hood because of his strict selflessness. Ironically, the name didn't really apply. Early in his tenure, Hood had discontinued adherence to the CCP. He tossed the rule book when he realized that it was the antithesis to intelligence work. All an adversary needed to do was get a copy of the CCP from the government printing office to know exactly what Op-Center was going to do in a given situation. That included enemies outside the country as well as rivals inside the U.S. intelligence community itself. When Hood retired the CCP, his nickname went with it.

Hood's door was closed when Rodgers arrived. The director's assistant, Bugs Benet, was sitting in a cubicle directly across from the door. Bugs told Rodgers that Hood was on a personal call.

"I don't expect it to be a long conversation," Benet said.

"Thanks," Rodgers said. The door was soundproof. Rodgers stood beside it and waited.

Hood was probably talking to his wife, Sharon. The two had recently reached an agreement on terms for their divorce. From what little Hood had confided to Rodgers, their primary goal now was the rehabilitation of their daughter, Harleigh. The young girl was one of the hostages taken by terrorists at the United Nations. After nearly a half year of intensive therapy, Harleigh was at last beginning to recover from the trauma she had suffered. For weeks after the crisis, she had done little more than cry or stare.

Rodgers understood what Harleigh was feeling. The general was luckier than the young woman. The difference between an adult and an adolescent was a lifetime of anger. "Impotent rage" was what Liz Gordon had called it. When a kid took an emotional beating, he tended to feel victimized. He shut down the way Harleigh had done. When an adult took a hit, it often tapped into buried resentment. He let it out. That aggressiveness did not heal the trauma, but it did provide fuel to keep the individual going.

"He's off now, General," Bugs said.

The general nodded. He did not have to knock. There was a small security camera in the upper left corner. Hood already knew Rodgers was there.

"Good morning, Mike," Hood said.

"Morning."

"Sit down," Hood said. He did not say anything else.

The general lowered himself into one of the room's two armchairs. He knew then that Hood was troubled. Whenever Paul Hood had bad news, he did not engage in top-of-the-morning chat. The only thing Mike Rodgers did not know was whether this was personal or professional. And if it was professional, which one of them it was about.

Hood did not waste time getting to the point.

"Mike, I received an E-mailed letter of resolution from Senator Fox early this morning," Hood told him. He regarded the general. "The CIOC has voted unanimously not to allow the NCMC to rebuild its military capacity."

Rodgers felt as if someone had driven a baseball bat into his gut. "That's knee-jerk bullshit."

"Whatever it is, the decision is final," Hood said.

"We can't restaff Striker?" Rodgers said, still in disbelief.

Hood looked down. "No."

"But they can't order that," Rodgers protested.

"They have—"

"No!" Rodgers said. "Striker is mandated by charter. Fox would need an act of Congress to change it. Even if we sent

Striker on an unauthorized mission, the CCP very clearly states that disciplinary actions are to be directed against the commanders in the field and at HQ, and not against the unit individually or in total. I'll send her the chapter and verse."

"They took pains to point out that this is not a disciplinary action," Hood told him.

"Like hell it isn't!" Rodgers snapped. Senator Fox had poked a hole in his rage. He was fighting to control it. "Fox and the CIOC doesn't want one, because if they investigate us under DA charges, the hearing has to be public. The press would put her against a wall and pull the trigger. We stopped a goddamn war. They know it. She has no reason other than pressure from other agencies to shut us down. Hell, even Mala Chatterjee had good things to say about us."

Mala Chatterjee was the Indian-born secretary-general of the United Nations. Before the Striker action in Kashmir, she had been fiercely critical of Paul Hood's handling of the United Nations situation.

"Mike, we stepped on the toes of the military and made things rough for the embassy in New Delhi," Hood said.

"Aw, I'm bleeding for them," Rodgers said. "Would they have preferred dealing with a nuclear attack?"

"Mike, what was going on between Pakistan and India was not our official business," Hood said. "We went in to reconnoiter, not intervene. Yes, you have humanitarian rights on your side. They have political ramifications on their side. That's why the CIOC is hitting us so hard."

"No, they're just hitting us low," Rodgers shot back. "They don't have the balls to hit hard. They're like my friggin' Uncle Johnny who didn't have a car but liked to take drives. He called realtors and asked them to show him houses. The CIOC doesn't have a car, or money, but they're working us."

"Yes, the CIOC is working us," Hood said. "And yes, they're doing it very quietly and very effectively."

"I hope you told them to stuff their little letter," Rodgers said.

"I did not," Hood replied.

"What?" Rodgers said. That felt like the small end of the baseball bat.

"I informed Senator Fox that the NCMC would comply with the resolution," Hood said.

"But they're cowards, Paul!" Rodgers yelled. "You kowtowed to a bunch of sheep."

Hood said nothing. Rodgers took a long breath. He had to reel it in. He was not going to get anywhere beating up on Paul Hood.

"Fine," Hood agreed at last. "They're cowards. They're sheep. But you've got to give them credit for one thing."

"What's that?" Rodgers asked.

"They did something that we did not," Hood replied. "They did this thing legally." Hood opened a file on the computer and swung the monitor toward Rodgers. "Have a look."

Reluctantly, the general leaned forward. He needed a minute to calm down. He looked at the monitor. Hood had brought up section 24-4 of the CCP manual. Paragraph 8 was highlighted. Rodgers read the passage. Even as he focused on the text, Rodgers could not believe this was happening. What had happened to Striker in the field was crushing enough. But at least they died in action. To be shut down and humiliated by a clutch of soft, self-serving politicians like this. It was almost unbearable.

"Seconding fresh troops from other military forces falls under the heading of 'Domestic military activity and procurement,' " Hood continued. "That is something the CIOC can and has preemptively denied. They've also blocked the hiring of retired military personnel for other than advisory activities. They used section 90-9, paragraph 5, to do that."

Hood jumped to that part of the CCP. It outlined the need for all recommissioned personnel to undergo field examinations at Quantico, which was where Striker had been stationed. The manual defined that as military activity that had to be approved by the CIOC.

Mike Rodgers sat back. Hood was right. He almost had to admire Senator Fox and her backstabbing colleagues. They had not only stopped Hood and Rodgers by the book, but they had done it without kicking up any dust. He wondered if they were also hoping to get his own resignation.

Maybe they would. He did not want to give them the satisfaction, but he also did not have the patience for this kind of bureaucracy anymore.

Hood turned the computer screen around and leaned forward in his chair. He folded his hands.

"Sorry I got a little hot," Rodgers said.

"You don't have to apologize to me," Hood said.

"Yes, I do," Rodgers replied.

"Mike, I know this is a tough blow," Hood went on. "But I've also been reading the CCP. This does not have to be a terminal blow."

Now Rodgers leaned forward. "What do you mean?"

Hood typed something on the keyboard. "I'm going to throw some names at you."

"Okay," Rodgers said.

"Maria Corneja, Aideen Marley, Falah Shibli, David Battat, Harold Moore, and Zack Bemler," Hood said. "What do those people have in common?"

"They're agents we've worked with over the years," Rodgers said.

"There's something else most of them share," Hood said.

"I'm missing whatever it is," Rodgers admitted.

"Except for Aideen, none of them ever served in the military," Hood said. "And none of them is in it now."

"I'm still not following you," Rodgers said apologetically.

"These people are not governed by the CIOC resolution or by CCP restrictions," Hood said. "What I'm saying is that we get back in the field, but we don't do it with a military team. We don't replace Striker."

"Infiltration," Rodgers said. Now he got it. "We defuse situations from the inside rather than the outside."

"Exactly," Hood replied.

Rodgers sat back. He was ashamed that he had been so slow on the uptake. "Damn, that's good," Rodgers said.

"Thanks," Hood said. "We have an absolute mandate to collect intelligence. The CIOC doesn't control that," he went on.

"So we run this as a black ops unit. Only you, Bob Herbert, and one or two others know about it. Our people fly commercial airlines, work with cover profiles, move around in daylight, in public."

"They hide in plain sight," Rodgers said.

"Right," Hood said. "We run an old-fashioned HUMINT operation."

Rodgers nodded. He was annoyed that he had sold his boss short. Yet this was a side of Paul Hood he had never seen. The lone wolf in sheepish team player's clothes.

Rodgers liked it.

"Any thoughts?" Hood asked.

"Not at the moment," Rodgers said.

"Any questions?" Hood asked.

"Just one," Rodgers replied.

"I already have the answer to that," Hood said. He smiled. "You start right now."

SEVEN

Okavango Swamp, Botswana
Tuesday, 5:36 P.M.

It felt good to breathe again.

For the first part of his ordeal, Father Bradbury was on the edge of panic. The man of the cloth could not draw breath easily nor could he see through the hood. Except for his own strained breathing, sounds were muffled by the mask. Sweat and the condensation from his breath made the fabric clammy. Only his sense of touch was intact, and he was forced to focus on that. The priest was hyperaware of the heat of the plain and the ovenlike convection inside the vehicle. Every bump, dip, or turn seemed exaggerated.

After lying in the vehicle for a long while, Father Bradbury forced himself to look past his fear and discomfort. He concentrated on drawing the air that was available, even if it was less than he was accustomed to. More relaxed, his oxygen-deprived mind began to drift. The priest went into an almost dreamlike reverie. His spirit seemed to have become detached from his weakened body. He felt as if he were floating in a great, unlit void.

Father Bradbury wondered if he were dying.

The priest also wondered if the Christian martyrs had experienced something similar, a tangible salvation of the soul as the flesh was consumed. Though Father Bradbury did not want to give up his body, the thought of being in the company of saints gave him comfort.

The priest was torn from his reflection when the vehicle stopped. He heard people exit. He waited to be pulled out. It never happened. Someone climbed into the vehicle. Father Bradbury's hood was lifted at the bottom and he was given scraps of bread and water. Then the hood was retied and was left there for the night. Though the priest kept drifting into sleep, he would invariably suck the cloth of the hood into his mouth, begin to choke, and wake himself. Or his perspiration would cool just enough to give him a chill.

In the morning, the priest was hauled from the vehicle and placed face forward on someone's back. As the men entered what was almost certainly a marsh, Father Bradbury's body returned, vividly alive. For a time, his shoulders, arms, and legs were hounded by mosquitoes and other biting insects. The humidity was greater here than on the plain. Breathing was even more difficult than the previous day. Perspiration dripped into his dry mouth, turning it gummy and thick. The paste caused his throat to swell, and swallowing became a chore. The clergyman once again succumbed to mortal despair. But he was too weak to struggle. Father Bradbury went where he was taken.

Whenever he opened his eyes, the priest saw dark orange instead of black. The sun was up. As the humidity increased, the priest became dehydrated. He found himself fighting to stay awake. He feared that if he lost consciousness, he would never regain it. Yet he must have passed out. When they stopped, the sun appeared to be much lower in the sky.

But he could not be sure. Even as he was walked across thick, almost muddy soil, his captor would not remove his hood. Once again, he would not tell the priest why he was brought here. It was not until Father Bradbury had been taken into a structure of some kind that he was given any information at all.

Unfortunately, not all of the communication was verbal. And none of it was encouraging.

Father Bradbury was led onto a rug and was ordered to stand there. The man who had brought the priest in released him. Through the hood, he saw a gauzy spot of light directly ahead.

"May I have a drink?" Father Bradbury rasped.

The priest heard a high whistling sound from behind. A moment later, there was a sharp snapping sound followed by a blaze of intense heat behind both knees. The fire jumped up through Father Bradbury's thighs and down to his ankles like an electric shock. He sucked a deep, involuntary breath. At the same time, his legs folded, and he dropped to his knees. When he was finally able to let the air from his lungs, he moaned miserably.

The burning grew worse as he lay there. He knew at once that he had been struck with a switch.

After several moments, he was hoisted roughly back to his feet and cuffed on the side of the head to get his attention.

"Do not speak," someone ordered.

The speaker was standing a few feet in front of the priest. His voice was soft but commanding. Father Bradbury's ear was ringing from the blow. He turned the side of his head toward the man who had just spoken. There was something compelling about his voice.

"This island has been sanctified with blood of fowl and day dancing," the man continued. "The voice of a reverend from outside the circle can only be used to advance or accept our faith."

The words made sense, but Father Bradbury was having difficulty concentrating on them. His legs were weak and trembling violently. He fell again.

"Help him," the voice from in front said.

Strong hands moved under the priest's arms. He was raised from the rug. This time the hands held him upright. The priest's breath was tremulous. The pain behind his knees settled into a regular, forceful throbbing. His head, overheated and aching for water, sagged forward. The hands released him after a moment. The priest wobbled but forced himself to remain standing.

The only sound the priest heard was his own breathing. And then, after a minute or two, the man in front spoke again. He was nearer now. Though the voice was barely more than a whisper, it was deep and compelling.

"Now that you understand my position, I want you to do something," said the speaker in front.

"Who . . . who are you?" Father Bradbury implored. The words were cracked. It did not sound like his own voice.

A moment later, he heard the terrible whistle. He cried out as he felt the bite of the switch. This time, it struck a little higher, along the backs of his thighs. The pain was so great that he actually danced forward several steps before collapsing. He fell on the dirt floor, panting and whimpering. He had a flashback to when he was a boy and had been hit with a strap by his father. This was how he sounded then. The priest lay writhing on his belly, hooting pain into the hood. He could not control what came from his mouth. His bound hands pulled against the ropes. But Father Bradbury was not trying to get free. His body had to move, to keep from letting the pain be his only stimulus.

"You were told not to speak!" someone yelled from behind. It did not sound like the man who had brought him here. This was some other tormentor. Perhaps they had brought in someone who was proficient with a switch. Many villages had people like that, men who were skilled at corporal punishment. "Nod if you understand the instructions."

Father Bradbury was curled on his side. He nodded. He barely knew what he was doing anymore. His body was in agony, yet his mind was numb. His mouth was dry, but his hair and face were greasy with sweat. He was struggling mightily with his bonds yet he had never felt so weak.

Only the priest's spirit was intact. It had been shaped and reinforced by over two score years of reflection, reading, and prayer. He needed that part of him to stay strong.

The switch nipped the backs of his bound hands. Father Bradbury yelped and stopped moving them. He thought of restless young boys whose knuckles he had rapped in catechism class and apologized to God. He was pulled back onto his feet. His knees folded inward, but the priest did not fall. The powerful hands continued to hold him.

"You must believe me," said the gentle man in front. He was leaning close again, his voice even more compassionate now. "I do not wish to hurt you. On my soul, I do not. The creation of pain is a black deed. It hurts you, and it attracts the attention of evil spirits. They watch us. They feed on evil, and they grow stronger. Then they attempt to influence us.

That is not what I wish. But for the sake of my people, I must have your cooperation. There is no time to debate this."

Father Bradbury had no idea what this man was saying. Everything around him was confusion.

"Now," the voice said as the man stepped away. "You will be taken to a telephone. We have been watching your seven deacon missionaries. We have the numbers of their cellular telephones. You will call them and tell these men to leave my country. When their departure has been confirmed, you will be permitted to leave our camp. Then you, too, will leave our Botswana. You and the other priests of a false divinity."

"He is not false," Father Bradbury said.

The clergyman braced for a blow that did not come. Then it came, just as he was relaxing. It struck his lower back. He felt the shock of the blow race up his back to his neck, and he whimpered loudly. No one said anything. There was no need. He knew the rules.

The hands holding Father Bradbury were joined by another set of hands. They pulled the priest forward. He could not keep his wounded legs under him. He did not even try.

The priest was dragged across the room. His legs were screaming, but he could do nothing to quiet them. His head was throbbing as well, not just from the blows but from thirst and hunger. One set of hands pushed him onto a stool. The edge of the seat brushed his leg where he had been hit. It burned terribly, and he jerked away. The men settled him back down. Another man untied the bottom of the hood. It was lifted to just above the priest's mouth. As warm as the evening was, the air felt wonderfully cool on his face.

"There is a speakerphone in front of you," said someone close to Father Bradbury. This was the man who had originally captured him. "The first person we are calling is Deacon Jones."

No one was holding the priest now. He slumped forward slightly, but he did not slip from the stool. His feet were spread wide, and his hands were still bound behind him. His arms served as a counterbalance to keep him from falling. His legs and hands burned furiously where he had been struck. His arms shook. Tears slipped from the edges of his eyes. His parched lips were trembling. He felt violated and forsaken. But Father Bradbury still had one thing neither pain nor promises could take from him.

"You will tell him to return to the church, collect his belongings, and go home," his captor told him. "If you say anything else, we will end the call, and you will be beaten."

"Sir," Father Bradbury croaked. "I am . . . Botswanan. So is . . . Deacon Jones. I will not tell him . . . to leave."

The switch came down across his slender shoulders. The heavy blow snapped the priest erect and bent him backward. His mouth flew open, but he made no sound. The pain paralyzed his vocal cords and his lungs. He sat there frozen, arched away from the telephone. After a few seconds, the little air that was left in his lungs wheezed out. His shoulders relaxed slowly. His head fell forward. The pain of the blow settled in as a now-familiar heat.

"Do you need me to repeat the instructions?" the man asked.

Father Bradbury shook his head vigorously. Shaking it helped him to work through the aftershocks of the blow.

"I am going to punch in the number," the man went on. "If you do not speak to the deacon, then we will have no choice but to go after him and kill him. Do you understand?"

Father Bradbury nodded. "I still . . . will not say . . . what you want," he informed the man.

The priest expected another blow. He was trembling uncontrollably, too unsettled now to even try to prepare for it. He waited. Instead of striking him, someone retied the hood under his chin. Then he lifted the prisoner to his feet. His legs seemed to be disconnected, and the priest began to drop. The man grabbed the meat of his upper arms and held him tightly. It hurt, but not as much as the rest of him.

The priest was dragged back outside. He was taken to another structure and tossed roughly inside. His hands were still tied behind him, so he tucked his head into his chest to protect it from a fall to the floor. The fall never came. Father Bradbury struck a corrugated metal wall and bounced back toward the door. He landed against metal bars that had been shut so quickly they literally pinned him to the wall. His legs were still wobbly, but that did not matter. His body sagged but did not drop. There was no room. He tried to wriggle to the left and right, but that was not possible. The side walls were as far apart as his aching shoulders.

"Lord God," he murmured when he realized he was in a cell, a cell so small that he would not be able to sit, let alone sleep.

Father Bradbury began to hyperventilate through the hood. He was frightened and rested his cheek against the metal. He had to calm himself, get his mind off his predicament, off his pain. He told himself that the man who had been leading this action, the man in the hut, was not an evil man. He could feel that. He had heard it in his voice. But Father Bradbury had also heard strong determination. That would cloud reason.

The priest folded the fingers of his bound hands. He squeezed them together tightly.

"Hail Mary full of grace the Lord is with Thee," he muttered through the damp cloth.

In the end, only the body dies. Father Bradbury would not stain his soul to save it. But that did not stop him from fearing for the lives of his friends the deacons, from acknowledging that he had no right to sacrifice them.

Yet he also feared for his adoptive home. Only one group spoke of white and black magic. A group as old as civilization and terrifying to those who knew of the pain black magic could cause. Not just supernatural magic, but dark deeds such as drugging, torture, and murder.

A group that had the power to subvert the nation and the continent. And then, possibly, the world.

EIGHT

Washington, D.C.
Tuesday, 5:55 P.M.

It was Mike Rodgers who informed Bob Herbert of Paul Hood's proposed new intelligence unit. The general had come to Herbert's office and briefed him about the meeting with Hood. Then he went off to contact the personnel he hoped would join his new unit.

Bob Herbert was not happy when he heard about it. He was pretty sure he understood why Hood did this the way he had. Rodgers had lost Striker twice. First in Kashmir, then in a wood-paneled office on Capitol Hill. The general needed something to get him back on his feet. The combination of briefing, pep talk, and eye on the prize seemed to have done that. Rodgers had been upbeat when he came in to talk to Herbert.

But Herbert was the intelligence chief. Hood should have consulted him. Herbert should have been briefed about this new unit at the same time that Mike Rodgers became involved.

Hood did not speak to Herbert about the new undertaking until after the routine five P.M. intelligence briefing. The briefings were held at both nine in the morning and again at five P.M. The first briefing was to keep Hood abreast of activities in Europe and the Middle East. Those regions had already been active for hours. The second meeting was to cover the day's intelligence activities involving Op-Center as well as events in the Far East.

After the fifteen-minute update, Hood regarded the Mississippi-born intelligence chief.

"You're upset, aren't you?" Hood asked.

"Yeah," Herbert said.

"About Mike's new operation."

"That's right," Herbert replied. "Since when is my input a threat?"

"It isn't," Hood told him.

"For that matter, since when is Mike's ego so delicate?" Herbert asked.

"Bob, this had nothing to do with letting Mike ramp this thing up on his own," Hood assured him.

"What then?" Herbert asked indignantly.

"I wanted to keep you clean," Hood said.

"From what?" Herbert asked. That caught him off guard.

"From the CIOC," Hood said. "My sense of what they decided last night was to try to push Mike to resign. Senator Fox and her allies can't afford public hearings, and they don't want Mike around. He's a loose cannon who gets things done. That doesn't work in their bureaucratic worldview. The solution? Terminate his primary responsibility. That gives him a disciplinary kick in the ass, and it leaves him without much to do."

"Okay. I'll buy that," Herbert said.

"So I had to give Mike something else to do," Hood said. "If I had made it part of your intelligence operation, that would have given the CIOC a new avenue to attack us. They could have gone after your budget, your personnel. What I did was give Mike responsibilities that fulfill both the CIOC action and his own job description. If Senator Fox decides she isn't happy with what I've done, and they question you about it, you can honestly tell them you had nothing to do with it. Your job or your assets can't be attacked."

Herbert was still pissed. Only now he was angry at himself. He should have known that Hood had a reason for doing what he did. He should never have taken it personally.

He thanked Hood for the explanation. Then Herbert returned to his office to do something constructive rather than brood. Emotion was a quality intelligence operatives were trained to avoid. It fogged the brain and impeded efficiency. Since he had taken an office job, Herbert often forgot that. One of the first questions Hood had asked Herbert before hiring him was a good one. Herbert and his wife had been working for the

CIA when they were caught in the Beirut embassy blast. Hood wanted to know whether Herbert would trade information with the terrorists who had destroyed his legs and killed his wife.

Herbert said that yes, he would. Then he had added, "If I hadn't already killed them."

If Herbert had thought this through, he would have realized that Hood was trying to insulate him. That was what the professionals did. They looked out for their people.

Herbert had just returned to his office when the desk phone beeped. His assistant, Stacey, told him that Edgar Kline was calling. Herbert was surprised to hear the name. The men had worked together in the early 1980s. That was when the Johannesburg native first joined the South African Secret Service. They shared information about terrorist training grounds on the African coast along the Indian Ocean. The SASS was responsible for gathering, correlating, and evaluating foreign intelligence with the exception of military data. Kline resigned from the group in 1987, when he discovered that SASS resources were being used to spy on antiapartheid advocates working abroad. The operative was a devout Catholic who did not approve of apartheid or any exclusionary form of government. Kline moved to Rome and joined the Vatican Security Organization, where Herbert lost touch with him. He was a good man and a solid professional. But he had also been a very difficult man to read. He told you only what he wanted you to know. As long as you were on his side, that was fine. He never left your ass exposed.

Herbert wheeled himself behind the desk and grabbed the phone. "Gunther Center for World Studies," Herbert said.

"Robert?" said the caller.

"Yeah, this is Robert," Herbert replied. "Is this really the Master of Ceremonies?"

"It is," said the caller.

MC had been Edgar Kline's code name. The CIA had assigned it to him when the then-twenty-three-year-old operative worked the coast along the Mozambique Channel. Kline used it whenever he called the Gunther Center for World Studies. That was a small office Herbert had set up to process intelligence information. Herbert had named it after John Gunther, the author of *Inside Africa* and other books that Herbert had read as a young man.

"You know, I've always said the best way to start a day is saying good-bye to a new friend," Herbert said. "Preferably of the opposite sex. But the best way to end a day is definitely saying hello to an old one. How the hell are you?"

"Very well," Kline told him. "What about you?"

There was no mistaking Edgar Kline for anyone else working in intelligence. His voice was still thick with its Afrikaans inflection. It was a unique accent, a hybrid of the English and Dutch that comprised Kline's Afrikaner heritage.

"I'm still cleaning up after the yakety-yak diplomats," Herbert replied. "Where are you calling from?"

"At the moment, from a commercial airliner en route to Washington," Kline told him.

"No shit!" Herbert said. "Does that mean I'm going to get to see you?"

"Actually, while I realize this is rather short notice, I was wondering if you might be free for supper."

"Tonight?"

"Yes," Kline said.

"If I weren't, I would make myself free," Herbert said.

"Excellent," Kline said. "I'm sorry about this being so last minute, but it's been difficult to make plans."

"Don't worry about it," Herbert assured him. "Tell me. Are you still with the same group?"

Herbert had to be careful what he said. Kline had made a point of informing him that he was on board a commercial aircraft. That meant the phone line was not secure.

"Very much so," Kline answered. "And obviously, so are you."

"Yeah, I love it here," Herbert informed him. "They'll have to blast me out of this place, too."

There was a short, pained moan on the other end. "I can't believe you said that, Robert," Kline told him.

"Why not?" Herbert asked. "That's how they got me out of the Central Intelligence Agency."

"I know. But still," Kline replied.

"MC, you've spent too much time with the wrong people," Herbert teased. "If you don't laugh at yourself, the only option is to cry. So where do you want to meet?"

"I'm staying at the Watergate," Kline told him. "I should be there about eight o'clock."

"Fine. I'll meet you at the bar," Herbert said. "Sounds like we need to put some hair back on your cheek."

"Would you mind meeting me in my room?" Kline asked. The South African's tone was suddenly more serious.

"Okay, sure," Herbert said.

"I'll be in the same room I had back on February 22 of '84," Kline told him. "You remember which one that was?"

"I do," Herbert told him. "You're getting nostalgic."

"Very," Kline said. "We'll order room service."

"Fine, as long as you're picking up the check," Herbert said.

"Of course. The Lord provides," Kline said.

"I'll be there," Herbert told him. "And don't worry, MC. Whatever it is, we'll fix it."

"I'm counting on that," Kline told him.

Herbert hung up. He glanced at his watch out of habit and immediately forgot what time it was. He was thinking about Kline.

Kline had not stayed at the Watergate in 1984. That was how they used to communicate room numbers or house addresses of terrorists. The date signified the number. In this case, February 22 meant that Kline was staying in room 222. Obviously, the VSO operative did not want Herbert asking for him. That meant he was not traveling under his real name.

Edgar Kline did not want a record of his being in Washington, D.C. That was also why he was not staying in the permanent rooms the Vatican kept at Georgetown University. If he did, he would be photographed by the campus security cameras. There was also a chance he might be recognized by someone he had worked with.

Herbert wondered what kind of crisis could require such precautions. He brought up the White House database on the travels of world leaders. The Pope was not planning any trips abroad in the near future. Perhaps there was a plot against the Vatican itself.

Whatever it was must have come up suddenly. Otherwise, Kline would at least have let Herbert know he was coming.

In any case, Herbert could use a good scrap right now. The CIOC action had left him frustrated. And it would be nice if he could help an old friend and colleague in the process.

While Herbert pondered the problem, he happened to glance down to his right to the pocket in his wheelchair, to something he had forgotten because he had been distracted and annoyed for most of the day.

To a possible answer to his question.

NINE

Okavango Swamp, Botswana
Wednesday, 1:40 A.M.

The hut was bank-vault dark, and the air was as stuffy and still. The swamp gave up the heat it had accumulated during the day. It was no longer as open-oven hot as it was under the sun. But it was still humid, especially inside the small hut. However hot he was, though, Henry Genet was certain of one thing. The stubborn Father Bradbury was warmer.

Dressed only in briefs, the bald, five-foot-nine-inch Genet sat down on the forty-eight-inch canvas cot. The bed was surrounded by a heavy white nylon lace mosquito net that hung from a bamboo umbrella and reached to the wooden floor. Genet pulled it shut. Then he eased onto his sunburned back. It had been too hot to keep his shirt on, and the sun had managed to find him, even through the thick jungle canopy. Beneath him was a foam mattress and pillow. They were not the king-size bed and down pillow to which he was accustomed, but both were surprisingly comfortable. Or maybe he was just tired.

The trappings were completely alien to the Belgian native. So was this remote swamp, this distant nation, this vast continent. But the fifty-three-year-old was thrilled to be here.

He was also thrilled to be doing what he was doing.

The son of a diamond merchant, Genet had lived in and around Antwerp most of his life. Situated on the busy Scheldt River, Antwerp was Europe's chief commercial city by the mid–sixteenth century. The importance of the Belgian city declined after its sacking by the Spanish in 1576 and the subsequent closing of the Scheldt to navigation. Its significance to modern times dates from 1863. Kings Leopold I and

Leopold II undertook a massive industrialization program and a modernization of Antwerp's port. Today, it is a very modern city and a major center of finance, industry, and the diamond trade.

For all of that, Henry Genet did not miss it.

Despite the history, the culture, and the conveniences, Antwerp existed for finance. So did most of Europe these days. So did Genet. Though he loved acquisition, it had ceased to become a challenge. That was why he had put together the Group. The others were as bored as he was. And boredom was one of the reasons they had come here.

In Botswana, the mentality was far different than it was in Antwerp. For one thing, the age of things in Africa was measured in eons, not in centuries. The sun witnessed the rise and fall of mountains and plains, not improvements in buildings and streets. The stars looked down on the slow workings of evolution, not the life span of civilizations. The people had a monolithic patience that was unheard of in Europe.

Here, Genet had found himself thinking bigger thoughts but with European impatience.

As ancient as this world was, it was also fresh and uncomplicated. There was a clarity of purpose. For the inhabitants it was dance or die. The predators had to kill their prey. The prey had to elude the predators. That simplicity also suited Genet's partner Beaudin. Unlike Europe, where there were attorneys and financial institutions to protect him, the risks here were intense and exciting.

It had been two days since Genet first arrived to oversee the expansion of the ministry. What he had discovered was that even sleeping here was a challenge. The noises, the heat, the mosquitoes that lived in the shallow waters on the shore of their little island. Genet loved being challenged like this.

Especially when the Belgian diamond merchant knew that, if he needed it, escape was just a few dozen yards away. Genet could always use the Aventura II to fly back to his private airstrip and then to civilization. He wanted excitement, but he was not delusional.

Not like Dhamballa. He was an idealist. And idealists, by their nature, were not realists.

Genet used the edges of his pillow to wipe sweat from his eyes. He turned gently onto his belly so the perspiration would run out on its own. Then he thought about Dhamballa, and he had to smile. This operation could not have been easier from conception to launch. And for all Dhamballa's ideas, for all his insights about faith and human nature, he had no idea what any of it was really about.

Eight months before, Dhamballa had been associated with Genet in a much different capacity. Then, the thirty-three-year-old Botswanan was known as Thomas Burton. He was a sifter in a mine Genet visited each month to do some of his buying. Sifters were men who stood beside the mining flumes—long wooden troughs with running water. These troughs were located inside the mines where the lighting could be kept constant. There were screens at different intervals. The water went through without a problem. Small rocks and dirt were trapped by the screen. If the sifters did not see any diamonds, they moved the screen so the detritus could be washed along. Each successive screen had a finer mesh than the one before. And each successive sifter was trained to spot diamonds of decreasing size. Even diamond dust had value to scientists and industrialists. Those people used the dust in microtechnology as prisms, cutting surfaces, or nano-thin switches. The diamond dust was removed from the sand by a fan operator, who blew the fine powder away from the significantly heavier grains.

Thomas had worked at the very end of the trough line. And he had a voice that could be heard over the rushing water and the hum of the fan. Genet knew this because every day, promptly at two o'clock, Thomas would speak about the ages-old teachings of *Vous Deux* or "You Two." While continuing to sift, the young man would extemporize on the beauty of life and death and their relation to the universe.

He would talk about the greatness of the snake, which cast off its skin and died without dying. He would explain how men could cast off death if they took the time to find their own "second skin."

The mine operators allowed Thomas to speak. The other sifters enjoyed hearing him, and they always worked more energetically after his ten- or fifteen-minute inspirational talks. During one visit, Genet listened to what Thomas had to say. He spoke about the gods and how they favored the industrious. He talked about "the white arts," the doing of good deeds, and how it spread light on those whom the practitioner loved. And Thomas spoke of the strength and character that was indigenous to the people of Botswana. It was all very general and very uplifting. It sounded to Genet as if Thomas's words could have come from any faith—Christian, Hindu, Islam.

It was only upon his return to Antwerp that Henry Genet discovered what Thomas Burton was talking about. Who and what he really was. As Genet drifted into sleep, he recalled how, over dinner, he had been discussing the speeches with five other businessmen. When Genet was finished, one of the men, Albert Beaudin, sat back and smiled. Beaudin was a seventy-year-old French industrialist who had his hand in a variety of businesses. Genet's father had invested heavily in several of his enterprises.

"Do you have any idea what you witnessed?" Beaudin asked.

"I don't understand," Genet told him.

"Do you know what you saw in Botswana, Henry? You saw a papa giving a sermon about Bon Dieu," the elderly industrialist explained.

"Who was doing what about whom?" asked Richard Bequette, one of the other merchants.

"A papa is a priest, and Bon Dieu is his supreme deity," Beaudin said.

"I still don't follow," Genet said.

"What you heard were lectures in Vodunism, the religion of white and black arts," Beaudin said. "Of good magic and evil magic. I read about it in *National Geographic*."

And suddenly Genet understood. *Vous Deux* was better known by its Anglicized name, voodoo.

Henry Genet and the other men at that meeting also understood something else. That what the Belgian had witnessed was like the mines he visited. The voodoo faith was deeper, older, and richer than most people knew. All it needed was for someone to tap its wealth. To speak directly to its traditional adherents and potential converts.

To unleash its power.

TEN

Washington, D.C.
Tuesday, 8:00 P.M.

The Watergate was Bob Herbert's favorite hotel. And not just his favorite in Washington. His favorite in the world.

It was not only because of the history of the hotel. The infamy attached to Richard Nixon and the break-in. Herbert actually felt sorry for the man. Virtually every candidate did what Nixon's staff had done. Fortunately or unfortunately, he got caught. That was bad enough. What affected Herbert was this smart man's too-slow uptake in the nascent art of spin control.

No, Herbert had a more personal connection with the hotel. It happened in 1983. He was still getting accustomed to life in a wheelchair, to life without his wife. His rehabilitation facility was several doors down from the hotel. After one frustrating session, Herbert decided to go to dinner at the Watergate. It was his first time out alone.

The hotel, the world, were not yet wheelchair-accessible. Herbert had a difficult time getting around. It was made more difficult by the fact that he was convinced everyone was giving him the "you poor man" look. Herbert was a CIA agent. He was accustomed to being invisible.

Herbert finally made it into the hotel and to a table. Almost at once, the diners at the next table engaged him in conversation. After a few minutes, they invited Herbert to sit with them.

The diners were Bob and Elizabeth Dole.

They did not talk about disabilities. They discussed the value of growing up in a rural area. They talked about food. They compared notes on TV shows, movies, and novels. It was one of those moments of kismet that transcended the practical value of what had transpired. The act of being asked to join the Doles made Herbert feel whole.

Herbert had come back often after that. The Watergate became a touchstone for him, a place that reminded him that a man's value was not in his mode of mobility but what was inside.

Of course, it did not hurt that they had installed ramps since then.

Herbert did not go directly to the elevators. He went to the house phones. There, he swung his laptop from the arm of the wheelchair and accessed the wireless Internet. As soon as he was on-line, he rang room 222. Intelligence people made enemies. Some of those enemies went to elaborate extremes to get revenge. Herbert wanted to make certain that it was Edgar Kline who had called and not someone trying to set Herbert up.

Kline picked up. "Hello?"

"Just making sure you're in," Herbert said.

"I got here five minutes ago," Kline replied.

"On what airline and flight?" Herbert asked.

If Kline were being held against his will, he might give Herbert misinformation to keep him from coming up.

"Lufthansa 418," Kline said.

Herbert did an Internet search for Lufthansa schedules. While he waited he asked, "What make of aircraft?"

"Boeing 747," Kline replied. "I was in seat 1B, and I had the filet."

Herbert smiled. A moment later, the Lufthansa web site confirmed the flight. It was supposed to land at 3:45 P.M., but it had been delayed. "I'll be right up," Herbert said.

Three minutes later, Bob Herbert was rapping on the door of room 222. A tall man with a lantern jaw and short blond hair answered. It was Edgar Kline all right. A little more rotund and leathery around the eyes than Herbert remembered him, but then who wasn't?

Kline smiled and offered his hand. Herbert rolled into the foyer and shut the door before accepting it. He glanced quickly around the room. There was an open suitcase on the bed. Nothing had been removed from it yet. A tweed sports jacket was draped over the back of the desk chair, and a necktie was slung over that. Kline's shoes were at the foot of the bed. Those were the first things a man would have removed after a long flight. The arrival looked legitimate. Kline did not appear to be trying to put something over on him.

Now Herbert turned toward Kline and shook his hand.

"It's good to see you, Robert," Kline said.

Kline spoke with the same reserve Herbert remembered so well. And though he was smiling, it was the kind of smile a professional gambler gave to a newcomer or to a flip comment during a poker game: polite, practiced, not insincere but not very expressive.

"I'm glad to see you, too," Herbert replied. "We haven't been together since I left for Beirut, have we?"

"No," Kline said.

"So what do you think of the new me?" Herbert asked.

"You obviously haven't let what happened over there stop you," Kline observed.

"Did you think it would?" Herbert asked.

"No," Kline replied. He nodded toward the wheelchair. "Does that thing have afterburners?"

"Yeah, these," he said, holding up his powerful hands.

Kline smiled his polite smile and gestured toward the main room. It bothered Herbert more than it used to. Maybe it was just because the intelligence chief was older and more cynical. Or maybe it was something else. Maybe his veteran spy antennae were picking something up.

Or maybe you're just flat out paranoid, Herbert told himself.

"Would you like a drink?" Kline asked.

"A Coke would be nice," Herbert said as he wheeled himself in. This was the first time he had been to one of the rooms. He stopped by the bed and watched as Kline went to the minibar. The South African turned the key and removed a can of soda.

"Would you like anything else?" Kline asked.

"Nope," Herbert said. "Just the Coke and an update."

"I promised you dinner," Kline said. "Shall I call for it?"

"I'm okay for now, and we know you just ate," Herbert said.

"Touché," Kline said.

"So," Herbert said. "Why are you here?"

"To talk to Cardinal Zavala here in Washington and Cardinal Murrieta in New York," he replied as he handed the Coke to Herbert. "We need to get more American missionaries into the field in southern Africa."

"Quickly, I assume?" Herbert said.

Kline nodded. Then his mood changed. The bright blue eyes lost a little of their light. The thin mouth tightened. He began to pace the room. "We're facing a potentially explosive situation in Africa, Robert," Kline said slowly. "And I do not mean just the Vatican."

"You're talking about the incident yesterday with Father Bradbury," Herbert said.

"Yes," Kline said. A hint of surprise crossed the poker face. "What do you know about that?"

"You first," Herbert said. He held up the can. "My mouth is dry."

"Fair enough," Kline said knowingly.

Bob Herbert never went first. Having more information than someone else, even an ally, was always a good thing. Today's allies could be tomorrow's adversaries.

"Father Powys Bradbury was abducted by a militia that was led by someone who we believe is Leon Seronga," Kline said. "Do you know that name?"

"Doesn't spark anything," Herbert said.

"Seronga is a former Botswana soldier who helped to organize the Brush Vipers," Kline said. "They were a very effective intelligence unit that helped Botswana break away from Great Britain."

"I know about the Brush Vipers," Herbert said. This was not what he had wanted to hear. If the Brush Vipers were back, in more than just name, it meant that what happened was probably not a small, isolated action.

"Seronga was spotted two weeks ago at the Botswana village of Machaneng," Kline went on. "He was attending a rally held by a religious leader named Dhamballa."

"Is that his real name?" Herbert asked as he unfolded his computer. "I mean is that a surname or a tribal name or an honorary title?"

"It's a variant spelling of the name of a god of the Vodun faith," Kline said. "We do not know more than that. And we do not have direct access to him. Nor is his image in our file."

"At least, not under that name," Herbert said.

"Correct."

"But this Dhamballa is the reason you had someone watching the rally," Herbert said.

"Yes," Kline admitted.

Herbert asked Kline for the spelling of the name. He made a note of it in a new computer file.

"We routinely watch all religious movements in Africa," Kline added. "It's part of the apostolic tool kit."

"Collecting intel about rivals," Herbert said.

"You never really know who your rivals are—"

"Or who they might be fronting for," Herbert said. Political activism often hid behind a new religious idea. That made it easier to sell to the masses.

"Exactly," Kline agreed. "We take digital pictures of events like these and load them into a master file. We like to know whether they originate at a grassroots level or elsewhere. Real religious movements tend to peak at a certain point and return to the underground. Sects concealing a political agenda tend to be well financed, often from abroad. They don't usually fade away."

"Making them more of a threat," Herbert pointed out.

"Yes, but not just to the Church's goals," Kline said. "They're a danger to the political stability of the continent. We take a very real interest in the lives, health, and well-being of the people to whom we minister. This is not just about the state of their immortal souls."

"I understand," Herbert assured him.

"After we ID'ed Seronga, we went back and checked photographs from previous Dhamballa rallies," Kline went on.

"Were these large rallies or small ones?" Herbert interrupted.

"Small at first, just about a dozen people at the mine," Kline said. "Then they began to grow as family members attended. He began holding them in village squares and in fields."

"Talking about?"

"The same things he discussed in the mines," Kline said.

"Gotcha," Herbert told him. "Sorry to interrupt. You were saying about Leon Seronga—?"

"That he was not the only member of the former Brush Vipers to have been present," Kline said.

"I see," Herbert said. "Which is really why you came to Washington. If this is the start of a new political action in southern Africa, you want Americans to help contain it."

"Let's just say I'd like you to participate in the process of containment," Kline said. "That can take many forms, though right now I need intelligence."

Kline seemed somewhat embarrassed by that. He should not have been. Herbert welcomed honesty. Everyone wanted America to become involved in international scuffles. The United States gave backbone to friends and took the heat from enemies.

"Edgar, do you have any idea why Father Bradbury was targeted?" Herbert asked.

"Not really," Kline said. "As I said, we lack information."

"Was there something special about his ministry?" Herbert asked.

"Father Bradbury presided over—forgive me. I mean, he *presides* over the largest number of deacon missionaries in the nation," Kline said. He shook his head and tightened his lips. "I can't believe I said that."

"It's a natural mistake," Herbert said. "I've probably done it a million times without being smart enough to catch it." He paused. "Unless you know something you're not saying."

"No," Kline said. "If we thought something else had happened, I would tell you."

"Sure," Herbert said. "Okay, then. Back to the still-presiding

Father Bradbury. Who has the next-largest number of deacon missionaries?"

"There are ten other parish priests, each with three or four deacon missionaries," Kline said. "They are all being watched."

"By?"

"Local Botswana constables and by undercover elements of the Botswana military," Kline said.

"Good," Herbert said. "And I assume no one at the Vatican has received a ransom demand?"

Kline shook his head.

"That means the kidnappers need him," Herbert said. "If kidnappers don't want money, they want the victim to do something for them. To sign a document, make a radio or TV broadcast, renounce a policy or idea. They may even want his dead body to scare converts or other priests. Do you have any idea where they've taken Father Bradbury?"

"No," Kline said. "And it wasn't for lack of trying. Within one hour, the Moremi Wildlife rangers were looking for the militia on the ground. The military was up in two hours doing an aerial search. They didn't find anything. Unfortunately, there's a lot of ground to cover. The kidnappers could have dispersed, hidden, or disguised themselves as a safari group. There are hundreds of those in the area at any given time."

"Did anyone talk to truck drivers, check with amateur radio operators?" Herbert asked.

"Both," Kline said. "The police are still talking to CB operators. It was silent running all the way. This was a well-planned operation, but we have no idea to what end." The VSO officer stopped pacing and regarded Herbert. "That's everything I know."

"Pretty much in line with other neopolitical grab-and-runs I've encountered," Herbert said.

"I agree," Kline said. "This is more like the act of rebels than religious acolytes."

"One thing I don't see is Botswana complicity with this militia," Herbert said. "The economy is strong, and the government is stable. They would have nothing to gain by this."

"I agree again," Kline said. "So what does that leave us with? Are we facing some kind of religious-military hybrid? The Brush Vipers fought to obtain the independence Botswana now enjoys. Why would they want to be involved with a potentially destabilizing force?"

"I'm not sure," Herbert said. "But I agree with what one of my coworkers said. General Mike Rodgers was the one who called the incident to my attention this morning. I believe a message was being sent. That's why this Leon Seronga moved against the tourist office in daylight. They had the weapons and personnel to have massacred everyone. But they did not."

"What kind of message do you think he was sending?" Kline asked.

Now it was Kline who was fishing. Since this part was speculative, Herbert did not mind going first.

"It could be any number of things," Herbert said. "They may have done it this way to assuage the government. To show them that while they had weapons, they did not use them. That will probably encourage a more moderate response from Gaborone."

"A wait-and-see approach," Kline thought out loud.

"Exactly."

"Even though a Botswana citizen was kidnapped," Kline said.

"The term *citizen* is a legal one," Herbert pointed out. "To most Botswanans, a citizen is probably someone who can trace his ancestry back hundreds, maybe thousands of years."

"All right," Kline said. "That's reasonable. What else could the form of this kidnapping signify?"

"Well, it can also simply mean that Dhamballa is not strong enough to engage in military action but will if they're forced," Herbert said. "That might also soften the government's response. They pride themselves on being one of the most stable regimes on the continent. Gaborone will probably try to present this as an aberration. Something that can be handled. Maybe they'll want to wait and see what, if anything, happens next before stirring things up."

"But at some point, the Botswana military must move against them," Kline said.

"Not if Dhamballa's end game is a modest one," Herbert said. "And we don't even know that this is Dhamballa. We also don't know what the master plan may look like, but I researched some of our databases before coming here. The Brush Vipers were one of four paramilitary groups that used to operate in that region of Botswana. Do you know where they got their weapons from?"

"Not from the Botswana military, I hope," Kline replied.

"No," Herbert replied. "Worse. They came from someone we dealt with years ago."

"Who?" Kline pressed.

"The Musketeer," Herbert replied. "Albert Beaudin."

ELEVEN

Paris, France
Wednesday, 3:35 A.M.

He had always worked late. Ever since he was a young man in occupied France.

Albert Beaudin sat on the terrace of his apartment overlooking Champ de Mars. The night was cool but pleasant. Low, thin clouds were colored a murky orange black by the nighttime lights of Paris. To his left, the aircraft warning lights of the Eiffel Tower winked on and off. The top of the tower flirted with the passing clouds.

Beaudin's earliest memory of the monument was also at night. It was after the Allies had come through Paris. That was when it was finally safe for his father and him to come to the city. What a night that had been. They had ridden for nearly twenty hours straight with little Albert sprawled in the sidecar of a stolen German staff motorcycle. Albert was used to being up at night. Much of the work he had done was in the dark. But that night was special. He could still smell the diesel fuel. He could still hear his father and himself singing French folk songs as they sped through the countryside. By the time they reached Paris, they had no voices left. Albert had no derriere left either, after bumping around in the sidecar.

But it did not matter. What a journey it had been. What a childhood he had lived.

What a victory they had won.

Maurice Beaudin had worked with Jean LeBeques, the legendary *Le Conducteur de Train de la Résistance,* the "Train Conductor of the Resistance." LeBeques ran a locomotive between Paris and Lyons. Lyons was where spare parts for the railroad were manufactured. Because of the city's central location and relative proximity to Switzerland, the French Resistance was also based in Lyons. Personnel could be dispatched quickly to other parts of the nation or smuggled to safety in a neutral country.

The Germans always sent a substantial military force with LeBeques. They wanted to make certain he was not bringing supplies to the *Die Schlammgleisketten,* as the Germans derisively referred to them. "The Mud Crawlers." The Germans were derisive, but they were not dismissive. From the time France surrendered in June of 1940 until the end of the war, the French Resistance was relentless. They sabotaged the German war effort and forced the enemy to keep much-needed resources in France.

Albert and his father were among the earliest members of the resistance. Maurice Beaudin was a widower. He had a small plant that manufactured the fishplates used to join sections of rail. Maurice had known LeBeques for nearly thirty years. Both men happened to share a birthday, March 8, 1883. One evening, shortly after arriving, LeBeques presented Maurice with a cake. Written on the paper doily underneath was a message asking *le réceptif,* the recipient, if he would be willing to fight for a free France. If so, he was to cut an X-shaped notch on the top left corner of the first crate he put on the train. Maurice did so. From that point forward, the men found ways to smuggle ammunition, spare parts for radios, and personnel on LeBeques's trains. By some miracle, both men managed to survive the war. Tragically, if ironically, LeBeques died in a train wreck late in 1945. He was busy transporting former resistance fighters home after the war.

Albert was just six years old at the time. He attended school until two in the afternoon then went to the small factory to sweep. It was important to collect metal filings every day. Iron was scarce, and the scraps were melted down and reused. To this day, in his own munitions factories, the pungent smell of oiled metal, fresh from the lathe, brought Albert back to his youth.

So did the idea of working with other dedicated individuals on a paramilitary undertaking.

Maurice had never hesitated to involve his young son in resistance operations.

If France remained enslaved, Maurice reasoned, what was the point of growing older?

Sometimes Albert had to distract soldiers by fighting with another boy or picking on a young girl. At other times he had to slip things onto the train while the adults created distractions. Throughout the rest of his life, Albert was never able to communicate to others the excitement of risking death. He had seen others, including his fourteen-year-old cousin Samuel, murdered for suspected acts of sabotage. He had watched men and women dragged in front of stone walls and shot, hanged from trees and streetlights, and even lashed to tractors or bales of hay and used for bayonet practice. Any of those things could have happened to Albert. He learned to accept danger as a part of life, risk as a part of reward. Those sensibilities remained with Albert after the war. Fearlessness enabled him to expand his father's business into aircraft in the 1950s and munitions in the early 1960s.

By the time he was in his midthirties, Albert Beaudin was a very wealthy man. But he had two regrets. The first was that his father died before he saw how vast the Beaudin empire had become. And the second was that France had failed to become a military and political force in the postwar world. The strongest free nation on the European continent, France was weakened militarily and politically by the defeat of its troops in Indochina in 1954 and then in Algeria in 1962. Hoping to restore French prestige in world affairs, France elected resistance leader Charles de Gaulle as president. De Gaulle made military independence from the United States and NATO one of his priorities. Unfortunately, that left France a virtual nonplayer in the Cold War. Instead of being embraced by the Soviet Union and the United States, France wanted to be independent. That left the nation mistrusted by both. The emergence of Germany and Japan as financial powers in the 1960s and 1970s was also something the French had not anticipated. That left France with wine, films, and posters of the Eiffel Tower as their legacy for the latter twentieth century.

But while the century was finished, Albert Beaudin was not. Growing up as a resistance fighter had taught Albert never to be afraid of anything. It taught him never to accept defeat. And it taught him how to organize a small but devoted band into a powerful force.

Albert heard a jet. He looked up. He watched as a low-flying aircraft threw cones of white light above the clouds. There must be severe storms to the south. Aircraft usually did not fly directly over the city this late.

Albert listened until the roar of the jet engines had faded. Then he let his green eyes move across the rest of the dark Parisian skyline.

There were indeed storms to the south. Storms that were going to sweep the world. Albert found himself staying up at night, recapturing the drama, risk, and excitement of the last great war he fought for his homeland.

However, the results of this war would be different. It would be fought without the loss of French lives. It would be fought in a foreign land. And it would show the world what ingenuity and stealth could accomplish.

It would also do one thing more. It would shift the center of world power from a handful of bellicose nations to a handful of men. Men who were impervious to bombs and sanctions.

Men who would restore their homeland to a prominence it had not known for over two centuries.

TWELVE

Washington, D.C.
Tuesday, 9:49 P.M.

After meeting with Paul Hood and briefing Bob Herbert, Mike Rodgers went to his office. For the first time in weeks, he was energized.

Over a year before, General Rodgers had talked to Hood about establishing a HUMINT team for Op-Center, one that would not only gather information but have the ability to infiltrate enemy units if necessary. Events had forced them to put the idea on hold. Rodgers was glad to be bringing it back. He knew that spearheading a new HUMINT team would not ease the loss of the Strikers. It would not change the general's perception that he had mismanaged aspects of the Himalayan operation. It would not accomplish that any more than remanning Striker would have done. But Hood's aggressive step reminded Rodgers that command was not a profession for the timid.

Or the self-pitying.

The first thing Rodgers did was to access the computer files of the agents he and Hood had discussed. Op-Center kept track of all the operatives who had worked with them. The "co-operatives," as Bob Herbert called them. The COs were not aware of the electronic surveillance. Senior Computer Specialist Patricia Arroyo in Matt Stoll's office hacked everything from credit card transactions to phone bills. They did this for two reasons. First, Op-Center needed to be able to contact freelance agents quickly, if necessary. Covert operatives often resigned. They frequently dropped out of sight, changed addresses, and occasionally changed identities. But even if credit card numbers were different, purchase preferences and phone contacts were the same. Those patterns were easy to locate and track to new credit cards or telephone numbers.

The second reason Op-Center continued to watch former COs was to make certain that potential partners were not spending time with potential adversaries. Calls placed to cell phones were very closely monitored. Patricia had developed software to cross-reference these numbers with phones registered to embassy employees. Nearly 40 percent of all foreign service workers were intelligence gatherers. Tax documents and bank accounts were watched to make sure the sums matched. The records of family members were also collected. Wherever possible, computer passwords were broken and E-mails read.

Even experienced, well-intentioned intelligence workers could be tricked, seduced, bribed, or blackmailed.

Locating Maria Corneja, David Battat, and Aideen Marley was not a problem.

The thirty-eight-year-old Corneja, a Spanish Interpol agent, had recently married Darrell McCaskey. McCaskey was Op-Center's NAFIL—National and Foreign Intelligence Liaison. He had returned to Washington while Maria settled her affairs in Madrid. She would be joining her husband in a week.

Forty-three-year-old David Battat was the former director of a CIA field office in New York City. Battat had recently returned to Manhattan after helping Op-Center stop a terrorist from sabotaging oil supplies in Azerbaijan. Thirty-four-year-old Aideen Marley was still in Washington. The former foreign service officer had worked with Maria Corneja, averting a Spanish civil war two years before. Now she was working as a political consultant for both Op-Center and the State Department.

The other operatives were living in different parts of the world. Twenty-eight-year-old Falah Shibli was still working as a police officer in Kiryat Shmona in northern Israel. A veteran of seven years in the *Sayeret Ha'Druzim*—Israel's elite Druze Reconnaissance unit—the Lebanon-born Israeli had assisted Op-Center in their Bekaa Valley operation.

Forty-nine-year-old Harold Moore divided his time between

London and Tokyo. Moore was a former G-man who had been recruited by McCaskey to help Op-Center with its first crisis, finding and defusing a terrorist bomb on board the space shuttle *Atlantis*. Feeling underappreciated, Moore had elected to take early retirement. He was now working as a consultant to both Scotland Yard's Specialist Operations Anti-Terrorist Branch and the Intelligence and Analysis Bureau of Japan's Ministry of Foreign Affairs.

Twenty-nine-year-old Zack Bemler was based in New York. Bemler was a magna cum laude Ph.D. graduate in international security from Princeton University's Woodrow Wilson School of Public and International Affairs. The young man had been courted by the CIA and the FBI but ended up working for World Financial Consultants, an international investment group. After rogue generals were prevented from overthrowing the legitimate government in Russia, then–political liaison Martha Mackall contacted Bemler. Bemler had dated Martha's kid sister Christine at Princeton. Together, Martha and Bemler worked to clean out the generals' bank accounts in Switzerland and the Cayman Islands. The twenty-five million dollars was used to fund joint intelligence ventures between Paul Hood and Sergei Orlov's Russian Op-Center.

Rodgers knew how to contact the personnel he wanted. He had the money to hire them. But numerous questions remained. Should he mix veterans with new personnel, combine new ideas with the old? Would these people consider working for Op-Center full-time, if at all? If so, where would they be based? Would it be practical to run an entirely freelance operation? Then there were logistic issues. They could not travel as a unit in a military transport, since those aircraft were routinely watched by satellite and on the ground. Upon arriving at an air base, they might be spotted and followed. But it was also unwise to put them on a single commercial flight. If one were identified, they might all be exposed.

Rodgers also had to figure out how to run the unit. Covert operatives were more like artists than soldiers. They were creative individuals. They did not enjoy working in groups or doing things by the book.

The general wanted input from Herbert. He also wanted to talk to the spy chief about the way the team had come about. After the meeting with Hood, Mike Rodgers could think of nothing but the new team. It did not occur to him until hours later that it probably upset Herbert to be excluded from this process. As a former spy himself, Herbert had a great poker face. He might not have let his displeasure show to Rodgers. Herbert was also a team player. He would not want to dull Rodgers's enthusiasm.

Unfortunately, Herbert had been busy for most of the day. Rodgers busied himself with the personnel files and other Op-Center business. That included daily military reports from around the world. Rodgers liked to keep track of former allies as well as potential enemies. A crisis management officer never knew when he would have to call on one group for assistance or fight the other.

The night team came on at six P.M. That left Rodgers free to concentrate on the team and possible sites for a shakedown operation. He did not want to talk to any potential agents until he had something concrete to propose to them.

It was shortly before ten P.M. when Bob Herbert finally returned Rodgers's call.

"You were right," Herbert said.

"Glad to hear it," Rodgers said. "About what?"

"Something is going on in Botswana," Herbert said.

It felt like it had been ages since Rodgers gave Herbert the newspaper. This had been a long day.

Rodgers listened as Herbert told him about the meeting with Edgar Kline. It sounded like a regional scuffle until he mentioned the name Albert Beaudin. In intelligence circles, Beaudin was known as the Musketeer.

"What does he have to do with this?" Rodgers asked.

"I'm not sure he does," Herbert said. "But there is a connection between him and the Brush Vipers of thirty-odd years ago."

Rodgers was concerned about that. He was also intrigued. Beaudin was a powerful but elusive figure. Since the early 1960s, the industrialist was suspected of using a worldwide

network to provide arms to rebels, rogue nations, and both
sides of Third World conflicts. His agents at customs check-
points, in police stations, in shipping offices, and in factories
enabled him to sidestep embargoes and arms bans. He provided arms to Central and South American rebels, to African
warlords, and to Middle Eastern nations. His willingness to
sell low-priced weapons to both Iran and Iraq was one of the
reasons their war lasted for eight years in the 1980s. Even if
he just broke even on the initial gun sales, Beaudin made
money on the steady demand for ammunition and spare parts.
Because rebel factions and smaller countries needed his weapons, they were never willing to help the United Nations, Interpol, or other international organizations investigate his
activities. Because of Beaudin's influence among French politicians and military officials, they were also unwilling to cooperate. Op-Center had always suspected that Beaudin was one
of the financial forces behind the New Jacobins, xenophobic
terrorists they had fought in Toulouse several years before.

"If Beaudin is involved, chances are we're probably not
looking at a small event," Herbert said.

"Or a short one," Rodgers added. "Whoever is behind this
had to know the Vatican would get involved."

"They were obviously counting on that," Herbert said. "The
Church won't surrender its ministries. Kline is afraid that if
this isn't an isolated attack, someone may be trying to create
a schism."

"Between?"

"Catholics and people of indigenous faiths," Herbert said.
"If someone pits religion against religion, you have a hot-
button issue that can blow up throughout the western world.
It could fuel arms consumption all over Africa, the Middle
East, Central Asia—"

"Giving Beaudin a damn near bottomless market for his
product," Rodgers said.

"Right," Herbert said. "That's assuming Beaudin's involved
in this, of course. There could be other people behind the abduction, international players we haven't even considered."

"I'm also not ready to make the leap from the abduction of

Father Bradbury to a regional war," Rodgers said. "These things take time to develop."

"True."

"And a short-term conflict would be chump change to a guy like Beaudin," Rodgers said.

"That said, all the war simulations in the regions show the potential for widespread pocket conflagrations," Herbert reminded him. "We might not see a pattern until local governments start falling. A religious war in Botswana would be the perfect trigger to start uprisings of all kinds among the disenfranchised."

"The war sims also show the major powers being forced to contain those struggles, the way we did in Kashmir," Rodgers noted. "Too many nations have big, blow-down-the-door weapons. None of us can afford to let those come into play."

"The good thing is, if Beaudin is involved, he can't afford that, either," Herbert said. "There's no profit for him. That's why we have to see if there are some major pieces still missing."

"What does Kline want to do?" Rodgers asked.

"I spoke to him again, told him there was no point trying to check up on Beaudin's activities through France," Herbert said. "They shut me down when I tried to link him to those nutcases in Toulouse."

"The Church might find a few more allies than we did," Rodgers pointed out. "There are more Roman Catholics in France than any other denomination. About ninety percent, I think."

"You're right, but they're also fiercely nationalistic," Herbert said. "Kline doesn't want to suggest that a Frenchman committed an anti-Catholic act."

"Even if he may have," Rodgers said.

"If he did, we'll have to find out through other means," Herbert said. "If that ever got out and we were wrong, the Vatican would have forty-five million very unhappy worshipers."

While Herbert was speaking, Rodgers reaccessed Patricia Arroyo's personnel database. He entered the name Ballon, Colonel Bernard Benjamin. The forty-something Colonel Ballon was a tough veteran officer with France's *Groupe d'Intervention de la Gendarmerie Nationale*. The Frenchman's anti–hate crime unit had worked with Op-Center to stop the New Jacobins from murdering Algerian and Moroccan immigrants in France. If they could bring in Ballon, maybe this would not have to become a national hot potato.

"My feeling is we're going to have to try to kite-tail Beaudin from the other end," Herbert went on. "We or the Vatican Security Organization should get someone close to the religion or cult or whatever it is as soon as possible. While we're watching them, we can also look for signs of Beaudin."

"Do you think Paul will go along with that?" Rodgers asked. "Not the idea but the haste."

"I think so," Herbert said. "If not for humanitarian reasons, then for simple intel. No one else is onto this yet, and it could be explosive."

"Paul may not want to take that heat," Rodgers said. "Not with the shit we're getting from the CIOC and Senator Fox."

"We may not have a choice," Herbert replied. "It's happening, and we've been asked to help. The VSO may not want the CIA or National Security Council involved. Our government doesn't like religious wars. Minority wars. Paul's answer has to be yes or no."

Given that choice, Rodgers knew what Pope Paul would say. He always put people ahead of politics. But Rodgers had been in this game long enough to know that even a successful mission could hurt. Instead of proving how invaluable Op-Center was, they could piss off all the intelligence units that did not have a Vatican contact, or had missed the significance of the *Washington Post* article, or who just didn't want Op-Center to succeed at any damn thing they did.

"If nothing else," Herbert said, "getting involved with the kidnapping will let your new team hit the ground running."

"That's true," Rodgers said. "Bob, I've been wanting to talk to you about the team—"

"There's nothing to talk about," Herbert interrupted.

"I think there is," Rodgers shot back. "Paul sprang the HU-

MINT idea on me this morning, and I ran with it."

"That's what you were supposed to do," Herbert assured him.

"Not over your still-breathing body," Rodgers said.

Herbert laughed. "Mike, I don't have the time, temperament, or experience to run a field force," the intelligence chief assured him. "You do. Now we've got more important things to deal with than protocol between coworkers who also happen to be good friends."

Rodgers did not believe that Herbert was as indifferent as he made it sound. But Rodgers thanked him just the same.

Herbert was about to call Hood and update him when the file on Colonel Ballon opened.

"Hold on," Rodgers said. "I just brought up the file of someone I thought might be able to help us."

"Who?"

"Colonel Ballon," Rodgers told him.

"Good idea," Herbert observed. "He's a tough nut."

"That's why I wanted to call on him," Rodgers said. "Unfortunately, he's MIA."

"You mean Patricia lost him?" Herbert asked.

"No," Rodgers said. He was sickened as he read the file. "I mean Ballon is gone. According to the GIGN payroll files, he stopped showing up for work nearly two years ago. There's been no trace of him since."

"He may have gone undercover," Herbert suggested.

"Possibly," Rodgers agreed.

It was also possible that Colonel Ballon ran afoul of someone he had crossed. The officer's disappearance occurred not long after the struggle with the New Jacobins. Rodgers was not ready to make that leap, either. But he could not ignore the possibility.

"I'll have Darrell check on this," Rodgers said as he composed an E-mail for the former FBI agent. "Maybe he can get an update from some of his European contacts."

Herbert said he would let Rodgers know what Hood had to say. Then he hung up. Rodgers returned to his list of operatives. He did not imagine that Hood would keep Op-Center out of this. American officials did not turn down requests from the Vatican. Not even unofficial requests. That meant that Rodgers might have to field a team sooner than he expected.

Rodgers had a sudden flashback to the moment he learned he had to take his green Striker team out to save the space shuttle *Atlantis*. The general had been sitting at this same desk, at about the same time, when the call came from Hood.

"Can you be ready to go at twenty-three hundred hours?"

Of course he could, he had replied. And Striker performed brilliantly that night.

They always performed brilliantly.

His eyes moistened, not with sorrow but with pride. Smiling for the first time in weeks, Rodgers went back to his files and to the job at hand.

THIRTEEN

Okavango Swamp, Botswana
Wednesday, 5:58 A.M.

For the first few hours, Father Bradbury had fought temptation. He refused to lick the damp interior of his hood.

During the trek to the islet, the priest's hair, hood, and clothing had become saturated with the swamp water. The temperature dropped during the night, causing the thicker grime to separate from the water. The remaining paste hardened, and the water dribbled down the inside of the hood.

At first, the priest refused to taste the water. But as thirst and exhaustion worked on him, his head grew light. It became difficult to focus on prayer or anything but his aching legs and his thirst. Reason was nudged aside. Finally, he used his tongue and lips to work the hood into the side of his mouth. He bit on the fabric and sucked out the water. The liquid was greasy and tart. Most of it was probably his own perspiration. It did not satisfy his thirst, but it made his body happy to swallow something.

The effort probably cost him more energy than it was worth. But he began to understand the desperation that drove shipwrecked men to drink seawater. Though it did more damage than good, the body gave you no choice. It craved something, anything. The need to survive transcended logic.

Because there was no room for Father Bradbury to sit, he leaned against the side of his prison all night. Sometimes he kept his cheek against the wall, sometimes his forehead. His tired eyes burned, and he kept them shut. He tried to imagine that he was somewhere else. His legs began to hurt, and he realized that he really did not walk enough. One had to drive on the floodplain to get anywhere. He would have to change that if he returned. Maybe he would get a bicycle instead of the motor scooter he used to go to shops in Maun. He thought about the multidenominational church in Maun and how nice it would be to talk to the priests who came in to conduct services. To discuss the Bible and faith and dogma.

For a moment, the priest smiled. Then he began to sob. He wanted to return to his parish. Thinking back on his life, he was not certain he had done everything he could to show his loyalty to God. He had never shirked a task, that he could remember, or doubted his faith. But was that enough? Were there ways in which he could have pushed himself harder?

Even in this matter, the recalling of deacon missionaries, Father Bradbury did not know what was the right thing to do. Protect the spreading of the word, or protect the bearers of the word?

Father Bradbury decided that this was not the time to contemplate his shortcomings. That would undermine whatever strength and resolve he had left. Obviously, that was the point of his being locked up here. They wanted him to make those calls to the deacon missionaries.

Now and then, the priest tried to work his hands free. Because they were behind him, he did not have much room to move in any direction. When the rope began to rub the flesh of his wrists raw, he stopped. He prayed in silence. The proximity of the walls prevented Father Bradbury from sinking to the floor, and he was not able to sleep. Irregular streams of perspiration tickled him with annoying regularity. After what felt like several hours, his legs began to cramp. The lack of air in the cell, inside the hood, also prevented him from relaxing.

His mind grew increasingly tired, and the anxiety returned. He could not help but think of cool water, fruit, food, sleep. The more he thought about it, the more he missed it. When he managed to pray it distracted him less and less.

By morning, when people came to get him, Father Bradbury was dizzy. He felt as if someone had stuffed cotton in his ears, in his cheeks, and behind his eyelids. He also had to be ripped from the wall of his prison. The muck from the swamp had solidified. The priest's hair stuck to the hood. Along with his clothes, the hood stuck to the wall. As he was led outside, the priest tried to stand, but his knees felt as if someone had hammered nails into the sides. The pain was intense when they tried to support his full weight. His legs folded, and Father Bradbury had to be held up by four hands. Two held him around the waist and two gripped his upper arms. He was pulled to wherever it was they wanted him. The hint of rich sunlight and sweet air that came through the hood was a tease. The priest inhaled deeply but got only a frustrating taste of morning.

Once again, Father Bradbury was brought to a structure of some kind. Maybe it was the same one he had been in the night before. He had no way of knowing. When they arrived, he was not permitted to sit. The men who had brought him here continued to hold him. One of them grabbed his bound wrists and pulled upward. Father Bradbury felt the tug in his upper back. It reminded the priest of reading he had done about strappado, a form of torture used during the Inquisition. The victim was bound in this fashion, lifted by rope, then dropped partway with a jerk. The action would dislocate the prisoner's shoulders.

Though he was warm and perspiring again, Father Bradbury began to tremble.

The idea of having his body broken was frightening. But the idea that he would be tortured for the wrong ideal was even more terrifying. He did not have the certainty of a martyr.

"Bring him closer," someone said from in front of him. It was the man who had spoken to him the night before. The man with the gentle voice. It sounded even calmer now. The priest wondered if it were the voice of a man who had just finished morning prayer.

Father Bradbury was urged forward. He tried hard to keep his legs under him. At the very least, he wanted to be standing on his own when he faced his own inquisitor. He failed. Sweat was collecting in the bottom of the hood. It was pooling faster than the fabric could absorb it. The priest wished they would at least take the hood off.

"Have you changed your mind?" the voice asked.

Father Bradbury stopped thinking. He answered from the gut. "No," the priest replied. His voice was a rough whisper.

There were sounds from ahead. Someone was coming toward him. Father Bradbury did not know whether to expect words or blows. Once again, he prayed silently for strength.

"You may relax," the speaker said. "I am not going to let anyone strike you. Not today. There must be a balance. Wrath and mercy. Otherwise, neither has any meaning."

"Thank you," the priest said.

"Besides, some men refuse anything they are *forced* to do," the voice said. "Even when these are things they would do willingly at another time."

The speaker was very close to him now. Even more than the previous night, his voice had a soothing, oddly comforting quality. It also sounded young. For the first time, he heard a hint of innocence.

"I would never recall missionaries who are doing God's work," Father Bradbury rasped.

"Never?" the voice asked.

Father Bradbury was too tired, too distracted to think back. Had he ever done that? He did not think so. Would he ever do it? He did not know. He could not answer the question.

"I am certain you would warn your people of an impending flood or hurricane," said the voice.

"Yes," Father Bradbury agreed. "But so they could help others, not save themselves."

"But you would not want them to stay and perish," said the man.

"No."

"You would tell the missionaries to leave because life is dear," said the speaker. "Well, your people are in danger. The gods want this land restored to them and their people returned to the olden temples. I am going to give the gods what they want."

"What about the wishes of the people?" Bradbury asked.

"You hear their confessions," said the speaker. "You know what many wish. They wish to sin. They wish to have an easy life. It is for the heralds of the gods to teach them a better way."

"Not everyone wants those things," the priest wheezed.

"You are in no position to say that," the speaker said.

"I know my parish—"

"You do not know *my* parish," the man shot back. "It is also for you to decide only whether you and your missionaries will be alive to preach elsewhere. Do not act from pride but with wisdom. But act quickly."

Father Bradbury could not help but think of Proverbs 16: 18. "Pride goeth before destruction, and an haughty spirit before a fall."

Perhaps it was the speaker's intention to remind Father Bradbury of that passage from the Bible. To make him doubt himself. Since the priest had been abducted, everything seemed designed to disorient him. But knowing that did not make it any less effective. Nor did it change the truth of what the man was saying. Father Bradbury did not have the right to keep anyone in danger's way. And what of his own soul, let alone his life? The priest asked himself the same question he had asked the night before. What would God think of a man who knew that others were at risk and did nothing to save them? The answer seemed clearer now. Or maybe his resistance had diminished. But he was not being asked to disavow his faith. He was being asked to help save lives.

A sudden sense of outrage flooded the priest. Who were these people to insist that he and the other clergymen leave their adopted home? Who were they to *demand* that the word of God Almighty be silenced? But the indignation faded quickly as the priest asked himself whether he had the right to make these decisions for the missionaries or for God.

He needed time that he did not have. Father Bradbury wished he could remove the hood and have a drink. Taste clean air. He yearned to sit down, to lie down, to sleep. He wanted the time to think this through. He wondered if he should ask for these things.

"I can't think," he muttered.

"You're not being asked to think," the speaker replied

coldly. "Make the telephone calls, and then you will be fed and permitted to rest. When you are refreshed, you will understand that you acted wisely. You will save lives."

"My job is to save souls," the priest replied.

"Then live, and save them—somewhere else," the man replied.

Even if Father Bradbury had the will to fight, he was not sure exactly what he was fighting for. Or against. Or if he was even fighting for the right cause. It was all too confusing. The man was right about one thing. He needed a clearer head. He needed time. And there was only one way to get that.

"All right," Father Bradbury said. "I will do as you ask. I will make your calls."

The priest felt hands working around his neck. He eagerly anticipated the removal of the hood. It only came up partway. The men tugged the front only as high as the top of his mouth. They lifted the right side above his ear. The cool air felt like a breath from Heaven. He was walked forward and gently lowered to his knees. It was a little kindness that he appreciated. He was given a short sip of warm water from a canteen. That, too, was a gift from God.

"The first call is to Deacon Jones," another man told him. Father Bradbury recognized the voice. It was the gruff-throated man who had brought him to this room the previous night.

Strong hands continued to hold his shoulders as numbers were punched. The clergyman remembered someone saying the night before that there was a speakerphone.

The priest was told to say that he was being well cared for. Then he was to give the deacon missionaries their instructions. He was to tell each missionary that he would join them soon at the diocese in Cape Town. He was to reveal absolutely nothing more.

Deacon Jones answered the phone. The young man was excited and relieved to hear from the priest. In as clear and firm a voice as he could generate, Father Bradbury instructed the missionary to return immediately to the compound, pack, and go to Cape Town.

"What is it?" Deacon Jones asked. "What is happening?"

"I will explain when I see you," the priest replied. He felt a reassuring squeeze on his shoulders.

"As you wish," Jones replied.

The deacon had never disputed the priest's judgment. Nor did Deacon March. Nor did any of the other deacon missionaries.

When Father Bradbury was finished making the calls, he was taken to a wicker chair. His legs were stiff, and his lower back was tight. It was difficult to sit. He jumped as the edge of the seat scraped behind his knees. That was where he had been struck the day before. The priest waited for the mask to be removed and his hands to be untied. Instead, he heard another chair moved beside him.

"You will be given water and food now," said the man who had done most of the talking. "Then you will be allowed to sleep."

"Wait!" said the priest. "You told me I would be released—"

"You will be set free when your work is finished," the man assured Father Bradbury.

"But I did as you asked!" the priest protested.

"For now," the man said. "You will be asked to do more."

Father Bradbury heard a door shut. He wanted to scream, but he did not have the energy or the voice. He felt betrayed, foolish.

A canteen was once again pressed to the priest's lips.

"Drink it or else I will," the gruff-voiced man said from beside him. "I have things to do."

Father Bradbury put his mouth around the warm metal. He drank as slowly as a thirsty man could. Then he sat while the man fed him pieces of banana, papaya, and melon. He sat and he thought.

Reason returned along with some of his strength. As Father Bradbury began to think back through the events of this morning, he began to feel extremely uneasy. He realized that he may have made the greatest mistake of his life.

He may have just been used to start the flood that was going to wash over Botswana.

FOURTEEN

Washington, D.C.
Wednesday, 6:00 A.M.

Paul Hood was shaving when Bob Herbert called. The intelligence chief was already at Op-Center. They had spoken about Edgar Kline just a few hours before. Hood told Herbert that they should give the Vatican representative any support he required.

"What did I interrupt?" Herbert asked.

"Just scraping my face," Hood replied as he finished up. "What's up?"

Op-Center's director pulled the hand towel from his bare shoulder. He wiped his cheeks and chin. He felt a sad pang as he thought back to when his young son Alexander used to watch him do this. He would not be there the day Alexander started shaving. How the hell did that happen?

Herbert's soft, Southern accent brought Hood back to the moment.

"I just got a call from Ed Kline," Herbert said. "Powys Bradbury has been working the phones."

"The priest?" Hood said.

"Father Bradbury, yes," Herbert replied.

"Is he all right?"

"They don't know," Herbert told him. "He telephoned each of his deacon missionaries, the guys in the field, and told them to pack up and go back to the diocese in Cape Town."

"Are they sure it was him?" Hood asked.

"Yeah," Herbert said. "One of the deacons asked him something about a conversation they had a few weeks ago. The caller knew what the two of them had spoken about."

"Did Father Bradbury give a reason for recalling the missionaries?" Hood asked.

"None," Herbert said. "Apart from saying he was okay and would catch up with them in Cape Town, the preacher didn't tell them anything else. Nothing about where he was, where he would be, or what comes next. Kline got the records of calls that were placed to the missionaries' cell phones."

"And?"

"*Nada,*" Herbert said. "The number was blocked. Stoll says someone probably hacked the local computers to erase the number as soon as it appeared. Or maybe it was blocked on the caller's end. Our own TAC-SATs do that."

"Which means these people have some technological talent either in the group or available to them," Hood said.

"Right," Herbert said. "We'll have to wait for this Dhamballa guy to surface again before proceeding. In the meantime, I want to do two things. First, we should get people into Botswana. We will need intelligence resources on the ground. Second, assuming Beaudin is part of this, I want to try to get a look at his possible end game."

"How?" Hood asked.

"Revolutions need two things," Herbert said.

"Guns and money," Hood said.

"Exactly," Herbert went on. "We need to try to find out if any of Beaudin's companies are funneling money to Botswana."

"Absolutely," Hood said. He thought for a moment. "There's someone I used to work with on Wall Street who might be able to help with that," he said. "Let me give her a call."

"I knew those years you spent in the exciting world of finance would come in handy," Herbert teased.

"It hasn't helped my stock portfolio," Hood said as he walked into the bedroom. He looked at the clock. When Emmy Feroche worked with Hood at Silber Sacks, she used to be in the office at four A.M. to check the Tokyo and Hong Kong exchanges. Now she worked for the FBI's Finance Division investigating white-collar crime. Hood had not spoken to

Emmy in over a year, but he bet that she was still an early riser.

"Do me a favor?" Hood said.

"Sure," Herbert said.

"Give Darrell a call," Hood said. "Tell him I'm contacting a friend at the Bureau. I don't want him upset because I'm playing in his sandbox."

"You've got to stop doing that," Herbert joked.

"Yeah," Hood replied.

Hood said he would call back as soon as he had spoken to Emmy. However, before he hung up, Herbert had one thing to add.

"When I came in this morning, there was a voice mail message from Shigeo Fujima."

"I know that name," Hood said.

"He's the head of the Intelligence and Analysis Bureau of *Gaimusho,* the Ministry of Foreign Affairs," Herbert said. "Fujima did the Japanese security follow-up on our North Korea operation."

"That's right," Hood said.

"Fujima wanted to know if we had any information on a guy named Henry Genet," Herbert said.

"Who is?"

"A member of the board of directors of Beaudin International Industries," Herbert said. "But that's not all he does. Genet spends a lot of time in Africa pursuing his main business."

"Which is?" Hood asked.

Herbert replied, "Diamonds."

FIFTEEN

Washington, D.C.
Thursday, 8:00 A.M.

DiMaggio's Joe was not the kind of place where spies did business. It was public, brightly lit, watched by security cameras, heavily trafficked, and generally loud.

That was precisely why Mike Rodgers asked Aideen Marley, David Battat, and Darrell McCaskey to meet him there. Any young job seekers or political junkies would be watching and listening for members of Congress, the State Department, or something high profile. Spies looking for intelligence typically went to bars. Not only was it dark, but people drank. Caution fell away. Information was often revealed, especially if free drinks or sex was used as bait. No one sold out their government for a mochachino.

Battat was the only out of towner who said he could come down immediately. The former CIA officer promised to take the first shuttle down from La Guardia and cab right over Thursday morning.

Rodgers was the first to arrive. He ordered coffee and a Danish and grabbed a corner table. He sat facing the front door. Darrell got there a few minutes later. The short, wiry, prematurely gray ex-FBI man looked tired. His leathery face was pale, and his blue eyes were bloodshot.

"You look like you haven't slept," Rodgers said.

McCaskey sat down with two double espressos and two raisin biscottis. "Not much," he admitted. "I was up most of the night seeing what I could find out about the disappearance of your friend."

"Ballon?" Rodgers said quietly.

McCaskey nodded. He leaned closer. "I called my contacts

in France and at Interpol," he said. "They swear that the colonel is not undercover. A couple of months ago, he went out to return a library book and never came back."

"You believe that?" Rodgers asked.

"These guys have never lied to me before," McCaskey said.

Rodgers nodded. He felt very sad about that. A man like Ballon made a lot of enemies during the course of his work. A man like Beaudin had the clout to mount a counterattack like this.

"So that's the story about Colonel Ballon," McCaskey said. "I had Interpol look for bank transactions, credit card purchases, phone calls to relatives and friends—nothing."

"Shit," Rodgers said.

"Yeah," McCaskey agreed.

"Well, thanks, Darrell," Rodgers said.

McCaskey took a sip of his first double espresso. "Then there's stuff with Maria," he said.

"What kind of stuff?" Rodgers asked.

"She's worried," McCaskey said.

"About being married, or coming to the U.S.?" Rodgers asked.

"I don't know. Everything, I guess," McCaskey grumbled.

"I wouldn't worry about it," Rodgers said. "Newlyweds always have a bout of PHSD."

"PHSD?" McCaskey asked.

"Post-honeymoon stress disorder," Rodgers replied.

"You're pulling my leg," McCaskey said.

"Partly," Rodgers said. "It's not a real syndrome. But I swear, Darrell, I've seen this in family members, friends, servicemen. It's when you get back from the Bahamas or Tahiti or wherever and realize, 'Holy shit. My dating days are over. I've enlisted for the duration.' "

"I see." McCaskey bit one of the biscottis, then took another short swig of double espresso. "Well, there's probably some of that. But I think it's more," he said. "Maria's afraid that when she's finished psychologically disengaging from Interpol, she'll have a really tough time getting adjusted to suburban D.C. and then finding something interesting to do."

"I thought she was ready for a break," Rodgers said.

"So did she," McCaskey replied.

"Did something change her mind?" Rodgers asked.

"Yeah. Bob called her early this morning," McCaskey told him.

"Bob called Maria?" Rodgers asked.

McCaskey nodded.

Rodgers was not happy. Maria Corneja was on his own short list of operatives to call on, and Herbert knew that. But Bob Herbert was a team player. Something must have happened over there, or he would not have contacted her. Because Rodgers's cell phone was not secure, he would have to wait until he got to Op-Center to find out what it was.

"What did he want?" Rodgers asked.

"He needed Maria to check on something at the Ministry of Defense," McCaskey said.

"Do you have any idea what it was?"

"Haven't a clue. But it didn't matter to Maria," McCaskey went on. "She got all juiced up having something to do, something that was important. She called me from her old office. She was psyched because she knew which people to talk to at the Ministry, she knew the area, and she knew exactly where to look. She felt plugged in."

"She's spent her life there," Rodgers said. "And going back home, right before you leave somewhere—that's rough."

"I know," McCaskey said. "But she also isn't a kid. We went through all this. She knew that moving here would be like anyone going to a new job, a new house in a new neighborhood, a new anything. There's a lot you think you're going to like about it. Then, like you said, after you make the commitment, you start to think about all the things it *doesn't* have."

"You go through withdrawal," Rodgers said.

"You got it," McCaskey replied. "That's what Maria had been going through. Or at least, that's what she was going through until four-thirty this morning, our time. She wakes me up with a call that goes something like, 'Darrell, I may have made a mistake. I don't know if I can give this up.' "

"I'm sorry, Darrell," Rodgers said.

"Thanks. I appreciate that," McCaskey said.

Rodgers took a swallow of coffee. He was not certain whether this was a good time or a terrible time to broach the subject of Maria becoming a part of the new unit.

Given the situation in Botswana, he decided he did not have a choice. He also thought of something that might appeal to McCaskey.

"So what are you going to do if she does want to go back into the field?" Rodgers asked.

"I don't know," McCaskey said. "I guess the question is: Where does she get that opportunity?" He leaned in closer again. "There was a rumor going around the clubhouse yesterday that you're going to spearhead a new HUMINT operation. Is that true?"

Rodgers nodded. Herbert must have slipped McCaskey the word. The intelligence chief hated keeping a brother at arms in the dark.

McCaskey sat back. "Damn, Mike. I would have appreciated some kind of heads-up."

"You would have gotten that today, right now," Rodgers said. "That's why I asked to see you this morning. Christ, Paul just hit me with this new operation."

McCaskey scowled.

"As for Maria, I don't know why Bob called her," Rodgers said. "The new group is my operation, not his. And I won't ask Maria to be involved with my team if it'll make things tough for you."

Even as he said that, Rodgers knew he should not have. He might not have anyone else he could call on in Europe. However, there might be a solution.

"I don't know, Mike," McCaskey admitted. "I love the woman. I always have. I gave Maria up once rather than worry about losing her in the field, if that makes any sense."

"It does," Rodgers said.

"But after talking to her this morning, I know she's not going to be happy working as a nine-to-fiver again, even for us," he said.

"How ya gonna keep 'em down on the farm after they've seen Paree," Rodgers said.

"Something like that," McCaskey replied.

"Maybe she won't have to," Rodgers said.

"What do you mean?"

"We might be able to work something out where Maria is in the field part-time," Rodgers said. "And when she does go out, we wouldn't send her into red zones."

Red zones were high-risk areas, such as going behind the lines in combat situations. A white zone action was the infiltration of an adversary's nonmilitary group. A green zone operation was the kind Maria was doing now, going into an allied area for information.

"That could work," McCaskey said. "Hell, I don't want to try to control Maria."

"As if you could," Rodgers said.

"Exactly. I just don't want her dead."

Rodgers glanced at the wall clock.

"Listen, Darrell, we can talk about this later," Rodgers said. "Having Maria work with me is not why I wanted to see you. I asked you here to tell you about the HUMINT group because I may need help from some of your people in D.C. and abroad."

"Then why did you want to meet at this place instead of the office?" McCaskey asked.

"Because two other people are joining us," Rodgers said. "I want to see how they conduct themselves in public."

"You mean how well they blend in," McCaskey said.

"Exactly," Rodgers said.

Just then, as if on cue, Rodgers saw Aideen Marley enter the shop. Actually, the first thing he saw was the young woman's brilliant red hair. It was longer than he remembered, framing a face that was not as full as he remembered. She was wearing a smart fawn-colored pantsuit and seemed taller somehow. Maybe working in the corridors of power had changed her. Either it gave a person new self-confidence, or it crushed them. He liked the fact that working as a political consultant clearly had enhanced the thirty-six-year-old's poise.

Rodgers waved to her, and both men stood. Aideen weaved

through the crowd. The smile she wore was genuine. That, too, was a rarity in Washington.

When Aideen arrived, she gave the general a warm hug. "How are you?" she asked.

"Not bad," Rodgers said. "You look terrific."

"Thanks," she said. She turned to McCaskey and offered her hand. "I hear you got married. Congratulations. Maria is a great, great lady."

"That she is," McCaskey said.

Aideen had worked closely with Maria and McCaskey averting a new, wide-ranging Spanish civil war.

McCaskey asked Aideen if he could get anything for her. She asked if he would mind getting a regular decaf and a croissant. He took one of his espressos with him and went back to the counter.

Rodgers regarded Aideen. "Decaf?" he remarked.

"I had three cups of coffee before I left home and another on the way," she said as she slid onto a stool. She put her shoulder bag on the floor, between her feet. "I get up and do most of my work when it's still dark out. Better for the concentration. I research and write my *Moore-Cook Journal* articles when my brain is still fresh, then cram for the day's meetings."

The *Moore-Cook Journal* was a quarterly about the impact of international affairs on domestic policy. It was published by a small, conservative isolationist think tank and was widely read in the intelligence industry.

"How's the consulting work going?" Rodgers asked.

"It's long hours, okay money, and crappy health coverage," she said. "But I like seeing new faces each day, and I love the learning curve. The trick is knowing things other people don't, then scaring them into hiring you."

"Information insurance," Rodgers said.

"Something like that," Aideen replied. "It would be nice to have a steady gig again, but I got out of line when I left Op-Center. I don't want to start over somewhere else."

There was a hint of bitterness in her voice. After the assassination of her mentor, Martha Mackall, Aideen needed time off—more than Op-Center could afford to give her.

Aideen went on quickly. "I was thinking on the way over, we haven't seen each other in over a year. How are you?"

"Okay," he said. "I assume you heard about the trouble in Kashmir."

The woman nodded once. "I was sorry to hear about that. How's Colonel August?"

"He's fine," Rodgers said. "That mission was my call, my black mark. Besides, he's always been able to look ahead."

"While you look back," she said.

"What can I say? I'm a history buff," he said.

"You can say that you apply what you learn to the future," Aideen answered. "Otherwise, what's the point of learning it?"

"I agree."

"What about Paul and Bob?" Aideen asked.

She is good at this, Rodgers thought. Aideen did not let a sore subject sit. She got in, made her point, and kept things moving.

"Paul and Bob are the same," Rodgers told her. "I suppose you heard that Ann Farris is no longer at Op-Center."

"Yes. I'm hoping she left due to natural causes," Aideen said. That was a euphemism for attrition or a change to a better job. What she was really saying was that she hoped Ann had left for professional reasons and not because of her relationship with Paul.

"It was not exactly that," Rodgers told her. "There were budget cuts. That's how I lost Striker, too."

"Not just the personnel? You mean the group?" she asked. Rodgers nodded.

That surprised the woman. Obviously, there had not been time for that one to hit the Washington grapevine.

"Mike, I'm so sorry," she said.

"It's okay. It was a kick in the pants," he admitted, "but we move on. Which is one of the reasons I asked you to come down here today."

McCaskey returned with Aideen's decaf. She thanked him without taking her eyes off Rodgers.

"I'm putting together a new group," he said quietly. "Very

low profile, doing the same kind of work you did with Maria. I was wondering if you'd consider being part of it."

She looked from Rodgers to McCaskey. "Will Maria be working with us?" she asked.

"We don't know yet," Rodgers said.

"I do," McCaskey replied. "When Mike asks that question, Maria won't hesitate. Not like she did when I popped mine."

"We haven't decided if Mike is even going to ask that question," Rodgers clarified.

Before they could discuss the team further, David Battat entered the café. Rodgers recognized him from his file photo and motioned him over. The general did not know what to expect from the man. He only knew what he had read in the dossier, that Battat had been a CIA liaison with the Mujahideen guerrilla fighters in Afghanistan. He worked his way up to running a field office in New York. He was sent back in the field when one of his operatives, Annabelle Hampton, helped the terrorists who attacked the United Nations Security Council. Stationed in Baku, Azerbaijan, he had recently worked with Op-Center to prevent war in the Caspian Sea.

The former CIA agent was short and scrappy, with none of the boot camp polish to which Rodgers was accustomed. But the general was not dealing with the military any longer. He felt like South Carolina's Edward Rutledge and the other Southern delegates to the Continental Congress must have felt when they first met their Yankee counterparts. No veneer, no respect for class or finery. Yet Rodgers reminded himself that they all managed to work together to gain American independence.

Battat reached the table. He was wearing a New York University sweatshirt and had the *New York Times* under his arm. He carried nothing else. Rodgers liked a man who traveled light.

Battat brushed back his short, thinning black hair. He introduced himself to Rodgers and McCaskey.

Rodgers introduced Aideen. Battat's heavy eyebrows rose behind his sunglasses.

"You must be the Aideen Marley who writes for the *MCJ*," Battat said.

"That's me," she said.

"I read your article on the impact of media hysteria on civic antiterrorist preparedness," Battat said. "We'll have to discuss it."

"You don't agree with my findings?" she asked.

"I do, as far as they go," he said. He pulled a stool underneath him and sat down. "You can't anticipate and preempt assaults. All you do is panic people, which can be worse than an attack itself. Hell, it *is* an attack itself."

"A mock attack," she said.

"Psychological assaults are not pretend assaults," Battat replied.

"No, but they are easier to defend against," she suggested. "Education always goes down harder than ignorance."

"Education is totally beside the point," Battat said dismissively. "Fear is the key. A dictator has to be afraid that he will lose his small kingdom if he attempts to expand it. Khrushchev didn't pull his missiles from Cuba because he suddenly thought, 'Hey, wait a minute! What am I doing?' " Battat said. "He was scared of mutual assured destruction. So forget that. You also can't just manage crises after the fact, which is what Aideen's article really suggests."

"What's your solution?" Aideen asked.

Rodgers was enjoying this. The great thing about pundits is that they were always right and wrong. There was no universal solution. But the debates were always fascinating.

"My solution is an aggressive offense," Battat replied. "An enemy hits a building, you knock out a city block. They hit a city block, you wipe out an entire town or city. They hit a city, you turn the country to landfill."

"What's wrong with the legal system handling the aftermath of an attack?" Aideen asked.

"Because that gives them a podium from which to spout their BS," Battat replied. "Who needs that?"

"It also lets people know that they are twisted individuals who need to be watched," Aideen said.

"You know what?" Battat replied. "TV is something you watch. I prefer our enemies dead."

"We *will* have to discuss this," Aideen said.

There was an edge in Aideen's voice. But again, the woman had been savvy enough to table the discussion before it became overly emotional. As for Battat, he sounded like any passionate Washingtonian with an opinion. That would not make him stand out. Just the opposite in fact. These two looked and sounded like ordinary citizens.

"David, can I get you anything?" McCaskey asked. "I mean, apart from a tactical nuclear weapon?"

"I'm good," Battat said. "They gave out cookies on the plane." He looked at Rodgers. "How have you been?"

"I'm alive," Rodgers replied.

"I read about what happened overseas," Battat said. "You did us proud. Americans *and* everyone in the business."

"Thanks," Rodgers said. "I was just telling Ms. Marley that because of what happened, we've been forced to make a few changes."

"Nothing the unappreciative, buck-passing bureaucrats do surprises me," Battat said. "How can I help?"

"We're putting together a different kind of sports team, and I'm sounding out possible players."

"I'm in," Battat told him.

"That's it?" McCaskey said.

"That's it," Battat replied.

"Great," Rodgers said. He looked at Aideen. "What about you?"

She hesitated before replying. "I'm very interested," she said. "I'd like to discuss this some more."

"Sure," Rodgers said.

Rodgers did not know whether her hesitation was bitterness toward Op-Center, a desire to run her own life, or maybe even impatience with Battat. Possibly a little of everything.

"What I suggest is that we go back to the office and have a real chat," Rodgers said.

Aideen nodded.

"Question," Battat said. "When were you thinking of fielding this team? Just so I can work things out schedule-wise."

Rodgers finished his coffee and looked at his watch. He replied, "In about six hours."

SIXTEEN

Washington, D.C.
Thursday, 8:12 A.M.

The list of people who Bob Herbert trusted was short. The list of people he trusted absolutely was shorter still.

Edgar Kline was never on the very short list. Now, Herbert was not sure he was on the short list. Kline also had self-interests to protect. The well-being of the Vatican and its inner circle was his top priority. Herbert understood and respected that. But Herbert also had interests to look after. That was why he called one of his freelancers, April Wright.

April was a professional watcher, one of the hundreds who walked the streets of the nation's capital every day. Some were hired by American agencies to spy on rival agencies. Others were hired by Americans to spy on foreigners and vice versa. They were dressed as delivery people, tourists, souvenir sales-men, or joggers. A few watchers worked in teams and pre-tended to be TV reporters or college kids making a student film. Some carried handbags that contained changes of clothes. If the watchers had to watch an area with a security camera, they did not want to stay in the same outfit all day.

April used to be an actress. She worked mostly in regional theater, so her face was not well known. She had been a close friend of Herbert's wife. Now the woman was married to a pilot and had a young daughter. During the course of a day, she went from posing as a nanny to being a mother out for a walk to being a homeless woman with a child. In all of her disguises, she carried a digital camera. When she was "home-less," she kept it hidden in the bottom of a brown paper bag. Whenever she needed to take a picture, she took a drink. April was good at what she did, and she loved it. It was also a secret only Herbert shared. April was only available when her husband was out of town.

Herbert asked April to keep an eye on the Watergate. He wanted to know where Kline went and who came to see him. She signed in at ten P.M. then came downstairs in her nanny guise and found a spot near the house phones. She rocked her baby until two A.M. and then became homeless, watching Kline's window from the outside. Shortly after dawn, she was an early-rising mom out for a few turns around the lobby. She always made sure she was near the phone when anyone used it. If Kline had left the hotel, she would have followed him. The driver that had brought her there waited for that purpose.

Herbert had arranged for Kline to come to Op-Center at eight A.M. and brief Hood. At two A.M., April made an interim report. At seven forty-five, she made her final report. Herbert thanked her and told her to go home. In the meantime, he had asked Matt Stoll's computer group to check the flights from Spain to Botswana. There was something he needed to know.

Kline arrived in a taxi. Herbert greeted his old friend at the main level and took him directly to Hood's office. Kline sat in the armchair in front of Hood's desk. Herbert parked his wheelchair inside the door. Hood had also asked his political liaison, Ron Plummer, to attend the meeting. The former CIA intelligence analyst for Western Europe arrived just a minute after Herbert. He shut the door and leaned against it, crossing his arms tightly. Plummer was a short man with thinning brown hair and wide eyes. He wore thick, black-framed glasses atop a large, hooked nose. He was an intensely focused man, which was fortunate. His work on the delicate situation in Kashmir had been the key to keeping it from exploding.

Herbert asked how Kline's evening had gone. The Vatican security officer said that it went well. He had met with Cardinal Zavala before Mass this morning. Kline said that when he was finished here, he was going directly to New York to meet with Cardinal Murrieta.

"Did you get what you wanted from the cardinal?" Herbert asked.

"I did," Kline told him. "We arranged to have Bishop Victor Max go to Botswana. He's flying to New York to meet me."

"Max is a big human rights advocate, isn't he?" Herbert asked.

"He is," Kline said. "The bishop is going to take Father Bradbury's place in a show of support. He will fly to Gaborone and then take a shuttle to Maun. We have asked two of the deacons not to leave but to meet him there."

"That could be dangerous for the bishop and the deacons, you understand that," Herbert said. *"They* understand that."

"Of course."

"Is there going to be press coverage?" Hood asked.

"We absolutely will not solicit coverage, but we will make an announcement," Kline said. "We want Dhamballa to know he cannot scare us away. We're sure some press will be in Gaborone, but there will be no additional statements, no press conferences. The Church has a narrow line to walk between supporting its mission and defying the will of a native faction."

"What kind of precautions are you arranging for the bishop's security?" Hood asked.

"We're working with local authorities," Kline said.

"Is that all?" Herbert asked.

Kline regarded the intelligence chief. "We have other options open to us," he replied. "The bishop will be safe."

"I have no doubt," Herbert said.

"Why is that?" Kline asked.

"Because, Edgar, I'm betting you've invoked the Madrid Accords," Herbert replied.

It was the first time Herbert had ever seen Edgar Kline seem surprised. "You've been busy," Kline said.

"We both have," Herbert replied.

"Back up," Hood said. "I'm not familiar with the accords."

"Three years ago, the Vatican signed a secret agreement with the *Ministerio de Defensa de España,*" Herbert said. "In exchange for aggressive support from the Vatican, the prince promised to provide ground troops in the event of action undertaken against the Church in any developing country."

Kline waved his hand dismissively. "The Madrid Accords are not a secret," he said.

"Not if you happen to read the Fraternal Vatican Minutes, which is not available on-line or outside the Hall of Records in Rome. Or you might have read about it if you had access to the Spanish Alliance file at the Defense Ministry in Madrid," Herbert pointed out. *"I only know about the arrangement because at two-fifteen this morning, I called one of our people in Spain. I asked her to look into the existence of any such agreements."*

"What prompted you to do that?" Kline asked.

"A visit you had from Deputy Chief of Ministry Rodriguez very early this morning," Herbert replied.

Kline's pleasant features darkened. "You had me watched."

"That's right."

"I'm very disappointed, Bob."

"So am I," Herbert replied evenly. "You asked for my help, but you didn't tell me everything."

"There wasn't much to tell," Kline replied.

"There was enough for you to withhold it," Herbert pointed out.

"We have security issues that I did not wish to discuss or disclose," Kline replied. "The ramifications of another nation lending that kind of support go beyond the current crisis."

"Gentlemen, now I'm the only one who's confused," Hood said. "Bob, would you tell me what's going on?"

"I've pretty much told you all I know for certain, Paul," Herbert said. "Edgar wanted our help locating Father Bradbury. I brought Mike aboard, set things in motion, then found out that there are other players. That this situation may be bigger than we were led to believe."

Herbert did not want to say anything to Kline about the call from Shigeo Fujima. For all he knew, there might not be a connection. If there were a connection, he wanted to keep that contact to himself.

Hood looked over at Kline. "Mr. Kline?"

"The involvement of the Spanish military is a very delicate

aspect of this 'situation,' as Bob describes it," Kline said. "The Vatican does have a defense arrangement with the Spanish military. The agreement does not affect the main body of the military. It is only with the *Grupo del Cuartel General, Unidad Especial del Despliegue.*"

"That's the Spanish military's equivalent to Striker," Herbert said. "A rapid deployment unit about two hundred commandos strong. They're based in Valencia, on the Mediterranean."

"Correct," Kline replied. "The only time we ever expected to call on them is if there were an imminent threat against His Holiness or the Vatican itself. I didn't tell you about their involvement because they're not going into Botswana in an official capacity."

"They're going to Father Bradbury's parish in Maun as tourists," Herbert replied.

Kline seemed even more surprised than he had been a minute before. "What makes you think that?" he asked.

"It makes a whole lot of sense," Herbert told him. "I knew you'd want the soldiers in place before the bishop arrives tomorrow. But you don't know who may be helping the Brush Vipers, so you couldn't risk sending in a Spanish military aircraft. I had our computer group check flights from Spain to Botswana. Reservations for several Spanish men came up on the hop from Valencia to Madrid and then to Gaborone. The names were aliases, but they used their personal telephone numbers for E-ticket security. That data was in the Pentagon's files from last year's war-sim exercises on the Mediterranean. They don't share tactical information with people they can't find again. The name that stood out was Major Jose Sanjulian. He's an antiterrorist specialist with the *Grupo del Cuartel General, Unidad Especial del Despliegue.*"

"Now you know everything I did," Kline remarked. "In fact, you knew more than I did."

There was resentment in his voice. Herbert was sorry to hear it. But this was not a profession where friendship could come before national security or the lives of one's coworkers. Kline was a professional. He would think about what Herbert had done, and he would recover. Especially if he wanted Op-Center to help in the search for Father Bradbury.

"Now that everything is on the table, Mr. Kline, what would you like from us?" Hood asked.

Kline regarded Herbert. "*Is* everything on the table, Bob?"

"You mean, have I done any other snooping?" he asked.

"No," Kline replied. "Is there anything else I should know to protect lives in Botswana?"

"Not at the moment," Herbert said.

Kline did not look as though he believed him. Herbert did not care.

"Edgar, what do you want from us?" Hood asked.

"Broadly, we would like any quiet intelligence assistance you can provide," Kline told Hood.

"That's a pretty big canvas to work on," Hood said. "We have the present activities of the perpetrators and whoever might be backing them, as well as the history of Mr. Seronga and his own associates."

"It's extremely big and volatile," Kline agreed. "We are dealing with what we see as a three-part problem. One is the situation involving Father Bradbury. That's the one we're most concerned with. Getting him back. But his abduction is obviously not an isolated action. Father Bradbury was provoked into asking his missionaries to leave Botswana. That seems to be a very clear prelude to an anti-Catholic movement relating to the activities of this Dhamballa individual."

"The cult leader," Hood said.

"Correct," Kline replied. "The second part of the problem is, if we cannot quickly secure the safe release of Father Bradbury, we need to know what Dhamballa's plans for him are."

"I assume there's been no contact between the cult and the Vatican?" Hood said.

"None at all," Kline told him. "Dhamballa does not have any kind of office or even a physical church that we are aware of. We don't even know what the man's name was before he founded this cult."

"What's the third problem, Mr. Kline?" Hood asked.

"That one is not so much a Vatican issue but a potential problem for Botswana and the rest of the region," Kline replied. "That's the problem you pointed out earlier, that of who may be backing Dhamballa. We do not know whether Albert Beaudin is involved in this movement. If he is, it's extremely doubtful he is there for religious enlightenment."

"He would want to stir things up for his own reasons," Hood said.

Kline nodded.

"Bob, do we know whether Beaudin has access to the same NATO files we used?" Hood asked.

"He probably does," Herbert said. "At the very least, whoever is behind this would probably assume that the bishop will not be unprotected."

"Mr. Kline, what does the Vatican risk by letting this play out a little longer?" Hood asked.

"A great deal. If this were simply about the return of Father Bradbury, I would agree to let the church go untenanted for a time," Kline replied. "But it isn't. It's about the credibility of the Vatican and its commitment to those who have literally put their faith in us, not just in Botswana but around the world. These are volatile, militant times. The Church cannot afford to be as passive as it has been in the past."

"Flip the question," Hood said. "Can Dhamballa afford to let Bishop Max take up where Father Bradbury left off?"

"We don't know," Kline admitted. "We're hoping the Vatican's resolve will discourage him from ratcheting this higher."

"You mean by attacking a bishop," Hood said.

Kline nodded.

"What if that's what Dhamballa wants?" Herbert asked. "What if he's looking to prove how bold he is by taking on the Church? How outsiders return to his land without hesitation."

"Then we will have an extremely grave situation on our hands," Kline admitted. "The Church is not willing to give up its missionary activities in Botswana or anywhere else."

Hood turned to his political adviser. "Ron, what kind of ramifications are we looking at if there's a civil war in Botswana?" Hood asked.

"A politically based war would be bad enough," Plummer said. "With that alone, you would run the risk of having tens of thousands of refugees clawing into South Africa and starting border violence there. But if we have a religious uprising, a situation where non-Christians are turning on Catholics, the Hindu and Islamic minorities in South Africa could be inspired—or encouraged—into doing the same thing."

"And make no mistake," Kline added, "if there is a conflict in the region, Johannesburg would have to move very quickly to shut the border and protect its people, its workforce. They cannot afford to lose the income from exports. Turmoil in South African industry would affect regional supplies of steel, corn, wool, metals, and the international market for diamonds."

Hood and Herbert exchanged glances at the mention of diamonds. Kline did not appear to notice.

"In the case of a religious war, you've also potentially got serious problems to the west, east, and north of Botswana," Plummer went on. "To the west, you've got Namibians, half of whom are Christian. The other half practice ancient, traditional beliefs."

"Those are the people who would be drawn to Dhamballa, whose cult draws from a variety of old sources," Kline pointed out. "It would be worse to the east, in Zimbabwe, where followers of traditional faiths outnumber Christians two to one. And we could well see open persecution in the north, in Angola. The majority of the Christians there are Roman Catholic, but they are still outnumbered nearly four to one by traditionalists. That could fuel tribal disputes that have nothing to do with religion."

"One well-placed flame, and the entire region could blow up," Plummer said. "And it will not just explode. It will be pulled in so many directions—political, religious, economic, and social—that it will be impossible to find the original pieces, let alone reassemble them."

"All right. Let's back up," Hood said. "What is the government of Botswana doing and likely to do to deal with this situation?"

"At the moment, they're doing nothing beyond a search," Kline said. "They interviewed the people at the lodge and are tracking the movements of the kidnappers. But until they know more about Dhamballa and where his cult is headed, they don't want to aggravate the situation by overreacting."

"Religious radicals and would-be rebels are not unknown outside the cities," Plummer remarked. "They have undoubtedly had to deal with things like this before, events that pass under the international radar."

"And if the struggle between the Vatican and Dhamballa escalates?" Hood asked. "What then, Ron?"

"If Gaborone feels that Dhamballa has built any kind of power base, they will probably negotiate with him," Plummer said. "As I said, cults are not uncommon over there. The big difference is that this one may have snatched a priest."

"The risk you run is giving Dhamballa added legitimacy by fighting him," Herbert said to Kline.

"Or negotiating with him," Kline replied.

"There are different levels of negotiation, Edgar," Hood pointed out. "Gaborone can open a dialogue without legitimizing his actions. Does the Botswana president—what's his name?"

"Butere," Kline said. "Michael Butere."

"Does President Butere know about the possible involvement of the Brush Vipers and foreign interests in Dhamballa's activities?" Hood asked.

"We have told him about the possible involvement of former Brush Vipers," Kline acknowledged. "But since they helped eject the British and remain heroes to an older segment of the population, he is not prepared to pronounce them rebels. We have not said anything to the president about Albert Beaudin."

"Why not?" Herbert asked. "The Botswana government might be the ultimate target. He should have that intelligence."

"We're more concerned about the Vatican's relations with France," Kline said. "We absolutely do not want to implicate a leading French industrialist until we're convinced that he's involved."

"Then let the French government know," Herbert said. "At least tell them your suspicions."

"That's a bad idea, Bob," Plummer said. "For all we know, there are people in power who are supporting Beaudin."

"That was our conclusion," Kline said, "and we don't want to risk turning key members of the government against our people in France. As I said, at the moment, our only concern is for the safety of our priests and missionaries."

"Which is as it should be," Hood said firmly.

Hood's remark was meant more to rein Herbert in than to support Edgar Kline. Hood was right to take the shot at him. He had to have noticed that Herbert was a little less controlled than he should be. The intelligence chief had been fidgeting and scowling and looking in all different directions. It was more than Herbert simply being annoyed at Kline for not having told him about the Spanish military unit. Herbert also wished that he were running the HUMINT aspect of this operation. With all of the countries and all the hot potatoes involved, there would be enough work to go around. Still, Herbert envied Mike Rodgers being able to field the team on this one.

Hood looked over at Plummer. "Suggestions, Ron?"

"I have two," Plummer replied. "First, Op-Center should move with considerable caution. We have domestic as well as international issues to consider. Anything we do has to be extremely low profile, invisible if possible."

"I agree," Herbert said.

"Having said that," Plummer went on, "we can't afford to let this blow up. As long as we have an exit strategy for our personnel and our involvement, we should give Mr. Kline any and all the intelligence support he requires."

"If we get involved, give me your nightmare meltdown scenario on the international side," Hood said.

"That's easy," Plummer said. "Someone who reports directly to us is apprehended in Botswana spying on the activities of a Botswana citizen. There's no way the United States can pick on a religious movement in a small African nation and come out of it looking good."

"If the French are involved with Dhamballa, you can be certain we'll get all the attention we don't want," Herbert said.

Hood's gaze shifted to Herbert. "Bob, how do we prep for that?"

"That depends on Mr. Kline," Herbert said. He looked at the Vatican security officer. "Ideally, we would send someone in with the bishop. Possibly disguised as a cleric. But I have a feeling his credentials would be checked by someone in the media."

"That's correct," Kline said.

"But there is another way in," Herbert said.

"How?" Kline asked.

"We can put someone in with the Spanish 'tourists,' " Herbert said. "Edgar, do you think there would be a problem with that?"

"There could be," Kline admitted. "I'm told that Major Jose Sanjulian doesn't work with outsiders."

"Brett August might be able to help us there," Hood told him. "The colonel has maintained a very good relationship with officers from most of the NATO countries."

"If the UED commander doesn't protest, I'm certain the Vatican will have no objections," Kline told him. "Who did you have in mind for the undercover operation?"

"A woman who just retired from Interpol and is probably entitled to a few weeks of vacation," Herbert replied. "Maria Corneja-McCaskey."

SEVENTEEN

Maun, Botswana
Thursday, 4:30 P.M.

The bus to Maun Center arrived at four o'clock. It had dropped off forty-two tourists and would wait for an hour before returning. Anyone who missed this bus would have to wait until eleven A.M. the following morning to leave the tourist center. Taxicabs were expensive, and there were very few of them after dark. Outside the city or off the highway, the uncertain terrain was not conducive to nighttime driving. Car rentals were mostly for foreigners who were driving the highways directly to Gaborone or the other major city, Francistown.

Thirty-eight-year-old Deacon Eliot Jones had arrived at the Church of the Holy Cross shortly after two P.M. It had taken him more than a day to make his way northwest from Tonota on the Zimbabwe border. It was necessary to ride his bicycle to Francistown and catch a tour bus that went west, around the Makgadikgadi Pan. Then he had to wait at the salt pan tourist center for another bus that took passengers to Maun. From Maun, he had to catch the bus to the tourist center, where the church was located. There, he and Deacon Canon would link up. They would make preparations to leave Botswana.

That order did not sit well with him. He did not like the idea of being bullied from his flock. Souls mattered more than his flesh. His work was to help save souls, not his own skin.

Several times during his trip, he had tried to phone Father Bradbury. The calls were not answered. Deacon Jones was deeply worried about his old friend and mentor.

Just minutes after he finally reached the church, he received a call from the archdiocese in Cape Town. There was a change of plans. Jones was to go to Maun the following afternoon. Only he would not be flying to South Africa. He was to wait for the arrival of Bishop Victor Max from Washington, D.C., and bring him back to the church. The personal secretary of Archbishop Patrick in Cape Town also instructed Jones to bring one other deacon with him. Patrick did not want the thirty-five-year-old bishop left alone when the deacon had to buy tickets, food, or collect his luggage.

Jones was delighted to hear that the church would not be abandoned. Perhaps the new bishop would allow Jones to stay. The deacon was also excited because he had never met an American bishop. Though the men would only be together for a few hours, Jones was looking forward to it. Foreign clergy often had different perspectives, different ideas. Americans on the whole were always more direct and often better informed. Perhaps the bishop would have news about Father Bradbury or comforting insights about what was happening in Botswana. If the archdiocese in Cape Town knew any more about the crisis than Deacon Jones did, they were not saying anything.

Apart from Deacon Jones, Deacon Samuel Holden Canon had made the longest journey. His ministry encompassed a string of villages on the 6,000-foot-high Tsodilo Hill, which stood where Botswana, Namibia, and Angola all met in the northwest. He had taken a mule, jeep, and bus to get to Maun. Because of his late arrival, the Johannesburg-born Sam Canon was the only other deacon who had not taken the morning bus for Cape Town. Jones relayed the archbishop's instructions to the twenty-four-year-old deacon. Canon said he would be honored to accompany Deacon Jones to Maun.

The men went to the quarters the deacons used whenever they came in from the field. After removing their dirty soutanes and showering away the dust of the journey, the men put on fresh cassocks. In the absence of Father Bradbury, they would be responsible for ministering to any tourists who might need them. Deacon Jones made tea in the small kitchen area and then took it onto the veranda. The two men sat in wicker chairs and looked out at the flat, sprawling floodplain. The afternoon was as dry, warm, and windless as usual for this time of year. The sky was cloudless, and the amber sun was low.

"Do you have any idea at all what's behind this?" Canon asked.

Eliot Jones had never been an especially political man. He had been raised in an upper-middle-class household in the Kensington section of London. Political history interested Jones only when it impacted on his two loves. Those were art and religion.

"I'm not sure," Jones said. "Have you ever read anything about the Mahdi of the Sudan?"

"Are you talking about the one who fought the British in the 1880s?" Canon asked.

"That's right," Jones said. "The British were under the command of General Gordon."

"I saw the movie *Khartoum* with Charlton Heston," Canon said, somewhat embarrassed.

Jones smiled. "In the video library at the archdiocese?"

Canon nodded.

"I saw it, too." Jones smiled. "I first became interested in the conflict between the two men when I was thirteen. Gordon was a very religious Christian who fought in the Crimean War, put down the Taiping Rebellion, and then went searching for Noah's Ark. That was something I always wished I could do. Read the Bible and other texts, look for clues, then search through the mountains. I found a copy of General Gordon's published journals and was fascinated by the quest. He finally had to give it up to undertake the defense of the loyal British subjects of Khartoum.

The Mahdi was Muhammad Ahmad, a forty-year-old Muslim religious leader. For years, Ahmad would preach to whomever would listen. Typically, they were the hungry, the homeless, people without hope. In 1881, Ahmad became convinced that he was God's vice-regent on earth. He was equally convinced that the ills of his people were due to the presence of infidels. He declared a *jihad*, a holy war, and from that point forth, he would go anywhere, slay or torture anyone who disagreed with his worldview. Only General Charles Gordon and a few hundred Sudanese soldiers were on hand in Khartoum to oppose him. The Mahdi slaughtered them and thousands of citizens who were loyal to him."

"The first radical Islamic fundamentalist," Canon said.

"Not really," Jones replied. "But he was the first one who made all the newspapers in England."

"So are you saying that you see parallels between that conflict and this one?" Canon asked.

"I do," Jones replied. "I don't believe Father Bradbury's kidnapping or the deacon missionaries being asked to leave has to do with national origin. It's clearly a religious issue."

"A Mahdi in the making," Canon said.

"That's what I believe," Jones told him.

"How do you know the government is not behind this for some reason?" Canon asked.

"The Church brings food, education, and health care to the villages," Jones said. "That encourages peace. The government of Botswana gains nothing by casting us out."

"Then how do you explain what Director Ndebele told me when I arrived?" Canon said. "He said that Father Bradbury was taken away by soldiers."

"Soldiers can be hired," Jones pointed out.

"But what kind of loyalty do they give you?" Canon asked. "What kind of courage?"

"Enough, if it gets the job done," Jones replied. "Especially if you hire enough of them. I also spoke with Director Ndebele. He said that forty or fifty men came to take Father Bradbury. That tells me the kidnappers were looking to make some kind of statement."

Canon shook his head slowly. "I really don't know about these things. My parents were always talking about politics, but I didn't get involved. It seemed to me that all the answers we needed were in the Bible. That was my guide. The word of God."

Jones smiled. "That's exactly how General Gordon felt. In the end, he could have used a few more bullets."

"What happened to the Mahdi?" Canon asked.

"His own success killed him," Jones replied.

"How do you mean?" Canon asked.

"His holy warriors slaughtered the defenders of Khartoum and left their bodies in the streets for weeks," Jones told him. "As a result, there was an epidemic of typhus. The Mahdi succumbed to the disease just a few months after securing Khartoum."

" 'Let evil hunt down the violent man speedily,' " Canon said.

"Psalms 140:11," Deacon Jones said.

"Yes," said Canon. "The Mahdi was doomed the moment he raised a sword against others. But it did not need to be that way; 1 Corinthians 2:15 says, 'The spiritual man judges all things, but is himself to be judged by no one.' If the Mahdi had been a truly spiritual man, devoted to God and not to glory, he would have preached instead of making war. He would not have been destroyed."

"To the contrary," Jones agreed. "He might have had a more lasting impact. Working among the people here, I have seen deep spirituality," he said. "Many of those who have not been persuaded by the teachings of Christ have held tightly to their own faith. I admire their conviction. Faith and truth must be the vehicles of change," he insisted. "Otherwise, the result is never permanent."

Canon grinned. "Have their beliefs ever made you doubt your own?" the deacon asked.

"No," he replied. "But they have made me reexamine it. And every time I do, I come away stronger."

The men sat in silence then, as they sipped their tea. The sun dropped, and the air cooled quickly. The chill felt good. The silence, settled upon such vastness, was humbling.

Deacon Jones's cell phone beeped. He jumped from the sound and quickly pulled the phone from the pocket of his cassock. He expected it to be the archbishop's secretary.

It was not.

It was Father Bradbury with a surprising request.

EIGHTEEN

Washington, D.C.
Thursday, 9:55 A.M.

The meeting with Bob Herbert, Ron Plummer, and Edgar Kline ended with Herbert going off to call Maria and Kline chatting with Hood for several minutes longer. Their conversation ranged from the financial and political health of Botswana to Hood soothing the lingering indignation Kline felt at having been put under surveillance. Hood behaved sympathetically because that was his job. The truth was, he felt a lot like he did when he was mayor of Los Angeles. City officials often expected to be exempted from tasks such as jury duty or waiting in line at amusement parks and crowded restaurants because of who they were. Kline expected to be above suspicion because of who he worked for. Hood rejected both attitudes. The only thing that mattered to him was his responsibility to the rights and security of his constituents. When Kline left to go to New York City, he seemed satisfied, though perhaps not entirely convinced, that Bob Herbert simply had been following Op-Center protocol.

As for Maria, Herbert came back into Hood's office to assure him that she would be ready for the challenge.

Hood had offered to brief Darrell McCaskey as soon as he arrived. Herbert asked to handle that.

"Darrell was not happy to hear that you were contacting a friend at the FBI," Herbert said. "But he's going to be a lot less happy when he hears what I'm going to do."

"I would agree with that," Hood said dryly.

"If he blows up at me, he can always complain to you. If he blows up at you, he may walk out on us. We don't want him to do that."

"But he *is* going to blow up," Hood thought aloud.

"Oh yeah," Herbert said. "It could be one big blast or a lot of small ones. I'm guessing small ones. He will want to do what's right for Op-Center, so that will stuff the big one down."

Hood gave him the go-ahead. Besides, there were other things Hood needed to do. His old financial colleague Emmy Feroche had been in a meeting. He left word on her voice mail to call him back. In the meantime, Hood wanted to talk to Shigeo Fujima.

As soon as Herbert left, Hood brought up Fujima's file. He scanned it quickly. The man was thirty-five, married, two children. He held an advanced degree in political science from Tokyo University and another in criminology from the Osaka School of Law. He had been with the Intelligence and Analysis Bureau for seven years. The man obviously had intelligence chops and political savvy. The Japanese were a hierarchical society. To be the head of the IAB at such a young age was very impressive.

After checking Fujima's file, Hood brought up the dossier on Henry Genet. The fifty-three-year-old Antwerp native was a diamond merchant. He was on the board of directors of Beaudin International Industries along with several other movers and shakers of French business and finance.

Hood punched in the telephone number Fujima had left on Herbert's voice mail. The head of the Japanese Intelligence and Analysis Bureau was in a meeting. He left it to take Hood's call.

"Thank you for calling back, Mr. Hood," Fujima said. "I'm honored the director of Op-Center would call personally."

The intelligence officer's voice was calm and respectful, and his manner was unhurried. But that did not mean anything. Japanese officials were always calm and unhurried.

Hood decided to get right to the matter at hand. He did not have time to get into what Martha Mackall used to call the "plastic bouquet liturgy," the back-and-forth exchange of insincerely sweet compliments that typified initial conversations with most Japanese officials.

"Your call interested me personally," Hood replied. "You had questions about Henry Genet?"

"Yes," Fujima replied.

"Let's see if I can help you," Hood prompted.

Fujima was silent for a moment. Within seconds the men had gone from empty, free-flowing compliments to the taciturn dance of intelligence personnel. This business was unlike any other Paul Hood had ever encountered. When the Japanese intelligence officer spoke, it was with care and precision.

"We have been watching Mr. Henry Genet because of several recent investment and business undertakings," Fujima began. "Over the past few months, he has increased the hiring of personnel in Botswana. At least, that is what it says on the tax forms filed in Gaborone."

"But you don't believe it," Hood said.

"I do not," Fujima said.

"What kind of personnel is he supposed to have hired?" Hood asked.

"Diamond buyers, security personnel for his purchases, scouts for new purchases—"

"In other words, the kind of employees that would not raise any flags," Hood said.

"Yes," Fujima agreed. "Yet we saw no evidence of such personnel in our surveillance."

Hood was curious what kind of surveillance the Japanese were using. HUMINT resources might be helpful to Op-Center. Yet even if Hood had asked, Fujima would not have told him. Putting the man on the spot would have served no purpose. Sometimes a man gained respect by not asking things he wanted to know. That was certainly true when dealing with the Japanese.

"During that same period, Genet has also withdrawn nearly one hundred million dollars from banks in Japan, Taiwan, and the United States," Fujima went on. "Genet has used some of that money to lease large tracts of land and invest in factories in both China and North Korea."

"That could simply be an investment decision," Hood said.

"The Chinese economy is expected to grow exponentially over the next twenty years."

"A reasonable assumption," Fujima agreed. "Except that Mr. Genet established several international holding companies to share the ownership of the property and apparently to conceal his involvement."

"What are the names of the companies?" Hood asked.

"The only one we know is called Eye At Sea," he replied. "It's incorporated in Holland and lists its business as venture capital. We believe that Mr. Albert Beaudin is part of that investment group. He should not have to conceal his participation. It is not illegal for Frenchmen to invest in China."

"Where in China has Genet leased land?" Hood asked.

"The property is in Shenyang in the Liaoning province," Fujima replied. "Are you familiar with that region of China, Mr. Hood?"

"I am," Hood said. "That's where the Chinese manufacture their advanced J-8 II fighter jets."

"That's right," Fujima said. "And that is why the purchase concerns us. They have a highly skilled, relatively inexpensive labor pool there. An international munitions manufacturer could make a great deal of money using that talent. Obviously, it's an area of enterprise that Japan must watch closely."

"Of course," Hood said. "Do you have any indication that Albert Beaudin himself was involved in the purchase or that he is looking to expand his operations into China?"

"None, Mr. Hood," Fujima admitted. "But we cannot ignore those possibilities."

"Of course not," Hood said.

Hood went back to the computer file on the Beaudin corporate structure. He reviewed the biographies of each individual. The entries were short and did not show the common origins, traumas, national agenda, or even ages that typically formed the basis for what was classified as PIGs—political intervention groups. Hood had always felt that was a fitting acronym for groups that backed terrorists, rebels, and coups.

"Have the other members of Beaudin's team made any significant financial transactions?" Hood asked.

"To date, we have only been watching Mr. Genet and Mr. Beaudin," the intelligence officer replied. "But you were in finance, Mr. Hood. Consider some of the names on Beaudin's board. Richard Bequette. Robert Stiele. Gurney de Sylva. Peter Diffring. Are any of them familiar to you?"

"They weren't until now," Hood admitted.

"You have files on them?" Fujima asked.

"I have very thin files," Hood said. "I'll forward them when we're done. They all appear to be low-profile French, Belgian, and German financiers."

"These are extremely low-profile gentlemen," Fujima agreed. "But directly they control nearly one billion dollars. Indirectly, through partnerships and through individuals who follow their investment leads, they control four to five billion dollars."

That sum was greater than the gross domestic product of Botswana.

"I am not convinced that we're witnessing the unfolding of a master plan," Fujima went on. "Nonetheless, I was hoping you might have some information on Genet, Beaudin, or their colleagues. We cannot ignore the potential for at least a financial assault on international economies."

Fujima's use of the term "at least" suggested his greater worry: that the European money, along with Beaudin technology, would be used to enhance the already formidable Chinese military machine. It was a justifiable concern.

What troubled Hood more was whether the events in Botswana were connected to the activities of Genet. Shaking up the flow of diamonds from the south of Africa would be significant to a portion of the world economy, but it would not be enough to help wage a "financial assault."

Hood received an instant message from Bugs Benet. Emmy Feroche was on the line. Hood wrote back and asked him to have her hold on.

"Mr. Fujima, I'm going to look into these developments for you," Hood said. "Bob Herbert or I will keep you informed. I hope you will do the same."

"I will," Fujima promised.

The Japanese intelligence officer thanked him. Hood told Bugs to forward the personnel files of the Beaudin board to Mr. Fujima. Then he grabbed the call from Emmy.

"Sorry to keep you waiting, Emmy," Hood said.

"Not a problem, Paul," she said. "It's great to hear from you! How has life been?"

"Eventful," he replied.

"I can't wait to catch up," she said. "God, it's amazing how 'Let's stay in touch' can turn into 'Has it really been that long?' "

"I know," Hood said. "How is the world of white-collar crime?"

"Overall, it's very busy," Emmy told him. "At the moment, it's completely insane."

"Why?" Hood asked.

"We're checking to see if there were any improprieties in several major stock deals," Emmy told him. "Have you ever heard of a German stockbroker named Robert Stiele?"

Hood felt a chill. "It so happens I have," he replied. "What did he do?"

"Stiele quietly pulled the trigger on some major deals early this morning, Euro time," she said. "He dumped one hundred and fourteen million dollars in blue-chip stock holdings, companies that were doing well, and put the money into three separate, privately held operations."

"Do you have their names?" Hood asked.

"Yes," she replied. "The first one is VeeBee Ltd., the second one is Les Jambes de Venus—"

"And the third is Eye At Sea," Hood said.

"Yes!" Emmy replied. She was obviously impressed. "How do you know that?"

"I can't tell you," Hood said.

"Well, Mr. Wizard, what *can* you tell me?" she asked.

"Look into Albert Beaudin," he said.

"Why?"

"Can't tell you that either," Hood said. "what are you doing about Stiele?"

"We're trying to find out if Mr. Stiele knows something about the blue chips that we don't."

"I wouldn't worry about the blue chips," Hood said. "This is about Stiele. He needed to get liquid."

"Why?" she pressed.

"That," Hood replied, "is a damn good question."

NINETEEN

Okavango Swamp, Botswana
Thursday, 6:00 P.M.

It was ironic. After being given food and rest, Father Bradbury's own tactics were used against him.

The priest had recalled the missionaries, as instructed. Then he was taken outside. He was not bound or hooded, and it felt strange to see the morning light, to feel fresh air on his face. He was allowed to use the little island's outhouse. After that, he was not returned to "the cage," as his captors called it. He was taken to a small hut. The window was shuttered, the walls were made of logs, and the roof was corrugated tin. Near the ceiling, a series of four small holes had been cut two feet apart in the walls on every side. They provided the small room's only light and ventilation. The door was bolted from the outside, and the floor was concrete. But there was a cot against the back wall, and Bradbury was given bread and water. After saying grace, he ate and drank greedily.

The air was humid and extremely hot. Following his modest meal, Father Bradbury stood on the cot and sucked the relatively cool morning air through one of the openings. Then, his eyes heavy, he lay down on his belly. He put his head on the towel that passed for a pillow. He reeked of dried perspiration and the smells of the swamp. Marsh flies scouted his sticky hands and cheeks. But the heat, the stench, the bugs, all of that vanished when the priest shut his eyes. He was asleep within moments.

The next thing Father Bradbury knew, he was being awakened by a firm tap on the shoulder and a gruff, unfamiliar voice.

"Get up!"

It was now very dark in the room and he had no idea how long he'd been asleep. The voice seemed to be coming from far away. The priest felt incredibly groggy. He was not even certain he was awake. He did not want to move, let alone stand.

Someone tapped him again. "Come on!" the voice said.

Father Bradbury tried to face the speaker. His arms were asleep, and it was a moment before he could move. He finally looked over at a shadowy figure. It was someone he did not know.

The man reached down and grabbed Father Bradbury's upper arm. He gave it a sharp tug. Obviously, the priest was not moving swiftly enough. Father Bradbury pushed himself off the cot and stood unsteadily, and his vision swirled from having gotten up too quickly. Still holding him, the man led the clergyman through the open door. The skies were blue black as they walked across the warm soil toward a hut. The structure was about thirty yards away. Father Bradbury had not seen Dhamballa's hut from the outside. The last time he was pulled in this direction, he had been wearing a hood. But he saw half-dragged footprints in the soil. They were probably his. And they led to this structure.

The island seemed deserted. There was only the one soldier to escort the priest. That did not surprise Father Bradbury. Even if he had the strength, where would an unarmed man go? Especially with predators hiding in the murky waters and along the moss-shrouded shoreline.

But flight was not what Father Bradbury had in mind. Sometimes the best escape was to change the prison itself.

"Whom do I thank for giving me food and allowing me to rest?" the priest pressed.

The man responded with silence. The priest was undeterred.

"May I know your name?" Father Bradbury asked.

The man still did not answer him.

"I am Powys Sebastian Bradbury—"

"Quiet!"

"I'm sorry," Father Bradbury replied.

The priest had not really expected the man to say anything.

Nonetheless, now that he had the strength, the clergyman wanted to try to engage these people in conversation. When talking to parishioners or taking confession, Father Bradbury found that trust often grew from the most banal or innocent exchanges. It was easy to evolve a conversation. To progress from learning a person's name to discussing the weather to asking how they're feeling. Now that the priest was rested and thinking more clearly, establishing a personal connection with his captors was a priority. It might not guarantee his safety or gain his release, but it might give Father Bradbury a clue as to what the Botswanans were planning. It might also tell him whether he should continue to participate.

But conversation was like a spear with two heads. If a man pushed too hard, he could impale himself on the backside.

The priest was taken inside the hut. Dhamballa was there. He was sitting on a wicker mat by the far wall. His back was to the door. There was a candle in front of him. It gave off a tart smell, like burning rubber. It was the only light in the room. There was a wooden bucket behind the man. Father Bradbury could not see what was inside.

The soldier sat the priest in a folding chair in the center of the room. Then the young man closed the door and stood beside it. There was a tray on the dirt floor to Father Bradbury's right. On it were a cell phone, a plate of fruit, a pitcher of water, and a glass.

"You may drink or eat, if you wish," Dhamballa said. He spoke without turning around.

"Thank you," Father Bradbury said. He filled the water glass and took a banana.

"You did both," Dhamballa remarked.

"Yes."

"But I gave you a choice," Dhamballa pointed out.

The priest apologized. He put the banana back.

"You kept the water," Dhamballa said.

"Yes."

"People will always choose drink over food," Dhamballa said. "Do you know why?"

"Thirst is a more commanding need, I would say," the priest replied.

"No," Dhamballa told him. "Water is the companion to air, earth, and fire. Men always return to the four elemental forces to nurture life, to find the truth, to understand themselves."

"Is that what you are doing out here?" Father Bradbury asked. "Searching for truth?"

"I am not," Dhamballa said. He looked back. His face was dark, but his head was haloed by the candle's orange glow. He looked very young, very innocent. "I have found the truth. I am preparing to bring it to others."

"Does that include me?" Father Bradbury asked.

Dhamballa now turned around fully. He stood. Dhamballa was a tall man, well over six feet. He was barefoot and dressed in a brown, sleeveless robe that reached to his ankles. "What do you know of Vodunism?"

The word itself made Father Bradbury feel unclean. He looked down at the cup of water. It reminded him of the Baptist. What is elemental to one is holy to another. That made him feel a little better. Besides, the Vatican had established guidelines that enabled missions to exist harmoniously with indigenous faiths. The most important was to open a dialogue with the leaders of those faiths. Not to remain a mysterious, threatening secret.

"I know nothing about Vodunism," Father Bradbury replied. He did not want to tell what little he knew about voodoo or the black arts. He could not risk misspeaking and insulting his host. As long as they kept talking, as long as they opened up to one another, the priest had hope.

"But you are acquainted with the term," Dhamballa continued.

"Yes," the priest admitted.

"What is your perception of Vodunism?" Dhamballa asked.

The priest considered his words carefully. "It is an ancient set of practices. I have read that your beliefs are rooted in nature. In the elementals, if you will. Your rites are said to employ herbal mixtures that can control the will, raise the dead, and perform other acts of the supernatural."

"That is part of it. Some of our 'practices,' as you describe them, are at least eight thousand years old," Dhamballa said.

"Your history is great," Father Bradbury agreed.

"Our history?" Dhamballa said. "We are more than an accumulation of years and events."

"Forgive me," Father Bradbury said immediately. "I did not mean any disrespect."

"In truth, priest, you know nothing about the *heart* of my faith," Dhamballa went on.

"No," Father Bradbury admitted.

"How can you know anything?" Dhamballa asked. "In the fifteenth century, your priests came to Africa, and later to the West Indies. They baptized my people to save us from a 'profound evil.' Growing up in Machaneng, I knew priests. I watched them. I saw how they promised the poor riches in the next life."

"They are there," Father Bradbury assured him.

"No," Dhamballa replied. "The riches are *here*. I saw them when I worked in the diamond mines. I watched as good Christians took our wealth from us, and the priests did nothing to stop them."

"It is not our job to restrict the actions of others," Father Bradbury said.

"You did not speak against it."

"Why would we? They broke no laws," the priest observed.

"They did not break your laws," Dhamballa said. "The laws that the British brought here and that subsequent governments retained. I do not recognize those laws."

Father Bradbury wanted to say, *Clearly you do not.* But that would not have helped him.

"I judge all men by one measure, and that is truth," Dhamballa said. "When I worked in the mines, I also saw the living faith of Vodunism. I saw men who could cure the hurt, the weary, the despairing with a touch, a prayer, a potion." He pointed a finger at Father Bradbury. "They explained to me that they practiced in secret because those whom you have converted also regard them as evil. And yet these are arts my ancestors took with them when they migrated to the Middle

East. They are skills that could very well have been used by your own Savior, Jesus Christ. White arts to heal, not black arts that hurt."

"The powers of our Savior belonged to Him because He is the Son of God," Father Bradbury said.

"We are all sons of God," Dhamballa replied. "The question is, which god? Jehovah or Olorun?"

The cult leader moved forward slowly. Father Bradbury noticed there were snakes tattooed on the backs of his wrists.

"My faith is as old as civilization itself," Dhamballa said. "It was ancient when your religion was not yet conceived. Our rites and our prayers have passed unchanged since the earliest days of man. Not just the black magic but the white magic, the arts your priests ignored as they had us flogged and hanged. We used mandrake to kill pain, rattles and drums to stimulate blood flow and cure illness, stimulated human glands by the consumption of animal meat and blood. Our priests do not just talk about miracles. They *work* miracles, every day, guided by Agwe, the essence of the sea; by Aida Wedo, the rainbow spirit; by Baron Samedi, the guardian of the grave; by Erinle, the heart of the forest; and by hundreds of others. The fortunate ones are taught in dreams and visions. These spirits give us the power and the wisdom to generate, to regenerate, or to destroy."

"Are you one of the fortunate ones?" Father Bradbury asked.

"I am among the blessed," the leader said with humility. "I am the priest of the serpent spirit Damballah. I have adopted a form of his name in tribute. My sacred task is to clean the nation of disbelievers. I must do that or else I must prepare the way for Ogu Bodagris, the great spirit of war. He wishes to reclaim the home that was once his."

Just a few minutes before, the idea of John the Baptist had brought Father Bradbury a feeling of peace. It was frightening to think that Dhamballa saw himself in that same way. John was a bringer of light and eternal salvation. Dhamballa was a harbinger of darkness and damnation. Even if it cost Father Bradbury his life, the priest could not allow this war to happen.

Words, he reminded himself. *Use them as you have in the past. Get him to open up.*

"There must be a way to resolve our differences without bloodshed," Father Bradbury said.

"There is, most definitely," Dhamballa replied. "Withdraw your people. Return our nation to us."

"But Botswana is home to many of us," Father Bradbury replied. "I am a citizen. So is Deacon Jones and many others. We have spent much of our lives in Maun."

"It cannot be your home because you came uninvited," Dhamballa replied. "You came here for one reason. To try to conquer the native faith of Botswana. Your people are the ones who have made war on us." Dhamballa pointed to Father Bradbury's forehead. "A war of ideas. They will be crushed."

"You speak of a different time, a different church," Father Bradbury assured him. "We respect other religions, other religious leaders. We wish to coexist with you."

"That is not true," Dhamballa replied.

"I tell you it is," Father Bradbury replied.

"Pick up the telephone," Dhamballa told him.

Father Bradbury was caught off guard. He walked to the table and lifted the cordless receiver. It was larger than any telephone he had ever seen. It looked more like a walkie-talkie.

"Call your parish," Dhamballa said. "Speak with your deacon. Ask who is coming to the church."

The priest did so. Deacon Jones answered. The missionary was surprised and excited to hear from Father Bradbury.

"God is merciful! How are you, Father?" Jones asked.

The deacon's voice was coming from the back of the receiver as well as the front. This was a portable speakerphone.

"I'm well," the priest replied. "Deacon, tell me. Is someone coming to Holy Cross?"

"Yes," the deacon replied. "A bishop is arriving tomorrow from Washington, D.C., to minister in your absence."

"A bishop?" Bradbury said.

"Yes, Bishop Victor Max," Jones said. "Deacon Canon and I are going to Maun to meet his plane when it arrives. Father, talk to me—where are you? Are they treating you well?"

"I am fine," the priest said. "Is anyone else coming to the church?" Father Bradbury asked.

"No," the deacon replied.

"Are you certain?" the priest asked.

"This is what I've been told," Deacon Jones informed him.

Dhamballa held out his hand. Father Bradbury handed him the telephone. The Vodun leader punched it off.

"You see?" Dhamballa said.

"A bishop is coming," Father Bradbury said. "A single clergyman. I'm certain he has been sent to tend to the needs of the people I left behind. My flock. My followers. He is no threat to you."

The priest spoke softly and with great compassion. But as he awaited Dhamballa's reply, Father Bradbury had an uneasy feeling, a sense that he had just made a terrible mistake.

"He is no threat," the voodoo priest repeated disdainfully. His dark eyes glared at the priest. "As I suspected, they will replace one with another."

"As you suspected?"

"They send one mightier in rank and from another nation, daring us to defend ourselves," Dhamballa said.

"You used me," the priest said angrily. "You didn't know anyone was coming—"

"They are daring me to go after him," Dhamballa said more to himself than to Father Bradbury. "But Leon expected this. We will postpone visiting the other churches to deal with this great man from America." His eyes shifted to the soldier. "Grinnell, return the priest to the hut."

The soldier took Father Bradbury by the arm. The priest tried to wrench it free.

"Wait!" the priest said. "What is going to happen now?"

Dhamballa turned back toward his mat. He did not answer.

Of all the hapless, trusting fools, Father Bradbury thought. The voodoo priest had done exactly what the priest himself had been trying to do. To engage his opponent and find out what he was thinking. Only Dhamballa had done it better. He had gotten the priest to open up, to hope, to trust. In so doing, Father Bradbury had told Dhamballa where and how to seize his next hostage.

As he was led from the hut, the priest wailed in despair.

TWENTY

Maun, Botswana
Thursday, 6:46 P.M.

It was as if no time had passed.

Most human bodies have a better memory than the mind. Skills once learned do not go away, whether it is assembling a rifle or holding a pencil. Reflexes and instincts work faster than thought. Even when the limbs age, they have the capacity to recall their abilities and execute many of them. The mind? Leon Seronga could not tell someone how to tie a shoe. But he could show them. He could not remember what he had for dinner two nights ago. But his fingertips could remember the weight of a switchblade he had learned to use when he was a boy. Whenever Seronga took the old knife from his pocket, his hand and arm could run a slash attack on their own.

Seronga sat on his motor scooter looking out at the tourist center. His body told him it was 1966. His senses were finely tuned. His muscles, only slightly impaired by age, were still at hair-trigger readiness. He and his companion, Donald Pavant, had driven to Maun and rented Malaguti Firefox F15 RR scooters. Dressed in white and blue Dainese scooter jackets, the men had pretended to be recreational bikers as they made their way across the floodplain. They raced through gullies and jumped small hills as they headed away from the city. Now that it was nearly dark, the men had stopped to keep an eye on the tourist center. If everything was all right, they would contact the men at the edge of the swamp. They would proceed to the Church of Loyola in Shakawe to kidnap the priest there. Seronga expected that he would be guarded now, probably by local police. The military would not want to give this a high profile. Not yet. But whoever was there, it would not matter. There was always a way in.

Seronga and Pavant had come here to keep an eye on any surreptitious developments at this church. The Brush Vipers wondered if the archdiocese in Cape Town, perhaps the Vatican itself, would let the violation of this place go unanswered. Would the Church respond with calm or would they send a battery of priests? Perhaps they would send nuns to see if women were vulnerable.

The secure phone provided by Genet beeped. The call from the Belgian gave Seronga his answer.

"Dhamballa just spoke with our guest," Genet informed the leader of the Brush Vipers. "As we anticipated, there is a new one coming over. We were told that a bishop is due in Maun tomorrow afternoon. Two individuals from your locale will be meeting him at the airfield."

"Is this new arrival traveling alone?" Seronga asked.

"That's what we were told," Genet informed him.

"Where is he coming from?" Seronga asked.

"The United States," Genet replied.

"Interesting."

"Very," Genet said. "That automatically makes it a global affair and guarantees the interest of international press if something happens."

Any move against him could draw America into this conflict in some capacity. Probably in a démarche, intense diplomatic activity. Possibly even a military one. There was a zero-tolerance policy for terrorism. A limited search-and-rescue operation could be called for. On the other hand, the clergyman might simply be bait to capture the abductors. The government in Gaborone might dispatch troops to protect him. Or perhaps the Vatican had made its own security arrangements.

Seronga thanked Genet for the update and hung up. The Belgian did not have to tell him what to do. That had been decided ahead of time. If a replacement were sent for Father Bradbury, he was to be taken. But not with a show of force this time. The abduction of Father Bradbury had been done that way to show the world that Dhamballa had soldiers to use if he wished. If Seronga had come back with his army, the Botswana president might begin to fear a brewing civil war. He would have no choice but to call on his own military. Dhamballa did not want that. This time, the kidnapping must be different. It must be very subtle. To slip the priest's replacement away would show Gaborone that this was not a war. It was a dispute. And the dispute was not with Botswana or its people. It was with the Roman Catholic Church. Only later, when Dhamballa had established a strong religious base among the general population, would he use his ministry to impact nationalism and politics.

Seronga briefed Pavant. The thirty-three-year-old was the youngest of the Brush Vipers. He was also one of the most militant. Born and raised in Lobatse on the South African border, Pavant was exposed to refugees from apartheid. Pavant believed that Africa was for native Africans and their descendants. He was one of the first men to discover Dhamballa and his ministry.

The men waited a quarter of a mile from the tourist center. They sat on their bikes, shielded by the darkness. They ate chicken sandwiches they had picked up in Maun and watched the dirt road for headlights. They did not speak. After five hours on the bikes, the silence felt good.

At a few minutes before nine o'clock, the evening bus from Maun pulled up to the front gate of the tourist center. Seronga asked for the binoculars. Pavant reached into the small equipment locker on the back of his bike. He removed the case and handed the binoculars to Seronga. The leader of the Brush Vipers peered across the dark, still floodplain.

There were several things odd about the group. The size, for one. There were about twenty-five new arrivals. That was a large number for this time of year. Most of the large tour groups came when the weather was cooler. Seronga watched carefully. They were all carrying duffel bags as well as having suitcases stored below. The bags had a sameness to them, as if the tourists had packed an identical amount of clothes, the same number of personal items. Individuals on a trip did not do that. Seronga also noticed that no one had plastic bags or souvenir caps, the kinds of things one typically picked up in airports or local gift shops.

And one thing more struck Seronga as very unusual. Most of the tourists were men.

"It looks as if a lot of people came in," Pavant remarked.

"Too many," Seronga remarked.

As Seronga watched, there were other things that made him uneasy.

Genet and Dhamballa had set out very strict guidelines for Seronga and his Brush Vipers to follow. Clergymen were to be captured as nonviolently as possible. None was to be martyred, even if it meant aborting a mission. Care was to be taken so that parishioners were never harmed.

Military or police action taken against Dhamballa or the Brush Vipers was to be met with deadly force. Dhamballa did not like killing. It angered the gods. But Seronga did not have enough soldiers that he could afford to lose any of them. He argued that self-defense was not an evil act. He also did not want his people captured. A prisoner who had been tortured, his brain rewired, could be made to say just about anything. A show trial could be used to discredit Dhamballa.

Reluctantly, Dhamballa had agreed to killing under those conditions. But neither man had expected things to reach that stage this early.

Seronga continued to study the group. The truth was, he had no way of knowing whether these were tourists or soldiers traveling incognito. He could not see if they were black or white. They might have come from Gaborone. Perhaps the United States sent them from the embassy to look after their cleric. The Americans had soldiers stationed there. These could have been selected from their ranks. Perhaps they would go touring when the deacons went to Maun to meet the American cleric. Perhaps the tourists would be watching for any attempts to abduct the new arrival. The bishop could not be allowed to reach the church and resume Father Bradbury's work. If he did, priests and field missionaries might be encouraged to stay. Dhamballa could not afford to let that happen.

"How is their posture?" Pavant asked.

"Excellent," Seronga said.

"Then they can't be tourists," Pavant said. "They always slump."

"Yes, and when these people got out, several did stretches," Seronga said. "They seem accustomed to traveling great distances." He handed his companion the binoculars. "And look at how they're moving."

Pavant studied the group for a moment. "They're passing each other bags as they unload them."

"Like troops," Seronga said. "Let's give them a while to settle in, and then we'll go over."

Seronga took the binoculars back. He continued to watch the bus until it pulled away. The more he saw of the dark figures, the more convinced he became that something was afoot.

He would soon know if that were true. And if it was, he would know what to do about it.

TWENTY-ONE

Washington, D.C.
Thursday, 11:47 A.M.

Darrell McCaskey left Mike Rodgers chatting with David Battat and Aideen Marley at DiMaggio's Joe. Within a half hour, the general had the two operatives revved up and ready to die for him. Rodgers's sense of purpose, and the quiet intensity with which he stated it, made people want to work with him. The genius of Mike Rodgers was that he was standoffish without being cold. He did not welcome new friendships. If others wanted to be with him, service was all they could give him. Colonel Brett August was the only one who had ever gotten close to Rodgers. And that had taken him a lifetime.

Darrell McCaskey was not like that. When he was with the FBI and out in the field, he had been ice. That was the only way to deal with the terrorists and drug dealers and kidnappers. He had to forget they were people with parents and siblings and children. His job was to uphold the law. If that meant arresting a single mother who was pushing heroin to support her kids, he did it.

When he was at the office or went home, McCaskey always did a one eighty. He let himself get close to people. He had to. He needed to keep his armor from becoming permanent. He opened himself up to superiors, subordinates, custodians, neighbors, shopkeepers, women he dated.

Inevitably, with that kind of emotional exposure came trust. Equally as inevitable, with trust came disappointment. And right now, McCaskey was disappointed in a man he had trusted.

Bob Herbert's call to Maria had gnawed at him during the drive from Georgetown to Andrews Air Force Base. Herbert knew that this was a sensitive area in the couple's relationship. McCaskey did not believe that Herbert had set out to hurt him. But his coworker, his friend, had not done anything to protect him, either. If Herbert had asked, McCaskey could have put him in touch with any number of Interpol agents in Madrid. They could have done the same job as Maria. McCaskey could not imagine what the hell the guy was thinking.

He tried calling his wife during the drive. Her cell phone voice mail took his call. He asked her to call back as soon as possible. She did not.

By the time McCaskey reached Op-Center, he was in a silent rage. The former G-man went directly to Bob Herbert's office. That was probably a bad idea, and he knew it. But Herbert was not a kid. He could take a dressing down. Hell, he had no choice. It was coming.

The door to Herbert's office was shut. McCaskey knocked. Paul Hood opened it.

"Good morning, Darrell," Hood said.

"Morning," McCaskey said. He entered the office. Op-Center's director shut the door behind him. Herbert was seated behind his desk. Hood remained standing. His white shirt-sleeves were rolled up and his tie loosened. Paul Hood was not a casual man. It must have been a tough morning. Or maybe Hood was just expecting it to get tougher.

"Everything okay?" Hood asked.

"Sure," McCaskey replied. He did not attempt to conceal the edge in his voice. But if Hood or Herbert noticed, they said nothing. They apparently had their own problems. McCaskey had spent nearly three decades in law enforcement. When the temperature of a room was off, he knew it.

"I was just bringing Bob up to speed on developments in Africa," Hood said. "You know what happened over there? About the kidnapping of Father Powys Bradbury?"

"I read the briefing on the Op-ED page before I left the house," McCaskey said.

"Bad news and a Danish," Herbert said.

"Something like that," McCaskey replied. Their eyes remained locked a moment longer than ordinary conversation

required. McCaskey realized just how angry he was at Bob
Herbert for having contacted Maria.

The Op-ED page was the Op-Center Executive Dossier
page, a twice-daily summary of NCMC activities. Written by
the daytime department heads, it was posted on the internal
web site. In that way, officials who did not normally interact
could stay on top of what was happening in different divisions.
It was also a quick way for the night crew to get up to speed.
The Op-ED program also cross-referenced names and places
with files from other U.S. intelligence agencies. If a company
owned by Albert Beaudin were involved in an investigation
over at the CIA, FBI, NSA, military intelligence, or some other
agency, the respective department heads would be notifed via
automated E-mail.

"There are a few things aren't on the Op-ED yet," Hood
said. "Have you ever heard of a diamond dealer by the name
of Henry Genet?"

"No," McCaskey said.

"Genet has financial ties to Albert Beaudin, the French industrialist," Hood told him.

"The Musketeer," McCaskey said.

"Right," Hood said. "As Bob and I were just discussing, the
most compelling reason for Op-Center to be involved in this
situation is to track whatever Beaudin might be doing. After
what we went through in France with the New Jacobins, we
can't afford to underestimate this guy."

"I agree," McCaskey said.

"The big question is whether these people have anything to
do with a religious cult leader named Dhamballa," Herbert
said.

"Where's the link?" McCaskey asked.

"A man named Leon Seronga," Herbert told him. "Seronga
is one of the founders of the Brush Vipers, a paramilitary intelligence group that helped Botswana get its independence
from Great Britain. The Vatican suspects Seronga of having
kidnapped their priest. He has also been seen at Dhamballa's
rallies. The MO of what went down in Maun is reminiscent
of how the Brush Vipers used to strike. In and out, surgical,

usually early in the morning when people were still groggy. We've promised to help Rome try to clear up some of these connections, maybe get some people over there."

"I think we're past the maybe stage," McCaskey said. "I was just with Mike, Aideen Marley, and David Battat. They're ready to go."

Hearing this, Herbert punched in the telephone extension of Barbara Crowe. Crowe ran Op-Center's documents department. This wasn't his operation, but he had never been one to fret over formalities. They would need counterfeit IDs, credit cards, and passports. Crowe could use photographs from their dossiers. Battat had been registered in a hospital in Azerbaijan. Marley had been involved in an assassination in Spain. The new identities would prevent their names from raising flags in any customs or airline databases.

While Herbert told Barbara what Marley and Battat would need, Hood continued the briefing.

"Apart from Beaudin and the missing priest, there is another immediate concern," Hood said. "The Vatican is sending a replacement to run the church in Maun, a bishop from D.C. He arrives tomorrow."

"Have they got resources to protect him?" McCaskey asked.

"Yes, which is what concerns me," Hood said. "He is going to be shadowed by undercover Spanish troops posing as tourists."

"How did Spain get involved?" McCaskey asked.

"They're in this because of the Madrid Accords," Herbert said as he hung up with Barbara Crowe. "That's a fairly recent alliance between the Vatican and the king of Spain. A dozen of the Spanish army's elite troops have gone over to Botswana. We tracked their flight. They're definitely on the ground and probably already on site."

"Paul, why is that a concern?" McCaskey asked.

"Because now you've got five political entities involved," Hood said. "The U.S. through the bishop. The cult. The Botswana government. The Vatican. And the Spanish."

"Ordinarily, coalitions are a good thing," Herbert said. "In this case, though, we feel that the Vatican should be walking softly, not hammering what may be a manageable crisis."

"Manageable by us," McCaskey said.

"It's worth a try," Hood said.

"What we should be doing is gathering intel to see if the priest can be rescued," Herbert said. "That should be done before anything else, including sending in a replacement."

"Would Maria be part of this intel gathering group?" McCaskey asked directly.

"Darrell, Bob and I were just discussing that," Hood said.

That was what McCaskey sensed when he entered the room. The chill between the men.

"I had called her to get me some information from the Ministry of Defense," Herbert said. "She got that. She said she wanted to do more."

"You asked her to go to Botswana," McCaskey said.

There was another long look. There was something in the intelligence chief's eyes. Something strong, as if he were braced for an assault.

"No, that isn't it," McCaskey said suddenly. "You already sent her."

"Yes," Herbert said. "She is en route."

"You recruited my wife to spy on the Brush Vipers," McCaskey said. As though saying the words would help him process them. "You sent her to track people who know Botswana better than we know D.C."

"She's not going to be alone for long," Hood said. "And she's been given very strict orders to gather data from secondary sources."

"As if my wife knows the meaning of *moderation*," McCaskey declared.

"Darrell, let's talk about this," Hood said.

McCaskey shook his head. He did not know what to do or what to think. But talking it out was third on his list of options. Beating the hell out of Herbert and walking out of the office were ahead of it, in that order.

"Darrell, I okayed the call to Maria," Hood said. "If she was going to get to Botswana in time for the bishop's arrival, she had to leave immediately."

"Traveling under her own name?" McCaskey said.

"No, under her married name," Herbert pointed out. "I made sure that she had already changed her passport. Maria McCaskey won't show up in any foreign databases."

"You still could have run it past me," McCaskey said. "You could have given me the courtesy of that."

"You weren't here," Herbert said.

"I have a cell phone—"

"This is *not* the kind of thing I wanted to tell you over a telephone, secure or not," Herbert replied. "That's how people cancel dinner reservations and dentist appointments. This needed to be face-to-face."

"Why?" McCaskey demanded. "How do you know I would have fought you on this?"

"Because you fought with Maria about it," Herbert replied. "Hell, you broke up over this a few years ago. I couldn't take the chance that you would hang up on me and call her. I didn't want her distracted or upset."

"Or have someone talking reason to her," McCaskey said.

"That was *not* an issue," Herbert insisted.

"Anyway, I thought this was *Mike's* operation," McCaskey snapped. "Mike thinks that, too. I just had breakfast with him."

"It will be," Hood said. "What Bob did was put Maria in a position where she might be able to help us. That's all."

"Look, Darrell," Herbert said. "The Spanish military group has experience in quick military strikes. They have not shown that they can conduct surveillance or work for extended periods undercover. I needed someone who can do that. Someone who was in the right hemisphere. Someone who speaks Spanish and can talk to the soldiers, if necessary."

McCaskey heard Herbert's words. They all made sense. But logic aside, he could not get past having been left out of the loop. This was his *wife* they were talking about sending into a potential combat situation.

Which was why Herbert did it this way, McCaskey told himself. Herbert had just said so. To avoid involving her in a debate like this. To keep the high emotions away from Maria. Reason told him that what Herbert had done was smart and professional. There were human interests, national interests at risk. But there were still conflicting personal and professional stakes. McCaskey could not think of a previous time when he had felt like this.

McCaskey continued to regard Herbert. As he did, something else eased into the equation. Something unexpected. McCaskey found it in Herbert's gaze. Those lively Southern eyes did not reflect the same hard determination McCaskey had seen a moment before. There was something new.

There was pain.

It was then that the realization hit McCaskey. It struck him hard across the chest, almost taking his breath away.

Bob Herbert was reliving his own fears, his own trauma. Everything McCaskey was feeling, Herbert must have felt each day he and his late wife were in Beirut. Yet then as now, Herbert had put his nation first. He had done his duty, despite the cost.

The furnace inside Darrell McCaskey shut down. A minute before, he had felt completely alone. That was no longer the case.

"I don't like this," McCaskey said, his voice low. "But I will say this much. You certainly called on one of the best undercover ops in the business."

Herbert seemed to relax slightly. "That I did," he acknowledged.

McCaskey took a long breath, then looked from Herbert to Hood. "I told Mike I'd do some prep work in case his people went to Africa. I need to find out if there's anyone they might be able to hook up with over there."

"Great," Hood said. "Thanks."

McCaskey turned from Hood to Herbert, then quickly left the office. Though McCaskey's manner was calm, he was far, far from being at peace.

TWENTY-TWO

Maun, Botswana
Thursday, 11:01 P.M.

The door of the church living quarters did not have a lock. There was no need for one. As Father Bradbury used to say, "Lions cannot turn knobs, and human guests are always welcome."

Tired from their journeys, Deacons Jones and Canon had retired at ten. Jones had spent over two hours on the telephone discussing his call from Father Bradbury. He had reported it, first, to a priest in Cape Town. Then he recounted the conversation to Archbishop Patrick himself. A few minutes later, he was telephoned by a security officer from the Vatican. After that, the deacon missionary received a call from a man named Kline in New York. Deacon Jones was glad for the many years he had spent memorizing lengthy passages of scripture. He was able to repeat the conversation accurately, word for word, to each man with whom he spoke. Yet except for the first priest in Cape Town, no one seemed to share his delight at having heard from Father Bradbury. The archbishop and especially the two men from the Vatican acted as if he had been phoned by the devil himself. Deacon Jones could not figure out why. Nor would anyone explain it to him. The conversation was brief, and it had seemed innocent enough.

The men from the Vatican both told him not to speak to anyone else about Bishop Max. He agreed.

Jones did not let the confusion trouble him. Ignorance was determined by how much information one had. It was not a measure of intelligence or character. At peace with himself, he went to the washroom, brushed his teeth, put on his pajamas, and returned to the sleeping quarters. He and Deacon Canon took linens from the closet.

There were four twin beds in the long, sparsely furnished room. Two of the beds were situated near windows. The deacons made those and opened the windows. Jones took the bed away from the veranda. Canon was a heavy sleeper. If any of the tourists took a late-night stroll, he would not hear them.

Jones knelt beside the bed and said his prayers. Then he gently parted the fine-mesh mosquito net and slid inside. The window was to Jones's right. The breeze was warm but soothing. It was good to sleep on a mattress with a clean, white sheet. In the field they usually slept on bedrolls, canvas cots, or patches of grass.

Deacon Jones fell asleep quickly.

There was a sharp prick at the top of the clergyman's throat. It felt like the bite of a female deerfly, which slashes the flesh and drinks the blood. Jones did not know if minutes or hours had passed. He did not want to know. He was groggy, and all he wanted to do was get back to sleep. He kept his eyes closed and went to brush the fly away.

His hand struck metal.

Jones opened his eyes with a start. It was not a fly at his throat. It was a knife. Behind it was a big, dark figure. The mosquito net had been neatly pulled aside, and the intruder was standing holding the tip of the knife firmly under Deacon Jones's chin. From the corner of his eye, Jones could see that the door was slightly ajar. He also saw someone standing over Deacon Canon.

"Have you ever met the American bishop?" the intruder asked in a low, rough voice.

"No," Jones answered. His mind was still fuzzy. Why did the man want to know that?

"What are your names?" the intruder pressed.

"I am Eliot Jones, and he is Samuel Canon," the deacon replied. "We are deacons at this church. What is going on?"

"Where is your cell phone?" the intruder went on.

"Why do you want to know?" Jones asked.

The intruder pushed down slightly on the knife. Jones felt

his flesh pop as the tip of the blade punched through it. Blood seeped around the metal and trickled down both sides of his neck. He could actually feel the sharp steel against the top of his larynx. Instinctively, the deacon reached for the man's hand to push it back. The intruder twisted the knife blade so that it could cut sideways now. He gave a tug to the side. The pain caused Jones's entire body to tense. His arms pulled back in the same reflex.

"The next thrust sends it all the way through," the intruder said. "Once again. Where is your cell phone?"

"Go ahead, cut my throat!" the deacon said. "I have no fear of death."

"Then I will kill everyone at this facility," the intruder said.

"That sin would be yours, not mine," replied the deacon. "And whatever you do to their bodies, their souls will be with God."

The intruder removed the knife. The next thing the deacon felt was a sharp sting, then a blazing pain in his right thigh. Even as the deacon reflexively sucked down air to scream, the intruder put the blade back at his throat. It took a moment for the deacon's brain to realize that he had been stabbed. His mind shifted from disbelief to shock to defiance.

"Where is your cell phone?" the intruder repeated. "Tell me, or I'll let your soul out in pieces."

"The soul cannot be harmed," the deacon whimpered. " 'Though I walk through the valley of death—' "

The knife pierced his forearm. The deacon screamed. The blade was worked around in a circle, digging into bone. This pain was not like the other. This one did not stop but kept going deeper into his body, as though molten lead had entered his veins. His head shook violently. His feet kicked on the bed. He could not control his body. Or his mind. Or his will.

"The phone!" the intruder said. "We don't have time—".

"It's inside my jacket!" the man screamed. "Behind the door! Oh God, stop! Take the phone! *Take it!*"

The intruder did not remove the knife. He continued to drive it down. Jones could feel his blood seeping into the sheets, along his leg.

"What time are you meeting the bishop from America?" the intruder demanded.

Deacon Jones told him. He would have told him anything he asked. How did the Savior bear it? It was incomprehensible.

The intruder removed the knife from the deacon's wrist. The deepest pain abated instantly, like waves pulling back from the shore.

A moment later, the intruder put the blade to his throat and pushed down hard. Deacon Jones heard a scream from somewhere in the distance. It was not his own voice. He knew that because he could not move his mouth. He felt an electric pain in the base of his tongue. He lurched. An instant later, the pain struck the roof of his mouth. That one hurt worse as the hard palate offered resistance to the blade. Jones was still trying to speak, but all that came from his mouth were guttural grunts and gagging. Then the man reversed his hold on the hilt so that his thumb was on top. He pushed the knife to the left, as though it were a paper cutter. The deacon's carotid artery was severed. Then he tore the blade back to the right. The internal and external jugular veins were cut.

The pain was intensely warm and cold at the same time. Jones heard gurgling from somewhere. It took a moment for him to realize that the sounds were his. He was trying to breathe. The deacon reached for his throat, but his hands were weak, his fingers tingling. He let his arms drop to his sides. His eyes sought his attacker. But by then he was unable to see anything. His vision swirled black and red. His head felt extremely light.

An instant later, Deacon Jones saw nothing at all. The heat and chill blended into a dreamy neutrality.

He went back to sleep.

TWENTY-THREE

Maun, Botswana
Thursday, 11:30 P.M.

Leon Seronga looked down at the bloody shape on the bed. To his right, Donald Pavant finished cutting the throat of Deacon Canon. The Brush Viper had placed a strong hand across his mouth. The man had died with a single, muffled scream.

"It is done," Pavant said to him with defiance. "You had no choice. We did what was necessary."

Seronga continued to stare.

"Prince, this is the way you used to do it, the way that things must sometimes be done," Pavant said.

"I promised Dhamballa this would be different," Seronga said. "No killing. No black magic."

"That man would have bled to death," Pavant replied. He was cleaning his own blade on the blanket of the other cot. "You showed mercy. And if you had not pushed him, he would not have told us what we needed to know."

"What we *needed* to know," Seronga said.

"Yes. We cannot allow the bishop to come here. It would undo everything," Pavant said. "Dhamballa would have been seen as small, petty, ineffective. Besides, no one need know about these two."

"They mustn't," Seronga said.

The leader of the Brush Vipers felt sick. He had been pushed to this extreme by this man's stubborn resistance. It would have been so much easier if the clergyman had cooperated. Instead, his words were his own epitaph. He had said that if Seronga killed, it would be on his own conscience. If that was true, these two deaths were on the deacon's soul. Had he answered Seronga's questions, they would have tied the men up. They would have hidden them here or in the field, in a cave, away from predators. When the kidnapping of the American bishop had been accomplished, they would have instructed authorities where to find these two.

The stupid, stupid man.

"I have the cell phone," Pavant said from behind the door.

"See if there are fresh bedsheets anywhere," Seronga said.

"I will," Pavant said. "But I *won't* listen to you blame yourself. We are lions. These men were prey. This is the way it had to be. This is the way you did it when you liberated the country the first time."

"That was different," Seronga said.

"No, it wasn't," Pavant insisted. "You were fighting an empire then. We are fighting an empire now."

"It was different," Seronga repeated. "We were fighting soldiers."

"These are soldiers," Pavant replied. "They fight with resistance instead of arms."

Seronga was in no mood to debate. He removed his own knife from the throat of his victim and wiped the blade on the pillow. Then he put the knife back in his hip sheath. He waited as Donald Pavant felt his way around the dark room. The only light came from the half-moon shining through the partly opened door. They had not shut the door for that reason.

"I have the sheets," Pavant said. He was standing by a closet in the back of the room.

The younger man hurried over. He set the sheets down on the floor. Then, together, the men prepared the bodies in turn. They removed the pillowcases and stuffed them in the wounds. That would help stem the leaking of blood. Then they wrapped the bodies tightly inside the bloodstained sheets on the bed. The blood was already soaking through, so they took blankets from the closet and lay them on the floor. The bound bodies were placed upon these. Then the beds were made.

Seronga decided that the bodies would be carried out into the floodplain. The sheets would be removed. They would be wrapped around stones and dropped in Lake Mitali. By dawn, there would not be much of the deacons. The authorities would suspect murder. But they would not be able to prove it. The soft tissue the knife had penetrated would have been eaten. And there were footprints everywhere. Those of Seronga and Pavant would not stand out. As far as anyone could prove, the deacons went for a walk and were attacked by predators. The Vatican would have doubts, but they would not have proof. Most importantly, they would not have martyrs. And as long as the other clergymen were held captive, there was a chance for a negotiated withdrawal. First of the Church, and then of all foreigners. The Botswanans would be able to profit from their own rich resources.

There was one last thing the two Brush Vipers would need: the vestments these men had worn. But Seronga did not want to carry them with the bodies. They must not be splattered with blood. He would come back for the garments when the deacons' remains had been disposed of.

While Seronga wiped up stray streaks of blood, Pavant checked the veranda. There was no one outside. The men slung the bodies over their shoulders. Even with the loss of blood, the corpses were lighter than Seronga expected. Obviously, Deacon missionaries did not eat very well. The dead men were also still very warm. Eager to get his mind off the killings, Seronga wondered if Dhamballa's ancient magic would be potent enough to rouse two such as these. Not just men who had died of natural causes but men who had been murdered. Seronga wished he could spend more time with their leader. He wanted to learn more about the few phenomena he had witnessed. About the ancient religion he had embraced on faith.

In time, he told himself.

For now, Seronga would continue doing things he did not enjoy. That was how Botswana had become free once before. Whether he liked it or not, that was how Botswana would become free again.

TWENTY-FOUR

Washington, D.C.
Thursday, 4:35 P.M.

It was a busy afternoon for Paul Hood, the kind of afternoon when information flowed so quickly that questions provided their own answers. And each answer generated two or three new questions.

Unfortunately, none of those answers provided the key the Op-Center director was searching for.

Still, Hood was happy to get out of the morning alive. For the first time in over a week, Senator Fox's office did not call and ask to see Op-Center's daily work sheet. That was the duty roster Congress used to apportion budgets. Evidently, Fox was satisfied with the cutbacks Hood had already made. Nor did any other members of the Congressional Intelligence Oversight Committee contact him. That meant Mike Rodgers had been able to keep his new intelligence operation under wraps for over a day. In Washington time, that was equivalent to a year.

Even the tension between Darrell McCaskey and Bob Herbert had been defused, at least for the moment. The only lingering problem was not Op-Center's. At least, not directly. That was the tension between Darrell McCaskey and his wife. The way Herbert described it, Maria Corneja took the assignment "like a pit bull at a rib roast." She was not going to give up fieldwork. They had all suspected that would be the case. Now they knew it. The fact that Maria had made this decision without consulting her husband made it even worse. It was ironic. McCaskey was a great listener in interrogations or conferences. He was without equal when it came to sifting answers for truths or following voice inflections to fertile new lines of questioning. But when it came to his personal life, McCaskey tended to do most of the talking and none of the hearing. That was going to have to change.

Look who's giving advice, Hood thought. He himself was a man who had listened to everything his wife had said. And meant to do most of it. He just never found the time.

But there had not been time to dwell on small triumphs or major shortcomings. Not long after returning to his office, Hood received a call from Edgar Kline. The Vatican security officer reported that Deacon Jones had heard from Father Bradbury. According to Jones, the priest was still a prisoner.

"Is he in good health?" Hood asked.

"Apparently," Kline informed him.

"You don't sound happy about that," Hood said.

"Father Bradbury asked about the parish," Kline went on. "Unfortunately, Deacon Jones told the father that a temporary replacement was en route from Washington."

"Shit," Hood said. Obviously, African missionaries had lost some of their tactical finesse since the closing years of the nineteenth century. In those days, the Boers used clergymen to spy on the location, movements, and strength of Zulu tribesmen. "That means Dhamballa knows about the bishop."

"One has to assume that," Kline agreed.

"Are you going to change his travel plans?" Hood asked.

"That would signal to Dhamballa that we are afraid of him," Kline said. "We will not do that."

"What about your Spanish undercover operatives? Have they arrived?" Hood asked.

"Yes," Kline replied. "The leader of the group is going to introduce himself to the deacons in the morning. Several members will shadow them and watch out for the bishop."

"That's good," Hood replied.

"I'd also like to send over our E-file of photographs that were taken at Dhamballa's rallies," Kline said. "There are some photographs of Dhamballa. We thought you might be able to search your own databases on the off chance that there's a match."

Hood agreed to do so. Then he told Kline about Richard

Stiele's activities. Kline did not seem overly concerned. Nor would he be. Whatever the Europeans were doing probably would not impact the Vatican directly. Hood told Kline that he would keep him abreast of any new developments, whether or not they appeared to relate to Father Bradbury.

"Just to keep you fully in the loop," Hood said pointedly.

Kline thanked him.

A few minutes after Kline hung up, Hood's computer beeped. He had received a file containing the address for the secure Vatican Security Organization web site. The download came with a password to access the Dhamballa file. The password was *adamas*. From four years of high school Latin, Hood remembered that was the word for diamond. Someone in the VSO had a clear sense of the region. Or else they knew more than Kline was letting on.

Hood forwarded the information to Stephen Viens. Until recently, Viens had been the Satellite Imaging supervisor at the National Reconnaissance Office. A college classmate of Matt Stoll, Viens had always given Op-Center's requirements top priority. For that reason, among others, Viens was scapegoated for two billion dollars in funding that did not reach its targeted black ops programs. Bob Herbert helped to prove the man's innocence. Op-Center was punished by having their needs given VLP status—very low priority. Fortunately, Viens still had friends at the NRO. He did not go back to his former post. He now worked as Op-Center's internal security chief. Viens's duties included setting up a photo analysis program for Hood. Hood also sent the Vatican address to Herbert and Rodgers.

As Hood finished sending the data from the Vatican Security Organization, Emmy called.

"Paul, that was a terrific lead you gave me about Albert Beaudin," she told him.

"How so?" Hood asked.

"It turns out Mr. Stiele wasn't the only Beaudin associate who liquidated assets within the last few days," she said.

"Who else?" Hood asked.

"Gurney de Sylva, who is another Beaudin board member,"

Emmy said. "He sold his minority interest in six different diamond mines yesterday."

"Where are the mines located?" Hood asked.

"Throughout southern Africa," she replied.

"How much did he net?" Hood asked.

"About ninety million dollars," Emmy replied. "He turned around and put most of that money into corporations that are invested in oil operations in Russia and Mexico."

"Maybe he thinks oil is a better long-term investment," Hood speculated.

"Possibly," Emmy said. "But some of the profits also went into the corporation that holds Stiele's land leases in China."

"So the oil deal could be a smoke screen to keep anyone from looking too closely at China," Hood said.

"Or he could pull those investments at some point and put them into China," Emmy pointed out. "He did not indicate his long-term plans in the filing. Then again, he is not the most forthcoming investor we've ever tracked. He once avoided capital gains taxes by donating millions of dollars to a charity for the homeless, the Rooftop Angels."

"Weren't they shut down in 2001 for money laundering?" Hood asked.

"They were," Emmy said. "For every hundred dollars they received, the Angels gave back eighty dollars in cash. It was distributed through safe-deposit boxes, traveler's checks, and other monetary media. We could never prove that Stiele received any of what was doled out. None of his accounts showed any unusual spikes."

"That doesn't mean anything," Hood said. "The cash could still be sitting somewhere. Hell, he could be using it for groceries."

"Absolutely," Emmy said. "But that's an ongoing investigation, which is why the red flag went up on his latest stock sales. So far, we haven't been able to find anything that violates international law. However, I did discover a tie between de Sylva and Peter Diffring that goes beyond the Beaudin board. One that has nothing to do with China."

"Oh?"

"With several local businessmen, Diffring co-owns the construction company that did geologic and environmental site surveys on hotel sites in Botswana," Emmy said. "The sale required a filing with the Land Valuation division of the Department of Surveys and Mapping."

"Who did they buy the land from?" Hood asked.

"It was purchased from a tribe, the Limgadi," Emmy told him.

"Did they indicate what the land was to be used for?" Hood asked.

"The stated purpose is to 'develop transportation facilities,' " she informed him.

"How long ago did Diffring buy into that construction company?" Hood asked.

"Four months ago," Emmy replied. "The land office in Botswana says that so far, Diffring's group has put in a small landing strip. Nothing more. All of this could mean absolutely nothing, Paul."

"I know," he said. But his gut told him otherwise.

"It's not exactly uncommon for people to set up synergistic businesses in areas they plan to develop," she said.

"Of course," Hood replied.

There was a vast distinction between the kind of conspiracy Hood was envisioning and sound business opportunities Emmy had just described. These activities might have nothing whatsoever to do with Dhamballa and his group. It could all be a trick of timing.

Then again, maybe it was not. Paul Hood and his team were paid to assume that whatever was on the surface was a front. Effective crisis management had to presume guilt, not innocence.

Hood thanked Emmy for her efforts. They made dinner plans for the following week. The woman had gotten married a few months before, and she wanted Hood to meet her husband. Hood was glad for her. At the same time, he felt sad for himself. This was the first time in twenty years that he would be odd man out at a social dinner.

As Hood was finishing up with Emmy, Mike Rodgers came

to the door. Hood thanked Emmy. They agreed to talk again later in the day. Rodgers entered and took a seat. The general looked better than he had in weeks. He seemed energized, engaged, focused.

"How's the team shaping up?" Hood asked.

"Aideen Marley and Dave Battat are ready to go over if we need them," Rodgers said.

"They got along all right?" Hood asked.

"They got along well enough," Rodgers replied. "They're not running off to get married, but they'll get the job done."

"Where's the rub?" Hood asked.

"David knows his stuff and likes to beat you over the head with it," Rodgers told him. "Aideen has a solid foundation, somewhat less experience, but a whole lot more tact."

"Who'd be the better mission leader?" Hood asked.

"In this situation? She would," Rodgers said. "I already made that call. She will interact with ordinary people better than he will."

"Battat is okay with that?" Hood asked.

"To get back in the field? Yeah, he's okay with that," Rodgers said.

Hood regarded the general. Military people looked at things differently than civilians. Hood liked to have harmony on his staff. Rodgers put the emphasis on efficiency.

"Don't worry about them, Paul," Rodgers said. "Battat knows that Aideen will be in charge. They'll be fine."

Hood hoped that Rodgers was right. He had not anticipated fielding the new intelligence team this quickly, but Op-Center needed people on site. Given the haste, Hood also hoped that he had been right giving Mike Rodgers this assignment. He respected the hell out of the general. He admired Rodgers's ability to command. But Rodgers had suffered a heavy blow with the loss of the Strikers. Psychologically, both Hood and Rodgers were in uncharted territory.

Until recently, Paul Hood had not believed in psychiatry. He felt that character came from dealing with your own problems. Then Harleigh was taken hostage at the United Nations. Op-Center's staff psychologist Liz Gordon and other mental health specialists helped see the girl through her blackest days. They gave Harleigh her life back, and they gave Hood his daughter back.

He changed his thinking about psychiatry.

The change prompted Hood to take an unprecedented step of involving Liz in his own decision-making process. A few days before talking to Rodgers about the new intelligence team, Hood had spoken to the psychologist about it. The question he asked her: Would an officer who lost his squad be overly cautious with the next one or more aggressive? Liz told him that it depended upon the officer, of course. In the case of Mike Rodgers, she thought he might be reluctant to take on a new command. He would not want to risk any more lives. If he did accept the post, she believed he might experience a mild form of substitution hysteria. The need to re-create a failure and make it come out right.

Fortunately, this was not a military operation. The participants did not have to stay until the matter was resolved. They collected intelligence until things became too dangerous. Then they left.

"Since everything seems to be set, it's probably a good idea to get them over to Botswana," Hood continued. "I suspect things are going to heat up when Bishop Max arrives tomorrow."

"We can get Aideen and Battat on a plane today," Rodgers told him. "Travel documents are being prepared. Right now, I've got them in Matt Stoll's section, reading what we have on the Father Bradbury situation. They're also going over files about Botswana and Albert Beaudin. Bob told me that he and his people might be involved."

"It's possible," Hood said.

"I also had a chat with Falah Shibli on the drive over," Rodgers said.

"How is he?" Hood asked. Falah was an extremely capable and humble man. Those were a good combination in any man. In an intelligence operative they were invaluable. They made him invisible.

"Falah's still working as a police officer in northern Israel, only now he's running the department," Rodgers said. "He said he has his hands full keeping peace on the Lebanese border, but he'd be happy to take a short leave of absence to do whatever we need."

"A Moslem from the Jewish state helping the Church," Hood mused. "I like that."

"So does he," Rodgers told him. "That's why he offered to drop what he was doing and join the team. I told him I'll let him know if that's necessary. I also talked to Zack Bemler in New York and Harold Moore in Tokyo. They're tied up for the next few days. After that, they said they'd be happy to work with us. But with Maria on the way and the other three ready to go, I feel we have a strong team to field."

Hood agreed. Those four intelligence operatives had exceptional abilities. Hood had to trust that their collaborative skills would surface when they were required.

When Rodgers was finished, Hood brought the general up to date on his conversations with Edgar Kline and Emmy Feroche. In the middle of that briefing, Stephen Viens called.

"Paul, I think you should come to Matt's office," Viens said.

"What have you got?" Hood asked.

Viens replied, "Your missing link, I think."

TWENTY-FIVE

Okavango Swamp, Botswana
Friday, 12:05 A.M.

According to the beliefs of Dhamballa's Vodun faith, midnight was the most spiritual part of the day. It was the hour when the body was weakest and the soul the strongest.

More importantly, it was a time of the greatest darkness. The Vodun soul shunned the day. Day was for the flesh so it could be warm and work. So it could be nourished. Then there was early night, a time dominated by firelight. That was the time for group prayer, for singing, drumming, and dancing. A time when animals were sacrificed to honor the loas. Revelers were asking the gods for health, wealth, and happiness in life. Occasionally, the celebrations led to pairings that created new life. It was a holy thing for children to be conceived within the energy and love of a celebration.

Yet all of that, too, were needs of the flesh. And the flesh was a prison for the soul. Daylight was also an inhibiting force. In the dark, the soul could enjoy a sacred, private communion with the earth. It could leave the material world and visit the black places of its forebears. Like the souls of the living, the souls of the dead dwelt beneath the surface.

Each midnight, before retiring, Dhamballa made time for this personal reconnecting with the voices of the past. That was how Dhamballa first became aware of his destiny. A Vodun priest, Don Glutaa, had guided him through a visit to the spirit world. There was not always a revelation, but he always came out of this journey with a reminder of why he was here: to serve as a mortal bridge between the Vodun past and future.

Dhamballa lay on his back on the rough wicker mat. He

was dressed only in white shorts. His eyes were shut, but he was not asleep. The hut was dark, save for the very faint glow of a ceremonial candle. The wick was made from rushes that burned like a cigarette. It smouldered rather than flamed, releasing smoke rather than light. The short, squat candle had a slightly rounded bottom. It was not made from wax but from tallow. Dhamballa had created the candle himself before coming to the swamp. He had gone to the ancient cemetery of Machaneng. There, he mixed shavings of belladonna and pinches of dried ergot with the melted fat of a male goat. He had blended them in the eye socket of a human skull, the traditional way to make the Lights of Loa, the light of the possessing spirit. The herbs were necessary to relax his body and open his mind. The tallow was employed to capture the spirits of the dead. Burning the candle released those spirits so they could guide him through the home of the dead.

The candle sat at the top of Dhamballa's bare chest, just above his breastbone. The tallow pooled below his chin, reinventing the shape of the candle. This act was important to the Vodun faith. It symbolized what was about to occur. The dead were going to give something to the living. The living would use it to make into something new.

The pungent yellowish smoke snaked into Dhamballa's nostrils with every breath. His breathing grew slow and shallow. As he inhaled the fumes, the young man felt more and more as if he himself were made of smoke. He felt as though he were floating just above the mat. Then, like fire and air, his spirit wafted downward, through the weave of the mat.

Into the earth, he thought, *home of the eternal spirit.*

Dhamballa began to move, snakelike, through the thickly packed soil of the earth. He descended faster and faster. If and when the spirits wished, they would stir from cracks in the boulders and from places beneath the stones. They would come to him to make their knowledge available.

Almost at once, Dhamballa knew that this night was different than other nights. The spirits came quickly tonight, faster than ever before. That meant they had something important to share with Dhamballa. The Vodun priest stopped his descent so the spirits would not have to pursue him. It was for the living to wait for the honored dead.

Dhamballa did not select those to whom he wished to speak. Rather, the spirits approached Dhamballa. They came to tell him what he needed to know. They did not tell him in words but in images, in symbols.

The spirits began to tell Dhamballa about the future. They showed him a hen become a rooster. Then they brought him a calf, bloodied and torn but not yet dead. One was a mothering force that became a potential rival. The other signified a child that would be tested before it could mature.

The spirits left. Dhamballa moved on.

The holy man drifted farther into the earth. He moved now through larger caves and fissures. Finally, he came to a large pit. He floated past the rim and saw a great horned snake coiled below him. The gods were speaking to him now. This was a rarity. Dhamballa swam toward the huge rust-colored beast. The reptile opened its mouth. Dhamballa floated inside. Save for the serpent's red tongue, everything was black. Suddenly, the forks of the tongue became white wings. Flocks of sparrows rose from beneath him. Dhamballa watched as the birds soared upward. The first ones to reach the sky became stars. Soon there were thousands of points of light. He watched with delight but only for a moment. As birds were still rising, the stars became sand and rained to earth. The grains pelted the birds, ripping them to pieces. The downpour formed a sprawling, endless desert of sand. Here and there were small oases of dead birds and blood.

Dreams of greatness are going to be tested, the holy man thought. *And those who follow the dreams will be tested as well.*

Suddenly, a lion with a fiery mane burst from beneath the sand. Dhamballa recognized him immediately. It was Ogu Bodagris, the spirit of war. His fangs and claws raked the empty skies. New stars appeared, blood red and expanding. They formed faces. Familiar faces. Soon everything was red. Dhamballa moved away from the flood. Slowly, the flood grew to a dull orange. Dhamballa's eyes were open now. He was staring into the flame of the candle.

Perspiration rolled thickly down the holy man's neck and forehead. Some of the sweat was caused by the heat of the smouldering wick. Some of it was due to the close, humid warmth of the night. But most of it came from inside. From fear. Dhamballa was not afraid of the unknown. Faith, courage, and the Vodun arts were all he needed to survive life's countless mysteries and the troubles they caused. What frightened him was the known. Especially the duplicity of men. Even at that, Dhamballa did not fear for his own safety. If he died, his spirit would join his ancestors. What worried him was the fate of his followers. Many of them would lose their way so early in his ministry. He also feared for those who had not yet been returned to the ways of their people.

Dhamballa raised the candle from his chest. It came away easily because of the perspiration. He sat up slowly. The day had been tiring. Now the vision had left him drained.

My allies are my enemies, Dhamballa thought.

Someone close to him was going to betray him. What he did not know was who, exactly. Or how. Or when. It could be someone he already knew. It could be someone he would meet during his next sermon or holy ceremony. All he knew was that it would happen very soon.

Dhamballa put the candle in a clay bowl on a small ledge beside the window. The white canvas shade was down. He used the hemp drawstring to raise it. The flame kicked up for a moment, dancing as the hot, muggy night air rolled in. Then it died to its customary glow. With the breeze came the sounds of the swamp animals. The bullfrogs sounded like unhappy dogs. The night birds seemed to be laughing or sighing. The occasional hiss of a snake. It was deceptively loud because the sharp sibilation cut through every other sound. Almost at once, the wings of small white moths began to flash around the candlelight. Beyond the dark treetops the stars shone clear and large.

Dhamballa had always known that one day there would be conflict. He knew he would have to fight for the diamond mines. He did not mind selling the gems to outsiders to build his nation. But the earth was the home of the dead. Only the faithful should be permitted inside.

Still, Dhamballa did not expect to have to face the matter so soon. The first thing he would have to do was make certain that Leon Seronga and the Brush Vipers were among those he could trust. Without them, the holy man would have to look elsewhere for strength of arms. Perhaps the spirits would guide him. Perhaps they would not.

He suddenly felt very alone.

Dhamballa lifted a ceramic pitcher and cup from the floor beside the mat. He poured himself water flavored with mint leaves. He drank slowly and chewed on the leaves as he stared at the sky.

The stars in Dhamballa's vision had told him of an impending future. The stars suspended in front of him told a different tale. They reminded Dhamballa of his forebears. Of the men and women who had looked up at the sky when the world was young. The stars spoke of a time when the spirits of men were few, and wisdom had to come directly from the gods themselves.

The stars gave him the courage to do what those men had done. To trust in the visions. To believe in the prophecies. And to find ways of making them come true.

Dhamballa had been given a remarkable gift. He had been given both the blessing and the curse of Vodun enlightenment. It was a blessing because he had the ideas and the voice to inspire a nation, to lead a people who had become fragmented. Who had lost their way. It was a curse because he would not be able to lead those people by spirituality alone.

He was a man of peace, yet he was going to have to fight a war.

A war in which, he feared, not all of the magic would be white.

TWENTY-SIX

Washington, D.C.
Thursday, 4:47 P.M.

As they headed toward Matt Stoll's office, Paul Hood and Mike Rodgers bumped into Liz Gordon. The psychologist was chomping hard on her nicotine chewing gum. She had recently given up smoking and was having a tough time of it. She asked to talk to Paul.

"Is it personal?" he asked.

"Yes," she replied. Her broad shoulders swayed, and her medium-length brown hair bobbed hard as she walked and chewed.

"Can we talk while we walk?" Hood asked.

"We can do that," the woman told him. "I've always been good at multitasking."

Hood smiled. "What can I do for you?"

"My half brother, Clark, is a poli-sci major at Georgetown," Liz said. "They're dealing with contemporary urban issues. He was wondering if you could talk to his class about your term as mayor."

"When?" Hood asked. It was jarring to shift gears from the global to the local. Liz was obviously better at multitasking than he was.

"Sometime within the next two weeks?" she asked.

"Sure, I'll do it," Hood said with a wink. "Too bad everything is not that easy."

"Thanks. Is it the Vatican problem?" Liz asked.

Hood nodded. "As a matter of fact, you might want to tag along if you have the time."

"Be happy to," she said.

Matt Stoll's space was different from the other offices.

When he first came to Op-Center, Stoll had commandeered a small conference room. He proceeded to fill it with a haphazard arrangement of desks, stands, and computers. As Op-Center's computing needs grew, the original disarray remained where it was. They were like old oak trees a village had grown around.

There were now four people working in the rectangular space. Stoll and Viens now worked back to back in the center of the room. Mae Won sat at the far end, and Jefferson Jefferson sat near the door. When Hood was in Los Angeles, all the eccentrics he knew worked in the film business. Scientists were a serious, conservative bunch. Now it was the movie people who wore short hair and understood complex mathematics and the computer programmers who were the oddballs. Mae, who was born in Taipei, had a ring through her nose and orange hair. J2, as they called Jefferson Jefferson, had no hair and a tattoo of a tree on his scalp. When the mood struck him, J2 added new branches and leaves to the tree.

In the 1990s, these individuals would never have made it past the first interview for a position with the federal government. Now, government agencies could not afford to lose good tech people to private or especially foreign employers. This was particularly true of intelligence and investigative operations. What the people looked like was less important than what they could do or the new technologies they might come up with. In their spare time, Mae and J2 were working on what they called omni ink. Paper saturated in their ink would change its display via pixel-sized microtransistors activated by wireless signals. The electronic charge would cause the ink colors to change in nanoseconds, allowing for immediate news updates, constantly changing want ads, and even on-demand help with crossword puzzles. Hood was not sure their pet name "oink" would work for the new technology. But the question might be irrelevant. He knew from the duo's employment contracts that while any patents would be issued in their names, the government would have a shot at developing and marketing the product. As Hood walked through the door, he could not help but wonder, suddenly, if J2 would try to apply oink technology to tattoos.

Viens glanced over as the trio entered the room.

"Good afternoon, everyone," Hood said. "What have you got for us, Mr. Viens?"

"A photo ID from the files of the IODM," Viens replied. "That's the International Organization of Diamond Merchants. I figured your guy must have had a job before he became a cult leader."

"Good job, Stephen," Hood said.

"Thank you," Viens replied. "The IODM had his personnel file on-line, as required by law. The computer says that the guy in the three-year-old ID photograph and the guy in that Vatican photograph you sent over are an eighty-nine percent match."

"The differences being some apparent weight loss around the cheekbones and neck, different hair length, and a change in the bridge of his nose," Stoll added. "Possibly due to a break."

"I'm very comfortable with that match," Hood said.

"It's a good one," Rodgers agreed.

"We hacked the tax records in Gaborone and got lucky right away," Stoll said. "Your man is named Thomas Burton. Until four months ago, he was a mine worker in Botswana."

"Did he mine industrial diamonds or gems?" Liz asked.

At her station, Mae Won wriggled the bare fourth finger of her left hand. Hood smiled at her.

"Yes, diamonds," Viens replied.

"There's the connection between Dhamballa and Henry Genet," Rodgers observed.

Hood looked at the ID on Viens's screen. There was a color picture attached to it. Below it was a photo Edgar Kline had sent over. "Are you sure this is the same guy?"

"We're sure," the heavyset Stoll said from his keyboard.

"I've got a small on-line newspaper report of the Dhamballa guy's first mention," J2 said. "It matches the time Thomas Burton stopped making calls from his home phone."

"I had a look at those phone records," Mae added proudly.

"Where did Burton live?" Rodgers asked.

"In a town called Machaneng," Viens told him. "They've got an industrial mine about five miles out of town."

"According to the file from Mr. Kline, that was where the rally photo was taken," Stoll pointed out.

"Anything else?" Hood asked.

"Not yet," Viens replied.

"We've only had Mr. Kline's file for about thirty-five minutes," Stoll reminded Hood. "Like Stephen said, we got lucky."

"Believe me, Matt, that wasn't a knock," Hood told him. "You guys worked a miracle. I appreciate it."

J2 and Mae each slapped the air, giving one another an across-the-room high five.

"Will you be able to access any of this man's medical records?" Liz Gordon asked.

"Yes, if they're in a computer file and that computer has an Internet link," Stoll said.

"Looking for anything in particular, Liz?" Hood asked.

"Psychiatric care," Liz said. "Nine out of ten known cult leaders were treated, according to the last World Health Organization study."

"That's compared to what percentage of the non-Waco-bound populace that's had their heads shrunk?" Stoll asked.

"Seven out of ten percent," Liz replied.

"That doesn't exactly put cult leaders in an exclusive club," the computer expert continued.

"I never said it did," Liz told him. "But there may be records that we can get our hands on. The Botswana government might be interested in helping shut down a cult before it can get started."

"He was never shrink-wrapped," J2 declared.

The others looked at him.

"According to Mr. Burton's employment file, he was a line leader in the mine," the young man said. "That meant he was the last person to see the diamonds before they left the mine. I'm looking at the qualifications IODM has on their employment site for double Ls. They can have no criminal record. No immediate family members can have criminal records. And there must be zero history of treatment for mental problems."

"Also, according to a footnote in this file, the Botswana average for psychiatric care is far below the international average," Mae added, still studying her own computer screen. "According to the WHO, shrinkage in Botswana amounts to three in ten people. And most of those folks are white-collar workers and military personnel."

"They probably can't afford psychiatric care," Hood said.

"Government subsidies are available," Mae said, still reading.

"Maybe I ought to move there," Stoll said.

"Well, I still want to try to get as much information on Dhamballa as possible," Liz said. "If we can come up with a reliable profile, we can make some intelligent guesses as to what his next moves will be. You'll need that, Paul, if this goes on for any length of time."

"I agree," Hood said.

"You know, people, there's also the whole voodoo angle to this thing," Stoll said. "I did some research on the net. It was recognized as the official religion of Benin in 1996. It also has an extremely large following in the Dominican Republic, Ghana, Haiti, Togo, and various places around the United States including New York, New Orleans, and Miami," Stoll said, as he read from the screen. "It's also widely recognized throughout South America, where there are a variety of sects like Umbanda, Quimbanda, and Candomble."

"Impressive," Liz remarked.

"Shows how parochial we are here," Hood said.

"The essence of it seems to be very similar to Catholicism, actually, except that the spiritual figures dwell in the earth instead of in Heaven," Stoll went on. "Both religions worship a supreme being and believe in a spiritual hierarchy. In Vodun the big guns are called loas, and in Catholicism they're saints. The loas and the saints each have attributes that are unique to them. Vodunists and Catholics believe in an afterlife, in the notion of resurrection, in the ritualistic consumption of flesh and blood, in the sanctity of the soul, and in clear-cut forces of good and evil, which they refer to as white and black magic."

"Interesting," Rodgers said. "And it makes sense."

"What does?" Hood asked.

"It helps to explain why Catholicism took hold in non-Islamic sections of Africa back in the seventeenth century," Rodgers said. "In the absence of a national Vodun church, Africans would have found the structure of the Catholic church familiar and comforting."

"The food and wine the missionaries brought probably didn't hurt their cause," Stoll said.

"That would have gotten people to sit down and pay attention," Rodgers said. "But I've seen army recruiters at work. You need more than a buffet to get people to actually commit to something."

"So now Dhamballa wants his people back," Hood said.

"That could well be the limit of Dhamballa's ambition," Rodgers said. "The larger question is what Beaudin wants. And what his associates may have promised Dhamballa."

"What would they want from him that they can't get now?" Liz asked.

"A puppet leader," Hood said.

"Or maybe they don't want anything from him per se," Rodgers suggested. "Maybe it's destabilization of the region that they're after."

"Possibly," Hood agreed.

"There's also the chance that Dhamballa is just doing a job for pay," Viens remarked.

"The voodoo equivalent of a televangelist," Stoll said. He shook his head. "That's pretty sad."

"Yes, but I would not spend too much time looking into that idea," Rodgers said.

"Why not?" Hood asked.

"Let's assume that Beaudin or someone else is underwriting the Vodun movement," Rodgers said. "They aren't likely to have gone out and cast the role of a religious leader. Training someone and convincing others that he's the real thing is tough and time consuming. It's like gathering HUMINT. Infiltration doesn't work as well as finding an individual who is already on the inside and turning him. What's more likely is that someone spotted Burton or Dhamballa, heard him preaching, and saw an opportunity. They found a way to dovetail his beliefs into a project that was already in the works."

"If that's true, then Dhamballa may not know he's being used," Hood said.

"That's right," Rodgers said.

Hood nodded. He looked at Matt and his team. "Thanks, guys. You did a great job."

Stephen Viens smiled, J2 and Mae high-fived each other again across the room, and Matt Stoll unfolded his arms. He went back to the keyboard and began typing. He must have had another thought. Stoll was rarely in the same mental space as everyone else.

Hood turned to Liz. "Do you have some time right now?" he asked.

"Sure."

"I'd like you to stay here and see if there's any other data you can pick up on Dhamballa," Hood said. "His family background, friends, people he may have gone to school with, or stood next to on the diamond line, that sort of thing. Work up a profile."

"Sounds good," she said eagerly. Liz was obviously enjoying the new respect Hood was giving her profession.

Stephen Viens had already started clearing boxes of diskettes and cables from a chair. He stacked them on the floor and rolled the chair next to his workstation. Hood thanked Liz, then left with Rodgers. The men made their way back to Hood's office.

"Profiling Dhamballa is not going to give us the key to defusing this crisis," Rodgers pointed out.

"No," Hood agreed.

"We need to get someone close to him. We need to get his ear somehow," Rodgers said.

"Tell him that the Europeans are using him," Hood said.

"At least plant the idea, make him trust a little less and maybe move a little slower," Rodgers said.

"I agree," Hood said.

"Then we'll definitely have Aideen Marley and David Battat airborne as soon as possible," Rodgers said. "They can be in Maun by tomorrow evening, about six P.M. local time."

"Good," Hood said. "Assuming we can find Dhamballa and get our people close, what do we do about Father Bradbury?"

"I don't think we can do anything right now except try to get close to Dhamballa," Rodgers said.

"Then it's strictly intel gathering," Hood said. "No rescue attempt?"

"Except for Maria, none of the three has had much experience with kidnap situations," Rodgers said. "And she can't go into this alone. Besides, I wouldn't want her tripping over those Spanish soldiers if they have some kind of rescue in the works. Unless you think you can work that out with Edgar Kline. And with Darrell," he added.

"I don't know if Kline will give us the kind of access we'd need to coordinate our movements with the *Unidad Especial del Despliegue*," Hood said. "As for Darrell, let's not rev him up unless we have to."

"I'm with you on that," Rodgers said.

"I don't suppose we'll be able to count on much cooperation from Gaborone," Hood said. "They haven't seemed to show much interest so far."

"No, and I've been thinking about that," Rodgers said. "If this were just a backwater cult, the government might have taken stronger action. But they have to be very cautious turning against a ten-thousand-year-old religion. Hell, there may even be Vodunists in the Botswana ministries and in parliament. They may want to nudge Gaborone toward embracing the faith the way Rome turned to Christianity in the fourth century A.D."

"The Vatican is definitely not going to like that," Hood said.

"Not a bit, which is why they're probably going to do a full-court press to get Father Bradbury back," Rodgers said. "Or at least force the government to move against Dhamballa."

They reached Hood's office and stopped.

"Mike," Hood said thoughtfully. "We're going to need to get Maria on site, aren't we?"

Rodgers nodded. "If nothing else, Maria speaks Spanish," the general said. "If she manages to hook up with the *Unidad Especial,* she'll be able to converse with them. That could give us access to information we won't necessarily get through Edgar Kline."

"I wonder if I can sell that to Darrell," Hood said, glancing behind himself to make sure the FBI liaison was not listening.

"You mean, the idea that his wife is going in as a glorified translator instead of as a spy?" Rodgers said.

"Yeah," Hood said.

"I don't think he'll believe that," Rodgers told him.

"I don't think so, either," Hood said. "Okay, Mike. You get Aideen and Battat going. I'll go and talk to Darrell."

Rodgers turned and left. Paul Hood went into his office. He sat heavily behind his desk.

Hood was tired inside and out. He also felt strange, though he did not know why. He was going to have that chat with Darrell. Then, because he needed to feel grounded, he was going to call home. He would see what kind of a day Harleigh and Alexander had. It would be refreshing to listen to problems that did not threaten to topple a government.

Home, Hood thought. Just thinking the word put tears in the back of his eyes. And he realized that was why he felt strange. This day had begun and now ended with Hood participating in disunions.

Paul Hood still thought of the house in Chevy Chase as home. It was not. He did not live there anymore. He pulled into the driveway on weekends to pick up the kids. Home was now a small apartment a half hour from Op-Center. It was a few bare walls and some furniture. Nothing personal except for a few photos of the kids and some framed letters from heads of state. Mementos from his days as mayor. Nothing with any real emotional history. Here he was, missing that terribly. At the same time, he was trying to stop Dhamballa from reclaiming his home. And he was helping to prevent Darrell McCaskey from starting a new life with his new wife.

When Hood was mayor of Los Angeles, when he worked in finance, he built things. He built roads, housing, corporations, portfolios, careers. He started and nurtured his own family. What the hell was he doing now?

Keeping the world safe for other families, he told himself.

Maybe. Maybe that was a party-line crock. Maybe it was true. In any case, Hood had to believe it. Not just think it but be convinced of it. Otherwise, he would not be able to pick up the phone and call Darrell McCaskey. He would not be able to ask for help that would turn up the heat in an African floodplain where McCaskey's wife was already at risk.

TWENTY-SEVEN

Maun, Botswana
Friday, 8:00 A.M.

Leon Seronga and Donald Pavant woke with the sun. By eight, they had been up for nearly three hours and were anxious to catch the bus to Maun. Seronga did not like sitting still.

He also did not enjoy impersonating a deacon. Seronga knew they could not simply assume the identities of Deacons Jones and Canon while they were here. The director of the center had certainly met them. What was more, the director had seen Seronga when he came for Father Bradbury. The man had seen him from a distance, but he still might recognize him. Seronga came up with a cover story in case they needed it. He hoped, instead, that he and Pavant could simply remain out of sight until the bus arrived.

It was not to be.

Nearly a dozen of the tourists went to the church that morning. Though the door was unlocked, no candles had been lit. No clergyman was in attendance. Shortly after eight A.M., the center's director, Tswana Ndebele, went to the deacons' residential quarters. Donald Pavant opened the door. He stepped through the doorway onto the veranda.

The creases of Ndebele's sun-baked skin deepened with surprise. "Who are you?"

"Deacon Tobias Comden of the Cathedral of All Saints," he replied. "And you are—?"

"Tswana Ndebele, the director of the center here," Ndebele replied. He was guarded, suspicious.

"I am happy to make your acquaintance," Pavant said pleasantly. He bowed slightly. He did not want to offer his hand.

His skin was rough and calloused. They were not the hands of a missionary.

Ndebele pulled on his curly white beard. "The Cathedral of All Saints," he said. "I am not familiar with that church."

"It is a very small church in Zambia," Pavant replied. The soldier did not specify where the mythical church was located. If Ndebele decided to look it up, he would have a lot of ground to cover. "We came in during the night."

"We?" Ndebele asked.

"Deacon Withal and myself," Pavant said. The soldier stepped aside so the tour director could see into the room.

Ndebele leaned forward. He peered into the darkness.

Seronga was curled on the bed. His back was facing the door. Tucked in the waistband of his vestments was a Walther PPK with a silencer. It was there in the event that Tswana Ndebele came over to the bed for a chat and recognized him from the abduction.

Accustomed to the brilliant morning light, the tour director could not make out details inside the quarters. After a moment, he stood back.

"How did you gentlemen get here, Deacon?" Ndebele asked.

"We came by Jeep," Pavant informed him. "Deacon Withal did most of the driving. That's why he is still sleeping. We got in very late."

"I did not see a Jeep," Ndebele said. His mouth twisted suspiciously at one end.

"Deacon Jones and Deacon Canon took it shortly after we arrived," Pavant replied.

Ndebele reacted with open surprise. "They left in the dark to drive to Maun? They know better than that. There are no roads, no lights."

Lying on the bed, Seronga felt his heart speeding up. This was not going well. He hoped that he would have a clear shot at the tour director. The last thing they wanted was for him to go away unconvinced.

"The deacons said they knew the way," Pavant told him. "It was felt that two sets of deacons should go to meet the bishop.

The kidnappers might still be watching. We will take the tour bus."

Seronga waited. He listened closely. Lying there, pretending to sleep, was one of the most difficult things Seronga had ever done. There was nothing so frustrating as having one's fate in the hands of another.

After a long moment, Ndebele nodded. "Well, that is probably a good idea," he said.

Seronga relaxed. There was conviction in the tour director's voice.

"Forgive all of the questions," Ndebele went on. He sounded a little ashamed now. "We have all been as anxious as zebras since Father Bradbury was taken away. We jump at any unfamiliar noise or a change in routine."

"I understand completely," Pavant replied. "Now, was there something you needed?"

"Deacon, I came back here because some of our guests wanted to light candles," Ndebele said. "I wanted to find out if that would be all right."

"Of course," Pavant replied.

"Father Bradbury usually lit the first ones each morning," Ndebele said. "Not being Catholic, I didn't know if that's the way it has to be."

"It will be all right if they do it," Pavant replied. "Unfortunately, I cannot join them. We were instructed to remain as invisible as possible. If the kidnappers are watching, we do not want them to move against us."

"Of course not," Ndebele replied. "Though two of them did ask if they might be able to meet with you privately."

"I don't think that would be a good idea," Pavant replied.

"I understand. I will tell them," Ndebele said. "They are Spanish and very devout. I will ask them not to bother you on the bus, either. Maybe I will tell them that you only speak Bantu."

"If you like." Pavant smiled. "I appreciate your help."

"I will do anything to help the church of Father Bradbury," Ndebele said.

The director left, and Pavant shut the door. Seronga turned

around. The Brush Viper commander sat on the edge of the bed. Pavant walked toward him. His easy manner and benevolent expression both vanished.

"I'm proud of you," Seronga said. "You handled that situation like a true diplomat."

"How would you know?" Pavant asked.

"I did not have to shoot him," Seronga replied. He removed the gun from his waistband and put it on the bed.

Pavant shook his head. "I hate words. They do not solve things. They only put action off."

"Well, my friend, that was all we needed to do this morning," Seronga pointed out.

"So you say," Pavant said. "All those gentle words about deacons, priests, and the bishop. I made myself sick. We should bring this place down, to finish the threat completely."

"Why spend energy to pull down what will fall on its own?" Seronga asked his partner.

"Because *these* need to play a role," Pavant said, shaking his fists. "They have been idle while outsiders cut the heart from our people, our nation. My hands need to be active."

"They will be," Seronga said. "To build, not to destroy."

As he spoke, Seronga had gone to his backpack and removed several maps. He unfolded them on the bed. Then he sat down with Pavant to review the route that would take them from Maun back to camp. They had already arranged for one of Dhamballa's followers to meet them at the airstrip.

Donald Pavant was still angry. Seronga could see it in the harsh turn of his partner's brow, in the tense set of his mouth. He could hear it in Pavant's clipped words. Growing up on the floodplain, Seronga had seen all kinds of predators. He had watched insect-eating plants, crocodiles, lions, and hyenas. He had observed aggressors from hounds to bees. None of them had the quality that too many humans possessed: the ability to hate and for that hate to feed the predatory instinct. Even when he had been forced to kill, Seronga had always been motivated by positive forces. The desire to hunt with his father. The hope of seeing Seretse Khama become president. The need to protect his nation's borders.

Some men are driven by dreams, while others run from their nightmares, Seronga thought.

However, Seronga did have one hope: that when the struggle was over, all Botswanans would be united. He prayed that they would be moved by something that had been missing from their lives for too many years. By something greater than animal needs.

By Dhamballa and perhaps the gods themselves.

TWENTY-EIGHT

Washington, D.C.
Thursday, 5:30 P.M.

The conversation with Darrell McCaskey had been flat. Paul Hood had expected that. Darrell did not tend to react to things immediately. He took them in, and then he reacted. As the former G-man sat in his office chair, the only thing that seemed to annoy him was that Hood had come by to tell him about Maria's new objectives in Botswana.

"This is Mike's operation, isn't it?" McCaskey had asked.

"Yes," Hood said.

"Then he should be the one giving me the heads-up," McCaskey said. "I mean, Bob was the one who called her in Madrid. Now you're here. What the hell is Mike doing?"

"He's prepping Aideen Marley and David Battat," Hood said. He was not going to let McCaskey take out his frustration on Mike Rodgers. "We felt it would be okay if I talked to you. Because if you want to be by the numbers official about it, Darrell, you didn't have to be notified at all. This is Maria's gig, not yours. I'm telling you because we're friends, and I think you should be involved."

That had taken some of the steam from McCaskey's engine. He settled down a bit, thanked Hood for the information, and got back to work researching Beaudin's operations.

Hood went back to his office. He called home. The children's line was busy. One of them was probably on the computer. Most likely Alexander. Hood called the house phone. Sharon answered. His former wife said that Harleigh was on-line, and Alexander was at a night soccer game. She told him to phone back after ten. The kids would be up late because there was no school the next day. Teachers' conference. Hood said he would call. He asked Sharon how she was. She was not in a mood to talk. Hood knew her well enough to know when she was measuring her words. He suspected that she had a gentleman caller.

Well, why not? he thought. *No one should be alone.*

Before leaving for the evening to be alone in his own apartment, Paul Hood visited with Aideen Marley and David Battat. They were in Ron Plummer's office. The international political expert had assembled files on Botswana for them to read. Aideen was obviously a little uncomfortable being there. Plummer had replaced Aideen's former boss, Martha Mackall. Aideen had been with Martha when she was assassinated.

Bob Herbert and Lowell Coffey III were also present. Coffey had already briefed the two agents on the laws and political structure of Botswana. When Hood arrived, Bob Herbert was providing an overview of the Vatican's activities in the search for Father Bradbury. Battat and Aideen were told to watch out for the Spanish "tourists." They were told not to make contact unless the soldiers initiated such contact.

"We don't want you getting in the way of any military operation they might undertake," Herbert said.

"Or be blamed for it, either," Coffey added.

"Or have us caught in the crossfire," Battat pointed out.

Barbara Crowe arrived to give the two their passports and told them about their new identities. They were Frank and Anne Butler, a Washington, D.C.–based couple on their honeymoon. Customs officials, police, service providers such as hotel clerks and waiters, and even ordinary citizens tended to be more tolerant of newlyweds. Barbara had an engagement ring and wedding bands for them both. Annie was a homemaker, and Frank was a movie critic. Battat had wanted to be a government employee or law enforcement agent of some kind. That was closer to what he really did. He said he would feel more comfortable if fellow travelers asked about it. But those jobs might raise flags at customs. Especially if some clown in line joked with the agent, "Hey, you better just let this guy through! He carries a badge." Botswana was proud of its stability and extremely reluctant to allow potential subversives or troublemakers into the country.

"Besides, everyone wants to know about American movie stars," Barbara pointed out. "Just say that you've met Julia Roberts, and she's very nice. Everyone goes away happy."

Except for David Battat. He had not been to a movie or rented a video in over a year. Battat said that he had hoped he could read about Botswana on the plane and then take a nap. Instead, he would be reading about Botswana and then reading *People* magazine and watching movies. He said he could think of nothing less exciting.

Neither could Hood. But that was irrelevant.

Hood ignored Battat's crankiness. The former CIA operative was a professional. He had accepted the assignment. Whether Battat liked it or not, he would do whatever was necessary to complete it.

Aideen was a delight, as always. She was eager to be involved in something important. At one point she half jokingly referred to herself and Battat as "paladins for religious freedom." Hood liked the name. Paladins became the code name for Rodgers's new team.

After the short but intense briefings, Battat and Aideen returned to New York. There, they caught an early evening South African Airways 747 bound for Gaborone via Johannesburg.

Hood headed to his apartment. He wanted to be in bed relatively early so he could get back to Op-Center by six-thirty. That was when Bishop Max was due to arrive in Gaborone, Washington time. Hood walked in and opened the window. The night air was refreshing. Then he opened a can of pasta with tiny meatballs and dumped it on a plate. While it warmed in the microwave, Hood went to the small desk near the window. He decided not to call the kids. Instead, Hood booted his laptop and made a web-cam call to the house. That was one of the advantages of working with Matt Stoll. Op-Center's computer genius could wire anyone to anyone else.

The line was free, and twelve-year-old Alexander got on. Hood was surprised to see the first signs of what looked like facial hair. Maybe the lighting was throwing shadows under his nose and along his cheekbones. Or it could be dirt. Alexander was still wearing his soccer clothes. Whatever it was, Hood suddenly missed him very much. He wanted to hug the boy's neck, which did not look as scrawny as he remembered it.

They talked about the soccer game the school had played. Alexander's team had won. He had not scored any goals, but he had assisted in a key one. Sometimes, Hood said, that was all you got. They talked about school and about a new video game system that Alexander had seen. But they did not talk about girls. Maybe the boy had not grown up that much.

Not yet.

As usual, fourteen-year-old Harleigh was much less talkative than her younger brother. She seemed to have put on a little weight over the last week or so, which was good. Her long blond hair had a few fashionable green streaks in it. That was her mother's doing, no doubt. The idea of streaking it might have come from Harleigh, but not the color. Green was also the opposite of the blood red that other kids were using to streak their hair. But Harleigh had trouble making eye contact. Liz had said that this was typical of people who had been in hostage situations. By not looking at the people who were holding them prisoner, hostages somehow felt invisible and safe. Because the trauma leaves victims feeling impotent and extremely vulnerable, they avoid eye contact even after being rescued.

Hood and his daughter exchanged a few terse words of greeting.

"Hey, I like your hair, hon," Hood said at last.

"You do?" she asked, without looking up.

"Very much," he replied.

"Mom thought green was a good color," said the girl.

"What do you think?" Hood asked.

"It reminds me of that hill I used to roll down when I was little," Harleigh replied.

"The one near Grandma's house in Silver Spring?" Hood said.

Harleigh nodded.

"I remember that place," Hood said. "Didn't we put Alexander in a cardboard box and roll him down that hill?"

"I think so," Harleigh said.

"You did!" Alexander yelled from offscreen. "You traumatized me. I can't go in small places now!"

"Alex, shut up," Harleigh snapped. "You didn't even know what a trauma was before Ms. Gordon told you."

"That doesn't mean I couldn't *be* traumatized, Harleigh," Alexander barked back.

"All right, kids. Stop," Hood said. He did not want his daughter pursuing this topic of conversation. "Harl, what's been happening at school?"

Harleigh returned to her one-word answers.

Classes were "fine." Other kids were "okay." Even the novel she was reading for English class had a one-word title: *Emma*. But Hood was grateful his daughter was talking at all. In the first few weeks after the UN crisis, Harleigh had barely said a word.

"How about Mom?" Hood asked. "How is she?" He was not sure he wanted to know. But Liz Gordon had told him it was important the kids think he was still interested in the family members.

"She's okay," Harleigh said.

The teenager was hiding something. He could hear the catch in her voice. Probably the fact that she had a boyfriend. But that was all right. If that were the case, it would come out when it was time.

Hood told Harleigh to take care of herself. He kissed his index finger and blew it toward her. He made certain he put his fingertip close to the tiny fiber-optic lens. That got a flash of eye contact from the girl and a tiny smile. The master screen returned as Harleigh clicked off.

Sharon had not come to the computer talk. Nor had Hood asked to chat with his estranged wife. They had gone from being emotionally and intellectually involved in whatever the other was doing to a state of aggressive neutrality. It felt strange and unnatural. What's more, Hood still had to deal with the guilt of not spending time with his kids. Only now it had been formalized. It was not, "Daddy is working late." It was, "Daddy does not live at home anymore."

Over the past few weeks, there was one thing Hood had learned. He could not dwell on what went wrong with his marriage. That only caused him to beat himself up. He had to look ahead.

Hood propped his two pillows against the headboard. He set the alarm clock for five A.M. and took off his shoes. Then he lay on the bed with his pasta. A thirteen-inch TV sat on the night table to his right. He punched it on. The Discovery Channel was showing a documentary about mummies. The Discovery Channel was always showing documentaries about mummies. Hood did not bother to change the channel. At least these were Aztec mummies instead of Egyptian mummies.

Hood was exhausted. After a few minutes, his eyes began to close. He put his half-eaten meal on the night table and turned off the TV. His brain told him to get out of his clothes. To turn off the light. To shut the window in case it got too cold.

His body did not want to move.

His body won, and in a few minutes, Hood was asleep.

TWENTY-NINE

Maun, Botswana
Friday, 8:21 A.M.

The bus to Maun would be arriving in a little over a half hour. Seronga and Pavant found peanut butter and bread in the pantry. They made two sandwiches each to eat on the veranda. They also made four more sandwiches to take with them. Once they met up with trucker Njo Finn and left with the bishop, they would not be able to stop for food.

At least they would not be returning to the belly of the swamp. Seronga was happy about that. Even though they were a few months short of the fall malaria season, the Okavango region was ground zero for the disease. When he had left for the tourist center, Seronga saw what he thought were a few of the distinctive, humpbacked anopheles mosquitoes that carried the disease. He was not so much concerned about his own health or that of the Brush Vipers. He was worried about Dhamballa. They could not afford for him to become ill and seem infirm.

The men would be joining Dhamballa at the southern edge of the swamp. They would hold a rally at the diamond mine where Dhamballa once worked. Then they would move their camp to Ghanzi, a town just north of the Kalahari Desert. The prisoners would remain behind on the island with a unit to watch over them. There, they would be relatively safe from detection. The tree cover protected them from the air. From the water, motorboats would be heard and a defense mounted. The Brush Vipers were prepared to take their own lives rather than be captured. There would be nothing to connect those men to Dhamballa. No uniforms. No documents. No religious artifacts.

And no witnesses. If the island were taken, Seronga had left orders that the priests would have to die. Like the killing of the deacons, that was one of the difficult choices a military leader had to make. Unlike Dhamballa, he could not afford to adhere exclusively to white magic.

Dhamballa had selected Ghanzi because it was close to the airstrip Albert Beaudin's people used when they visited Botswana. Supplies could be brought directly to them. If necessary, personnel could also be quickly evacuated. The town of 400 was where the priest would establish the first *hounfour,* a Vodun temple. There would be no permanent physical structure in Ghanzi. A portable *poteau-mitan* would be erected, the pole through which the gods and spirits communicate with the worshipers. Symbolically, however, the pole-raising ceremony would be significant. It was to be the first public Vodun sanctification of African ground in hundreds of years. If local *houngans* and *mambos,* male and female priests, had done their job, thousands of faithful would be in attendance. With that one act, Dhamballa would become a figure of national stature. A day after thousands had proclaimed their devotion, tens or even hundreds of thousands would be emboldened to join the movement.

As the men were finishing their sandwiches, two young men walked over to the veranda. They were dressed in wide khaki shorts, short-sleeve shirts, sunglasses, and Nikes. They wore big, white, Australian outback shade hats. They looked like any members of a photo safari.

They were not.

One man stood a little over six feet tall. The other was a much broader five foot seven or eight. They both had extremely swarthy skin and ramrod-straight posture. They stopped just short of the veranda. The taller man removed his hat and took a step forward.

"Buenas días, diáconos," he said in a strong voice.

Seronga smiled pleasantly at the speaker. He assumed the man had said "good morning," but he was not sure. When you weren't sure what had been said, it was best not to answer.

"¿Puedo hablar con usted por un momento, diáconos honrados?" the man went on.

Seronga had no choice now but to answer. "I'm sorry, my friend, but I do not understand," the Brush Viper informed him. "Do you happen to speak English or Setswana?"

The shorter man stepped forward and removed his own hat. "I speak English," he replied in a gentler voice. "I'm very sorry. We thought missionaries were required to speak many languages."

"It is helpful but not a requirement," Seronga replied. He had no idea if what he had just said were true. But he said it with authority. For most people, that was usually enough to make something true.

"I see," the man said. "May we speak with you both for a moment, honored deacons?"

"For a moment, yes," Seronga told him. "We have to prepare for our trip to Maun."

"That is what we wish to talk to you about," the man told him.

The small of Seronga's back began to tingle.

"I am Sergeant Vicente Diamante, and this is Captain Antonio Abreo," the man went on.

Captain Abreo bowed slightly at the mention of his name.

"You are vacationing soldiers?" Seronga asked.

"Not vacationing, sir," Diamante replied. "We and our comrades are special forces soldiers with the *Grupo del Cuartel General, Unidad Especial del Despliegue,* out of Madrid."

Pavant sneaked a glance at Seronga. Seronga did not have to look back to know what was in his eyes. The same fire that was there when he urged Seronga to kill the two deacons.

"Special forces soldiers," Seronga said. He tried his best to sound impressed, even honored. He wanted to get the man to talk. "Are you expecting a military assault?"

"We do not know," Diamante admitted. "Our unit has been sent to safeguard the bishop who is coming from America. We will do whatever is necessary to support that mission. What we wanted to tell you is that we consider the tour bus to be a potential target."

"Thank you," Seronga replied.

"But do not worry," Diamante went on. "Two of us will be in the tour bus with you. If anything happens, all we ask is that you do your best to keep out of the way."

"We will," Seronga replied. "Tell me. Do you have any special reason to expect that something will happen on the bus or anywhere else?"

"We have no knowledge of a plot against the bishop," Diamante told him. "But after what happened to Father Bradbury, we are taking nothing for granted. We will be armed and watching for any unusual activity."

"Armed," Seronga said with a shudder. "We put our trust in the lord. In what do you put your trust? Machine guns? Knives?" Seronga had to know what he might be up against.

The sergeant lightly patted a bulge under his left arm. "Our M-82s will help the lord to protect you."

"That is gratifying. How many of you are there?" Seronga asked.

"Twelve," Diamante replied. "We've arranged with *Señor* Ndebele to borrow one of the safari cars. Four soldiers will follow the bus in that. The other four will remain here to make sure this area stays secure."

Seronga put his hand on his chest. He lowered his head gratefully. "Although I hope these precautions will not prove to be necessary, Sergeant Diamante, they are appreciated."

The sergeant nodded back. "We will not acknowledge you on the bus except in passing, as fellow travelers. I hope you are correct, Deacon. That the journey will be a safe one."

The two men left. When they had disappeared around the corner of the church, Pavant got out of his wicker chair.

"None of these bloody devils understands!" Pavant said angrily.

"I know," Seronga answered calmly. Part of his mind was here, dealing with Pavant's rage. The rest of it was looking ahead three hours, trying to figure out what to do.

"They think they can call in even more foreigners and swat us down. They don't understand that this is our country," he struck his chest with his fist, "that this is our faith we are fighting for. Our history, our birthright."

"They're wrong," Seronga assured him. "They will find that out."

"We have to alert Njo," Pavant said.

"I agree," Seronga replied. But that was all Seronga knew for certain. He looked down.

"What is it?" Pavant asked. "What's wrong?"

"The question is, what do we tell Njo?" Seronga said. "It is one thing to defend the island from an attack that probably will not come. This is different. We have to decide how far to escalate this conflict militarily."

"Do we have a choice?" Pavant asked. It was more of a statement than a question. "As soon as we take the bishop toward Njo's truck, they're going to realize that something is wrong."

"I know that," Seronga said.

"Either we need backup to cover our retreat from Maun, or we must make a preemptive strike against the Spaniards," Pavant decided.

"A retreat would not work," Seronga said. "Even with the bishop as a hostage, they would follow us to camp."

"Then we must attack," Pavant said forcefully.

"Lower your voice," Seronga cautioned, looking around. He gestured toward the church. For all they knew, the Spanish soldiers were standing there, having a smoke.

"I'm sorry," Pavant said. The Brush Viper bent closer. "We must make sure that they do not leave the bus station. They must not trace us to Dhamballa. They must be killed."

"Or eluded," Seronga said.

"Why?" Pavant asked. "Dhamballa will have to understand—"

"It isn't just Dhamballa that I'm worried about," Seronga said. "If we attack these men, the Spanish government will insist that it was unprovoked. They will say the soldiers were tourists. They will brand Dhamballa and his followers as terrorists. Our own government will be forced to hunt us in earnest to protect international relations, business investments, and the tourist trade."

Pavant stared at Seronga. His dark eyes lost some of their fire. "Then what do we do?" he asked. "We can't bring the bishop here. That will invigorate this parish. The Church will win."

"They will also find out that we are not real deacons," Seronga added. "We will be hunted relentlessly."

"So we cannot come back to the church, and we cannot let the Spanish soldiers follow us to Dhamballa's camp," Pavant said. There was renewed anger in his voice and frustration in his dark eyes. "That does not appear to leave us very many options."

"No," Seronga agreed.

In fact, there was only one thing to do. Regardless of the consequences, they would have to fight. Seronga would not let Dhamballa know now. He had already decided that sooner rather than later, the Brush Vipers would have to separate themselves from Dhamballa. The Vodun leader wanted to be known as a man of white magic. His credibility would suffer if the death of the deacons were tied to the Brush Vipers. Seronga could still help him, but from a distance. He thought of the Middle East, where leaders publicly denounced radical military organizations while benefiting from their violent activities. That separation could occur within weeks when, hopefully, Dhamballa would have enough bodies around to protect him from government interference. There would be followers who moved around with him as well as foreign journalists who covered his rallies. The Europeans had promised to bring in reporters as soon as the Vodun movement had its first major rally.

The leader of the Brush Vipers rose. *Everything old eventually returns,* he thought. During his decades of service to the government, Seronga had engaged in various small-scale engagements, from border skirmishes to ambushes. Most of those times, the Brush Vipers had been the perpetrators. Occasionally, they had been the targets. So it would be again.

Seronga knew the small-unit offensive and defensive drills

by heart. He also knew the area where the bus would be bringing them. If it came down to self-defense, he would have to have a plan.

Seronga entered the living quarters. While Pavant stood by the door to make sure no one entered, Seronga went to the bed. He opened his backpack and withdrew his cell phone. He called Njo Finn. The truck driver was about sixty miles northwest of Maun. The signal was not very strong, and Seronga made the message as succinct as possible. Seronga told the man exactly where to meet him. Using code words that were known to all the Brush Vipers, Seronga also told Njo what to have ready when the tour bus arrived.

It might not be the cleanest or best-planned operation the Brush Vipers had ever undertaken, but that did not matter to Seronga. He only had one concern: that it worked.

THIRTY

Washington, D.C.
Friday, 5:03 A.M.

It was not a restful night for Paul Hood.

He dreamed that he was trying to prop up the *Hollywood* sign. It was an endless task. One of the big white letters would begin to tilt forward, and he would rush over to it. He would push it back up, and another would immediately start to drop over. The rate of fall did not change, but the order did. There was no respite, nothing that could be done by rote. Hood woke around three-thirty A.M., wired and perspiring. Is that how he viewed his life? Constantly propping the same things up, minute after minute after minute? Was it all superficial, like Hollywood? Or was that his own past as the mayor of Los Angeles coming back to nag at him, to tell him that this was all he was good for? Bureaucratic management.

Hood flicked the television on and turned on the History Channel. The subject was World War II, the European Theater. The subject was always World War II, the European Theater. Hood watched for a while, then decided there was no point. He was not going to get back to sleep. He showered, dressed, and headed for Op-Center.

The night team was not surprised to see him. Since the separation, he had been there late at night and early in the morning. And Hood was not surprised to find Liz Gordon still in her office. She was there with J2 and Mae Won. Those two had the energy of the young. They were sitting around her desk, working on networked laptops. The smell of coffee hung in the open door like a scrim.

Hood rapped on the jamb. "Good morning."

J2 and Mae both returned the greeting. Liz did not look away from her monitor.

"Paul, I'm beginning to think you've got a very serious problem in Botswana," Liz said.

"More than just a Vatican problem?" he asked.

"Very much so," she said.

"Talk to me," Hood said. He walked toward her.

Liz's shoulders were slumped. She rubbed her eyes and looked over. "There are events in history that trigger what we call 'mass movements.' Examples are the American Revolution. The Communist Revolution. The French Resistance during the Second World War. Even the Rennaissance, though that was less clearly defined. It's the result of a collection of people whose imaginations are stirred to action by a person or an event or even an idea."

"Stowe's *Uncle Tom's Cabin*," Hood said.

"That or Upton Sinclair's *The Jungle*," Liz agreed. "You get an emancipation movement or a sweeping overhaul in the meat industry. Incited by one thing or another, people come together with a common goal, their collective efforts producing seemingly impossible results."

"The whole is greater than the sum of the parts," Hood said.

"Exactly," Liz replied. "I think we're looking at something that is being positioned very much like that."

"Let's back up a second," Hood said to her. "I assume this is based on a profile you worked up on Dhamballa?"

"Yes," Liz said. "He is definitely not a stereotypical cult leader. That's why I'm looking at this as a social phenomenon instead of an aberration."

"You're that sure?" Hood said.

"Absolutely," Liz told him. "J2 and Mae were able to get into the computers at Morningside Mines Ltd. and access his personal records."

"Morningside Mines?" Hood said. "Where are they based?"

"Antwerp," J2 said. "So are about a million other diamond companies that I found."

That information might or might not tie Burton to Henry Genet.

"Our man Thomas Burton is thirty-three," Liz said. "He has no history of mental illness. To the contrary. He is remarkably focused. Over the course of nine years as a mine worker, he was promoted quickly and regularly. He went from working the hoses that wash the mine walls for drillmen to drilling to running the line itself."

"The line?" Hood asked.

"That's where the diamonds are sorted and cleaned," Mae said.

"So he was competent and hardworking," Hood said. "Where's the jump to religious leader?"

"We don't have that link yet," Liz went on. "It could be from someone he knows, something he read, or even a holy revelation."

"Like God talking to Moses," Hood said.

"It almost doesn't matter what it was," Liz replied. "Burton is committed to this."

"Could it be a sham of some sort?" Hood asked.

"Unlikely," Liz replied. "Someone could be using him, for sure, but Burton himself is honest. His employee file contains quarterly performance reviews. They describe him as intelligent, conscientious, and absolutely trustworthy. The mine owners routinely send out private investigators to watch people who work on the line. They want to make sure the workers are not pocketing diamonds and selling them privately. The investigators actually do things like paying clerks in shops or restaurants to give the subject too much change."

"Just to see what they do," Hood speculated.

"Right," Liz said. "Our man gave it back. Every time. There is a philosophical consistency about an honest man who eventually turns to preaching. One is a statement to a single individual. The other is a statement to a group." She shrugged. "But both are about truth. That doesn't mean he wasn't pushed into this or encouraged by someone else," Liz added. "But he, himself, believes in what he is doing. I am sure of that."

"What about family?" Hood asked. "Any crises or vendettas that might have motivated him?"

"Burton's father is dead, and his mother lives in a nursing home in Gaborone," Liz said.

"Paid for by her son?" Hood asked.

"Yes sir," J2 said. "I checked his bank records."

"Do we know how the father died?" Hood asked.

"Malaria," Liz replied. She added, "The elder Burton died in a state-run hospital, not in a missionary hospital. Thomas Burton is not acting out against the Church."

"Are there any siblings?"

"No brothers or sisters," Liz said. "And no wife."

"Is that unusual in Botswana?" Hood asked.

"Being unwed? Very," J2 said. "I looked it up." He leaned forward in his seat and looked at the monitor. "Only four percent of males over eighteen are single. Those stats are pretty much spread one percent each over the military, the clergy, widowers, and miscellaneous."

"But Vodun clergy are permitted to marry," Mae added. "I put together the file on the religion."

"There are other reasons Burton might not have married," Hood said. "Having his mother to support could be one of them. Mae, what are the qualifications for Vodun priesthood?" Hood asked.

"A male priest is called a *houngan,*" Mae said, "and in order to become one, a man must communicate with spirits in the presence of another *houngan.* Sort of a religious conference call. Women priests or *mambos* have to do the same thing with a senior *mambo.*"

"I suspect that's a way of proving both men are hearing the same things," Liz suggested. "Either that, or it's a way of ensuring that the ranks or priests are joined only by those whom the priests approve."

"Everything is political," Hood observed.

"That's true, but we don't know whether Burton ever became a *houngan,*" Liz went on.

"How could he not?" Hood asked.

"Burton is claiming to be the embodiment of the powerful snake deity Dhamballa," Liz said. "We don't know if the usual rules of ascension to the priesthood apply."

Hood stared at her. "Are you saying that Thomas Burton thinks he's a snake god?" he said flatly.

"That's right," Liz replied.

Hood shook his head. "Liz, I just don't know about this. Do you think that Burton could be playing the part of Dhamballa? Faking it? He was a poor mine worker. Perhaps he's being paid to serve the political needs of Albert Beaudin and his partners."

"He didn't take money from people in the market," Liz said. "Why would he take it from Beaudin?"

"Mothers in nursing homes can become expensive," Hood said.

"I did the math," J2 said. "His salary was enough to cover that."

"Beaudin and his people may be using Burton," Liz agreed. "But I don't think he's acting."

"Why?" Hood asked.

"Two things," Liz told him. "First, Thomas Burton's epiphany would not have taken place in a vacuum. Even if he had no religious training, he would have gone to someone who did. Someone who could explain what he was thinking, feeling. The experience was obviously so powerful that any *houngan* or *mambo* Burton might have visited was convinced that he had been blessed. At least, no one questioned him or stood in his way."

"Do we know that for sure?" Hood asked.

"We're surmising it," Liz said. "Only a few weeks passed between Burton quitting his job at the mines and Dhamballa holding his first small rally. If there had been any serious resistance from Vodun priests, it would have taken months or even years to sort out. And it probably would have resulted in the use of black magic against him."

"Black magic," Hood said. "Are you talking zombies now?"

"Mae?" Liz said.

The young woman nodded. "We are. Only the word is really *nzumbie,* which means 'ghost.' "

Once again, Hood had to fight a sense of condescension. The fact that this was not his world or set of beliefs should not make it invalid. He had a flashback to when he was mayor of Los Angeles. He was hosting a movie industry dinner and was seated between two powerful studio heads. They were earnestly debating which of their studios was on top of the next big trend: talking animal movies or films about the post-apocalyptic era. Hood had brought the executives together to discuss internship programs for underprivileged city youths. He could not get worked up over the subject of *Babe* vs. *Waterworld*. But to the producers, with hundreds of millions of dollars at risk, it mattered.

To the Vodunists, this mattered.

"The zombies we're talking about are not the stiff, vacant-eyed killers we've seen in the movies," Mae went on. "From everything I've read, they are conversant, very active beings. No blood drinking, no flesh eating, no mindless mayhem."

"But are they still, like, slaves to masters?" J2 asked.

"No one is sure whether they're slaves or just willing subjects," Mae replied. "Either way, they are extremely devoted to the *houngan* or *mambo* who created them."

"These zombies may also be victims of sleeping potions and mind control drugs," Liz said. "Over the last fifteen or twenty years, there has been a fair amount of scientific debate about the subject in the psychiatric and medical journals. The consensus is that they do not die but are artificially placed in a deep narcosis and then revived."

"Mind control drugs," Hood said. He was glad that there was finally something he could hook into. "Could the Brush Vipers be victims of chemical brainwashing?"

"It's possible but unlikely," Liz replied. "Working as a soldier in the field requires the ability to act independently in a crisis. That brings me back to exactly what black magic is. To a Vodunist, it is not necessarily the supernatural. It is simply bloodshed."

"Which is why we don't think this Dhamballa man believes in it," J2 pointed out. "If the Brush Vipers had used violence to set him up, it would definitely have shown up as a blip on some of the South African intelligence reports from the region. I checked those. All the fights and arguments our people noted were about boundaries and trade and that sort of thing. Nothing about religion."

"Maybe the Brush Vipers kept people in line for him," Hood suggested.

"They didn't start showing up until after Dhamballa held his first rally," J2 said.

"All right," Hood said. "So Burton had this revelation and started his ministry with a core of people who believed in what he was doing, probably in his home village and possibly at the mine."

"Correct," Liz replied.

"At which point the mine owners and Genet might have become aware of him," Hood went on.

"Yes," Liz said. "We're not sure whether Burton was still working for them when he adopted the Dhamballa personality or whether they watched him after he left. Whenever anyone quits suddenly, the PIs watch them for a while. Make sure they did not sneak some diamonds out."

"I see," Hood replied. "Liz, you said there was a second reason you did not think that Burton was acting."

"Right," Liz said. "It ties in with the sanity issue. A man who is unbalanced, a man who has a god complex, has a very specific need. He wants to be the absolute ruler. He wants to be Jesus Christ or Napoleon or—Mae, who's the supreme god in Vodun?"

"Olorun," Mae replied as she consulted the monitor. "He is 'the remote and unknowable one.' His emissary god on earth is Obatala. He's the god who reports on human activities."

"From what we've been told and what little we've read, Burton is not making claims of that sort," she said.

"No," Hood replied. "Dhamballa is just saying that he's the incarnation of a snake god."

"We have to be more precise about that," Liz said. "Vodun priests do not claim to be an embodiment of gods so much as a representation. A spokesperson, if you will."

"He's still hearing voices in some fashion," Hood said. "You consider that sane?"

"You mentioned Moses a minute ago," the woman replied.

"What makes you think that Thomas Burton is any less rational? How do you know he is not what he says?"

Hood wanted to answer, *Common sense.* But something in Liz's voice made him hesitate. Her tone was not critical of Hood but respectful of Thomas Burton. In that moment, Hood realized he would never have said either of those things to Edgar Kline.

Hood felt a flush of shame. Liz had been right to ask that question. It was not the right of Paul Hood or anyone else to make qualitative judgments about the Vodunists or people of any faith.

"Let me ask you this, then," Hood said. "If Burton believes he is a god in some form, why does he need the Brush Vipers? Wouldn't Olorun come to his aid if he needed it?"

"Doubt is common to prophets and messianic figures, especially in the early stages of a ministry," Liz replied. "And a support system is helpful. Moses had Aaron, Jesus the apostles."

"But Moses and Jesus did not need to kidnap priests," Hood said.

"It makes sense if you don't think of it as an aggressive act but as a policy statement, so to speak," Liz said. "What the Brush Vipers did, almost certainly with Burton's approval, was merely an expedience. It was a way to announce his arrival and his target."

Hood felt that Liz was making several leaps where she did not have facts as a bridge. But that was all right. He did not have to agree with her, but this is what she was paid to do. Explore possibilities.

"I hear what you're saying," Hood said. "And the bottom line is we're dealing with a committed but probably nonviolent man. What we do not know is the extent to which Dhamballa controls the Brush Vipers and to what extent they are interested in religion or simply in power."

"Exactly," Liz said. "But you may find that out relatively soon. At some point early in any ministry of this type, the miraculous must occur. Moses and the plagues, Jesus healing the sick. Burton knows he has to produce something significant. Barring divine intervention, he is probably counting on a ground swell of support. By taking on the Church, he may be hoping to fire some long-dormant sense of religious zeal in his fellow Botswanans."

Hood was silent for a long moment. "Well," he said, "this has been quite an education."

"For all of us," Liz said.

Hood nodded. "You all did a very good night's work. Thank you."

Hood turned to go. Liz called after him. He looked back.

"Just remember something, Paul," she said. "These people are proud of their heritage. And as the Jews in the Diaspora and the early Christians under Rome showed, the Vodunists have one great advantage."

"What's that?" Hood asked.

Liz replied, "Faith can never be defeated by threats and force of arms. It has to be beaten by a better idea."

"Or from within," Hood said. "That's a much easier thing to do."

THIRTY-ONE

Maun, Botswana
Friday, 1:30 P.M.

She had given up smoking cigarettes for her husband. She had agreed to relocate to the United States for him. She loved him, and she was willing to give up a great deal to be with him. But Maria Corneja knew now that she could not give this up for him.

The field.

The woman had flown from Madrid to Gaborone. Within ten minutes of landing, she and a handful of fellow tourists were headed to Maun on board a two-prop British plane, a Saab 340. The trip took a half hour. The single landing strip was located outside of Maun. It was nestled in a flat region of short grasses. There was a modern, three-story control tower as well as a separate wooden tower on the opposite side of the runway. This was for sharpshooters. The marksman watched for herds as well as solitary animals that might wander onto the tarmac. If a herd were spotted, the man in the tower would fire until they left. Usually it took just one shot for the lead animal to turn and run. The rest of the animals invariably followed. If it were a single animal, it could be sick or old. If it did not leave, the sentry would shoot it with a tranquilizer dart. Then it was netted by a tractor that was parked behind the tower. The animal was hauled off the strip and taken to a local refuge for evaluation.

Tourists who came to the region by air were not bused to the heart of Maun.

They had to take individual taxis. The Ministry of Works, Transport, and Communications had given this route to the family that owned the land on which the airstrip was built. The family decided to open a taxi service. This gave the drivers ten minutes or so to talk to the new arrivals. They took pictures of the foreigners as they stepped off the plane, sold them mementos, and offered their services as personal tour guides.

Maria had intended to rent a car at the airport. Instead, she ended up with a driver named Paris Lebbard. The airport taxi stand was located near the airport car rental. Lebbard had stepped in front of Maria as she approached. He introduced himself with a smile and a bow. He said that he would charge her less than a rental car. He also told her that he would guarantee the safety of a woman traveling alone and could point out things that the tour books missed.

Maria looked him over. Paris was a very dark-skinned wisp of a man in his early twenties. He was dressed in a white short-sleeve shirt, tan shorts, and sandals. He wore a black kerchief and sunglasses. He spoke impeccable English, French, and Spanish. Maria had an idea. She decided to give him a short trial. She asked him to drive her to Maun. If she were impressed, she said, she would hire him. If not, he would have to drive her back to the car rental, free of charge.

He accepted the offer enthusiastically.

"You will hire me," he said. "I will make this trip even more special for you. Plus," he added, "I can take pictures with you *in* them. They will not just be scenery and animals."

On the way to town, Maria learned that Lebbard had been educated by missionaries. He was a boyhood friend of the grandson of the man who owned the taxi company. She was a good judge of character. He seemed sincere, hardworking, and honest. When they neared Maun Center, Maria told him that she would be delighted to take him up on his offer to drive her around.

Paris was elated. He told her that the minimum engagement was five hours for a total of fifty American dollars. She accepted. He told her that for an extra fifty dollars, she could have him for the entire following day. She said she would think about it.

The shiny black cab reached the busy heart of the village. It pulled up to a crowded taxi stand on the side of the market.

Maria got out. So did Lebbard, who stood beside the cab on his cell phone. The young man was eager to relay the news to his dispatcher, that he would be staying with his fare for the rest of the day, possibly for the following day.

While he called, the driver reassured the woman that she would learn a lot and that she would also be very safe with him.

"No wild animals and no wild Botswana men will bother you," the young man had insisted with a back and forth wave of his index finger. He told her he carried a .38 in the glove compartment and a rifle in the trunk.

While Lebbard made his call, Maria was eager to get to work. She began walking around the market. The plane carrying the American bishop was not due for another ninety minutes. Right now, she wanted to familiarize herself with the area. See for herself what the police presence was like. What the streets were like. Whether it would be easy to get in and out of here in a cab or on foot. Whether back doors were locked and how many children there were. Where they played, in case there was gunfire. Whether the kids had bicycles. Whether there were adult bicycles in case she needed one.

Maria Corneja moved with the litheness and power of a natural athlete. She stood slightly under five foot seven inches but seemed taller because of the way she held her head. It was set high and confident, her square jaw forward ever so slightly. She looked like a Spanish princess surveying her realm. Her brown eyes were clear and steady, her nose straight, and her thin-lipped mouth set. Her long brown hair hung down her dark neck. Wearing jeans, a black blouse, and a green windbreaker, Maria did not stand out among the more exotically dressed mix of international tourists.

The bazaar was a tourist attraction, with renovated cobble streets and stalls made of handmade fabrics. It was nicknamed Old Maun, and it was set in the heart of a small but modern city. It was approximately 300 feet wide and 700 or 800 feet long. Hundreds of years ago, this had probably been a caravan stop on a trade route. A convenient stop on an L-shaped bend in the Thamalakane River. The town simply grew up around it and remained. Today, the bazaar was crowded with visitors and locals, including a few roaming beggars. They reminded Maria of the homeless people she had seen in places like Calcutta and Mexico City. They were not just poor and unkempt, they looked sickly and broken. She put money in the paper bag of one woman who passed.

The market was also a curious blend of the traditional and the new. It offered everything from fresh produce to the latest electronic devices. There were wooden stands with canvas canopies. They stood on asphalt covered with windblown sand and dead grasses. All around was the quiet clack of laptop computers. The merchants used these to keep track of their sales and inventory. Beyond the market were new, white brick apartments and municipal offices. Stuck between them, in alleys and odd angles, were shanties with warped, discolored shingles. Several of them had small satellite dishes on their sloping roofs. She could see the glow of color televisions through the windows.

At the far end of the market was a building that served as a multidenominational chapel. It was empty. Maria wondered if that had anything to do with the attack on the church at the tourist center. On the opposite end of the market was a bar. It appeared relatively empty as well. Perhaps it was too early in the day for Maunans to drink.

The town was very different from Madrid. The air was different. It was clean and dry. The sunshine felt different, too. There was no smog to filter the heat and brilliance. Maria loved it. She simultaneously felt free and plugged in. And plugged in was not simply a figure of speech. There was electricity under her skin. It was in her fingertips, along the back of her neck, at the peaks of her high cheekbones. Some of the excitement came from being part of a great intelligence machine like Op-Center. But most of it arose from something else. It was something the woman had enjoyed ever since she was four years old, the day when she was seated on her first horse.

Risk.

In her thirty-eight years, Maria had learned that two things made any moment particularly sweet. One was sharing it alone and uninterrupted with your loved one. That had happened once far too many times in her life. With Darrell McCaskey it had happened repeatedly, becoming richer and more textured each time. Maria had grown tired of *once*. That was why she had made the commitment to her new husband.

But the other most precious times in life were knowing that any given moment could be your last. Every part of one's being came to life in those instants. You could feel it begin to build days before. A sharpening of the senses, memory, intellect, every physical and emotional resource at your command. When Bob Herbert called her the day before, Maria made a decision. She decided there was no reason she could not have a life with both intimacy and danger. Darrell would have to learn to live with that. After all, he was asking her to do the same.

Maybe, she thought, the risk was what made those other moments so wonderful. Once before they went after a militant group of Basque Separatists, a fellow Interpol agent had said to her, *"Tonight we make love, for tomorrow we may die."* She was not in love with the man, but it was a very intense night.

Even if nothing exciting happened in Maun, Maria was thrilled to be here. Just being involved in a major, evolving operation was exciting. Before leaving Spain, Maria had pulled the Interpol files on Botswana. The history and leadership profiles brought her up to speed on the nation. In a region beset by ethnic squabbles and hungry warlords, Botswana was the self-declared "Gem of Africa." It was a stable, democratic region of economic growth. Pertinent to her own trip, she noticed the laws against women loitering. They were extremely strict. According to a file from the Botswana Directorate on Corruption and Economic Crime, murder, drug dealing, and prostitution were zero-tolerance crimes. First-offense prostitution carried a mandatory prison sentence of not less than two years. Nor were the laws against prostitution and drugs based solely on the local ethic. Eighteen percent of the nation's adult population was infected with HIV. The laws were an effort to keep the disease from spreading.

Maria did not intend to linger anywhere. She had been sent to keep a surreptitious eye on the American bishop. But before leaving Spain, she had been informed that a dozen elite soldiers with the *Grupo del Cuartel General, Unidad Especial del Despliegue* had come over on the previous flight. The Spanish military could look out for the well-being of the bishop. Maria had another goal. She wanted to try to find Father Bradbury. When David Battat and Aideen Marley arrived, she wanted to have leads.

When Paris was finished with his call, he came after Maria. He found her standing beside a stand that sold handmade scarves. He asked Maria what she would like to do.

"The first thing I want to do is go to my hotel and wash up," she informed him.

"Naturally," Paris said. "I assume you are staying at the Maun Oasis."

"Yes."

"I knew that," he told her, snapping his fingers as if to say that had been an easy one. "Otherwise, you would be staying at the tourist center. In which case you would have been part of a group. So that I may make plans, what is the second thing you wish to do?" he asked.

She looked at him and smiled. He smiled back. But only for a moment. Her request both surprised and confused him.

"I'd like to go back to the airport," she said.

THIRTY-TWO

South African Airways Flight 7003
Friday, 12:03 P.M.

Something was bothering David Battat, something he could not pin down nor put from his mind.

Battat and Aideen Marley were sitting in the wide, soft seats of the 747 first-class cabin. They were in the first row along the port-side bulkhead. Battat had the aisle seat. There was nothing in front of them but upholstered wall. There was nothing to Battat's right but a permanent serving table. The flight deck was located one flight up. They did not fly first class for comfort. It was a matter of security. They were reviewing sensitive material on their laptops. The seats were far apart in first class, and Battat kept the back upright. It would be difficult for anyone to see what they were doing. He kept the overhead fan turned off so he would hear if anyone approached from behind. If they did, he had to make sure he closed the file in a slow, natural manner. He would not want to alarm a flight attendant with sudden, suspicious gestures.

The jet engines created a pleasant white noise, making it easy for Battat to concentrate on the files. He went through the 400 pages of material in just over three hours. Battat reviewed the thin case files on Father Bradbury, Edgar Kline, and the Madrid Accords. He was surprised. Not so much by the pact between the Vatican and Spain but by the fact that other nations had not joined. Or perhaps, wisely, the Church did not want other allies. That might tweak the temptation to build an international coalition. The world community might not react favorably to the prospect of another Crusade.

Battat had also studied the general intelligence files on Botswana as well as the personal dossiers of Maria Corneja and

Aideen Marley. Maria was a top Interpol agent. She had been
involved in everything from surveillance to infiltration. He was
glad to have her on the team. As for Aideen, he was encouraged to read that she had not been trained in field work. Aideen
had been thrust into it by the assassination of Martha Mackall,
when the two of them were on a mission in Madrid. The fact
that a junior political officer had helped to stop a civil war
showed that she had superb instincts.

When Battat was finished with the other files, he came to a
diskette labeled IP. That stood for Information Pool. It was
provided to everyone who was working on a particular operation. The file consisted of odds and ends that might pertain
to the operation at hand. It was updated twice a day and was
filled with names, places, and institutions that had been mentioned in passing or details that had come up in background
searches. Opening the file one looked for possible connections,
coincidences, or anomalies to follow up on. Often, a seemingly
incidental fact might trigger a link in the operative's mind—
something others had missed.

That had happened when Battat opened the IP file. And now
it was bothering him. What frustrated the former Central Intelligence Agency operative was that he knew *what* was
wrong. He just did not know *why*.

Unlike most of the personnel who worked at Op-Center,
David Battat had not spent most of his career on a military
base, at an embassy, in a think tank, or in a government office.
He had been "on his feet," as it was euphemistically referred
to. He had been in the field. Battat knew people. And, more
importantly, he knew how people of different nationalities behaved.

Before being stationed in the CIA's New York field office,
Battat had been all over the world. He had spent time in Afghanistan, Venezuela, Laos, and Russia. Because he spoke
Russian, he had even done a four-month tour in Antarctica,
from the beginning of spring to the middle of the summer.
There, he was responsible for listening to Russian spies who
were posing as scientists. The Russians were there to make

sure the Americans were not using their own research stations as military bases.

Battat liked the Antarctic work because, ironically, it was the most comfortable place he had ever worked. It was called a "listening post," but it was really a "listening folding chair." Several radio consoles hung from hooks on the cinder block walls. He sat on a metal bridge chair beside the speakers. He spent his days listening for any activity picked up by wireless microphones planted in the ice. Mostly, he just heard the wind. When the Russians did come out, he heard a lot of complaining. That was the real value of the experience. Battat realized that for the Russians, working in the South Pole was a somewhat humiliating experience. Antarctica was perceived as a surrogate Siberia. It was exile, a comedown. Men did not do their best work when they felt like prisoners.

Human nature was fundamentally the same around the world. But Battat was aware of how cultural influences affected people. They brought out different traits in different people to different degrees. And he was bothered by something he had read in Paul Hood's log. It was a passing reference, something that seemed to be off of everyone else's radar.

The entry had to do with Shigeo Fujima, the Japanese Foreign Affairs intelligence chief. As far as the Japanese knew, they had a mole in the CIA. She was Tamara Simsbury, a young American. She had been approached by the Japanese Defense Intelligence Office, *Jouhou Honbu,* when she was a student at the University of Tokyo Graduate School of Law and Politics. They offered her a rich yearly stipend if she would go to work for the CIA and slip a DIO liaison officer information they requested pertaining to China and Korea. The woman went to the CIA and told them what the DIO wanted. The Agency hired her. Unknown to her Japanese colleagues, she told her superiors everything Tokyo wanted to know. If Fujima needed information from American intelligence, he could have gotten it without asking Paul Hood.

No, Battat thought. *Shigeo Fujima had contacted Op-Center for another reason.* The Japanese intelligence officer had wanted to establish a personal connection with Paul Hood.

Something he could use later. That meant Fujima knew more than he was saying. He knew there would be a "later," something that would involve Japan.

And, most likely, the United States.

THIRTY-THREE

Maun, Botswana
Friday, 3:00 P.M.

Leon Seronga stood in the small, open observation area at the far end of the airstrip. The viewing deck was marked as such with a painted sign. The wooden plaque hung on a tall, ten-foot-wide chain-link fence. To either side were cinder block walls topped with barbed wire. There were five other people waiting at the fence, three of them children. They could not wait to see Granpapa, who was flying in from Gaborone.

At the moment, the only things to see were two small planes. They were parked on a small asphalt patch on the other side of the field, near the observation tower. The larger one was a twin-engine tour plane owned by SkyRiders. Seronga had seen this particular aircraft flying over the Okavanga Swamp. Tourists who did not have a lot of time to spend in Botswana could be flown over or to sites they wished to see. The other plane was a small, white, single-engine Cessna Skyhawk. It was a private plane.

The pilot was checking it over. Seronga wished he had access to a small craft like that. It would be so much easier to fly the bishop out of here and land at the edge of the swamp. Mr. Genet had airplanes at his disposal, but he did not offer them to the Brush Vipers. Seronga suspected that the diamond merchant wanted to keep a safe distance from the group's activities.

Roughly two dozen other people were standing by the road on the other side of the control tower. The first floor of the tower housed the airport's modest terminal. It consisted of a small refreshment stand, a ticket counter, and the baggage claim area. Except for the taxicabs and the shuttle bus, there was not a vehicle on the road. There was a single entrance leading to the airfield. A security officer hired by the airline stood just inside the doorway. He was armed with a 9 mm pistol and a surly expression.

Seronga had bought a bottle of water at the refreshment stand. He took a sip. The Brush Viper's own automatic was tucked in his shoulder holster, but he was trying not to look intimidating, unhappy, or uncomfortable. He wanted to appear a proper deacon. That was not easy.

Since they had arrived here a half hour before, Seronga had found it extremely difficult to focus. Physically, he was being baked by the direct sunlight and the uncustomarily heavy clothing. He was perspiring heavily from the forehead to the knees. Though a wind was blowing lightly from the northwest, it only added to his discomfort. It swept sand and grit from the tarmac into the eyes of those waiting for passengers. The marksman in the tower wore thick goggles to protect himself. When the jet landed, the assault was much worse. The engines kicked up whatever the wind had deposited and blasted it toward the crowd.

Emotionally, it was even worse. Seronga had once heard the expression, *"War is hell."* It was said by an American, and it was true. But there was something worse than combat: waiting.

Inactivity did not fill the mind with visions of the things that could go right. Rarely did tension suggest good new ideas. It fueled the nerves with things that could go wrong.

Seronga had come to Maun with a simple plan. He and Pavant had taken the shuttle bus to the airfield. The shuttle would take them back to Maun with the bishop. There, Seronga and Pavant would link up with Njo Finn. That much was certain. But two of the Spaniards had come out to the airfield as well. They claimed to have left a small bag at customs and wanted to see if it was still there. The presence of the soldiers complicated the plan. *What if* the Spaniards decided to chat with the bishop at the airfield? *What if* they wanted to stay close to the clergyman when they reached Maun? *What if* Seronga or Pavant did something that a deacon would never do? *What if* that made the bishop suspicious? *What if* the Spaniards noticed the bishop's uneasiness?

Seronga could not consider every possibility. Yet he knew that he had to be prepared for all of them. That was the definition of a professional. All he knew for certain was that he and Pavant had to leave Maun with the bishop. One way or another, they would.

Still, waiting to start was like running a car in neutral. Seronga was eager to get going.

Seronga was squinting out at the dusty black tarmac. Pavant was beside him, facing the control tower. After a few minutes, the lights of the airplane finally appeared in the cloudless sky. Seronga watched as the aircraft touched down. The jet's big wheels kicked up dust. The twin tawny clouds trailed the aircraft, and the wind carried them toward the spectators. The mother of the children pulled her youngest one to her, protecting his eyes.

As the jet taxied, Pavant nudged Seronga in the side.

"Look," Pavant said.

Seronga glanced behind them. The two Spanish soldiers had been inside the terminal since getting off the shuttle. Now they were walking toward the observation area.

"What do you think they're doing?" Pavant asked.

"Reconnaissance," Seronga replied. "They probably checked the faces in the crowd. Now they'll probably make sure they can get over the fence quickly. The bishop could be vulnerable before he reaches the terminal." Seronga pointed to the far side of the airfield. "Maybe they're afraid someone in those small planes will come after him."

"I hadn't thought of that," Pavant admitted.

"I didn't, either, until now," Seronga said. He grinned. "It's different when you know how things are going to happen."

"They're going to stay close to us, aren't they?" Pavant asked.

"That's very likely," Seronga agreed. "Don't worry about it, Donald. We'll get through this."

Seronga turned back to the airfield. So did Pavant.

The men watched as the jet taxied and the two screaming

engines were shut down. Before the dust had settled, the ground crew was already rolling over the silver white stairway. A fuel truck growled and pulled away from the control tower. There was a fire truck parked beside it with a small Red Cross emblem on the door. The firefighter was also probably a medic. That was the extent of the rescue services in Maun.

The door to the main cabin was opened. A moment later, the door to the luggage bay came down. A tractor rolled over, tugging four stainless-steel carts. Working swiftly, two men hoisted the bags onto the luggage transport. To the right, some-one boarded the Cessna. He had obviously been waiting for the jet to come in. Either he was waiting for a passenger or waiting for clearance. Meanwhile, the passengers began filing out. They moved slowly down the wind-buffeted stairway with their carry-on bags. They were a diverse mix of families, bus-inesspeople, and tourists of all ages and nationalities.

The bishop was one of the last people off the plane. At least, Seronga assumed it was the bishop. He was the only passenger wearing a simple black shirt and slacks with a white collar. His vestments and other belongings would have to come through customs.

The man in black waved to Seronga. Seronga waved back.

"Come on," Seronga said to Pavant.

Pavant grabbed Seronga's arm. "Wait," he said. "I just thought of something."

"What?" Seronga asked impatiently.

"What are we supposed to do when we greet the bishop?" Pavant asked. "Do we have to kiss his ring?"

"I don't know," Seronga admitted.

"We'd better do it," Pavant suggested. "Something like that could expose us to the bishop or the Spaniards."

"No," Seronga said. "Let's not worry about protocol. If we miss any formalities, we can apologize later. We'll explain that we wanted to get him inside the shuttle, where he will be relatively safe."

The two men left the observation area and went to the other side of the control tower. The Spaniards passed them going the other way. The soldiers did not make eye contact. Seronga stole a glance back. The Spaniards looked at the fence. Then they turned toward the tower and took pictures with a digital camera. That made sense. The soldiers were doing more than checking the crowd and planning a possible rescue. They were trying to get images of the people waiting for the airplane. If anything happened, they would be able to upload the images to Spain and have them checked against file photographs.

Seronga turned unhurriedly. He took another swallow of water. He wondered if he was in any of those security files. Probably not, he decided. He had never done anything to merit international attention. He also wondered how the deacons wore this damn outfit in the field. Maybe they were like the flagellants he had once heard about, the ancient Catholics who scourged themselves as a form of penance.

As if being a man or woman of principle was not punishment enough, Seronga thought. Whether one was Catholic or Vodun, a patriot or a rebel, a hunter or a conservationist, to do what you believed was right, against all reason, was a terrible burden. Seronga wondered, in passing, if the bishop was a man like that. Would he go passively like Father Bradbury, or would he struggle? There was another *what if*, another imponderable.

Seronga and Pavant reached the front of the control tower. The two men entered the packed terminal. They headed toward the airstrip doorway. As they made their way through the crowd, Seronga turned sideways to sidle through two large groups. In fact, he wanted to see if the Spaniards had entered the terminal. They had. They were only a few steps behind him. Seronga wondered, suddenly, if the bishop knew the soldiers were here. Not that it mattered. Whatever it took, Seronga was determined to accomplish his mission.

The bishop was just making his way inside. He smiled and waved again when he saw Seronga. As the clergyman crossed the threshold, the security officer suddenly turned toward him. The guard's pistol was drawn. He put it against the back of the clergyman's neck.

An instant later, he fired.

THIRTY-FOUR

Maun, Botswana
Friday, 3:07 P.M.

Seronga watched helplessly as Bishop Max died.

The clergyman's head jerked back, even as his body was propelled forward. The first thing that died were his eyes. Seronga could see the light go out of them. A moment later, the bishop fell facedown on the tile floor. Blood ran with ugly speed from a hole at the base of his skull. The guard's pistol had been so close that its flash had blackened the flesh around the wound.

In an instant, the terminal became a madhouse.

People have the same reaction when anything dramatically unexpected occurs. There is a moment of paralysis after the fact. If the danger passes, such as a car accident or an explosion, people tend to resuscitate slowly. The mind tells them there is no longer a risk. It gives them a long moment to process the situation, to adjust to the disorientation. If the danger persists, such as a fire, flood, or storm, the mind steps aside. It recognizes the danger and allows instinct to override the shock. People are free to seek a safe haven. The only ones who routinely suppress both instincts are professional bodyguards, such as members of the Secret Service. At the first sign of trouble, they are trained to launch themselves between the problem and the desired effect.

Gunfire is not like a bomb blast or car crash. It usually comes in a stream. When the airport guard fired his pistol, self-preservation took control of most of the people in the terminal. They cried, they shouted, and they ran. There were three exceptions.

One exception was the guard himself. After firing the single shot into Bishop Max, the big man turned and ran onto the airstrip. That told Seronga two things. It told him that the guard was an inexperienced assassin. It would have taken only a moment to put two or three more bullets into the body. People had been known to survive a single head wound. Additional shots would have made sure that the bishop was dead. The single shot also told him that it did not matter if the clergyman actually died, only that he was violently assaulted. Otherwise, a professional would have been engaged to do the job.

The small plane that had been preparing for takeoff was taxiing toward the terminal. The guard was running to meet it. The door on the passenger's side was open.

The second person who did not need time to recover was Leon Seronga. He had been lucky. The gunman became the focus of his attention. That kept Seronga from going into a traumatic pause. Within an instant of the bishop having struck the floor, Seronga was running after the guard.

Seronga did not know exactly why he ran. He himself could be shot and killed. He knew that his cover as a deacon would almost certainly be undermined. But he had to try to catch the gunman. Not simply for justice. It was more personal. Someone had prevented the Brush Viper from completing the mission he had been sent to do. Seronga had to know why. He also had to try to find out who wanted the American bishop dead.

Seronga pushed the panicked passengers aside as he rushed past. He reached the tarmac as the guard made his way to the oncoming Cessna. There was a man in the wildlife observation tower. He did not have a clear shot at the plane or the guard. The larger aircraft was in the way. Seronga noted the identification number on the rear end of the fuselage. Not that he really thought it would help him. The plane would fly low to avoid radar. It would land in a field, and someone would probably hide it. Repaint it. Seronga would never see a plane with this number again.

The guard glanced over his shoulder. He could not have heard Seronga's footsteps over the howl of the airplane engine. It was probably just a precautionary glance. The guard did not stop when he saw the oncoming Brush Viper. He simply pointed his pistol over his left shoulder and fired several quick, wild shots behind him.

Seronga dropped to the tarmac. He lifted his body slightly and thrust his hand down the front of his loose-fitting shirt. Reluctantly, he drew his weapon. Seronga could not afford to die here. The authorities would find out who he really was. They might tie the Brush Vipers to Dhamballa. That would hurt the Vodun cause. If the Spaniards asked, Seronga would tell them that he carried the weapon to protect himself from wild animals. Perhaps they would believe him. Not that it mattered. He would not be going back to the church.

The guard turned back toward the plane. Seronga got up. As he rose, he heard a muted *pop-pop* from the cabin of the Cessna. The guard slowed, and then his right leg folded. A moment later, he dropped to his knees. The back of his white shirt began to show a red stain.

No! Seronga screamed inside.

Of course a nonprofessional was hired to kill the bishop. Whoever was behind this never intended for him to leave.

Seronga began to run to the plane. An instant later, there was another *pop*. The guard twisted to the right and fell to his side. There was a red blotch in the center of his forehead. The pilot was a professional. He had not been satisfied with a single bullet.

Puffs of dirty white gunsmoke drifted from inside the cabin of the Cessna. They were quickly dispersed by the propeller. The pilot tossed his revolver onto the empty passenger's seat and leaned toward the door. He pulled it shut. Seronga did not get a good look at the man. Earlier, he had only seen the man from behind, which was obviously what the pilot had intended.

The airplane swung toward the airstrip. The Cessna was picking up speed. Once it had lifted off, he did not want to fire. It was a tough shot. But if he happened to disable the pilot or the plane, the Cessna could easily tumble toward the tower.

Seronga reached the body of the guard. He dropped beside it and felt for a pulse. He was not surprised to find none. The man had been shot in the heart and the head. The dead man's eyes were open. Seronga passed his hand over the guard's face to close them.

Pavant ran up behind Seronga. He helped his fellow Brush Viper up.

"Are you all right?" Pavant asked.

Seronga nodded. He quickly put his gun back in its holster.

"We've got to get away from here," Pavant told him. "There will be questions we cannot answer."

"I know," Seronga replied. His left hand was covered with blood from the guard's face. He tore open his shirt and wiped the blood on his arm.

"What are you doing?" Pavant asked.

"We'll tell people I was hurt and that you have to get me to the doctor in Maun," Seronga said.

"That's a good idea," Pavant said.

Pavant put his arm around the "wounded man" for support. They turned and started hobbling toward the terminal. Sergeant Vicente Diamante and Captain Antonio Abreo were running toward them. Both of the soldiers were holding their M-82s. The weapons were clutched close to their chests, concealed from the people in the terminal.

"What happened?" Diamante asked as they neared.

"The guard shot at me," Seronga said. "He grazed my arm."

Diamante stopped in front of Seronga and Pavant. Captain Abrero continued on toward the body of the guard.

"Let me see the wound," Diamante insisted. He reached for Seronga's bare and bloodied arm.

The Brush Viper twisted his body slightly. "It is not serious," Seronga assured him.

"It is badly grazed, that is all," Pavant added. "We will take a taxi to the hospital. I will bandage it on the way."

"Are you certain?" Diamante asked. His eyes shifted toward his partner as the captain reached the body.

"Yes," Seronga replied. "Sergeant, tell me. How is the bishop?"

Despite the fact that he wanted to get away, Seronga felt that was a question the deacon would have asked.

"The wound was mortal," the sergeant replied. "I'm sorry.

We tried to position ourselves as close as possible—"

"I saw what you were trying to do," Seronga interrupted. "There was nothing you could have done to prevent this."

"Let's go, Seronga," Pavant said.

They began walking back toward the terminal. Diamante walked backward, alongside them.

"One more thing, Deacon," Diamante said. "Did you happen to get a look at the pilot or notice the serial number of the aircraft?"

"I'm sorry, I did not," Seronga replied. "After the guard fired at me, I covered my head. Forgive me."

"That's entirely understandable," Diamante said.

The sergeant headed off to join his partner. The men continued toward the terminal. Suddenly, Diamante stopped and turned.

"*Señor* deacon!" the sergeant yelled.

"Yes?" Seronga said.

"The tour director told me your name was Tobias," Diamante shouted after him.

"It is," Seronga said. What had they done wrong? Something inside his belly began to burn.

"The deacon just called you 'Seronga,' " the Spaniard said.

Seronga felt Pavant's fingers dig into his side. Neither man had caught the slipup.

"You are mistaken," the Brush Viper replied. "He said 'lion.' That is my nickname."

"I see," Diamante said. "I'm sorry. *Esté bien*, be well," he added. "I will see you later at the church."

Seronga and Pavant continued toward the terminal. He was glad Diamante had been distracted enough to believe that and not to notice that part of his shoulder holster was visible through his torn shirt. He pulled the ripped fabric higher to cover it up.

"I'm very sorry for what happened out there," Pavant muttered as they reached the door. "That was very careless of me."

"Now we've all apologized for something," Seronga said. "Let's just get out of here."

The body of the dead bishop had been covered with a large

shawl. The thick weave was soaking up the dead man's blood. It was the white and black zigzag pattern of the Kava tribe of northeastern Botswana. The tribe members were mostly Vodun.

No one in the terminal was the same person they had been just a few minutes before. They would never be the same. They would be unable to forget the moment, the shock, the sights, smells, noises.

People were either subdued or animated. Strangers had become instantly bonded by the tragedy. Some were frightened, others relieved. A few people were talking. Others were standing around, quiet and unmoving. Some were tearfully hugging new arrivals. Still others were trying to get a look at the body. The short, lanky ticket agent was doing his best to keep people away. The statuesque woman from the refreshment stand was helping. A Spanish soldier asked if he could help Seronga, but the Brush Viper insisted he was all right. He had only been grazed. Seronga and Pavant were able to slip through the terminal without being stopped.

But they were noticed.

THIRTY-FIVE

Maun, Botswana
Friday, 3:18 P.M.

A third person had moved when the guard fired at the bishop.

It was Maria Corneja.

The woman had left Paris Lebbard sitting at the curb in his taxi while she went into the terminal. She saw the shooting. It was done in close quarters with eyewitnesses who could have ID'ed the killer. An amateur. She saw the deacon run onto the airfield, pursued by two swarthy men. All three men moved like soldiers. She did not need a cast list to know who everyone was.

Maria followed the Spaniards toward the tarmac. The plane was airborne before she could reach the field. Instead of continuing outside, she doubled back to the cab. She grabbed her camera and snapped several digital pictures of the airplane in flight.

Lebbard had jumped from the cab when he heard the shots. He ran toward Maria.

"What happened?" he asked.

"A passenger was shot," she said. "Go back to your taxi. You'll be safer there."

"What about you?" he asked.

"I'll be there in a minute," she told him. "Just *go!*"

Paris did as she commanded. Meanwhile, Maria waited. She listened to random pieces of conversation. The assassin was the airport security guard. Maria was not surprised to hear that he had been gunned down. If he had not been shot on the tarmac, she had half expected to see his body fall from the airplane. He was not only expendable, he was a liability. When the local authorities checked, Maria was sure they would find a bank box stuffed with cash. It would probably be American currency. A down payment for murder. The woman did not know local law, but she was willing to bet the money would be confiscated by investigators. And, in time, the cash would find its way into other bank boxes.

Maria stood beside the front door. She watched as the deacons emerged from the terminal. She noticed two things at once. First, the man with blood on his arm was only pretending to be wounded. Maria had seen people who had been shot. A gunshot wound was body wide. It could be seen in the victim's posture, in his expression. It was reflected in the concern of others. This man's pain stopped short of his eyes. And his companion was not doing much to support him. He seemed more anxious to get out of the terminal than anything else. Second, the way the man was leaning, there appeared to be a bulge under his left arm. That was where a holster would be for a right-handed man.

Maria walked alongside them as they headed toward the curb. She coughed to get the man's attention. He glanced over. It was the same face from the photographs she had seen.

It was Leon Seronga.

Maria headed back to the cab. She watched as Seronga and his partner got into a taxi. Then she got into her own cab.

"Paris, do you see the white car at the front of the line?" she asked.

"Yes, that is Emanuel's car," he said.

"I want you to follow it," she said.

"Follow it?" he asked.

"Yes," Maria said. "Keep a car or two between you, if possible."

"We may not encounter any other cars on the road," Paris pointed out.

"Then keep a two-car distance," she said. "I don't want it to seem as if you *are* following it."

"I see," he said. "What about the person you came here to meet?"

"He's in that cab," she said.

"You mean the bleeding man?" Paris asked.

"Yes."

"And you don't want him to know you are here?" Paris asked.

"That's right. And I don't think he was really hurt," Maria added.

"I am puzzled," Paris said. "You came to meet someone who you don't want to meet. And now you think he isn't hurt even though he is bleeding."

"Please just drive, Paris," Maria said. "It will be easier on both of us."

"Of course," Paris said. "I will do whatever you ask." He sat tall. He gripped the steering wheel tightly. He was trying to regain some of the professional dignity his questions and confusion had cost him.

Seronga's car pulled onto the road. A moment later, so did the taxicab of Paris Lebbard.

"You know, I can always call and ask where they are going," Lebbard said helpfully. He held up his cell phone.

"If you do that, and Emanuel answers, it may be the last thing he says," Maria informed him.

"I see," the Botswanan said. He fell silent and slouched slightly. His dignity had vanished again.

As for Maria, she felt vindicated. And fired up. She wished that she were driving the car herself. Or better yet, she wished she was on her motorcycle. Or on horseback. Doing something where she was able to move. Burn off some of her energy.

For the moment, though, Maria would have to contain herself and do something that would give her deep satisfaction of a different sort.

She had to call Op-Center with an update.

THIRTY-SIX

Washington, D.C.
Friday, 8:40 A.M.

Since the Striker debacle in Kashmir, Mike Rodgers had not spoken very often with Colonel Brett August. When the two men did chat, it was over the telephone or on-line. It was never in person. They simply did not want to look into each other's eyes. They never said that was the reason. They did not have to. They knew each other too long and too well.

And they never mentioned the death of nearly everyone in the unit. The risk of death came with the uniform. The ultimate responsibility for those deaths came with the stripes. There was no official blame. Officially, there was no mission. There was just guilt. Though the two men had to look ahead, the loss still hurt. It hurt them every moment they were not busy. They both knew it would hurt until they could no longer feel a damn thing.

Ironically, by avoiding the subject, each man had to think about it more. He had to consider what to say, what not to say. That served to reinforce the loss and sense of failure both August and Rodgers were feeling. They each took the hit because they did not want to inflict it on the other.

Colonel August had accepted a temporary transfer to the Pentagon. He was stationed in Basement Level Two for SATKA. That was the multiservice department of Surveillance, Acquisition, Tracking, and Kill Assessment. August worked as a liaison between the Pentagon and his former co-workers at NATO. He studied data that came from potential combat regions and helped to determine the force necessary to contain the struggle or crush it. The desirability of such a response was left to his superiors. It was not an assignment August would have selected for himself. But he had run an unauthorized covert operation in Kashmir. Even though he prevented a nuclear war between India and Pakistan, someone had to take the fall for exceeding mission parameters. The Pentagon picked him. It could just as easily have been Rodgers.

August knew he could have turned this assignment down. He could have requested a transfer back to NATO. But implicit in the Pentagon position was a promise. If Colonel August stayed off the radar for at least half a year, there would not be a military or congressional investigation into his actions in Kashmir. Members of all the elite forces took exceptional risks in their work. They were not only the first ones into enemy territory. Sometimes they were the only ones into a region like Iran or Cuba. Groups like Striker conducted recon, sabotage, search and rescue, and ran surgical strikes. The military could not afford to undermine their morale. Away from the attention of the media, the so-called "centurion line" looked after their own.

Being hidden in an underground data processing center was absolutely not August's favorite place to be. That was why he had called Mike Rodgers. Not to complain but to stay connected. To talk to someone in a place where things were not simply discussed. They happened. August knew that his life-long friend would understand.

The men chatted about their work and about people they both knew. August told him that he had bumped into Colonel Anna Vasseri, who worked on the president's Intelligence Oversight Board. Years before, in Vietnam, August had gotten himself an unofficial reprimand for writing new lyrics to the old standard, "The Anniversary Waltz." He called his version "The Anna Vasseri Waltz." Then–Private Vasseri wrote for *Stars and Stripes* at the time. The lyrics speculated about what happened during a night she had spent just outside Saigon with another private who worked on the newspaper. A storm and flash flood had stranded them on top of a small hill. When they were rescued the next morning, all they had with them were the blankets and bottle of Jack Daniel's they had taken out with them.

"Has she forgiven you?" Rodgers asked.

"No," August replied. "Which doesn't surprise me. From the look of her, that was probably the last time her uniform was off. What the hell was the name of that cat mummy we saw in the British Museum?"

"Bast," Rodgers replied. He did not know where the hell in his memory the name was stored, but there it was.

"Right," August said. "Bast. Well, this woman is wrapped as tight as that cat mummy."

Rodgers whistled when he heard that. It was good to look back at happier times. And at mistakes that did not cost so damn much.

Rodgers also talked a little about the team he was putting together. He did not tell August he had already put three members in the field. August would not have approved of that. Experienced lone wolves could be more dangerous to each other than inexperienced team players. But circumstances did not always give a leader the luxury of choice. With the help of the operatives themselves, Rodgers and Paul Hood had made that choice.

The conversation was interrupted by a call from the outside. Rodgers told August he would be in touch later in the week. Maybe they would get together for dinner. It was long overdue.

Rodgers punched the button to switch phone lines. "General Rodgers," he said.

"General, it's Maria," the woman said. She did not use her last name because she was calling on a nonsecure phone line. "The American bishop was just assassinated."

"How did it happen?" Rodgers asked.

The general fought his first, involuntary reaction. The one that went back to stories his grandfather used to tell about jinxed platoons during World War I. Units where the new lieutenant or the guy about to be mustered out or the sergeant who just had a kid always died. Rodgers refused to believe that Op-Center was cursed.

"It was right after the plane landed," she said. "The airport guard shot the bishop in the back of the head as he entered the terminal. A Cessna taxied over, and the killer ran toward it. Then the pilot opened the door and shot him. The guard died on the tarmac, and the plane took off. I managed to take a few digital photos of the tail markings."

"Can you download them?" Rodgers asked.

"As soon as I can get to a computer," Maria told him. "I'm in a taxi right now."

"Was anyone else hurt?" Rodgers asked.

"No," she said. "Most of the people in the terminal ducked behind chairs and counters. That's how I was able to see what happened next."

"Which was?" Rodgers asked.

"There were two deacons waiting for the bishop. They ran onto the field to try to stop the killer. One of the deacons had a gun."

"Was he one of the Spanish representatives?" Rodgers asked.

"No," she replied. "Both deacons were black men."

Rodgers had seen the file on the *Grupo del Cuartel General, Unidad Especial del Despliegue*. None of the soldiers was black.

"I'm almost certain one of them was the man whose photograph was in the file," Maria added.

Apart from Dhamballa, the only black man pictured in the file was Leon Seronga. "Did you get a picture of him?" Rodgers asked.

"Yes, but it's not a very good one," she replied. "He was facing away from me most of the time."

"What happened to the deacons?" Rodgers asked.

"The gunman fired at one of them," Maria went on. "The deacon was not hit, but he pretended to be."

"Are you sure?" Rodgers asked.

"Very," Maria said. "The two men said they were going to the hospital and left in a taxi. I am following them now."

"What did the Spanish do?" Rodgers asked.

"They stayed at the field," she said. "I think they believed that the two men were deacons."

"Were there any police officers at the airport?" Rodgers asked.

"Not that I saw," she replied.

Rodgers brought up his computer file on the Maun airfield. He looked at the map of the surrounding area. The nearest police station was back in the city itself. That meant it would be at least a half hour before authorities could get to the airfield. Anyone who had been involved in this by accident or design would have plenty of time to get away. And several routes to do it.

"What road are you on?" Rodgers asked.

Rodgers heard Maria ask the driver. "He says we're on the Nata Road," she told him.

"The police will be coming along the Central Highway," he said. "Our deacons obviously know that."

"I'm sure they do," she said. "On the other hand, they may not be headed toward Maun."

"True," Rodgers said. He should have thought of that. He glanced at the computer clock. "Your associates from Washington should be reaching Maun in about three hours. Can you keep the taxicab?"

"I've hired a driver for the day," she said. "He's a good man."

"All right," Rodgers said. "I'll make sure the others hook up with you along the way. Try to check in every half hour. And Maria?"

"Yes?"

"Be careful," Rodgers said. "And thank you."

Maria thanked Rodgers for giving her this opportunity. Then she hung up. The general did not bother to replace the receiver. He hit Paul Hood's extension. He felt as if Maria had lit the afterburners. He collected his thoughts as Bugs Benet put the call through.

An American clergyman had been killed. Edgar Kline and the president would have to be informed. So would Aideen Marley and David Battat. Then Op-Center would have to do two things more. They would have to find out who wanted this situation to spin out of control.

And then prevent that from happening.

THIRTY-SEVEN

Maun, Botswana
Friday, 3:44 P.M.

Upon getting into the taxi, Leon Seronga told the driver to head out along the Nata Road. Seronga told him they would be taking the highway toward the town of Orapa. The driver pulled away from the curb. As he drove, he used his cell phone to call his dispatcher in Maun.

Seronga was oblivious to the driver's conversation. The air-conditioning grumbled loudly beneath the dashboard. The muffler hacked under the car. Seronga heard none of that either. His senses had shut down to everything but lingering shock over the assassination. It held him like nothing he had ever experienced. He had seen men killed before, but he had never been caught by surprise like this. And he had never been faced with a greater crisis.

Someone obviously wanted to frame Dhamballa, possibly draw him out to defend himself, Seronga thought. Until this moment, he had not realized how truly vulnerable Dhamballa was. Not necessarily to physical attack but to being under-mined. His ministry could end before it had truly begun.

In time, support for the Vodun leader would have grown exponentially. That was when Dhamballa intended to take a very strong public stand on the question of outsiders influencing or controlling Botswanan religion, culture, and industry. But that would not happen for many months. At the moment, Dhamballa was not yet well enough known to become a martyr for the Botswana cause. If he were connected to the attacks against the Church and blamed for the death of the bishop, their cause would be irredeemably lost.

Protecting Dhamballa over the next few hours and days was

only part of the problem. There was also the matter of finding out who was actually responsible for the killing. In Seronga's mind, anyone from government moles to the Spanish soldiers to the Vatican itself would have had cause to kill the bishop. But whoever was behind it, the result would be the same. National opinion would come down heavily on the side of aggressive action. To show that they were still in control of the nation, the government would be forced to redouble their efforts to find Father Bradbury and crush the Vodunists. The Brush Vipers would have to try to prevent that. They would have to stop the government, find the real perpetrators, and protect Dhamballa.

There was also a separate issue: what to do about Father Bradbury. Releasing the priest would invite prosecution as well as the inevitable return of the missionaries. Their work would be undone and resistance to it strengthened. The priest might just have to disappear the way the two deacon missionaries had.

Dhamballa had always wanted his ministry to be a contest of native esteem and ideas. Not bloodshed. Seronga had hoped that would be possible. His heart told him that peace and tribal allegiances were incompatible, whether they were local tribes or international ones. Still, he had hoped that Dhamballa could unite people in a Vodun Botswana. The nation would be joined out of pride, not economic necessity or the fear of military reprisals.

The old taxi pulled onto the empty, sun-baked highway. As he sped up, the driver regarded the men in the rearview mirror. "May I ask you something, Eminences?" the driver asked.

When Seronga did not answer, Pavant gently nudged him in the side. Seronga looked at his surly companion. Pavant motioned forward with his eyes. Seronga noticed the driver's questioning gaze in the rearview mirror. The man must have asked him something.

"I'm sorry, I did not hear you," Seronga said. "Would you mind saying it again?"

"I said that I would like to ask you something, Eminence!" the driver said loudly.

"Of course," Seronga replied.

"Do you need medical care?" the driver asked.

"Excuse me?"

"A doctor," the driver said. "I only ask because I noticed that there is blood on your sleeve."

"Oh," Seronga said. "Thank you, no."

"If you are hurt, I have a first aid kit in the trunk," the driver went on.

"This isn't my blood," Seronga told him. "A passenger was shot by a guard. I tried to help him."

"A passenger?" the driver said. "Was it serious?"

"He died," Seronga said.

"Ah," the driver said. "I wondered why people ran out. As you can imagine, I could not hear very much inside this car."

"I do not have to imagine," Seronga replied.

"Did you know the victim?" the driver asked.

"I did not," Seronga answered truthfully.

"What a sad world we live in," the driver said. He shook his head and concentrated on his driving.

"How would you make it better?" Seronga asked.

"I do not know," the driver admitted. "Maybe everyone should have children. Then we would want to stop shooting each other. Or maybe we should spend time *making* children. That would keep us too busy to shoot." He glanced in the mirror. "I am sorry, Eminence. That is something you are not permitted to do. But you are not the one who needs to learn peace."

If he only knew, Seronga thought. The driver returned to driving, and Seronga went back to thinking.

He had been talking to Dhamballa a great deal over the past few weeks, learning about the Vodun faith. It just now struck the Brush Viper that they had experienced the Vodun ideal of *veve.* A perfect, symmetrical pattern. Death in, death out. The blood of two deacons had allowed Seronga and Pavant to get into the situation. And the blood of the American bishop had given the Brush Vipers an excuse to get away from the airport.

To get away and do what? Seronga asked himself.

That was the real question. The attempt to kidnap the American clergyman had been a disaster. Neither Seronga nor Dhamballa nor any of their advisers had anticipated this outcome. A kidnapper did not expect an assassin to hit the same target at the same time.

Seronga had never failed before. He did not like the way it felt. It was distinctive by the stillness it radiated. An individual who failed suffered a system-wide internal crash. The skin felt dead. Failure slowed the heartbeat and respiration. The mouth stayed shut, the jaw powerless. The brain sat motionless, unable to get past the event. Nothing moved, nor did it want to.

But the brain has to move, Seronga told himself. There was too much to do. And there would not be time to procrastinate.

Seronga turned back to the side window. He stared out at the flat, sun-washed fields of grass toward the distant mountains. They seemed so far away. Everything did. A half hour before, Seronga had been poised to turn up the pressure on the Church. Now the scenario had changed. Seronga wanted to talk to Dhamballa, but he could not call. They were out of range. Not that it was crucial. Louis Foote monitored radio broadcasts from Gaborone at the Okavanga camp. He would hear about this soon enough and inform Dhamballa. Hopefully, the Belgians would help put together a plan of action. Still, he would have liked to inform Dhamballa himself.

Seronga wondered briefly if he should call Njo to alert him, at least, that they would be arriving alone. He decided against it. It had always been the plan for Njo to get them out of Maun as fast as possible. The only difference now was that they would not have a captive. And they would not be running from anyone. At least, not anyone they knew about.

Now that Seronga had opened his mind, thoughts flew at him. He wondered about the plane that had taken off. Where was it going? Who owned it? He thought about going back to the tourist center and talking to the Spaniards. Perhaps they had gathered additional information. But that would be too risky. The bodies of the two deacons could have been found and identified. Or they might check with the hospital in Maun and find out that he had never gone there.

No, he decided. *It is best to get to Dhamballa.*

Beside Seronga, Pavant was simply angry. He was breathing heavily through his nose, his hands fisted in his lap. He obviously had things to say but did not want to discuss the incident in front of the driver.

After they passed the exit for the Maun police barracks, Seronga told his driver to cut over to the Central Highway.

"Are you sure you want to do that, Eminence?" the driver asked. He was an elderly man with white hair and sun-cracked skin.

"I am," Seronga replied tersely.

"That will not take us to Orapa," the driver said. "It will take us to Maun, Tsau, and Shakawe."

"I know," Seronga replied. "I changed my mind. I've decided I would like to go to the church in Maun."

"Ah, I see," the driver said apologetically. "I will take you there. But then I must charge you for two zones, Eminence."

"We will pay for the longer trip," Seronga assured him. "Just take us there, please."

"Of course," the driver replied. He called his dispatcher to let him know the change of destinations.

After the taxi had gone a few miles, Seronga noticed the driver glancing repeatedly into his rearview mirror. A minute later, the driver picked up his cell phone. Seronga leaned forward slightly and listened. The driver called a number and spoke in colloquial Setswana. It was a language that native Botswanans used to speak with longtime friends. Otherwise, they spoke English. That was how the driver had spoken to Seronga.

"What are *you* doing, Paris?" the driver asked.

Seronga could not hear the other man's response.

"I know you are working," the driver said. "But why are you taking this route?"

The Brush Viper turned casually and glanced back. There was another taxi behind them. It was one of three other cars on the deserted road.

"Oh," the driver said in response. Then he chuckled. "I thought you were following me."

Seronga did not like the sound of that.

The driver and his friend chatted for a few moments more. When the driver hung up, Seronga leaned closer to the front.

"May I ask why you called the other taxi?" Seronga said.

"Paris Lebbard turned off the Okavanga road at the same time we did," the driver told him. "It is unusual for two people to take this route to Maun. I asked Paris why."

"What did he tell you?" Seronga asked.

"He said that he was engaged to show someone around for the day," the driver replied. "He thought this would be a scenic route. It isn't, though. Maybe he is just trying to add extra miles."

"Did Mr. Lebbard say who his passenger is?" Seronga asked.

"A Spanish woman," the driver told him.

Seronga did not like that, either. "Did he say anything else?" the Brush Viper asked.

"Nothing else, Eminence," the driver said. His voice was beginning to show some concern. As if he had done something wrong. "Do you wish me to call him back and find out more?"

"No," said Seronga. He did not want to risk giving her any information. "Just drive on. Don't worry about it."

"Yes, Eminence."

Seronga sat back. The blood on his sleeve was beginning to dry. It occurred to him that he had rarely felt caked blood. When men died in the field, either they were quickly taken away or left behind. If they were left behind, they were invariably eaten by carnivores. It was strange, the things an old soldier had not experienced after all these years.

He returned to the problem at hand. *A Spanish woman,* he thought. It could mean nothing. She might be a tourist. Or she could be part of the military group that had gone to the tourist center. Perhaps Seronga and Pavant did not get away as clean as they had imagined.

Pavant obviously had the same thought as Seronga. The younger man leaned toward him. The driver would not be able to hear them over the clank of the air-conditioning and rattling muffler.

"We should stop and let the other driver pass," Pavant whispered.

"No," Seronga said.

"What if they are following us?" Pavant demanded.

"We can watch them better if they don't suspect what we're doing," Seronga told him.

"We can watch them better if they are in *front* of us," Pavant said.

"We will do it this way," Seronga insisted. "If they are following us, they will stop in Maun. We will take care of them there."

Seronga slumped down. The back of his black shirt was thick with perspiration. It clung to the air-chilled vinyl seat. Seronga felt the coolness. It moved along his arms and up the back of his neck. He began to come back to life. But he was revived by more than that. Seronga was encouraged at having a possible target, a potential link to whoever was behind this.

If so, there was another job still to be done.

And this time, he would not fail.

THIRTY-EIGHT

Washington, D.C.
Friday, 9:00 A.M.

The call from Mike Rodgers was a shocker.

Before Rodgers phoned with news of the assassination, Bob Herbert, a very tired Liz Gordon, and political adviser Ron Plummer had spent nearly an hour in Paul Hood's office. They had been discussing the imminent arrival of the American bishop in Maun. Darrell McCaskey was supposed to attend, but he was busy talking to his Interpol connections in southern Africa. He said he would come by as soon as he was finished.

The Op-Center brain trust agreed that there would be an attack. Hood felt that the Brush Vipers would not strike for at least two or three days. They would wait for the bishop to settle in, to establish a routine. A clean, successful abduction required that a kidnapper tap into his intended victim's pattern. It also allowed them to study any defenses.

"That makes sense, but not everyone is as cautious or careful as you are, Paul," Plummer said.

Hood had to admit he had a point.

Herbert and Plummer thought the Brush Vipers would strike again immediately. He felt that they had to show they could come and go unhindered in their own country. They also could not allow the clergyman to reestablish a presence in Maun. If that happened, his arrival would be viewed as a successful, even defiant return of the Catholic Church to Botswana.

Liz had a different view altogether. She did not look at the situation from a political perspective. To her, it was a question of creating what she called a "higher drama zone." The Brush Vipers needed that.

"They can't use the same scenario twice," Liz insisted.

"Psychologically, to simply abduct another clergyman from the tourist center is equivalent to standing still. That would be viewed as yesterday's soup warmed over."

"A one-note repertoire," Plummer said.

"Right," Liz agreed.

"Maybe they'll just kill him," Herbert said.

"I don't think so," Liz said.

"That goes back to what you were saying before about white magic?" Hood asked.

Liz nodded.

"What does the method matter, if they move closer to ousting the Church?" Herbert asked.

"It matters to their own sense of self," Liz said.

"Yeah, assuming these guys will think it through the way you have," Herbert said.

"This isn't something you necessarily think about," Liz said. "It's something you just do. Dhamballa and his people have shown good psychological instincts so far. Don't forget, their faith includes aspects of mind control that have been refined over ten thousand years. If they are true Vodunists, they know a great deal about human nature."

"If you're right," Hood said, "the Brush Vipers will have to hit the bishop before he reaches the church."

"Yes," Liz said. "If they don't strike quickly, if they have to follow him back to the church, then they will be forced to do something more dramatic than abduction."

That last statement was still hanging in the air when the phone rang. It was Mike Rodgers. Hood put the call on speakerphone. Rodgers gave Hood the information about the assassination just as Maria had given it to him. He told the group about Maria's immediate plans.

"Mike, this is your operation now," Hood had replied. "You want to tell Darrell?"

"Yeah," Rodgers had said. "Got another call to make first. Meanwhile, you've got to let Lowell Coffey know what's going on. If there were security cameras, I don't want Maria Corneja exposed to any legal fallout from leaving the scene or pursuing Leon Seronga."

"Good point," Hood said.

Hood told Rodgers that he would call Edgar Kline in New York.

The news about the assassination stunned everyone but Liz Gordon and Bob Herbert.

"Is that dramatic enough for you?" Herbert asked Liz.

She did not need to reply.

The others left the room so Hood could phone Kline. As Bugs Benet placed the call, Hood's reaction was deep frustration. All four of them had been wrong about the next step.

Or had they?

Hood and Liz had agreed that the Brush Vipers were not likely to be involved in an assassination attempt. The way Maria described it, someone other than Seronga had shot the bishop. Perhaps it was someone who was not associated with the Vodunists. Hood found that even more troubling. Time and energy would be wasted pursuing the Brush Vipers when the real adversary was elsewhere. Perhaps the enemy was attached to Beaudin and Genet in some way.

But why would the Europeans have been supporting Dhamballa until now? Hood wondered. To ensure that he would take the blame for this killing? How did Beaudin benefit from that?

Hood hoped that Edgar Kline would have some insights. As Hood waited to be put through to Kline, he wondered if the Vatican security operative had expected an ambush. He also wondered if that would benefit Rome in some way. The situation in Botswana was religion on the outside but politics in the center. It was a struggle for control of the nation's soul. In politics, death was a tool like any other. A martyr could help the Church get back into Botswana. Or perhaps the Vatican felt that if the Brush Vipers attacked an American, the United States would be drawn into the struggle on the side of the Vatican.

There were many possibilities. Unfortunately, there was not yet sufficient intelligence to support any of them.

Edgar Kline was in an office of the Permanent Observer of

the Holy See to the United Nations in New York. Hood was not surprised to learn that he already knew what had happened at the airfield in Maun. Kline said that the leader of the Spanish group had informed him. He added that he was about to phone Bob Herbert when Hood called.

"I was extremely sorry to hear about the shooting," Hood said.

"We were all caught off guard," Kline replied. "No one expected the kidnappers to ratchet things up like this. Now we have to accept that they may have killed Father Bradbury as well."

"Not necessarily," Hood said. "No one here believed that the Brush Vipers would kill Bishop Max. I'm not convinced they're behind this."

"Who else could it be?" Kline asked.

"I don't know," Hood admitted. "Let's talk about that."

"Botswana has never been on anyone's list of security risks," Kline pointed out. "The government prides itself on the nation's stability. Everyone who wants a job has one."

"Obviously, Dhamballa and his followers feel there's room for change," Hood said.

"Economy masquerading as religion," Kline said.

"What do you mean?"

"Botswana's greatest asset is its diamonds," Kline said. "They produce two hundred million dollars' worth each year. No outside entity is going to stir things up for that. They'd go after drugs or weapons-grade uranium, something that could net them billions."

"What makes you think Dhamballa and the Brush Vipers are after the diamond mines?" Hood asked.

"Someone is," Kline remarked. "Otherwise, Dhamballa could have started this crusade in a nation with a much higher rate of indigenous religious affiliation. Mozambique, for example. Angola is half Christian, but even they have a smaller Roman Catholic population than Botswana. The fact is, no one wants to corner the cashew or banana markets."

Kline had a point. But Hood could not help but think this

was about more than diamonds. He was not the only one who thought so. The Japanese Ministry of Foreign Affairs thought so as well.

"Were the Spanish soldiers at the site?" Hood asked.

"They were there," Kline said. "At a discreet distance."

"Were the soldiers able to give you any insight into what happened?" Hood asked.

"Nothing," Kline replied. "They did not see very much. They had positioned themselves well away from the tarmac. They didn't want to seem like bodyguards. They weren't supposed to be there."

Which possibly cost the bishop his life, Hood thought. He wondered if the Spanish soldiers might somehow have been involved with the assassination. Or at least been aware of it.

"Where are the soldiers now?" Hood asked.

"The ones who were at the airport are still there," Kline replied.

"Incognito?" Hood asked.

"No," Kline said. "We wanted to be able to recover the body. Get a look at the bullet. See if it can give us any leads. The soldiers have identified themselves as special Vatican envoys and are talking with police. They are trying to get some background on the dead guard. Also, there is some confusion about the identity of the deacons who were waiting at the airport. Apparently, they were black men. The only black men who worked with Father Bradbury had already left Botswana and are in Cape Town now. What about your people?" Kline went on. "Were any of them there?"

"Yes," Hood told him. "Maria Corneja."

"Where was she?" Kline asked.

"Close enough to have made a tentative identification of one of those 'deacons,' " Hood said. "She believes that the man she saw was the leader of the Brush Vipers."

"Leon Seronga?"

"Yes," Hood said.

"What else did she tell you?" Kline demanded. "Does she know where he went?"

"She's following him in a cab," Hood said. "I was hoping we could get some of your people to watch out for her. She's alone over there."

"I'll get right on it," Kline said. "Are you in touch with her?"

"Yes," Hood said.

"What is her present location?" Kline asked.

"She's headed back into Maun," Hood said.

"In a taxi, you say?" Kline said.

"Right."

"Maybe the soldiers can rent a helicopter at the airfield and track her," Kline said. "Or the local police must have a small plane they can use."

"I do not want you to do that," Hood said.

"Why?"

"If the deacons are Brush Vipers, or operatives of any ability, they'll notice a spotter," Hood said.

"Does that matter?" Kline asked.

"It does if you want to recover Father Bradbury," Hood said.

"Assuming he's still alive," Kline said.

"He's alive," Hood said confidently. "If the Brush Vipers were behind this killing, they knew they would need a hostage. If they weren't, they have no reason to kill him."

Kline was silent. Hood began to wonder if they had been disconnected.

"All right," Kline said at last. "I'll buy that."

"If the Brush Vipers think they're being tailed, my guess is they'll try to get their hands on the plane or chopper and its pilot." Hood accessed the topographical map on his computer. "If they manage to do that, we'll have a tough time picking them up again. We can tap into South African radar, but it may not be able to find them if they fly low in the Okavango Basin."

"That may be true, Paul, but how the Brush Vipers are tracked is out of my hands," Kline told him. "Now they've killed a man. According to the leader of the Spanish team, both the local police and the national police will be moving against the assassins."

Hood swore.

"Based on their conversations with the local authorities," Kline went on, "the Botswana National Police have taken over the case from the police in Maun. Apparently, attacking a local individual remains a local matter. Once an international figure is involved, the state becomes involved."

Hood noticed Mike Rodgers's instant message about the church on his computer.

"Edgar, let me ask you something," Hood said. "Is there a church in Maun proper?"

"There's a multidenominational chapel," Kline replied. "It started out as a Catholic church. We opened it to other faiths when we established the Church of the Holy Cross at the tourist center. It was a show of good faith."

"Do you happen to know if the church has Internet access?" Hood asked.

"I can find out for you," Kline said. "Why do you ask?"

"If the police are closing in, we may need to send our people data at a place where they won't have to look over their shoulders," Hood said. He did not want to tell Kline about Maria's photographs. The Botswanans might want to confiscate the camera.

"Hold on," Kline said.

"While you're looking," Hood went on, "what is the name of the dead security guard?"

"Festus Mogami," Kline said.

"Are they sure that's his real name?" Hood asked.

"Pretty certain," Kline said. "He's been at the airport for at least two years, according to one of the ticket agents."

Hood instant-messaged that name over to Bob Herbert. It sounded, on the surface, like the kind of mob hits he used to see in Los Angeles. An outsider was hired to kill an important figure. Then he was shot by the backup gunmen or the people who were supposed to get him out.

"The church in Maun does have an E-mail address, so obviously they're on-line," Kline said.

Kline provided the E-mail address. He also gave Hood an up-to-date list of the pastors who held services at the chapel.

Hood sent all the information to Herbert as well.

"Is there anything else you can tell me?" Hood asked.

"What are you looking for?" Kline asked.

"Details about the shooting, anything about what our people might be facing over there," Hood told him. "Because we *are* in this now. Not just Op-Center but the United States. I don't think the president will do anything except condemn the action, but you never know."

"Paul, I don't have any other information right now," Kline told him. "I wish I did."

"Can we talk to the leader of the Spanish team?" Hood asked.

"I'll find out for you," Kline replied. "Your agent in Maun is Spanish, isn't she?"

"Yes."

"Depending on what region of the country she's from, that could work for her or against her," Kline said. "The soldiers are serious loyalists."

"Maria's not a separatist, if that's what you're asking," Hood said. "She was with Interpol for years."

"That's good," Kline said. "I'll call over there. They may want to talk to her directly. I'll let you know as soon as possible."

Hood believed that Kline would press the soldiers to cooperate. He would want all the help he could get.

"Before you go, Edgar, there is one more thing I would like to ask you," Hood said. "Does the Church believe that what's happening in Botswana is the will of God?"

"That's an odd question," Kline said.

"Not from a doctrinarian member of the Episcopal Church," Hood said. "We believe that God's hand is in everything."

"Catholics believe in free will," Kline said. "It is the privilege of an intelligent being to act or not act. There is no compulsion from outside. God did not will the kidnappers to do what they did nor the assassin to do what he did. The choices were their own."

"And God would not have intervened to stop either of those events," Hood said.

"He would not have," Kline said. "He did not save His own Son. Murder is the province of—"

Suddenly, Kline stopped.

"I have another call," the Vatican official said. His voice was noticeably different now. It was clipped, urgent.

"Is everything all right?" Hood asked.

"I don't know."

"Then we'll talk later," Hood said.

"No, I'll call you right back," Kline insisted urgently.

"Why?" Hood asked. "What happened?"

"The incoming call," Kline said. "It's news from Father Bradbury."

THIRTY-NINE

Washington, D.C.
Friday, 9:00 A.M.

Before phoning Darrell McCaskey, Mike Rodgers needed to put in a call to his friend Lieutenant Colonel Matt Mazer at the Pentagon. Rodgers wanted Mazer to call ahead to the airport in Gaborone. He wanted to make sure the plane carrying Aideen Marley and David Battat to Maun was given a thorough security check. The airfield as well. Maybe it was an attack on the bishop himself. Or maybe someone was shooting Americans. Rodgers wanted to make sure Aideen and Battat were protected.

Rodgers had just hung up with Mazer, when Darrell McCaskey swung into his office.

"Mind if I come in?" McCaskey asked.

"No. I'm glad you're here, Darrell," Rodgers said. "I was just going to give you a holler."

"What about?" McCaskey asked.

"I've heard from Maria," Rodgers replied.

"And?"

"She's doing all right," Rodgers said.

"Just 'all right'?"

"No, she's fine," Rodgers said. This was not coming out the way he wanted. Rodgers had been in combat situations that were easier than this.

McCaskey eyed the general warily. "I hear a 'but' there, Mike," McCaskey said.

"What you hear is frustration, Darrell, because I feel like a genie in a goddamn bottle," Rodgers said.

"Mike, what the hell are you talking about?" McCaskey asked.

"I'm talking about things happening on the outside that affect what we do," Rodgers said. "The bottle gets rubbed, we jump into service with all our resources, and we have very little control over any of it." He took a short, deep breath. "Yes, Maria is all right. But she was at the airport in Maun when a security guard, or someone posing as a security guard, killed the American bishop."

"What?" McCaskey declared. "They killed the bishop who just flew over there?"

"Yes," Rodgers said.

"How did it happen?" McCaskey asked as he eased into a chair. His voice was flat and professional. For the moment.

"He was killed by a gunshot at close range," Rodgers told him. "When the killer tried to board a small plane that was apparently waiting for him, the pilot shot him."

"A patsy," McCaskey said.

"No doubt," Rodgers said.

"And Maria?"

"She was on the sidelines, but she's pretty sure she ID'ed one of the men who was on site," Rodgers said. "She thinks it was a Brush Viper. She's following him in a taxi."

"Did the Brush Viper participate in any way?" McCaskey asked.

"Not that she could see," Rodgers said.

"I see. Does Maria have backup?" McCaskey asked.

"Aideen Marley and David Battat will be arriving in Gaborone shortly," Rodgers told him. "They'll be in Maun in about three hours. I left a message for Aideen on her cell phone. Calls are being relayed by our consulate in Gaborone. She'll call before they catch the connecting flight, and I'll bring them up to speed."

"What about local police?" McCaskey asked.

"They were not present, and she left without them," Rodgers said. "It would have taken them about a half hour to get there."

"But you'll let them know where Maria is," McCaskey said.

"She doesn't want that," Rodgers replied.

"Does that matter?" McCaskey asked.

"Yes, it does," Rodgers said. "Maria is hoping the Brush

Viper may lead her to Dhamballa and Father Bradbury. She doesn't want to do anything to signal her presence."

"Mike, it doesn't matter what she wants," McCaskey said. "She isn't running this mission. The Maun police can pick up the Brush Viper and get the same information she can. Botswana peace officers can be pretty aggressive when they want to be."

"Then how do *we* get the information?" Rodgers asked.

"Why do we need it?" McCaskey asked. "The police can find Father Bradbury."

"Not if the target sees them closing in and signals ahead," Rodgers said. "You know better than that, Darrell."

McCaskey stared at Rodgers. The look was pure G-man: steady gaze, neutral mouth. It was an expression that agents practiced to keep adversaries from knowing whether they had touched a weak spot in a confrontation or interrogation. Or that they had let an important piece of information slip. Rodgers did not think McCaskey was trying to keep his feelings a secret, but the former FBI agent was trying to keep them in check. McCaskey could not have liked what he just heard about his wife.

"What about you, Mike?" McCaskey asked.

"I don't follow," Rodgers said.

"What do you want?" McCaskey pressed.

"I want Maria to be safe," Rodgers replied. "I also want to complete the mission she undertook."

"In that order?" McCaskey pressed.

There was something accusatory in McCaskey's tone. Rodgers did not appreciate it.

"Very much in that order, Darrell," Rodgers replied. "I've already lost my allotment of Op-Center personnel for this year."

McCaskey looked like he'd been hit across the back with a two-by-four. There was an awkward, deadly silence. McCaskey lowered his eyes. Some of the anger seemed to leave him.

Mike Rodgers was still pretty pissed off, himself. But not because McCaskey had raised the subject of Rodgers's priorities. If he were in McCaskey's position, he would have asked the same question. And not as diplomatically. He would have done it for two reasons. First, to make sure his wife was not taking reckless chances. And second, to blow off pressure at having been left out of the decision-making process from the start.

No, what bothered Rodgers was one of the same things that bothered McCaskey. Maria was being forced to improvise an entire recon operation. There was no playbook for Maria to follow. And there was no exit strategy. The least they could do was to try to get her some blockers.

"Let's get back on track," Rodgers suggested.

McCaskey nodded weakly.

"One of the reasons I was going to call you is that we've got an orphan agent in the field," Rodgers said. "Who do you know over there?"

"No one we can use," McCaskey replied. "I already checked. There's an Interpol office in Johannesburg, but that's a dry well."

"They don't have anyone free, or they won't help?" Rodgers asked.

"Interpol South Africa needs authorization from Botswana to operate within their borders," McCaskey said. "That will take days to obtain."

"They can't go in unofficially?" Rodgers asked.

"They won't," McCaskey replied. "Unlawful police actions are code-one crimes. Federal crimes that carry a minimum of life imprisonment. South Africans don't get very favorable treatment in Botswana courts. It's a holdover from apartheid."

"There's no one else we can ask?" Rodgers asked.

"All of my dealings in that region were with ISA," Mc-Caskey said. "Botswana was never a hub of intelligence activity."

"Which could be one of the reasons the perpetrators struck there," Rodgers thought out loud.

"First rule of starting a revolution," McCaskey said. "Always start where the resources are on your side. Speaking of which, Bob told me that the Vatican Security Organization has undercover personnel in the area. Members of the *Grupo del Cuartel General*."

"That's true," Rodgers said.

"Can't we get them to help Maria?"

"Paul's going to ask Kline about that," Rodgers replied. "We don't know what their mandate was. I'm also not sure how far to trust them. They didn't do a very good job protecting the bishop."

"No," McCaskey agreed.

"If it doesn't work out, I need some other options," Rodgers said. "What about newspaper offices over there? Do you know anyone in Maun?"

"I might be able to find someone who knows someone," McCaskey said. "Why?"

"Maria took pictures at the airport right after the shooting," Rodgers said. "I want those. We'll need someone in the heart of town who has a computer and modem that can take Maria's digicam software."

"I'll look into it," McCaskey said. "In the meantime, you might try the local church. They're probably hooked into the Vatican by PC. I'm sure your friend Kline can get you access."

"Good idea," Rodgers said. He turned to his computer and immediately sent an instant message to Hood.

"Thanks, General," McCaskey replied. "You want another really good suggestion?"

"Sure," Rodgers said.

"Recall Maria," McCaskey said.

He was serious.

"Do you think she would bail if I did?" Rodgers asked. "Or would she know that you put me up to it?"

"I don't care," McCaskey said. "At least she'd be back here."

"Maybe not," Rodgers said. "You don't divert a laser gunsight from seven thousand miles away."

"You do if you're a good gunner," McCaskey said.

Rodgers didn't like that. But he didn't let it get to him. McCaskey was not thinking. He was reacting. If Rodgers did the same, there would be even angrier words and probably worse.

"Look, Darrell," Rodgers said. "No one knows that Maria is in Botswana. I'm sure she will not do anything to call attention to herself."

"I know that," McCaskey said. He was exasperated, and it showed in his expression, his voice, his posture. "But hell, Mike. Maria isn't even armed. She turned in her handgun when she resigned from Interpol. Even if she had a weapon, she wouldn't have risked packing it in her luggage. Not without a license. A scanner might have picked it up at the airport. There would have been questions, she would have had to say who she was, there might have been a leak. She's too professional to have let that happen."

Mike Rodgers did not know what else to say to his friend. Even if he did, there was not a lot of time to say it. Rodgers did not want to spend any more time on hand-holding. He wanted to check in with Bob Herbert and Stephen Viens. Make sure they were doing everything possible to support Maria.

"Darrell, we're going to do everything we can to help her," Rodgers said. "But we're in this now, and we have to let it play out."

"We?" McCaskey said. "She's the one who's out there on her goddamn own." He rose and turned to go.

"Darrell?" Rodgers said.

McCaskey turned back.

"I heard everything you said," Rodgers said. "I'll get her out of there as soon as possible."

"I know you will," McCaskey said. He thought for a moment. "And I'm sorry if I hit you hard."

"I can take it," Rodgers said.

"Yeah," McCaskey said with the hint of a smile. "Anyway, you're in the intel-gathering business now. I needed to tell you what was on my mind."

"Fair enough," Rodgers said.

McCaskey left the office, and Rodgers immediately phoned Hood. Bugs Benet told him that the boss was still on the phone with Edgar Kline. Rodgers told Benet to make sure Hood looked at the instant message before ending the call.

Then he called Matt Stoll. Rodgers wanted to make sure they had conversion software to upload to Botswana. He wanted to be certain Maria's camera would interface with whatever computer they located.

As Rodgers made the call, he had an unsettling whiff of the future. He had the very strong sense that the next wars would be fought this way. Not by soldiers looking for the correct range for their artillery. Not even by massive armies, financial institutions, and diplomats working in tandem, the way they had in the War on Terrorism. Wars of the future would be fought by people behind desks searching for the right software to fire off. A combination of cyber-hits, intelligence, and microsurgical strikes.

Mike Rodgers was not sure he was prepared for that future. A future in which, conceivably, any nation could be a superpower.

Even Botswana.

FORTY

Okavango Swamp, Botswana
Friday, 4:39 P.M.

Father Bradbury had spent nearly twenty-four hours in a small hut in the center of the tiny island. The only items in the room were an aluminum-frame cot, a hanging lantern, and a straw mat. The priest's left ankle was cuffed to the frame of the cot. He had been fed stew three times during that period. They left him with a canteen of warm water to keep him from dehydrating. The priest had been taken to the outhouse twice. The shutters were still closed, and the room was ferociously hot, though it was not as stifling as his first prison had been. He had been left with one thing to occupy himself. It was a slender pamphlet containing the reflections of Dhamballa.

Bradbury lay on his side on the canvas cot. He had sweated so much that the fabric was clammy. His outer clothes were so rank with swamp water and sweat that he had removed them. They were lying on the dirt floor, where he hoped they would dry. The ground was slightly cooler than the air.

Occasionally, people would pass the hut. It was difficult to hear anything that was said outside. Bradbury wondered if he were the only one being held on this small island. He wondered what was happening in the outside world. How the Church and his deacons had reacted to his abduction. He hoped his friend Tswana Ndebele was all right. Now that Father Bradbury had time to reflect on what had happened, he realized how many people would be worried about him.

He also had time to reflect on the suffering of Jesus and other Christian saints and martyrs: Saint John the Evangelist beaten, poisoned, and placed in a cauldron of boiling oil; the young convert Felicitas, taken to an arena and trampled by a wild cow; Saint Blaise, raked with iron combs and beheaded; so many others. In John 16:33, Jesus warned that there would be tribulation in this world. Father Bradbury would not complain about his.

The priest also took time to read the Vodun booklet several times. He was happy to have it. Perhaps it would give him a means of communicating with the Vodun leader. When they met, nothing he said had any impact. If the Bible taught him anything about zealots, it was that reason seldom worked on them. Perhaps there was some other way they could communicate. Perhaps if he knew more about the man's faith, he could find something they had in common.

They came for him again. There were two men, dressed in camouflage fatigues and carrying rifles. Only this time, there was an urgency Father Bradbury had not seen before. While one man unlocked his leg, the other held his arm tightly. Father Bradbury did not resist.

"Please let me get my clothes," the priest said. He pointed to them as the second man took his other arm.

The men allowed Father Bradbury to dress. Then they pulled him toward the door.

"The booklet—" he said. He gestured to the pamphlet, which had fallen on the ground. The men ignored him.

The priest did not bother to ask where they were going. It was still light enough in the leaf-filtered twilight for him to see their faces. They seemed anxious. As they headed toward the center of the island, the priest became aware of other activity. Men were gathering things up inside huts. On the far side of the island, moss, leaves, branches, and canvas were being removed from motorboats. The vessels had been kept there under heavy camouflage. A small airplane was being stocked beyond them.

Obviously, the camp was being abandoned. Quickly. The priest had seen films of occupied towns and concentration camps being evacuated. Papers, extra supplies, and evidence of crimes were destroyed. Witnesses and prisoners were executed. Father Bradbury had a sudden, strong sense that the men were taking him out to shoot him. He began to murmur through the Eucharistic prayer. He never imagined this was how it would be, administering the last sacraments to himself. So much of his life had been stable and predictable.

The men led Father Bradbury to Dhamballa's hut. It was dark, lit with just a few candles. It seemed funereal. They brought him in and released his arms. The Vodun priest was standing in the center of the room. His posture was as ramrod straight as before. Another man was with him. A bald man, short and hefty, stood beside him. He was slouching slightly. Both men wore unhappy expressions. The smaller man, a white man, was sweating heavily. The priest could not tell if that was a result of the heat or anxiety. Probably both.

The soldiers released Father Bradbury's arms. They left the hut and shut the door. Physically and psychologically, Father Bradbury felt stronger than he had the last two times he was here.

All right, the priest thought with some relief. *The soldiers are not going to kill me.*

At least, not yet. Father Bradbury wondered what Dhamballa would want him to do this time. The priest had already recalled his missionaries. He lacked the authority to do anything else.

Dhamballa stepped closer to the priest. Their faces were only inches apart. There was fierce intensity in the Vodunist's eyes. He pointed toward the telephone on his table.

"I want you to call your diocese," Dhamballa told him.

"The archdiocese in Cape Town," Father Bradbury said.

"Yes," Dhamballa replied.

Something must have happened. The Vodun leader's voice was tense, angry. He pointed a long finger toward the phone on his table. Then he pointed toward Father Bradbury.

"What do you want me to say to them?" Bradbury asked.

"That you are alive," Dhamballa said.

"Why would they think I am not?" the priest asked.

The other man jostled the priest. "This is not a negotiation," he complained. "Make the damned call!"

The man had what sounded like a French accent.

Father Bradbury looked at him. They had starved and struck

him so much that his body seemed to be in pieces. And when
there was no body, only one thing remained: spirit. That could
not be hurt from the outside.

"Why?" the priest asked.

"I will tell you," Dhamballa said. "Your replacement was
executed when he landed at the Maun airport."

"The bishop?" Father Bradbury asked.

"Yes," Dhamballa replied.

"Because of my call to the deacon?" he asked.

"No," Dhamballa said. "We had nothing to do with this."

The priest felt weak. Martyrs were a part of history. That
was fact. But there was nothing inspiring about it. Not when
you were living it.

He pushed Dhamballa away and stepped back. He did not
want to hear any more.

"I want people to know that you are well," Dhamballa said.
"And I want you to tell them that we did not do this."

"Of course you did it," Father Bradbury replied. His statement bordered on accusation.

"You idiot!" said the other man. He struck the priest.

"Stop that!" Dhamballa yelled.

"He makes accusations, but he knows nothing!" the man
charged.

"I know that you started a process of discrimination," the
priest went on. "You forced it upon people who love the Church.
Perhaps you've given courage to others who do not share the
views of the Church—"

"All I know, priest, is that we killed no one," Dhamballa
insisted. His tone was more moderate, yet there was menace
in it. "But if we are forced, we will do whatever is necessary
to preserve our heritage."

There was often a very thin line between someone being
confident and someone on the verge of being overwhelmed.
The priest heard it in the confessional booth time after time.
He could tell when an individual was contrite and afraid of
damnation. He could also tell when a person was simply feign-
ing atonement. Dhamballa and the other man were desperate.
Father Bradbury did not know what their scheme was to ex-

tend the influence of Vodunism. In his lucid moments, he hoped it would be done by peaceful means, by what Dhamballa described in his writings as "white magic." But that was no longer the only thing at risk. Their lives might be in jeopardy. Father Bradbury could not ignore that. Nor did he have any reason not to make the phone call and tell the truth. He *was* alive.

"If I make the call, they are going to ask me questions," Father Bradbury said. "They will want to know how I am and how I have been treated."

"You may tell them anything except where we are," Dhamballa replied. "They must understand that while we have our differences, we are men of peace."

"They will say that men of peace don't take other men by force," the priest pointed out.

"Men of your sect inflicted the Inquisition on men of peace," Dhamballa said. "What is it that you say? Let he who is without sin judge me."

The Vodun leader had anticipated the question. This was not the time to debate the point.

The priest looked over at the cordless phone. He looked at Dhamballa. "I read your pamphlet. There is room for everyone."

"That is true," Dhamballa said. "But not in Botswana."

"We don't have *time* for this," the other man snarled. "Make the damned phone call."

The priest went over to the small table. As he crossed the cool, damp soil, he looked at the telephone. It was covered with droplets that glistened in the dull daylight. Perspiration, no doubt. This was where the bad news had been received. As Father Bradbury walked toward the phone, he said a short, silent prayer for the murdered bishop.

"You will have no more than three minutes to deliver the message," Dhamballa cautioned. "I will not give the authorities time to triangulate the call. We will also be listening," he added.

Dhamballa punched the speakerphone button. A loud, strong dial tone filled the room. Father Bradbury had not noticed before, but the dial tone sounded extremely clear. The camp must have had their own uplink.

Father Bradbury's ordeal had cost him his focus. It took the priest several moments to remember the phone number of the archdiocese. He began to punch it into the keypad. Perspiration blurred his vision. He entered the number slowly. It hurt to move his fingers. He just now noticed how severely swollen they were. No doubt that was a result of the heat and humidity. Perhaps the salt in the stew had caused it.

So many things have changed out here, the priest thought. Yet Father Bradbury did have one wondrous realization. His mind, his body, and his emotions had all undergone degrees of metamorphosis. Through the ordeal, however, his faith had remained unaltered.

"Hurry!" snapped the man who might be from France.

Father Bradbury glanced over at the European. The man's expression was agitated. He looked at his watch.

The activity all over the island, the priest thought. *The European's urgency.* Father Bradbury realized that these people were suddenly on an extremely tight timetable.

Despite the stiffness in his joints, Father Bradbury entered the numbers more quickly. He finished entering the number. Then he turned and rested against the table. Dhamballa stood directly beside him. The priest's own sweat fell on the black receiver. As he waited for someone to answer, Father Bradbury wondered what the European was doing here. His language and demeanor did not suggest that he was a holy man. His reasons for being in Botswana had to be political or economical. Power and wealth were the only other reasons faithless men embraced religion. Even in his own Church.

A lay secretary answered the phone. Father Bradbury introduced himself and asked to be put through to the archbishop as quickly as possible.

"Of course, Father!" the young man practically shouted into the receiver.

In less than half a minute, the archbishop was on the phone with his heavy, distinctive Afrikaner accent.

"Powys, is it truly you?" Archbishop Patrick asked.

"Yes," Father Bradbury replied.

"Praise to God," the archbishop sighed. "Are you well?"

"I am—"

"Have you been released?" the archbishop pressed.

"Not yet, Your Eminence," Father Bradbury said. "My captors are with me, in fact," he added. The priest wanted the archbishop to know that they were not free to speak.

"I see," the archbishop replied. "Gentlemen, if you *can* hear me, please talk to me. What must we do to secure the release of our beloved brother?"

Dhamballa did not respond. He stood still, glaring impatiently at Father Bradbury.

"Your Eminence, my freedom is not why I've called," said the priest. "I have been asked to tell you something."

"All right," the archbishop said. "I'm listening."

"My hosts insist that they were not responsible for the death of the American archbishop," Father Bradbury said.

"Do you believe them?" the archbishop asked.

"I have no reason to doubt what they have told me," Father Bradbury replied.

"Do you have reason to *believe* them?" the archbishop pressed.

The priest regarded the dark-eyed Vodun leader. "They have fed me and given me shelter and water," Father Bradbury said. "They do not seem to want blood upon their faith."

"I see," said Archbishop Patrick. "If they are good men, as you say, then when may we expect your safe return?"

The priest was still looking into Dhamballa's eyes. There was no hope, no answer to be found in them.

"Soon, I pray," the clergyman replied.

Dhamballa took the handset from Father Bradbury. He hung it up.

"Thank you," Dhamballa said. But the hardness in the Vodun leader's eyes was unchanged.

"Good," the European said. "Since that is done, I'm going out to see about the preparations."

The French-sounding man left. Father Bradbury turned away from Dhamballa. The priest leaned on the table, his shoulders slumping. He shook his head sadly. After a moment, he slipped his hands into his pockets and turned back. When he spoke, his voice was quiet but firm.

"Please," Father Bradbury said. "I do not know what you're planning. I do not want to know. But I recognize fear, Dhamballa."

The Vodun leader said nothing.

"You're afraid, and so is your friend," the priest said as he cocked his head toward the departing European. "Talk to me. Not as a prisoner but as a friend," he implored.

"As a confessor?" Dhamballa asked.

"If you like."

"I do not like," Dhamballa replied.

"Dhamballa, I don't care what your plans are for me," the priest said. "But I *am* worried about your followers. They are my countrymen, too, and I care very much about them."

"If you care about Botswana, then make no trouble for me," Dhamballa replied.

"I've tried to be cooperative, have I not?" the priest asked.

"As the termite who looks out from your wall and says, 'But I did not eat your table,' " the Vodun leader replied. "Sabot, Alfred!"

"Don't you understand?" Father Bradbury said. "More can be accomplished through talk than through fighting. Don't force a confrontation you cannot win."

The soldiers came back into the room. They awaited instructions. Dhamballa looked at Father Bradbury.

"We are the ones being forced," Dhamballa told the priest. "We've been forced from our roots and now we've been forced from a measured, peaceful plan. At the moment, Father, we have nothing to lose."

Dhamballa told the soldiers to take the priest back to his shack. Then he left the hut.

Father Bradbury sighed as the men took hold of his arms. He did not struggle as they led him out. The sun had gone down. The men moved the priest quickly across through the thickly shadowed twilight. Activity around the island seemed more intense than it had a few minutes before. Perhaps that

was because everything was now being done by lantern light.
Battery-powered lanterns were suspended from tree limbs and
hooks on the hut walls. Each soldier had a brilliant glow
around his station. Their open jackets fluttered lightly in the
gentle air that rolled in from the swamp.

The angels of Vodun at work, Father Bradbury thought.

The priest was returned to the shack. Once again, his left
ankle was chained to the cot. Father Bradbury remained standing as the men left. They locked the door behind them. The
priest listened. When he was sure they had gone, he reached
into his pocket.

Father Bradbury had counted the footsteps from Dhamballa's hut to his own. By his measure, it was about two hundred steps. That was about fifty yards. It might be too far.

The priest reached into his deep pocket. He would know in
just a few seconds. He had to act quickly if he was going to
prevent a disaster from befalling these people. The darkness
in the hut had shielded his actions. But it would not be very
long before Dhamballa noticed what Father Bradbury had
done.

Leaning close to the light of his own lantern, Father Bradbury looked down at the telephone receiver. The priest had
placed his hand on the cordless unit when he turned his back
to Dhamballa. It had been easy to step close then and conceal
the fact that he was slipping it into his pocket.

Now he put it to his ear. He was not too far from the receiver. There was a dial tone.

His heart pumped blood to his brain and made his senses
hyperalert. Even his fingers seemed more alive than before as
he hit Redial and pressed the phone to his ear.

The irony of what he was doing did not escape him. The
soldiers had seemed like angels to him. Now he was a tactician, a de facto warrior. Father Bradbury did not even recognize his own somber voice as he spoke to the archdiocese
secretary and asked to be put through to Archbishop Patrick.

A moment later, the priest's feet were set on a path from
which there was no turning back. He prayed it was the right
one.

FORTY-ONE

Gaborone, Botswana
Friday, 4:40 P.M.

As the South African Airways 747 was making its final descent into Gaborone, the chief flight attendant went to the front of the cabin. He announced gates for connecting flights. If passengers were bound for Cape Town in South Africa or Antananarivo in Madagascar, their flights would be departing on time. If they were headed to Maun, there was an indefinite delay.

As the flight attendant made his way back to the galley, Aideen stopped him.

She asked what the problem was in Maun.

"The airfield has been closed," the middle-aged attendant informed her.

"What's the problem?" Aideen asked.

"They did not tell us," the attendant replied.

"We've got family waiting for us," Aideen lied.

"I'm sure an announcement will be made at the terminal," the attendant said. Smiling politely, he excused himself.

Aideen glanced over at Battat. His mouth twisted unhappily.

"Maybe they've got some kind of animal infestation up there," Battat suggested. "Migrating storks or gazelles or an insect swarm. Something that will pass quickly."

"I'm pretty good at interpreting airport-speak," she said. "This was the kind of announcement they make when there's an ongoing situation like a fire or a bomb threat. I was also watching the flight attendant. I really don't think he knows why there is a delay."

"But he *would* know if it were weather- or animal-related," Battat said.

"Exactly," Aideen replied.

Ten minutes after the jet touched down, Aideen was standing outside the gate in the big, open terminal. She accessed her cell phone voice mail. There was a message from Mike Rodgers. He had left Aideen the access code to the general-purpose voice mail box at Op-Center. Obviously, General Rodgers had not wanted to leave information on the automated answering system of her cell phone. If someone else accidentally entered her code, they would be able to get the information. That could compromise security.

The message told Aideen why the Maun airport had been shut down. It also instructed her to get to the village as soon as possible. Maria Corneja was chasing a pair of Brush Vipers with no backup. Rodgers's message included Maria's cell phone number.

Aideen put the cell phone away. She quickly briefed Battat. There were security officers by the gate and along the corridors. Aideen did not want to act suspiciously. Since one airport was attacked, she assumed that others would be on heightened alert. She pointed at overhead signs while she and Battat spoke, acting as if they were discussing which way to go.

Battat did not seem surprised by the killing. Aideen asked him why.

"There seems to be a lot more to this situation than what we've been told," Battat said.

"In what way?" Aideen asked.

"The Belgians, the Chinese, the Japanese, the Vatican, us," Battat said. "There are too many people interested in a very small battleground. It's like Vietnam."

"A stage for superpowers," she said.

"That would be my guess," he remarked.

"Why?" she asked.

"I'm not sure," he replied, "but I'll bet Dhamballa or people close to him have some of those answers."

Aideen told Battat to go ahead and rent them a car. They only had carry-on luggage. She said that she would take the wheeled bags through customs and meet Battat in front of the airport.

The young woman pulled the two bags through the modern, air-conditioned terminal. She was edgy, unsettled, but she did not know why. It was more than just the dangerous business at hand. There was something about the environment that bothered her.

She looked around.

For one thing, she had noticed a sharpness about the security personnel that she had not seen in her travels through the United States or Europe. Their posture was perfect, and their uniforms were crisp and immaculate. They were alert, yet their expressions were calm, almost spiritual. She had read in the Op-Center files that Botswana was like the Middle East. Church and state were not separate. Religion was an integral part of the national, political, and individual character.

That was an alien concept to the young woman. And it created a subtle, unpleasant disconnect. Aideen did not even believe in her own Protestant faith. Not because she did not want to. She had never trusted anything that could not be sensed or measured. She realized that she did not know how to deal with these people. That scared her.

The gates fed into a narrower corridor that took passengers to customs. As Aideen entered the hallway, a flash of light caused her to turn to her right, to the west. As she walked, she looked out the large, double-pane picture windows. The view was epic. The bottom half of the sun rippled as it neared the absolutely straight horizon. Aideen had never seen the sun so large or so crimson. Ahead, to the north, were sharp-edged mountains. They were blue gray and featureless except where the setting sun struck snow-topped peaks. For just a moment, the amber rays sparked and danced off one cliff, then another. It was like a distant cascade of flame.

A bloodred sun and a mountain of fire, Aideen thought. If she were spiritual, if she were superstitious, those would be troublesome omens.

Aideen rounded another corner and found herself in the luggage claim area. Beyond the three crowded carousels was the customs area. It was already jammed with people who had brought only carry-on luggage. Aideen looked for Battat and did not see him.

Good, she thought. He was able to get through before the crowd hit. They would be on their way to Maun shortly.

Aideen crossed the baggage area and entered the customs hall. She selected one of the four lines and stood in it. It was a dramatic change from the quiet of the plane and the open terminal.

Strange languages assaulted her. The sights were both familiar and new. There was American-style clothing from suits to T-shirts as well as bright, traditional African attire. There was movement everywhere. People fanned themselves with ticket folders and open hands. Children ran tight circles around their mothers as if they were maypoles. On the other side of the customs counters, vendors sold newspaper, candy, and beverages from small pushcarts.

As she waited, Aideen was surprised to find her confidence returning. Then she realized why. Despite the new sights and sounds, she was back in a world she understood, a world like the one she left behind.

A world of organized chaos.

FORTY-TWO

Maun, Botswana
Friday, 5:22 P.M.

The streets were darkening quickly as the rattling taxi arrived in Maun. Leon Seronga was glad it was dark. Only the main road had streetlights. Neither Njo Finn nor his truck would be visible to casual passersby. Finn had said he would park on a narrow side street near the town's movie theater. The doors did not open until six-thirty. No one would be there now. After six-thirty, Finn would have moved to the soccer field at the north end of the town. Only a few people were out there at night, kicking a ball by flashlight or lantern. There was a small picnic area where Finn could have parked and waited, unseen.

Seronga had not wanted to go to the soccer field. If he did, others might see what he was going to do.

The Brush Viper had the taxi driver drop them in the square at the center of town. The shops were winding down their activities. Buses were growling down the main thoroughfare. The newer green buses were carrying tourists back to Gaborone. The older ones, lopsided and rusty with patchwork paint jobs, were bringing villagers back to remote areas of the floodplain.

The old Maun theater was across the street. Seronga saw Finn's truck parked in the shadows.

"Are you certain you will not need me for anything else, Eminences?" the driver asked.

"I am certain," Seronga said. The Brush Viper walked around to the window and paid the man. The fare was seventy pulas, the equivalent of twenty-seven American dollars. Seronga gave the driver twenty-five pulas above the amount on the meter.

The driver looked up. He smiled widely. "Thank you, Eminence. You are very generous."

Despite the pressure of the moment, Leon Seronga took a long look at the man's face. He looked at flesh baked by years of heat. At eyes bloodshot from long hours and a long, hard life. But what a magnificent face it was. The face of a man, a pillar of this nation, of their race. These were the people that the Brush Vipers were fighting for. Hardworking Botswanans.

"You deserve this and more," Seronga replied warmly.

The taxi pulled away. Leon Seronga stepped onto the sidewalk and joined Pavant. The other Brush Viper was standing behind a telephone booth, away from the lights of the taxi. He was scowling as he watched for the taxi with the Spanish passenger.

"It's coming," Pavant said.

Seronga stood beside him. They looked down the two-lane road. There were a few bicyclists. They were probably local workers on their way home. There were virtually no cars left on the road. The taxi was approaching slowly. Its identification number glowed red in the plastic display on top of the vehicle.

"I want you to do something," Seronga said. "Cross the street in front of the taxi. Act as if you're in a hurry, but make sure they get a good look at you in the headlights."

"And then?" Pavant asked.

"Go to the alley and wait behind the truck with Finn," Seronga said. "I'll stay here. If the woman follows you, I'll come in after. If I don't think she's coming in, I'll join you in a few minutes."

"Do we want a hostage or a casualty?" Pavant asked.

The question was asked casually, but it was not a casual question. Seronga considered their options. A woman's life was at stake. But Seronga also had to consider the future of Botswana.

"If she enters the alley, do what it takes to silence her and get us out of here," Seronga told him.

"What if she decides to stay in the taxi and follow us?" Pavant asked.

"Then we'll wait until we're outside of town and take them," Seronga said. "I don't think she'll do that, though."

"Why?" Pavant asked.

"Right now, the woman does not know that we're aware of her," Seronga replied. "She does not know about the truck. She has to try to find out why we're here."

Pavant nodded in agreement. He waited until the taxi was a little closer. Then he walked briskly into the street. The taxi stopped as he crossed. Pavant turned toward the driver. The Brush Viper's face was clearly illuminated by the headlights as he passed.

Meanwhile, Seronga had stepped away from the battered old phone booth. He stood in the recessed doorway of a bakery that had closed for the night. The taxi slowed some fifty meters ahead. It pulled to the curb on the same side of the street as the movie theater. A woman got out. She spoke with the driver for a moment. Then she strolled back toward the theater. The taxi left. The woman went past the movie theater for about thirty meters. Then she turned and walked back.

Seronga was anxious to get going. He lowered himself to his left knee. He withdrew the nine-inch hunting knife from its leather sheath on his right shin. He shielded the exposed blade with his left hand. Seronga did not want to risk it glinting in a streetlamp or passing headlights. He rose slowly and held the knife behind him. He watched to see what the woman did.

She passed the movie theater again. This time, she looked across the street. Seronga did not care whether she saw that someone was there. What mattered was that she not see him clearly. The woman would have to come to Seronga to find out whether he was a deacon, whether he was with the other man. Fighting a defensive battle was easier than fighting an offensive one. The attacker always led with strength. Once that strength was exposed, weaknesses were also revealed. That was where the defender struck.

The woman passed below a streetlight. This was the first time Seronga saw her face. She looked to be in her midthirties. She did not appear to be anxious. She also did not appear to have any backup. Perhaps the woman did not expect to find trouble here.

Or maybe she's smarter than I gave her credit for, Seronga thought.

The woman stopped and looked at the handwritten card propped in the box-office window. She glanced at her watch. She was acting as if she were waiting for someone to show up.

To take her to a movie, Seronga realized.

The woman had only seen one deacon. She must have seen both of them in the taxi. Maybe she was waiting for the second to arrive. Or maybe she was going to wait until people began arriving for the film before she went into the alley.

In either case, Seronga did not have the time to wait for her. Sometimes even a cautious soldier had to take the offensive.

Keeping the knife concealed behind his back, Seronga stepped from the doorway and strode toward the alley.

FORTY-THREE

Maun, Botswana
Friday, 5:31 P.M.

Maria Corneja had been with Interpol long enough to know when she was being set up.

Back on the highway, Maria had heard the conversation between Paris Lebbard and the other taxi driver. When it was over, Lebbard filled her in on what the other driver had been asking. Maria knew two things then. First, that the two "deacons" were going somewhere and did not want to be followed. And second, that they would be watching her.

When Maria reached Maun, she became even more convinced that the men had a very specific plan for her. Over the years, Maria had attended dozens of Interpol seminars on profiling. She had started when it was still a nascent science called "psychological evaluation studies." People who committed crimes, or feared they were suspected of crimes, did not present themselves to potential captors. Not unless they were sociopaths who yearned for a confrontation. Watching them at the airport, these men did not seem to be unusually aggressive or careless, yet the deacon had made a point of staring at her as he crossed the street. That could only mean one thing. The man wanted her to see him. He wanted her to follow him. And that could only mean one thing.

The deacons wanted her out of the way. The fact that the men did not stay hidden, watching her, suggested that they did not have a lot of time to waste. Their actions told Maria how to react. She would quickly reconnoiter and then kill time. That would force them into the open.

Obviously, the deacon wanted to see if she would follow him down the street beside the movie theater. A truck was

parked well down the road there. Perhaps it was their truck.
Or perhaps they were meeting other people inside the theater.
The man who had walked in front of the taxi was not Leon
Seronga. That was probably the man who was watching from
across the street. It was clear to her that these men did not
think she was a seasoned intelligence officer.

Maria decided to wait in front of the theater. That way, she
could watch both the alley and the man in the doorway across
the street. But there was a time limit. She had checked the
schedule in the box office. People would be arriving soon to
open the theater. The laws in Maun were strict about women
loitering. If nothing happened by six o'clock, she would have
to go into the alley and hope she wouldn't be seen there. She
did not want to risk being confronted by police. If the deacons
tried to slip away, she would not be able to follow them.

Fortunately, Maria did not have to wait until six o'clock.

The man standing in the doorway suddenly came toward
her. There was blood on his sleeve. As the man passed under
a streetlight, she knew for certain that it was Leon Seronga.

Seronga walked purposefully, his eyes on her. Maria could
tell at once that he had a weapon. The man's arm was held
stiffly at his side instead of swinging. She did not know if it
was a gun or knife.

Maria waited by the movie theater. She pretended to pay
the man no attention. If she walked toward him, he might feel
challenged. That could provoke him. Perhaps he was not certain she was interested in him at all. Maybe his determined
approach was a way of testing her.

If so, Maria had a surprise for the man. It had nothing to
do with the small can of pepper spray she had palmed. If
necessary, using the spray would help to protect her. But it
would not get Maria what she came for. She had to lead Seronga carefully and precisely to the point she wanted. He had
to trust her with the location of Father Bradbury.

Seronga slowed as a truck clattered by. It was followed by
two men on bicycles. The deacon continued forward as the
traffic passed.

Maria looked toward the alley. As far as she could tell, no

one was standing there. That was important. She did not want to find herself being approached from two sides. For all she knew, these people had one or more accomplices waiting in another building or down another side street.

Seronga was about five meters away. Maria waited until he had halved that distance. Now she was going to get him to do what she wanted. She was going to get him to walk her safely into that side street.

"I know that you did not kill the bishop," she said.

Seronga stopped. "Who did?" he asked.

"I don't know," she replied. She did not want to tell him about the photographs she took. Not yet.

"Are you one of the Spanish soldiers?" Seronga asked.

"No," Maria replied.

"Then who are you?" he asked. "Why did you follow us?"

"I want to help you," she stated.

"Why?" Seronga demanded. He was growing tense, impatient.

"Because I believe in what you're doing," she lied.

Seronga hesitated. Maria did not want to say much more. Yet she needed him to be curious enough to take her with him. She needed for him to trust her.

"I want to help, even though you tried to get me to follow your partner into that dark side street," she said. "Even though you are holding a weapon behind your back."

"Are you unarmed?" he challenged.

She opened her palm. "A purely defensive tool," she said. She raised her arms. "Go ahead and check. I have nothing else."

Seronga glanced toward the alley. "All right," he said. "Walk ahead of me, and do as you're told."

Maria acknowledged with a nod. Then she walked toward the alley.

The nod had not been for Leon Seronga.

FORTY-FOUR

Washington, D.C.
Friday, 11:18 A.M.

Maria Corneja had told Mike Rodgers that she would get in touch with him as soon as she knew where Leon Seronga was going. According to the map on Rodgers's computer, Maria should have reached the city by now. He tried not to worry. She was a professional. Unfortunately, she was still a professional who was pretty much on her own.

Since Maria had telephoned, Rodgers had conferred with McCaskey and Herbert. Lowell Coffey joined them as well. He wanted to be able to alert them to any possible infractions of international law.

The men discussed getting help in the area from FBI, Interpol, or CIA sources. The only help available was ELINT from the CIA. The agency could provide electronic intelligence by monitoring wireless communications in the region. Rodgers asked Herbert to request the surveillance. It would be handled by listening posts at the United States embassies in Gaborone and in Cape Town, South Africa. Though these were one-person operations, it was possible that something might turn up.

Even though Rodgers was in charge of the new HUMINT division at Op-Center, he asked Herbert to make those calls.

"You're better at finessing those drop-everything requests than I am," Rodgers said.

"It's easy," Herbert said. "All you have to do is grovel with a little steel in your voice."

"Amazing what is in Bob's incomparable diplomatic arsenal," Coffey remarked.

"Lowell, that *is* my diplomatic arsenal," Herbert replied.

"That and threatening to go on *The Dugout* and name the bastards who are looking for votes and appointments instead of looking after their constituents."

"The Dugout?" Coffey snickered. "Stuttering Matt Christopher doesn't let his guests get in more than three words before cutting them off."

"Three words are all I need," Herbert said. " 'Barbara Fox, bureaucrat.' That's my *targeted* diplomatic arsenal. Plant the idea and it takes root on its own. It's like when an attorney says something in a courtroom and the judge tells the jury to ignore it. Like they do, right? All people have to do is hear my calm voice before Matt starts blathering."

Coffey laughed.

Rodgers had never considered himself much of a diplomat. He was a tactician and a commander. Right now, he was not feeling competent in those areas, either.

What concerned Rodgers most was that Maria still had no support on the ground. Aideen Marley and David Battat had landed in Gaborone. But Aideen had called to inform him that they were driving to Maun. The trip would take serveral hours.

Rodgers also feared that Aideen and Battat would end up being in the wrong place. Everyone was assuming that Leon Seronga was headed to Maun. What if he were not?

Shortly after the meeting ended, Rodgers finally received a call from Botswana. It came through on Maria's calling card. The caller had the correct ID number to enter the private Op-Center telephone directory. Once there, the caller was able to input Mike Rodgers's name and receive the correct extension. Without the ID, the caller had to go through the switchboard. That enabled the electronic operator to trace the call. The system kept crank calls to a very low minimum.

But the caller was not Maria.

The man on the phone identified himself as Paris Lebbard. Rodgers did not recognize the name, but the accent sounded almost Egyptian.

"What can I do for you, Mr. Lebbard?" Rodgers asked. The general said nothing more. Maria's cards had been lost or stolen. If that were the case, Rodgers did not want to let the caller know who he had reached or who she was.

"I am your friend Maria's driver," Lebbard said. "In Botswana. She gave me her calling card and your number."

"Is Maria all right?" Rodgers demanded.

"She nodded to me that she was," Lebbard replied.

"She nodded? I don't understand," Rodgers said.

"That was our signal," Lebbard said. "I dropped her off to meet the man from the airport. Then I parked around the corner and sneaked back. I watched as she spoke with the man. If she had not nodded, I would have gone to the police station to report a kidnapping."

"I see," Rodgers said. The general experienced the same gut-burning fire he had felt in Kashmir. The one that told him he may have acted recklessly. The desire to get Maria on-site backup had gone from necessary to desperate.

"She told me you would be concerned, sir," Lebbard added. "But I like her very much. And I know she has a husband who loves her. I also know she is trying to keep peace in Botswana. If I had any doubt about her safety, I would have gone for assistance at once."

Rodgers was not entirely convinced. But the general had to take his cue from the people in the field. And right now, Paris Lebbard was the only person in contact from the field.

"Thank you, Mr. Lebbard," Rodgers said. He swung toward his keyboard and prepared to type. "Can you tell me what the man looked like?"

"It was dark, and I was too far to see his face," Lebbard said. "But he was dressed like a Christian clergyman."

"Where did they go?" Rodgers asked.

"They walked to his truck, which was parked on Bath Street," Lebbard said. "Then they drove away."

"When did Maria leave with the man?" Rodgers asked.

"Less than five minutes ago," Lebbard said.

"Can you describe the truck?" Rodgers asked.

"Yes," the driver reported. "They drove right past me. It was a Chevrolet. Maybe ten years old. The cab looked olive green. It was dented, with a lot of rust. It had a canvas back and no markings on the side."

"Were you able to get the license number?" Rodgers asked as he typed up the description.

"No," Lebbard said. "It was covered with mud."

"Do you have any idea where they went?" Rodgers asked.

"That is difficult to say," Lebbard replied. "The truck did not get on the highway but took local roads."

"Meaning?" Rodgers asked.

"The driver does not want to be followed," Lebbard said. "At night, on the dirt roads, he will pass only villages. He will know if anyone is tailing him."

"Which direction was the truck headed?" Rodgers asked.

"North," Lebbard replied. "Though there is one thing."

"What's that?" Rodgers asked.

"It has not rained here for over a week," the driver said. "There was not only mud on the license plate of the truck. It was also on the fender, tires, sides, and flaps. It was dark mud. That's the kind of mud you find in and around the swamps to the north."

Rodgers made a note of that. He immediately E-mailed the description of the truck, its location, its heading, and its possible destination to Stephen Viens at the National Reconnaissance Office. There was a chance the NRO might pick the truck up by satellite. He also sent a copy of the E-mail to Aideen Marley.

"This is very helpful," Rodgers told him. "Was there anything else, Mr. Lebbard?"

"Yes," the driver went on. "Maria gave me other instructions."

That took Rodgers by surprise. He smiled slightly. The driver was very well organized. Rodgers also felt a flash of vindication. He had been right to select Maria for this assignment. She had obviously made a big impression on this man.

"Go ahead," Rodgers said.

"She left me with a camera and a computer diskette," the man said. "She said I should send you the photographs she took. She also said you might know where to find a computer."

"I do," Rodgers informed him. "Where are you now?"

"I am at a pay telephone at Nhabe, two blocks from the eastern bank of the Thamalakane River."

Rodgers brought up the map of Maun. "That's perfect," Rodgers said. "Do you know the multifaith chapel in the center of Maun?"

"Of course," Lebbard replied. "It's to the west of the Mall. The Chapel of Grace."

"Right," Rodgers said. "Go there. I'm going to call someone who will get you access to a computer. Do you know how to use the software?"

"Maria told me to insert the diskette," Lebbard said. "She said there would be instructions telling me what to do next. I have read maps for years. I am very good at following directions."

"I'm sure you are," Rodgers said. "Go there, Mr. Lebbard, while I make a few calls."

"I will," Lebbard replied. "Sir, Maria did not tell me who she works with. She is Spanish, but you sound American. Are you with the United Nations?"

Rodgers did not want to respond without knowing how his answer would be received. "What if we were?" Rodgers asked. "Would that make you happy?"

"It would make me very happy, sir," Lebbard replied. "When I was a young child, nurses from the United Nations came to my village. They gave us injections against smallpox and polio. They gave us food. They gave me the first chocolate I ever tasted."

Rodgers thought for a moment. He wanted Paris Lebbard to be happy. But he did not want to lie to an ally.

"We are not the United Nations, Mr. Lebbard. But we have worked with them," Rodgers said.

That seemed to please the Botswanan. Rodgers was glad.

Maybe he had the makings of a diplomat after all.

FORTY-FIVE

Okavango Swamp, Botswana
Friday, 6:20 P.M.

Father Bradbury had not bothered to turn on the lantern when the soldiers returned him to the room. The priest knelt by the foot of the cot and prayed. When he was done, he sat on the edge of the cot. He peered into the darkness. He let his mind move through the rich past and the uncertain future. Whichever way he looked, however, he came to the same place.

Life was about choices.

Years before, Father Bradbury had decided that the most dangerous thing in the world was to have a choice. When he was an altar boy, thirteen-year-old Powys Bradbury had found himself in a rectory fire. A spark had jumped from the fireplace while he was stoking it. An open Bible caught fire, a burning page fell on the rug, and within seconds, the room was ablaze. The youth looked around. There was no time for guilt or self-reproach. He tried to decide what Father Sleep would want saved.

Photographs? Books? Earthenware that had been dug up from Bethlehem? Black smoke began to cloud around the boy. Young Bradbury's throat began to thicken. After a few strained breaths, it was nearly impossible to inhale. His eyes teared, and he could not see. That was when he found it easy to prioritize. Bradbury needed to get out.

Forty-nine years ago, Powys Bradbury had a choice whether to risk his life or not. Now he did not have that luxury. Yet there were still choices to make. In a way, they were more important than deciding what to take from a burning rectory.

These choices were not about whether to escape. They were about how to accept his fate.

Neither Dhamballa nor the European had indicated that Bradbury's life was in jeopardy, but the soldiers and their leaders were breaking camp. The priest had already seen people rushing about. Now they were shouting and hurrying about. The departure was going to be hasty.

He was excess baggage.

The shadows around Father Bradbury seemed especially deep. At a time when he should be contemplating spiritual matters, he found himself thinking about physical things. He would have all eternity to contemplate the spiritual. This was the time to savor the shell that God had given to him, to enjoy the wonder of the senses: the simple act of breathing, a gift passed from the nostrils of God Himself through Adam; the beauty of the heart working at its steady, dependable pace; all of it functioning in miraculous unison. It was, on reflection, a masterpiece of the Creator's art. One that no man had the right to destroy.

Yet men kill and torture each other every day, he thought. That was why people such as Father Bradbury were needed. Only the peace of God could stop violence.

The priest began to pity the cultists who might be ordered to kill him. They were indirectly causing the suffering of others the priest might have saved. Father Bradbury also forgave the soldiers. The men would not understand what they were doing. And not understanding, they could never sincerely repent. They could not be saved.

The priest moved from reflection to the world around him. As he contemplated what might be his last minutes, Father Bradbury had no trouble admitting that he did not want to die. He drank in the beauty of even these dismal surroundings and the wisdom God demonstrated by letting men grow old. God had designed humans so that their senses and bodies dimmed over time. The world became more and more selectively available to them. Aging, people could only savor what their dimming senses could see, hear, taste, smell, or feel. God made the choice for them. He showed people how to enjoy, even cherish the things close to them. But God did not intend for life to end all at once. That was why He had put in His Commandments that it was wrong to murder. Father Bradbury wanted to experience God's choices over time.

The door of the hut flew open. The two soldiers had returned. He could only see their silhouettes framed by distant lantern light. Their posture was different than before. Their knees were bent slightly. Their shoulders were hunched. They were more aggressive.

They were holding their handguns.

One of the men came in. He released the priest's ankle from its metal cuff. Then he poked Father Bradbury in the side with his gun. That was the only order the soldier gave.

The priest rose. His legs were unsteady, due to exhaustion and fear. He fell on the shoulder of the soldier. The man did not pull away.

"Thank you," the priest said.

It took a moment for Father Bradbury to regain his footing. His knees were trembling, and his thighs felt weak, but he remained standing.

Choices, he thought. He could not think about the future. He thought about the moment. His heart was racing. The back of his neck was clammy. And his legs were like harp strings. But he was suddenly overwhelmed by the magnitude of God's gift to humankind. As he walked from the hut, the soldier put a hand on his shoulder. He forced the priest to his knees. He stepped behind him.

Father Bradbury felt cold. He was aware of nothing else but his heart hammering high in his chest and the sudden flow of tears. He looked up at the early evening stars. He was grateful for his life, thankful for all life. If it were possible to have an out-of-body experience without leaving his body, the priest was experiencing one now. He felt entirely at peace. Perhaps this was God's way of easing men into death.

"No!"

The shout broke the moment. Father Bradbury looked across the small island. Dhamballa was striding toward them. He had to have found out about the phone.

Or had something else happened? Something to distract him? His stride was quick, but it did not seem hostile.

"Put your weapon down," the leader commanded. "The priest is coming with us."

The soldier behind Father Bradbury backed away. The priest felt his heart drop from his throat. Blood began to subside from his temples and extremities. He stopped counting what was left of his life in breaths.

Dhamballa stopped beside Father Bradbury. "Why were you doing this?" he demanded.

"We were following instructions," the soldier replied.

"Instructions from whom?" Dhamballa asked.

"Leon Seronga," the soldier told him.

"Seronga?"

"Yes," the soldier said.

"Is he here?" Dhamballa asked.

"No," the soldier replied. "He called on the radio set five minutes ago."

"He had the code word?" Dhamballa asked.

"Yes," the soldier said.

"And he ordered you to execute the prisoner?" Dhamballa went on.

"He told me to do it personally, before we left," the soldier said.

"Did he say why?" Dhamballa asked.

"No, *houngan,*" the man told him.

Even in the dark, the priest could see that Dhamballa was surprised. It was in his stiff posture, the way he stood still and silent for a long moment.

"But you did not think to check with me," Dhamballa said.

"You are our religious leader," the soldier said. "He is our military commander." There was a hint of defiance in his voice.

"You did not question the order?" Dhamballa pressed.

"I asked him to repeat it, that is all," the soldier said.

Dhamballa moved closer to the man. "Do you know what happened today in Maun?"

"Yes, *houngan,*" said the soldier. "Another Catholic holy man was killed."

"He was shot in the back of the head, as you would have done," Dhamballa said. "That changes things for us. When we move into Orapa, we must show the world that we are not murderers. This man must be with us."

"I understand," the soldier replied.

"You will see to it, then?" Dhamballa asked. "You will see that he arrives safely?"

"Yes, *houngan.*"

"If Seronga contacts you again, let me know," Dhamballa added. "We leave within the hour."

Dhamballa left, and the soldiers helped Father Bradbury to his feet.

As they walked toward the shore, the priest found it strange to be back in his body. He felt tired and hot again. Thirst and hunger returned. But whether it was to make him brave or more pious, Father Bradbury knew one thing.

God had showed him the edge of eternity for a reason.

FORTY-SIX

Okavango Swamp, Botswana
Friday, 6:42 P.M.

Dhamballa shut the door of his hut. He was surprised to notice that his forearms were weak, his fingers shaking, as he turned on the lantern. He felt disoriented and alone.

The Vodun leader did not want to believe what the soldier had told him—that Leon Seronga had ordered the killing of the priest. The man Dhamballa knew would not give such a command. Not only was it bloodthirsty, it was against everything the peaceful revolution they had worked to achieve stood for.

Yet, do you really know Seronga? Dhamballa thought ruefully. *He is an officer, and officers yearn for promotions, for power.*

But Dhamballa must not think about that now. It was time to put the material world aside and let the gods speak.

Dhamballa removed a tiny chest from inside his desk. He set it down on the mat, knelt beside it, and raised the lid. Carefully, he removed a white cloth. He set it on the mat and unwrapped it. There were five chicken bones inside the cloth. A source of sustenance and fertility, the chicken was sacred to Vodunists. These were bones that Dhamballa had dried himself when he began studying the art of the *houngan*. He had baked them in the sun and in heated sand, drawing out all the moisture and making them hard, like ivory.

He reached into the chest and removed a pouch. He undid the drawstring and took out a pinch of cornmeal. This powder, known as *ma-veve*, represented a direct connection with the healthy and fertile earth. He spread the powder over the cloth, then steepled three of the bones on top of it. Only the largest of the bones was marked. It bore notches in the surface from top to bottom. Then he palmed two others and gently rolled them between his palms. He closed his eyes. The noise of the breaking camp seemed distant. The rolling of the bones often put the Vodunist in a trancelike state. Dhamballa's own *houngan* mentor had once told him that the man was the real medium. The bones were simply a totem to focus and guide the spirit of the *houngan*. During this brief journey, they did not provide detailed information about the future. Rather, they read currents in the river of human endeavor. They foretold where the currents would lead. The details were for a *houngan* to discover through deed and meditation.

Dhamballa released the bones. While they were still airborne, the gods breathed upon them. The Vodun leader could feel the breath as it rushed past him. The two tossed bones struck the other three.

Dhamballa opened his eyes. He studied the pattern in which the bones fell. They confirmed his fears.

Until tonight, the bones had landed in patterns that suggested peaceful trials for himself and his adversaries. Trials of religious resolve, of philosophy, of endurance. They pointed to the moon or sun to tell whether the ordeals would come during the night or day. They pointed east, west, north, or south to tell him from which direction the challenges were coming.

But something had changed.

The house of bones had fallen with all of the pieces crossing one another. That meant chaos was in the offing for the Vodun leader.

There were two more throws to make. The first toss told him how the future would be if the currents went unchanged. The second toss was a look at whether the events might be changed. If the bones landed exactly as before, then the future was fixed. First, there was something he must do.

Dhamballa picked up the largest of the bones. This was the bone with the hash marks cut in its surface. He tugged a hair from his head and carefully worked the strand through a small slit in the base of the bone. Then he wound the rest of the hair through the other notches cut in the bone. There were slashes representing the eyes, the heart, the stomach, and the loins. Dhamballa fit the free end in a slit on the top of the bone. When the Vodun leader was done, he picked up the rest of the bones and tossed them all again.

The other four bones landed on top of the bone with his hair.

The gods were telling Dhamballa that there was only one way to prevent the chaos. He must take the entire burden upon himself. He must deal with the issues and come up with the solutions.

The Vodun leader scooped the bones into his hand. He gave them a final throw. This last toss would tell Dhamballa whether it was possible to find a solution to the chaos. It would also suggest whether that solution could be peaceful or whether violence was inevitable. He did not bother praying. The gods were there to advise, not listen.

He leaned forward as the bones came to a stop. If none of the bones had touched, then peace was possible. That was not the case. Two of the bones lay by themselves. That meant some participants did not want to confront Dhamballa or each other. Two other bones lay crossed atop the element representing Dhamballa. The gods were telling him that while a peaceful solution was possible, those participants would be against it.

He bent and looked more closely at the cloth. The smallest bone was lying directly across the heart of the Dhamballa bone. That told him something significant.

His gravest enemy was also the unlikeliest one. Until now, he would have thought that was Leon Seronga. But if the prince had not betrayed him, it had to be someone else. Genet was gone and would not be present at the mine. Yet he and his partners stood to lose a great deal if Dhamballa failed. They were going to become Botswana's exclusive diamond merchants on the international market. They would have half of the 500 million dollars the diamonds would generate.

Dhamballa picked up the bone with his hair. He carefully removed the strand and tossed it aside. In its present form, it was an effigy, a crude doll that could impact his own life. If he broke the bone or shut it in darkness, those afflictions would be visited upon him. After shaking the cornmeal from the cloth, Dhamballa rewrapped the bones and placed them back in the chest. In a moment, he would leave the hut to join his soldiers. First, he knelt on the mat and sought to find his center. He could not allow anger or fear to unbalance him.

Dhamballa had not expected events to unfold as they had. But one of the fundamental teachings of Vodunism is that nothing is guaranteed. Even prophecy and magic can fail if the practitioner is careless or distracted.

This is the situation that exists, he thought.

He would not have the time to build a larger following. To get enough attention so that the media would be watching. To present a strong, unified force to the government. To demand that the people of Botswana not be led to the worship of new gods. To insist on the control of industry by Botswanans, not foreigners. He did not even know if the leader of his soldiers had betrayed him.

Nothing is guaranteed, but one thing is certain, Dhamballa told himself. He had to go to the mine. He had to preach as he had planned. There was still a chance that he could rally the loyal. Perhaps he could start a fire that would bring others to their side. With luck, they could draw sufficient numbers to hold off the military in a peaceful way. If they failed, Dhamballa would be assassinated. Even if he were not shot, it was Thomas Burton who would be arrested and tried. His words would be stifled by the leaders, his cause twisted by government attorneys. It would be years before the Vodun movement would have another chance to present its case to the people.

And for Dhamballa, there would be no other chance at all.

FORTY-SEVEN

Washington, D.C.
Friday, 12:00 P.M.

Matt Stoll had once told Paul Hood about the electron factor. It was knowledge that Hood thought he would never use. Like so many things, however, he was wrong.

The science lesson had been given two months ago. The senior staff had taken Hood to dinner for his birthday. It was Ann's idea to have the postmeal celebration at a bar near Ford's Theater. Bob Herbert, Stephen Viens, and Lowell Coffey joined them at a booth in the empty tavern. Stoll went, even though he was not a drinker. He said he liked watching other people drink.

"Why?" Ann asked.

"I like seeing who they become," Stoll said.

"That sounds a little condescending," Ann remarked.

"Not at all," Stoll replied. "It's inevitable. Everyone and everything has two natures."

"You mean you, too?" Herbert asked.

"Sure."

"The old Superman, Clark Kent thing?" Herbert asked.

"There's the timid or the heroic, the benevolent or the bestial, countless yins and yangs," Stoll said.

"Oh yeah?" Herbert remarked. He raised his beer in the direction of the Capitol. "I know some people who are just stinking rotten all the time, thank you very much Senator Barbara Fox, you disloyal, budget-cutting Ms. Hyde."

"She was also a loving mother," Stoll replied.

"I know," Herbert said. "We helped her find out what happened to her daughter. Remember?"

"I remember," Stoll said.

"That's something she seems to have forgotten," Herbert said.

"No. It's the duality that is a fact of life," Stoll insisted. "It's the result of physics."

"Physics?" Hood asked. "Not biology?"

"Everything comes down to physics," Stoll told him. "I call it the 'electron factor.' "

"Is this your own theory?" Herbert asked.

"It's not a theory," Stoll replied.

"No. He said it's a 'fact of life,' " Ann said, grinning and slapping Herbert on the wrist. "Facts are not theoretical."

"Sorry," Herbert replied. "All right, Matthew. Tell us about the electron factor."

"It's simple," Stoll replied. "When an electron is doing its thing, spinning around the nucleus of an atom, we don't know it's there. It's just a cloud of force. But when we stop an electron to examine it, what we're studying is no longer an electron."

"What is it?" Hood asked.

"Basically it's a 'Hyde' electron," Stoll said. "An electron is defined by what it does, not what it looks like or how much it weighs. Remove it from its natural habitat, from its orbit, and it becomes a particle with nothing to do."

Stoll went on to say that everything in nature had that double personality. He said that people could be one thing or another at any given time. Loving or angry, awake or asleep, sober or drunk. But not both. He said he enjoyed watching the change. He wanted to see if there would ever be someone who could be two things at the same time.

"Sure," Herbert said. "How about annoying and boring?"

Stoll pointed out that those were not occurring at once. It was obvious that the scientist was annoying Herbert. Therefore, Herbert was not bored. As for Stoll boring someone else, that was purely speculative. And if he were boring them, then he was not annoying them.

Ann was sorry that she had brought the subject up. She ordered another chocolate martini. Herbert ordered another Bud.

Hood continued to nurse his light beer. He was fascinated.

Hood remembered the conversation now because he *was* that electron. The stationary electron. The one without a purpose.

Hood stood in the small washroom at the back of his office. The door was shut. Physically, he was as isolated as he felt. He rubbed water on the nape of his neck and looked in the mirror on the small medicine cabinet. Incredibly, there was only one decision he had to make at the moment: whether to go to the local greasy spoon or the pizzeria for lunch. And Hood was not even that hungry. It was simply something to do.

Isolated and useless, he thought, *at forty-five years of age.*

Mike Rodgers was running the field operation. Bob Herbert was handling the intelligence gathering and liaising with Edgar Kline. Matt Stoll was on top of the ELINT. Liz Gordon would be refining her profile of Dhamballa and Leon Seronga.

Even the former accountant in Hood was restless. Senator Fox had done all the budget slashing for him. He could probably stay in here the rest of the day, and everything would run just fine. Even Bugs Benet, God bless him, was on top of things. Hood's assistant was dealing with a lot of the operational details, paperwork, and E-mails the director had been handling. Benet even found time to take care of some of the press matters Ann Farris used to handle.

It was not just here Hood felt a sudden disconnect. Right now, his kids would be eating the lunch their mother had prepared. There was a time when Hood knew what was in those sandwiches. Or in the juice boxes. What kind of snack they were having. What brand of chips. Who they would be sitting with at school. Hell, he did not even know what their class schedules were.

Some of that was their age. They were not in elementary school anymore. Some of it was circumstance. Hood was not at the house anymore. If he called each morning to ask what the kids were having for lunch, they would not see it as Dad connecting. They would think it was weird.

Whether or not this was a momentary lull or the shadow of

things to come, Hood had to do something. The leaner Op-Center was still feeling its way. His divided family was still finding its own new personality. Hood had to do the same. If things were quiet here this afternoon, maybe he would drive over to the school and pick up Harleigh and Alexander. Or he could stay and watch Alexander play ball, if that was what he was doing.

Hood was about to splash water on his eyes when the phone on the washroom wall beeped. Maybe Lowell Coffey was bored and thinking about going to lunch.

It was Mike Rodgers.

"Are you free?" Rodgers asked.

"Yes," Hood replied.

"We may have to blow the situation in Botswana to the next level," Rodgers replied. "We're meeting in the Tank in two minutes."

"I'm on my way," Hood said. He hung up the phone, wiped his neck, and tightened the knot of his tie. Then he opened the washroom door.

And, gratefully, Paul Hood began to move again.

FORTY-EIGHT

Maun, Botswana
Friday, 7:00 P.M.

The lights of Maun vanished, swallowed by the dirt kicked up by the truck. The vehicle bounced and rocked as it made its way over the dirt roads outside the city.

The cab of the truck was dark. Maria Corneja was crowded between the driver and Leon Seronga. Pavant sat in the back of the truck. He was armed with a rifle and night-vision goggles.

Soon Leon would contact the base camp. That was when they would reach the fork that took them north to the swamp or west toward the diamond mine. Leon needed to know where Dhamballa wanted to rendezvous. One of the Brush Vipers monitored military and police bands. Seronga was certain the Vodun leader had already heard about the bishop's murder. Seronga also needed to assure Dhamballa that he had nothing to do with that.

As the truck pushed through the dark, Seronga turned to the woman seated beside him.

"Shall I introduce myself?" Seronga asked. "Or do you already know who I am?"

"You are Leon Seronga, commander of the Brush Vipers," the woman answered.

"How do you know all of that?" he asked.

"I cannot tell you," she said.

"You're not being very helpful," Seronga said.

"It's not my job to be helpful," she replied. "All you need to know is that I can help."

"By revealing who killed the bishop," Seronga said.

"I have taken steps to find out who was responsible for the shooting," Maria told him.

"Can you tell me what kind of steps?" Seronga asked.

"I took photographs at the airport," the woman replied. "I've arranged for the pictures to be analyzed. Hopefully, my colleagues will be able to trace the identity of the people involved."

"Colleagues in Spain?" Seronga pressed.

Maria did not answer.

"But you *will* use that information to help us?" Seronga asked.

"I said I would use the information to clear you," Maria replied, "nothing more."

"That will help us," Seronga pointed out.

Maria acted as if she had not heard. "But I will do that only if you give me what I want," she said.

"Which is?" Seronga asked.

"You must release your captive, Father Bradbury," she replied.

"What if that is not possible?" Seronga asked.

"Everything is possible," Maria replied.

"But your cooperation depends upon that?" he asked.

"Absolutely," she answered.

"Unfortunately, I do not have the authority to promise what you say is possible," Seronga informed her.

"Then get it," she said.

"That isn't going to be easy," Seronga said.

"If political upheaval were easy, everyone would do it," Maria replied. "Without my help, your movement will die within days."

"You're certain of that," he said.

"Yes." Maria looked at him. "Whoever ordered the death of the bishop wants that. Assassinating an American prelate is a harsh opening move. I can only imagine what will follow if they do not get their way."

"And you say you have no idea who they are?" Seronga said.

"None," she replied.

"Would you tell me if you did know?" he asked.

"I don't know," she admitted.

Seronga sat back. He gazed out the passenger-side window. A thin coat of pale mud made the moon a featureless blur. That was fitting. Nothing was in clear focus right now. Except the woman. She had the confidence of a cheetah. He turned back to her.

"What do you know about our movement?" Seronga asked.

Maria shrugged. "Not much."

"Then let me tell you," Seronga said.

"Why?" Maria asked.

"You may be swayed by the righteousness of what we are doing," he said. "I was."

"Mr. Seronga, I am from Madrid," Maria said. "I have listened to the arguments of Basque separatists and monarchists from Castile, all of it very passionate and at times persuasive. But when they break the law, I don't care what they have to say. I take them down." She looked at him. "I'm here to secure the release of Father Bradbury. That is my righteous cause. I won't be stopped. If you want my help, that is the price."

"What if cooperating with us is the only way you will survive the night?" Seronga asked. He did not like being ordered around by someone he did not yet respect.

The woman looked ahead. A moment later, she jammed her left foot on top of the driver's foot. The accelerator was crushed to the floor and the truck sped ahead. Njo Finn's shouts filled the cab as he struggled to steer. At the same time, Maria thrust her long thumbnail into the small of Seronga's throat. The nail rested just above the sternum. Seronga tried to push her back, but she used her free arm to brace herself against the driver's shoulder. That action also pinned Njo Finn against the door. The harder Seronga pushed, the more Finn was pinned. Finn could not interfere with her and steer at the same time.

Maria pushed harder on Seronga's throat. He gagged. He could feel her long nail break through his flesh.

The Brush Viper raised his hands. Maria released both men. She raised her foot from the accelerator.

"That was madness!" yelled Finn. "I almost ran into a tree!"

Pavant pounded on the back of the cab. "What happened? Is everything all right?"

"Everything is under control!" Finn shouted back. He looked at Seronga. "Isn't it?"

Seronga nodded.

Finn looked at Maria. She did not answer.

"I'll take that to be a 'yes' from the lady," Finn said.

The three sat in silence. Seronga raised his right hand slowly. He did not want to alarm her by moving quickly. He touched a finger to his throat. There was blood. He lowered his hand to his side.

"Mr. Seronga, a killer for a *familia* in Spain once asked me the same question you did," Maria said. "He posed a threat veiled as a question. Well, I am here. He is with the devil."

The tone of Maria's voice was unchanged from before. This woman was as cool a warrior as Leon Seronga had ever encountered. But Seronga had been a soldier for a long time. He had nothing to prove to her or to himself. He had underestimated her. She had impulsively, foolishly put him on notice. He would not give her that kind of freedom again.

The Brush Viper had slid his right hand into the leather pouch on the door. That was where Njo Finn kept an automatic. Seronga wanted to make certain the weapon was there. It was.

Seronga relaxed and looked ahead. In a few minutes, he would call base camp for instructions.

He believed that this woman might be able to help them. He did not want to jeopardize that or hurt her. But there was too much at risk to let her determine policy.

He had already killed in the name of the faith. He had slain the two deacon missionaries.

If necessary, he would kill again.

FORTY-NINE

Washington, D.C.
Friday, 12:05 P.M.

"Edgar, Paul Hood just arrived," Bob Herbert said.

Herbert was talking into the speakerphone on the desk of the conference room, which was familiarly known as the Tank. The Tank was surrounded by walls of electronic waves that generated static to anyone trying to listen in with bugs or external dishes.

"Good afternoon, Paul," Kline said.

"Hello," Hood said. He strode behind Herbert and stopped there. Mike Rodgers, Darrell McCaskey, and Lowell Coffey were also in attendance. The men looked grave.

There was a thin monitor built into the arm of Herbert's wheelchair. When he was in the Tank, he jacked his computer and phone into a land line. He angled the monitor toward Hood and pointed toward the screen. There was a photograph of a small airplane. Herbert typed on the keyboard, *"Just in from Maun. Assassin's getaway plane. Tracing number now."*

Hood patted Herbert's shoulder.

"Paul, I was just telling Mike and the others that the Vatican wants to move against the people who are holding Father Bradbury," Kline said. "We are under a lot of pressure to take action."

"Your office or the Vatican?" Hood asked.

"My office," Kline replied. "Officially, the Vatican is calling for patience and a peaceful resolution to the crisis. Unofficially, they want the assassins caught, Father Bradbury released or rescued as quickly possible, and his captors apprehended and tried."

"I can understand why," Hood said.

"We found the driver who took the two 'deacons' to Maun," Kline said. "His description pretty much confirmed what we suspected. They were not affiliated with Father Bradbury's church. We are looking into the whereabouts of all the deacons who serve or have served in Botswana, though we are relatively certain these men will not be among them. It looks like your agent may have been right. They could very well be Brush Viper imposters."

"Could they have stolen vestments from one of the church residences?" Hood asked.

"Easily," Kline replied. "We may have more information soon, however. The driver did tell us where he dropped them. The entire Spanish unit is converging on the area. The driver also put us in touch with the man who brought your agent to Maun. He won't tell us anything."

"Maybe he doesn't know anything," Hood pointed out.

"I don't believe that," Kline said frankly. "He won't even tell us where he dropped your agent. Surely he knows that."

"I can't answer for what he does or doesn't know," Hood said. "Maybe he doesn't want to be involved in this. He could be afraid." That would not surprise Hood. Either Maria had terrified the driver or charmed him. Either way, he would not be talking.

"Paul, I gave you access to that church to use as a data drop," Kline said. "I have told you what we know. As I was just telling Mr. Herbert, I thought we were cooperating on this."

"Mister?" Herbert muttered. He scrunched his face.

"Edgar, we *are* cooperating," Hood said.

"Then I'll ask you the same thing the other members of your staff refused to answer, Paul," Kline said. "Where is your agent now? Is she still in Maun, or has she followed the two Brush Vipers?"

Hood looked at Rodgers.

"Edgar, this is Mike," Rodgers said. "As I told you a minute ago, we don't know where Maria is. She has not contacted us."

"You have an agent in the field, closest to the scene, and

she has not called in to let you know where she is?" Kline said.

"I have to assume she's been very busy," Rodgers said.

"Either that, or she's not in a position to talk to us," Herbert said. "She could be hiding in a goddamn closet somewhere, eavesdropping."

"Edgar, what reason would we have to withhold information from you?" Hood asked.

No one said anything for a moment. Hood could think of many reasons. No doubt Kline could as well. But this was not the time to go into them. Which was why Hood had asked the question.

"You've got other agents en route," Kline said. "How are they going to rendezvous with her?"

"We're hoping she *will* contact us so we can relay the information to them," Rodgers said.

"Well, while you're waiting for that, we're going to find the Brush Vipers," Kline said.

"I wish you luck, Edgar," Hood said. "I sincerely do."

"We're going to find them and do whatever it takes to stop them from terrorizing our missionaries. What I don't want is for your people—*more* of your people, General Rodgers—to be caught in the crossfire in a foreign land."

That last dagger was a reference to the loss of Striker in Kashmir. The general took the hit impassively. Hood did not.

"If you want our cooperation, Edgar, you'll address my people with a little more tact," Hood said.

"What I will do, Paul, what I am *concentrating* on doing, is bringing down the people who are attacking my Church," Kline said. "If anyone gets in our way, I'm sorry if they get clipped with a little tactlessness. They'll recover."

"What about Father Bradbury being caught in the crossfire?" Herbert asked. "How much does that matter?"

"I'm not even going to answer that," Kline said.

"No, you wouldn't," Rodgers said. "Because you and I both know how the *Grupo del Cuartel General* and their *Unidad Especial del Despliegue* work."

"Explain," Hood said.

"Paul, those soldiers hit hard," Rodgers said. "And they protect their own. They would sooner take out everyone in the line of fire than suffer any casualties. If you pursue your publicly stated policy of patience and peace, our people might be able to get Father Bradbury out safely."

"And the Brush Vipers?" Kline asked. "How do we keep them from attacking us again?"

"That's the responsibility of the government of Botswana," Hood said. "The United States government will push for intervention over the death of the bishop. There's no need for a skirmish."

"Unfortunately, that call will be made by Rome, not me," Kline said. "And they feel they have to respond in order to protect missionaries in other lands. My job is to get them any assistance I can. What I need to know is whether you will provide assistance."

Hood looked at the others. He did not see a consensus in their eyes. He punched the mute button on the phone.

"Do we need to talk about this?" Hood asked.

"Yeah," Herbert said. "We do."

"Do we have Edgar's number?" Hood asked.

Herbert nodded.

Hood deactivated the mute. "Edgar, we'll call you back in ten minutes," Hood said.

"I'll be waiting," Kline said and hung up.

Hood moved from behind Herbert. He leaned on the table. "All right. First, where is Maria?" he asked.

"She's heading north, off-road, to points unknown," Herbert said. "Her driver, Paris Lebbard, saw where Maria went."

"Is he following them?" Hood asked.

"No," Herbert replied. "But Lebbard saw the off-road direction they took. That was all we needed. We had Viens look for them with the GOSEE-9."

The GOSEE-9 was the Geosynchronous Observation Satellite and Electromagnetic Eavesdropping platform. The bus-sized satellite was positioned over southern Africa. It had wide bandwidth audio eavesdropping capabilities. Maria, Aideen, and Battat had each been given an OLB, an orbiter locator beacon. It was a device that looked like a pen and never caused a problem at customs. The OLB sent out a high-frequency pulse every thirty seconds. The GOSEE-9's onboard computer placed the pulse on a map and sent the exact location to a corresponding map in the NRO's computer.

"What was Maria's last reported position?" Hood asked.

"She was about four miles north of where Lebbard had reported seeing them," Herbert said. "We left that information on voice mail for Aideen and David. They rented a car in Gaborone. Their cell phone can't reach Op-Center."

"Hell of a roaming charge if they could," Coffey said.

"The towers in Botswana are too remote for a direct call," Herbert said. "However, they were able to call the satellite line at the United States embassy in Gaborone. The communications officer there is going to pipe them into a U.S. trunk line so they can collect their messages."

"Why can't they just call Mike directly?" Coffey asked.

"They can," Rodgers said. "But they may be in a place where they're free to listen but not talk. Or maybe they don't want their voices picked up and recorded by electronic eavesdropping."

"Any call longer than two minutes is relatively easy to pinpoint through triangulation," Herbert explained.

Coffey nodded with understanding.

"According to the OLB signal tracked at the NRO, Aideen and Battat turned west before they reached Maun," Herbert went on. "They appear to be on an intercept course."

"So there's a chance they can actually reach Dhamballa and get to Father Bradbury," Hood said.

"Well, without knowing how and where the priest is being kept, that's difficult to say," Rodgers answered. "In theory, yes. That's why we want to give her a shot before the Spanish army goes rolling in."

"But a clean rescue like that doesn't satisfy the Vatican's needs," Hood observed.

"No. They got into this to crush a rebellion," Rodgers said. "We got in to save a priest and help an ally."

"Still, we may end up with a war," Herbert said. He tapped

the photograph of the airplane. "We still don't know who shot Bishop Max or why."

"Put aside the ethics of this for the moment," Hood said. "Does preventing the removal of the Brush Vipers and Dhamballa from Botswana hasten or delay a war? Does it buy us time?"

"You mean, if there's a third party involved?" Herbert asked.

"Right," Hood said.

"I would say it slows things down," Herbert said. "Whoever killed Bishop Max obviously wanted Dhamballa to take the fall for the murder and get crushed for it," Herbert said.

"So an attack by the Spanish soldiers against the Brush Vipers helps whoever killed the bishop," Hood said.

"This is all very speculative, but yes," Herbert said. "For all we know, the Spanish could have done it. Or the assassins could have been sent by Gaborone. Maybe they were looking for a reason to shut down Dhamballa."

"Excuse me, but aren't we obligated to support the legal government?" Coffey asked.

"Is a government that murders an innocent American citizen lawful?" Rodgers asked.

"That's assuming Botswana had a part in his death," Hood said.

"I said *legal* not *lawful,*" Coffey pointed out. "We all know that legal governments sometimes do unlawful things."

"I'm shocked," Herbert said.

"Look, that's not a minefield I want to cross if we don't have to," Hood said. "Right now, I want to focus on our people."

"Hear, hear," McCaskey said.

"Do we let them go ahead on their own, do we abort this thing, or do we allow them to lead the Spanish soldiers to the target?" Hood asked.

"If the Spanish are killing Botswana citizens, we don't want to be a part of that," Coffey said.

"Why not?" Herbert asked. "The president might view that as a viable coalition."

"Spain and the U.S. ganging up on Botswana?" Rodgers said.

"No," Herbert replied. "Two nations surgically striking against the rebels, who are holding a Catholic priest as a hostage. Botswana will thank us for not having to move against their own people."

"I'm not so sure of that," Rodgers said. "None of us has been given permission by the 'lawful' government to stage any action."

"We'll get that authority after the fact, assuming it all works out," Herbert said. "They'll be happy to give it to us."

"Mike, I'm inclined to agree with Bob, but not for the reasons stated," Hood said. He was looking at the photograph. "A third party, as yet unknown, killed Bishop Max. Maybe Spain, maybe Gaborone, but maybe someone else. The *someone else* is the one that scares me. Especially with Beaudin on the perimeter. It would suggest that there is something larger going on. The sooner the Brush Vipers and the Vatican are removed from the equation, the sooner we can find out who is behind the killing."

"You're assuming the Brush Vipers *can* be removed from the equation," Rodgers said.

"They haven't fought for years," Herbert said.

"True. But there are dozens, possibly hundreds of them," Rodgers said. "And they will be fighting on terrain they know well."

"Yes, but we have an advantage they do not," Herbert said.

"Which is?" Rodgers asked.

"We have someone on the inside," Herbert said. "Someone of whom they are unaware."

"Someone who isn't going to be risking her life to stop what smells like a revolution we have no business in," McCaskey said.

"Darrell, she has no instructions to intervene," Hood said. "We'll monitor this closely, I promise."

McCaskey's arms were folded tightly across his chest. He leaned back in the chair and was rocking. Hood considered ordering him home. He would see how things developed.

"You know, I'm missing something here," Coffey said. "How does having Maria on site help us? We can't contact her directly."

"Aideen and Battat will be able to do that," Herbert said. "And we'll make sure they are fully briefed via voice mail. They'll check for instructions and fresh intel before they do anything."

"Gotcha," Coffey said.

"We'll let them know the Spaniards are going to move in," Rodgers said. "Their job will be to get to Father Bradbury, if possible. Get him out if they can. That accomplishes our original goal, and it gives us the moral high ground."

"In other words, our people get in and out before the shooting starts," Coffey clarified.

"Either that or they lay very, very low," Herbert said.

Rodgers's hands were folded on the conference table. He was staring at them intently. "I do want to make this observation," he said. "This started as an intelligence-gathering operation. It now has a potential political objective with a military component. The military end will be undertaken by soldiers who will not have the time nor inclination to check passports before they open fire. The people we have sent are not qualified to participate in that kind of operation. I don't want them involved in any way."

"Maria speaks Spanish, doesn't she?" Coffey asked.

"Yes," McCaskey said. "But Mike is right. They should not be interfacing with the Spanish soldiers."

"I didn't mean to suggest that," Coffey said. "Only if it comes down to that, she can communicate with them."

"Yes," Rodgers said. "Communicate. Not collaborate." He looked at Hood. "Are we on the same page about that?"

"Unless I'm mistaken, it's your call," Hood said.

Herbert made a face. "I have a couple cents to put in, too, Mike. Darrell's not going to like this, but safety aside, they are our only resource in the region."

"For intelligence," McCaskey reminded him.

"Yes, but only if we exclude the one objective we have not discussed," Herbert said.

"Which is?" Hood asked.

"Whether our people can prevent bloodshed," Herbert said. "We aren't just there for the greater glory of Op-Center. I believe that part of our mission is to try to save lives."

"Starting with the lives of our team," McCaskey said. "You heard Kline. He wants them to lead his soldiers to Dhamballa."

"That doesn't necessarily mean 'For a bloodbath,' " Herbert said. "Our people can be a moderating force. And for that matter, the Spanish soldiers can help to protect them."

"Like they protected the bishop?" McCaskey asked.

Hood held up his hands. "People, these are all good points. But I'm thinking that maybe we can do both."

"Do both what?" McCaskey asked.

"Keep the peace and free Father Bradbury," Hood said.

"How?" McCaskey asked.

"Aideen and David will be intercepting Maria before long," Hood said. "Suppose they tell her and Seronga what is coming. If they can persuade him that the cause is in serious jeopardy, they may convince him to split up. One or two of our people go with Seronga to free the priest. The other one or two lead the Spanish soldiers off-trail. Meanwhile, we work with Kline to convince Gaborone that the Brush Vipers were not responsible for the killing of Bishop Max."

The Tank was silent for a moment.

"Not bad," Herbert said.

"What if Seronga is not as reasonable as you think?" Rodgers asked. "He's a soldier. If he decides to fight, we could be leading the Spanish soldiers and our own people into an ambush."

"Seronga cannot want that kind of a showdown," Hood said. "Especially if Maria can convince him that we're on the trail of whoever it was that really did kill Bishop Max."

"It's not risk-free, but it's solid," Herbert said as his wheelchair phone beeped. "I like that better than cutting bait and running." He picked up the phone and wheeled himself from the table.

Hood turned to Rodgers. "Mike?"

Rodgers thought for a moment. "There are still a lot of variables," he said.

"When are there not?" Hood asked.

"True, but the biggest is what three men will do—Seronga, Dhamballa, and Beaudin, if he has any influence in this. Religious zealots are not known for rational behavior. Even when it comes to survival. And industrialists are not known to give up plans for mega-expansion, if that's what he has in mind."

"Nothing's guaranteed," Hood agreed.

"And of course, it's not *our* asses on the line out there," Coffey added.

"No, but we're going to get them through this," Hood said as Herbert wheeled back over. "Bob, you want to get Kline back on the phone?"

"In a minute," Herbert said. He tapped the photo of the airplane. "That was my guy at Air Force Intelligence. He tracked the identification number on the airplane and located the registration."

"And?" Hood asked.

"It was rented from a local company named *SafAiris*," Herbert said. "The plane landed in a field and was abandoned."

"Who rented it?" Rodgers asked.

"The name they gave was Don Mahoney of Gaborone," Herbert said. "I'm willing to bet there's no such person."

"Fingerprints?" Rodgers asked.

"If there are, we may not be able to get to them before the plane is impounded by the Botswana military," Herbert said. "Police in the region have already spotted the aircraft. Anyway, it probably wouldn't tell us much. People this thorough don't forget to wear gloves."

Hood knew the intelligence chief well. There was something else on Herbert's mind. "Out with it, Bob," Hood said. "What's the rest of it?"

"The rest is a real kick in the head," Herbert said. "Air Force Intelligence Signal Surveillance picked up a transmission from those same coordinates at four-thirty-one P.M. Botswana time."

"Why were they listening to that area?" Rodgers asked.

"They weren't. They picked something up because they've

been monitoring our outgoing calls," Herbert said.

"Come again?" Coffey said.

"It seems that since the showdown in Kashmir, the AFISS has been keeping track of *our* foreign communications," Herbert said.

"What are they doing?" Coffey asked. "Making sure that we behave ourselves?"

"On the books, they probably want to make sure we don't field any military missions that might backfire," Herbert said. "Trigger something that could involve more U.S. forces."

"We haven't done that so far," Coffey said.

"That's a bullshit reason," Rodgers said. "The Air Force is doing this because they don't want us showing them up."

"That would be the off-the-books reason," Herbert agreed. "Look—the fact that our own people are spying on us is not what surprised me. It was the nature of the signal they received."

"What about it?" Hood pressed.

"The AFISS routinely monitors radio transmissions that are sent to major intelligence agencies around the world," Herbert said. "Even if they can't decipher the code, they keep track of activity. Not just content but volume and frequency are also important."

"Like a surge in credit card activity sending up flags," Coffey said.

"Bingo," Herbert replied. "That's how we knew when the Russians were going to move into Chechnya. Increased communication. The radio transmission from the landing area in Botswana was noticed by the AFISS computer because it matched a foreign office we've been calling."

"Which one?" Hood asked.

Herbert replied, "Shigeo Fujima at the IAB."

FIFTY

The Trans-Kalahari Highway, Botswana
Friday, 8:07 P.M.

Battat was at the wheel as he and Aideen left Gaborone in their rented Jeep Wrangler Sahara. They got on to the Trans-Kalahari Highway. Almost at once they were struck by the scope of the countryside. Battat had been across Texas and had taken the Trans-Siberian railroad. When he was a teenager, he had crossed the ocean working on a yacht for some international oil tycoon. But he had never seen expanses as level and featureless as these. On both sides there was nothing but scrub, rock, and tawny earth to the horizon. Occasionally, the setting sun would catch a snow-topped mountain. But the peaks were so remote they were quickly hidden by the dusty winds that blew across the veldt.

As the Americans began their drive toward Maun, Aideen called the embassy at Gaborone to access the voice mailbox at Op-Center. Battat was surprised to hear that they had received new instructions. They were no longer going to be linking up with Maria Corneja in Maun.

"Is something wrong?" Battat asked.

"Maria managed to sneak off with Leon Seronga," Aideen said. "They believe he's taking her to Dhamballa's camp."

"Damn, that woman gets around," Battat said.

"There's more," Aideen told him. "Undercover Spanish troops are searching for Seronga and Dhamballa. Op-Center is inclined to assist them."

"What about assisting Maria instead?" Battat said. "We have an agent on site who may be in a position to defuse the situation."

"That's international politics for you," Aideen said. "I suspect we're helping the Vatican, not Spain. The United States needs to maintain good relations with Rome and, through them, help keep peace in Africa. We don't want another Somalia."

"Whoever we're helping, Maria is with Seronga. That puts her in the line of fire," Battat said.

"Maybe not," Aideen went on. "Hood wants the Spanish soldiers delayed. That's why we have to get to Maria first. We'll split up, one party going with Seronga, the other taking the Spanish along a different route. Whoever goes to the Vodun encampment is to try to get Father Bradbury away. That has to happen before the Spaniards arrive to take him by force. Ideally, we would also convince the Brush Vipers to lay low."

"Cornered and desperate men do not always do what you want," Battat remarked.

"But there's a chance they might," Aideen said.

"Yeah, and there's a chance an elephant stampede will save us the way it used to save Tarzan," Battat said.

"They might do it if Seronga or Dhamballa do not see another way out," Aideen said.

"Do we know exactly where Maria is?" Battat asked.

"Op-Center is going to send her coordinates through the embassy to my laptop in a few minutes," Aideen said.

"God bless wireless," Battat said.

"They're going to take a little longer getting that same data to the Vatican Security Office," Aideen added.

"Did Rodgers give any indication which of us is supposed to lead the Spaniards off course?" Battat asked.

"No," she replied. "I suppose Maria has to be part of the group that goes with the Spanish soldiers. Her countrymen may be more willing to follow her."

"Why?" Battat asked. "Because she's Spanish?"

"No," Aideen replied. "Because she's a great-looking woman."

"God bless the male libido, too," Battat remarked, shaking his head slowly. "And did the Op-Center brain trust tell you where we're supposed to lead the Spanish army?"

"General Rodgers said the field operation is under my direction," Aideen told him. "He wants to try to give the other team, the one that sticks with Seronga, a minimum of two hours to work with Dhamballa."

"That's just great," Battat said.

"What is?" Aideen asked.

"Never mind," Battat said.

"You don't like the plan?" Aideen pressed.

"No, it's fine," he lied. He did not want to get into it. Complaining wouldn't change anything.

"If you want, we can call Rodgers through the embassy," she suggested. "I'll ask him to clarify things."

"No," Battat replied. "He'll just tell us to use our initiative. And he'd be right."

"General Rodgers said he would feed Maria's locater beacon into the computer beginning at half past eight," Aideen went on. "That way we can be sure to intercept Maria. The general said the map coordinates would be refreshed every three minutes."

Battat glanced at the car clock. The download was just over fifteen minutes away.

"General Rodgers also said Op-Center was instituting an SSB," Aideen continued. "I did not see that term in any of my files. Do you have any idea what it stands for?"

"It's a simulated systems breakdown," Battat told her. "American intelligence agencies share locater beacon technology with several international intelligence services, including Interpol. Interpol has a Spanish division. Rodgers obviously does not want the information being accessed by Spain or the Vatican Security Office prematurely. He needs at least a half hour to purge the download system of cooperative links. The beauty of SSB software is that it allows them to lock out our allies without making it look as if it's intentional. There will be static, wireless disconnects, software crashes, a whole menu of impediments. It spares hurt feelings and mistrust in future dealings."

"I see," Aideen said. "That should give you some idea of

how many different issues they're dealing with over there."

"While we, luckily, have just one problem," Battat said.

"Father Bradbury," she said.

"Sorry, that's two problems," Battat said. "Father Bradbury is number two. Number one is getting out of Botswana alive. This was supposed to be simple recon, not search and rescue and deceive elite Spanish soldiers."

Aideen frowned. "I'm not going to worry about that," she said. "We've read the material, we've studied the maps. We're prepared."

"Are we?" Battat asked.

"As prepared as we can be," she replied.

"Exactly. There's always the stuff you can't plan for," Battat said. "I've had some experience with that. A couple of months ago, I was hunting for one of the world's most elusive terrorists."

"The Harpooner," Aideen said.

"That's the SOB," Battat said. "I wanted to be the one to bring him down. I needed to redeem myself. I collected data, zeroed in on where the bastard had to be, searched the region yard by yard, and waited. The bastard was literally one hundred and eighty degrees from where I thought he'd be. He coldcocked me. He would have killed me except that he needed me alive. We're improvising on a stage where there's no room to screw up."

"We won't."

"How can you be sure?" Battat asked. "Tell me something. If this car had been a stick shift, could you have driven it?"

"What does that have to do with anything?" Aideen asked.

"Just answer me," he said.

"No," she replied. "Could you have driven it?"

"Yes," he replied.

"So where's the problem?" she asked.

"My point is, at any given moment, we are going to face those kinds of unknowns even *with* a plan," Battat said. "Without a game plan or a playbook, the risks are extreme."

"Then we have to be that much more alert," Aideen said. "We have knowledge, and we have skills. That's why General

Rodgers put the two of us together. We obviously make a good team."

"Aideen, we were the only ones who showed up in time to be shipped here," Battat reminded her.

"It wasn't just that," the woman replied.

"Oh?"

"Mike Rodgers would not have sent us if he didn't think we could pull this off," Aideen said.

"Mike is a general, and generals have to field armies, or they have nothing to do," Battat said.

"He's not like that," she insisted. "Besides, I think you're looking at this all wrong. We have options. We have the right to exercise our own judgment."

"Do we? If I wanted to turn around and go back to Gaborone, is that what we would do?" Battat asked.

"You would," she said.

"And what would you do?" he asked.

"I would stay here," she said. "I'd walk."

"You'd be dead before morning," Battat said. "This is Africa. There are predators that don't check passports."

"I would take my chances," she said. "Don't you get it?"

"Obviously not," Battat replied.

"Most people would kill for the kind of freedom we've been given out here," Aideen said.

"Speaking of which, we may have to do that, too," Battat said.

"Do what?" Aideen asked.

"Kill people," Battat told her. "Are you prepared to take a human life? Will you push a knife into a person's back if you have to, or crack their head open with a rock?"

"I faced that question in Spain," she replied.

"And?"

"If it's my life or someone else's, they're dead," Aideen said.

"What if it's *my* life or someone else's?" he asked.

"We're a team," Aideen replied. "They're dead."

Battat smiled. "I'm glad to hear *that,* anyway."

"Don't doubt my resolve," Aideen said sternly. "I'm here. I'll do whatever the job requires."

"Fair enough," he said. "What about Maria Corneja? Is she as tough as everyone's been saying?"

"The first person I worked for at Op-Center was Martha Mackall," Aideen said. "Martha was a tough, tough lady. No bullshit. She was confident and strong as steel."

"She was the one who was killed in Madrid?" Battat asked.

"Yes, a drive-by shooting, totally unexpected," Aideen said. "Interpol became involved, and Maria was assigned to the case. I was asked to tag along and help her find the assassins. If Martha was steel, Maria is iron. Not quite as polished, but I never saw her break. I can't even imagine that happening."

"That means she'll want to make all the decisions when we hook up," Battat said.

"She'll want to, but she'll follow the orders Op-Center sends over," Aideen said. "Including who is in command."

"*Orders,*" Battat said. He shook his head. "I'm sure this whole thing would look real solid in the computer simulations. Or at least plausible. We have state-of-the-art intel simulation in Washington. There are respectable agents working in the field. And there's a relatively modest target. Hell, it sounds almost easy. But there's always the unknown. I was lucky in Azerbaijan. Here, they could dump your body, and you'd be a meal not a crime scene."

"As if that matters," Aideen said.

Battat snickered. "I suppose you're right." He shook his head. "You asked me why I was complaining a minute ago. I'll tell you. We don't really have freedom. What we have is a blueprint for scapegoating. What 'freedom' really means here is, 'If you screw up, it's your ass.' "

"Op-Center doesn't work like that," Aideen said.

"What makes you so certain?" Battat asked. "You weren't with them very long."

"Like I said a moment ago, I was there long enough to know that Paul Hood, Mike Rodgers, and the rest of them are not run-of-the-mill bureaucrats," Aideen told him.

"If you say so," Battat said dubiously.

"If they were, I wouldn't be here," she said. "I was happy working as a political consultant. And I was safe. No one was shooting at me." She paused. "Not with bullets, anyway."

The woman's voice sounded wistful when she said that. Battat smiled. Finally, they appeared to have something in common.

"You got a lot of sniping in the Washington press?" Battat asked.

"Not just me but my causes," Aideen said. "That hurts even more. They were my babies."

"Unfashionably liberal causes, I'm guessing?" Battat asked.

"Let's just say *inconvenient,*" Aideen replied. "Women's rights abroad, mostly."

"Forgive me, but that doesn't quite jibe with using Maria as Mata Hari," Battat observed.

"The question is not using sex appeal as a tool," Aideen said. "The issue is having the option to do so."

"It still sounds like a contradiction," he said. "You want to hear something ironic?"

"Sure."

"I got hit by the press because I gave a woman too much freedom," Battat told her.

"Annabelle Hampton?" Aideen asked.

"That's the gal who was spying for terrorists," Battat said. "There were Op-ED pieces suggesting that 'her superiors' be investigated for treason. There were slurs in the conservative press. Always blind items, but everyone knew who they meant. Especially after they found out I was in Moscow at the time."

"Yet you had the will to come back from that," Aideen said. "Pretty impressive."

"Either the will or the fear," Battat said. "I didn't want to leave government service with that on my record."

"I think it was character," Aideen said. "I learned something back in college. I had a twelve-to-two A.M. radio talk show. It was called *The Late Aideen.* Ironically, I got at least two death threats a week. What I realized was that you have to do your job regardless of what people think, say, or do. It's either that or do something safe, boring. I never want to do that."

"Well, it won't be boring here," Battat said. "The Spanish and the Brush Vipers won't be using innuendo and mud. They'll be using 9 mm clips."

"My attitude will be the same," she said.

Battat hoped so. When he was being fired on in Baku, he felt a lot different than he did when he was spying on the UN from a CIA office in New York. The knowledge that being discovered will cause you to be reassigned is different from knowing that a mistake could be fatal. Some people flourish under fire. Battat did. Others wither. Aideen said she had faced armed enemies before. Obviously, she had held up all right. Otherwise, Mike Rodgers would not have sent her back into the field.

The two sat quietly until eight-thirty. Consulting the computer map, Aideen switched on the decode program.

"It's downloading," she announced.

It took less than a minute for the data to be received from Op-Center. Aideen quickly calculated their new route. It was off-road. Not the kind of journey either of them wanted to take at night. But no mission had ever been designed for the comfort of the operative.

The Trans-Kalahari Highway took Battat and his partner to the Meratswe River. The wide, seasonally low river was located on the outskirts of the Central Kalahari Game Reserve. There, the Wrangler left the modern turnpike for the off-road trails. If they had a chance of intercepting the truck with Maria and the Brush Vipers, they would have to cut through the barren salt pan. A dirt road marked the way. It was difficult to say whether the trail had been pounded out by buses or years of migrating animal herds. Possibly both.

The soft top of the vehicle was down. The only sounds were the well-tuned I-6 engine, the air rushing by, and an occasional loud bounce when the Wrangler hit a shallow ditch. Fortunately, the vehicle's sophisticated suspension minimized the jolt to the lower spine.

Crossing the plain was not like driving in New York City. Or Moscow. Or even Baku, Azerbaijan. Driving here reminded Battat of sailing. For one thing, darkness came very quickly in the flat pan. Or maybe it only seemed that way because so much flat terrain became black all at once. For another, there was a sense of freedom. He could continue north on the path marked with signs. Or he could venture to the east or west. The grass was low enough to go off-road. But there was also a clear and ever-present danger.

The blackness.

Outside the cone of the Wrangler's headlights, the sky was actually brighter than the ground. It also seemed closer, in a way. That was because the Milky Way was clearly visible as it arced across the sky. Battat did not even have to avert his eyes to see it clearly. The other stars were even brighter as were the occasional shooting stars. Whenever Aideen saw a shooting star, she wished for more light. They did not get it. As a result, Battat did not dare to proceed at more than thirty to forty miles an hour. There was no telling when they would run into a ditch, a flat boulder, or a yellow ANIMAL CROSSING sign. These were scattered throughout the region, bearing the silhoutte of a trumpeting elephant, a rhinoceros, or a lion. Wild animals were something they had to watch out for. Most of the larger predators were on game preserves. But there were still rogues, strays, and packs of wild dogs, hyenas, and other nocturnal hunters.

On the other hand, because it was so dark and because the plain was so utterly flat and featureless, Battat did not imagine they would have much trouble spotting another vehicle.

There was still one thing that troubled David Battat. He worried about it more than the ditches and the boulders, more than getting lost in the darkness. The former CIA agent worried whether the Brush Viper truck would be in a position to spot them first.

And what Seronga would do if he did.

FIFTY-ONE

Washington, D.C.
Friday, 1:08 P.M.

Darrell McCaskey stepped into Mike Rodgers's office unannounced and unexpected. McCaskey wanted information. In
retrospect, he realized he wanted something else. A fight.

He got it.

The FBI liaison was angrier than he had been the day before. He had not slept very much that night. The more he had
thought about what happened, the more his rage had built. The
people close to him had done what was expedient. They did
not do what was right. He was furious at Rodgers for asking
Maria to go abroad. He was mad at Maria for having accepted.
And he was disgusted with Paul Hood for having allowed her
to go. McCaskey and Maria had just gotten married. She had
given up intelligence work. *What the hell were they all thinking?* At what point did the human factor enter into decision
making? Where was loyalty to old friends, concern for their
well-being?

McCaskey had come to Rodgers's office unannounced
because he wanted to see the general's face. Rodgers was not
a man who admitted concern. Not to his coworkers, not even
to his friends. McCaskey had heard that the only one Rodgers
confided in was his childhood friend and fellow officer Colonel
Brett August. But Rodgers was also not a man who could
disguise what he was feeling. It was always there in his eyes,
in the turn of his mouth. McCaskey did not want to see any
of that hidden for his benefit.

Rodgers was sitting at his computer. He glanced over as the
FBI liaison walked in. Years with the FBI had taught Mc-
Caskey to size up a person in an instant. To read expressions,

posture, perspiration levels. The concern in Rodgers's face was considerable.

"What's the latest?" McCaskey asked.

"I was just reading the confirmation from Matt Stoll," Rodgers replied. His expression became neutral. Mike Rodgers was back in control. "The download for the OLB has been received in Botswana. Aideen and Battat are en route to meet your wife."

"When do they expect to link up?" McCaskey asked.

"I estimate that should happen in about two hours," Rodgers told him. "What have you been up to?"

"Paul showed me the photo Maria took at the airport. He also gave me the AFISS phone data," McCaskey told him. "I'm looking into the possible involvement of Shigeo Fujima. Paul wants me to find out what the IAB could possibly gain by killing the American bishop. Or at least by implicating Dhamballa in the assassination."

"And?"

"Nothing yet," McCaskey told him. "The Japanese have zero interest in Africa in general and Botswana in particular. They certainly don't gain anything by moving in on the diamond industry. The income would be a blip on Japan's gross national product. My people are looking into other possibilities involving Beaudin and Genet. We'll see what turns up."

"Could the Japanese have made the hit for some other party?" Rodgers asked. "Someone we haven't considered?"

"That's one of the possibilities I've been checking," McCaskey said. "It would help if we knew whether the assassination was aimed at the Vatican, at this bishop in particular, or at Botswana."

"It's easier when you've got nations fighting over borders or commerce or thousands of years of enmity," Rodgers said. "We don't know what the core issue is here. But I don't think it's religion."

"So what happens next?" McCaskey asked.

"In Botswana?" Rodgers asked.

McCaskey nodded.

"In about ten minutes, Paul is going to send Edgar Kline

the same coordinates Matt gave Aideen," Rodgers said. "A few minutes after that, the Spanish soldiers will begin heading toward the spot as well."

"Have you heard anything from over there?" McCaskey asked.

"Aideen?"

McCaskey nodded.

"Nothing."

"Have you given them any additional instructions?" McCaskey pressed.

"No," Rodgers said.

McCaskey gave Rodgers a moment to add to that. He did not, damn that stubborn son of a bitch. Rodgers knew what McCaskey wanted to hear. That Maria could withdraw at that point.

"Do the Spaniards know that my wife is with this Leon Seronga character?" McCaskey said.

"Kline has been told," Rodgers assured him. "He will pass that information along. It's to the advantage of the Vatican Security Office to have a Spanish-speaking ally on site. Especially one who has been trailing Seronga."

"Look, Mike, there's something I've been wanting to ask you," McCaskey said.

"Shoot."

"I assume Maria will make the call whether to terminate, not the greenhorns?" McCaskey asked. The FBI liaison was getting angry again. He could feel it in his shoulders, in his arms and fingers, along the line of his jaw. He wanted to move, to strike out.

"Aideen decides for the team, but Maria can decide for herself," Rodgers replied. "And Darrell—I need you to do something for me. I need you to back off David and Aideen."

"Why?" McCaskey said. "Last time I looked, I was still drawing pay from Op-Center. I've got a voice here."

"You do," Rodgers said. "But it's an emotional one, and that doesn't help us. Battat and Aideen are good people."

"They're green," McCaskey insisted.

"Darrell—"

"I've read their dossiers," McCaskey went on. "They haven't logged enough solo field hours to qualify for a CIA junior recon post."

"Battat has," Rodgers said.

"Right," McCaskey said. "The guy the Harpooner clocked in the field."

Rodgers did not look happy. McCaskey did not care.

"Aideen Marley spent a few days in the field with Maria," McCaskey went on. "A few *days*. That was less than ninety-six hours in a support capacity. And yeah. Technically, Battat has put in the time. If you count his entire career, which has a big midsection where he sat in an office in New York City. Over the last five years, he spent even less time in the field than Aideen, a total of three days. That was also in a support capacity."

"They distinguished themselves in both cases," Rodgers said.

"How do you figure that? Maria did most of the work in Spain, and Battat barely survived in Baku," McCaskey said.

"Battat's opponent did *not* survive," Rodgers said pointedly. "That's a win in my book. And Aideen proved she's a quick study. Maria personally commended her work in Europe."

"Then why does having them out there with my wife fill me with very little confidence?" McCaskey asked.

"I'm not going to answer that," Rodgers said.

"I will," McCaskey said. "Because I know Maria. If you let her stay with this mission, she's going to watch *their* asses, not her own!"

"I don't agree, but we won't get anywhere debating any of this," Rodgers said. He rose. "Darrell, you've been looking for a fight on this ever since it started. I'm not going to give you one. Now, I've got to go see Paul—"

"Mike, I need you to do me a favor," McCaskey said.

"Darrell, I won't order her back," Rodgers said.

"You have to," McCaskey said. "Maria's carried this far enough. I want you to get her out."

"I can't," Rodgers said emphatically.

"Why?" McCaskey shot back. He leaned on the desk.

"Mike, you don't need my wife over there. You can have her link up with the Spanish soldiers, and she can brief them. Then you can ask them to ship her the hell out. They can handle this thing with our other two people."

"It's not that simple," Rodgers said.

"It can be."

"There's more to this than just manpower," Rodgers insisted. "We need to buy time. Someone has to get to Dhamballa and convince him to release Father Bradbury. If not, the Spanish may go in there shooting. They need to discourage other attempts on missionaries."

"Why can't Aideen or Battat carry that message?" McCaskey asked.

"They can," Rodgers said. "But we also need someone to keep the Spaniards away from the camp."

"Then I'm really confused, Mike, because I'm doing the math, and you're not making sense," McCaskey said. "Aideen does one job, Battat does the other. You said they're capable. Maria goes home. It's easy."

"It's easier with three people than with two," Rodgers said. "And I owe it to Aideen and Battat to give them all the support I can. They're the ones at the front line. Besides, Maria is not going to come home before her mission is completed. She just won't do that."

"She might, for me," McCaskey said. "If not, maybe she'll do it for you. When the Spanish get to Maria, you can *order* her back."

"I just told you I won't do that," Rodgers said. "Not unless I know she's in danger."

"*Screw* the job for just a minute, Mike!" McCaskey implored. "We're talking about my wife!"

"I understand that, Darrell—"

"Christ, do you know I haven't even seen her since we got married!" McCaskey said. "She was coming here to be with me, not to go to Africa. You want to talk about owing someone something? You owed me that courtesy."

"I owed you?" Rodgers said. "For what?"

"For friendship," McCaskey said.

"Friendship has nothing to do with this," Rodgers said. "We needed an agent. Maria is a damn fine one. End of story."

"No, Mike, the story is just getting started—"

"Not for me, it isn't," Rodgers insisted. "Whether Maria broke a promise to you, I don't know. Whether you should have ever *asked* for that kind of promise, I also don't know. Whether Bob and I should have talked to you first was a judgment call. Unfortunately, we didn't have a lot of time for back and forth. What I *do* know is that this matter is between you and your wife. And you can talk to her when she gets back."

"That's your answer?" McCaskey asked.

"Pretty much," Rodgers said.

" 'I'm only doing my job'?" McCaskey said.

"Yeah. And don't make it sound dirty," Rodgers warned. "You're really starting to piss me off."

"I'm pissing *you* off?" McCaskey said. He felt like throwing a punch. "We've been through the wars down here for nearly eight years. We've gone through crises, personal and professional losses, all kinds of shit. Now I need a friend and a favor, and I can't get either."

"That's bullshit. Ask me anything else, and I'll do it," Rodgers said. "But not this. I need the assets I have."

" 'Assets,' " McCaskey said. "You sound like Joseph Goddamn Stalin throwing peasants against trained German troops."

"Darrell, I'm going to let that slide," Rodgers said. "It'll be safer for us both." Rodgers came around the desk. "Excuse me."

"Sure," McCaskey said. He didn't step aside. "Go to Pope Paul. He'll absolve you. He'll give you a shot of that 'for the cause' crap. He'll say the job comes first, and you're doing the right thing keeping Maria in the field. Me? I care more about the lives of my teammates than the life of a priest who knew the risks of the work he was doing. Who wasn't even our responsibility in the first place!"

Rodgers walked around McCaskey. McCaskey grabbed his arm. Rodgers glared at him.

McCaskey released him, not because he was afraid, but because beating each other bloody was not going to get Maria home.

"Mike, please," McCaskey said.

Rodgers looked at him. His gaze was softer now. "Darrell, you think I don't care about our people?"

"I don't know," McCaskey said. "I honestly don't know."

Rodgers stepped right up to McCaskey. McCaskey could not remember seeing such a look of betrayal in someone's eyes.

"Say it again, Darrell," Rodgers demanded. "Tell me again that I don't care about them. That I didn't care about Bass Moore or Charlie Squires or Sondra DeVonne and Walter Pupshaw and Pat Prementine and the other people I lost in Kashmir. I want to hear it when you're not yelling. I want to hear it when you're actually thinking about what's coming from your mouth."

McCaskey said nothing. When he had spoken, he was not thinking about the Striker members who had been killed over the years. He was only thinking about his wife.

"Say it again!" Rodgers yelled.

McCaskey could not. He would not. He looked down. All the emotion that had built up in the last day was gone. Unfortunately, he had let it loose on the wrong target. And at that moment, Darrell McCaskey knew who he was really mad at. It was not Mike Rodgers, and it was not Maria. He was mad at himself for the reason Rodgers had said. McCaskey should never have tried to get Maria to agree to give up her work.

"Mike, I'm sorry you took it that way," McCaskey told him. "Shit, I'm sorry."

Rodgers continued to look at him. The men were silent for a moment longer. Finally, Rodgers looked away. Once again, he turned and headed toward the office door.

"I'll be back here after the Kline download," Rodgers said softly. "Let me know when you've got something about the Japanese."

"Sure," McCaskey said. "Mike?"

Rodgers paused and looked back. "Yeah?"

"For what it's worth, that isn't what I meant," McCaskey said. "I know how you feel."

"I know what's in your heart, pal," Rodgers said. "It's been a tough time for everyone. Right now, we're both a part of your wife's support system. Let's see what we can do to make that work in the best way possible."

Rodgers turned away and left the office. He did not look back at McCaskey. It seemed very, very quiet.

McCaskey made a fist and drove it into his open hand. The slap sounded like lightning. Which was appropriate. He had done what he had really come for. He had let out the pent-up energy. But he had dumped it on an old friendship. One that he feared would never be the same.

FIFTY-TWO

Maun, Botswana
Friday, 10:09 P.M.

Except for the occasional bounce, it was silent in the cabin
of the truck. Leon Seronga did not complain. The Spanish
woman was staring ahead, and Njo Finn was silent. He was
gripping the wheel tightly. After the encounter with Maria, the
driver seemed glad to be in control of something.

The windows were open. The night air was not cool, but
the strong wind felt good. A half hour before, Pavant had
passed a six-pack of warm Cokes from the back of the truck.
Seronga had offered one to Maria, but she had declined. Seronga was nursing his second can. Each sip of the warm bev-
erage burned his mouth, but the caffeine was helping him to
stay awake. There was an open map on Seronga's lap. His left
hand was resting on the map to keep it from blowing away.
Seronga had drawn a circle with a seventy-five-mile radius.
The Vodun base camp was located at the center.

The passage through the dark veldt had given Seronga time
to think. And now that he thought about it, this was a very
strange place for him to be. Not the plain but the war itself.
Until now, Seronga had never felt that he was fighting a religious war. He believed he was fighting a war for Botswana.
Yet he was beginning to wonder about that. He was starting
to think that Dhamballa might be right, and he could be wrong.
It was not a bad feeling, though. To the contrary. It was comforting to think that 10,000 years of spirit might be greater
than the African continent and its civilizations.

Decades before, in the years of the quiet revolution to oust
the British, the Brush Vipers did everything that was necessary
to free Botswana. Back then, Seronga's vision was clear. So

were his methods. Above all, there was strength of purpose: the desire to be free. It was backed by strength of arms and the patience to use them only when necessary.

Seronga had felt those same stirrings of purpose when he first heard Dhamballa speak. Religion had not entered into it. The man's words were about Africa and Africans. The truth was, Leon Seronga had no use for religion.

Since childhood, Africa had been his god. There was nothing to compare to the majesty of this land, the terrible beauty of the predators and the serenity of the prey. Or the moods of the place, which were unfathomable. Some days were epic and clear. They made life joyous. On others, depending upon the mood of the land, weather moved in with force or seductiveness. Sometimes rain and wind came from nowhere. Other times they were announced by gentle breezes and cool drizzle. There were baking droughts that lasted for weeks or horrendous floods that came so suddenly people drowned in their sleep. Then there were the nights. Sometimes, like tonight, the skies were so vast and vivid that a man felt as if he were weightless and airborne. Other nights were so close, so choking, that Seronga felt as if he were the only man on earth. On such nights even the crickets seemed as though they were on another world.

If the land had been his god, the lives and accomplishments of his people had been his religion. People invented other gods, he believed, because they feared death. For Seronga, death had always been a normal, accepted part of life. Since he was lucky enough to be part of Africa, he had to accept being part of that cycle. He had never resented it. He had never asked for extensions. Too much of life could be wasted on preparing for death.

Leon Seronga did not doubt the righteousness of what he was doing here. Even if he did not succeed, he would not question what he had done. But for the first time in his life, he wondered if he had been wrong about religion. He wondered if the Vodun gods were behind the spirit of Africa and his people.

Or maybe it is not wonder, he thought. *Maybe it is hope.*

For the first time in his life, Seronga felt a sense that things were out of balance. He felt like an outsider in his own land, in his own battle. There were Spanish soldiers in Maun. Priests from a diocese in South Africa. Observers in Rome. Allies in Belgium, France, and even China. More and more tourists on the roads and in the fields. Africa was no longer that pure physical entity he had once known. It was a park for the rich. A battleground for the ambitious. A source of souls and revenue for Rome. And he thought it had been minimized by the United States, when it became a cause for environmentalists and a laboratory for ethnologists. As if it needed aid and study to stay Africa.

But if Dhamballa was right, maybe Seronga had been finding Africa in the wrong place. Maybe the land and the people were just the manifestation of a greater identity.

Or maybe a veteran Brush Viper is just getting old and scared, Seronga had to admit.

That thought came with a little smile. He did not like to think of himself that way, but maybe it was time. Seronga had seen old lions stand in the brush and watch young members of the pride lead the hunts. He often wondered what those elder warriors were thinking. Did they not want to show how slow they had become? Were they too tired to get into the fray?

Or maybe it was something else, Seronga thought.

Maybe a voice inside the old lion was telling him to pick the time and place for a final hunt. There would be a better time for the warrior to become legend. Seronga wondered whether animals, like people, were powered by legends. And maybe those legends were the real essence of a people.

That was what led Seronga to wonder if Dhamballa might be right.

The gods of which Dhamballa spoke might be nothing more—or less—than ancient warriors who fell in combat and were immortalized in stories. After all, Seronga asked himself, what were gods but idealized beings? They were entities who could not be challenged or assailed, whose purpose was clear and perfect. Whether they were fancy or spirit did not matter.

By keeping these memories alive, the nature of a people could be sustained. Even if the land was conquered and the inhabitants enslaved and shipped to other continents, the stories could not be erased. The gods could not be destroyed.

"We're almost there," Finn said.

Seronga had constructed giants and eternities in his mind. The driver's very real voice startled him.

"Thank you," Seronga replied. He took a swallow of Coke. The tingle brought him back to the moment. He looked at the map.

The point they were approaching was within the reach of Dhamballa's radio. Even if he had left the base camp, the route he would take would keep him within the circle. As the truck entered that circle, they would finally be able to contact Dhamballa.

Seronga was not sure what he would find when that happened. He did not know how Dhamballa had reacted to the assassination. He did not know how that would affect their next rally.

They passed a small, kidney-shaped lake. The stars shone back at themselves from its surface. A few minutes later, Seronga spotted the dark silhouette of Haddam Peak. The 2,000-foot mountain stood alone in the northeast. Seronga recognized the distinctive hooked tor blocking the stars. It was the last landmark on the map. The truck was entering the call radius. The Brush Viper opened the rusted glove compartment. He replaced the map and removed a slender, oblong, black radio. It was a Belgian Algemene-7 unit. Used by the federal intelligence and security agency *Veiligheid van de Staat,* it was a secure point-to-point radio with a range of seventy-five miles. Dhamballa had the only receiver.

Seronga pressed the green Activate button on the bottom right of the unit. A red Speak button was to the right. A blue Terminate button was located to the left.

Seronga placed his thumb on the red button. He raised the hooded mouthpiece to his lips.

And stopped. He looked around.

"What's that?" Seronga asked.

Finn peered ahead. So did Maria.

"Where are you looking?" the driver asked.

"At one o'clock," Seronga said. He used the radio to point to his right.

"I don't see anything," Finn said.

"I do," Maria replied. "It's a car. A Jeep."

The woman was right. A small vehicle glinted faintly in the headlights of the truck. It was about one hundred yards away.

Finn slowed.

"Are you expecting anyone?" Seronga asked.

"Yes," Maria said.

Seronga glared at her. "Stop the truck," he said.

Finn crushed the brake. The truck stopped with effort, skidding slightly toward the passenger's side. That left Seronga staring out his open window, directly at the Jeep.

Seronga put the radio in his lap. He slid his hand beside the seat and withdrew the gun. He did not let Maria see it. Not yet.

Pavant poked his head around. "What's wrong?"

"Ahead," Seronga said.

"I see them," Pavant replied. "Do you want me to get the night-vision goggles and intercept?"

"Not yet," Seronga said. He regarded Maria. "Who are they?"

"Two of my associates," Maria replied.

"What do they want?" Seronga asked.

"They're here to help."

"To help *who?*" Seronga pressed. "You?"

"No. To help you and your people survive the night," she replied. Her voice was chilling in its calm prediction of disaster.

Seronga looked ahead. The Jeep remained stationary.

"How did they know we were going to be here?" Seronga demanded. "Do you have a signaling device of some kind?"

"That isn't important," Maria replied.

"It is to me," Seronga insisted.

"What matters is that there is an elite Spanish unit searching for your leader's camp," Maria told him. "These people may have news about them. I suggest we hear what they have to say."

Seronga saw Finn running his hands anxiously along the wheel.

"It's going to be all right, Njo," Seronga said.

"I'd like to get out of the truck," he said. "I *need* to get out."

"It will be all right, I promise," Maria assured him. "But you had best trust me quickly."

Seronga raised the gun. He let Maria see it but did not put it on her. The woman was obviously a skilled fighter. In tight quarters like this, it would be easy for her to neutralize the weapon by moving close to Seronga. He also did not want to risk firing wild.

"We'll all get out," Seronga said. "We'll go to the Jeep together. Pavant?"

"Yes?"

"Do you see anyone watching from the sides or back?" Seronga asked.

Pavant looked around. "No. There's no place *to* hide," he replied.

"All right. You stay where you are and cover us," Seronga said. He cracked the door and eased out. His shoes crunched on the rocky terrain. "Let's go," he said to Maria.

The woman slid out beside him. Seronga stepped back. He allowed her to walk several yards ahead. Finn jumped out on the other side. Seronga was glad the driver did not have a gun. He was a good and loyal man, but he had never been in combat. He had not trained extensively for it. The damn thing was, Seronga had not expected to be in combat, either. This was supposed to be a peaceful revolution. A war of ideas, not bloodshed.

The three walked toward the Jeep. Seronga did not even think to doubt what the woman had told him, either about the Spanish soldiers or that the people in the Jeep wanted to help them. It was a remarkable individual to command that kind of trust having said so little.

Finn stayed close to Seronga, behind the woman. Seronga

watched for signs of movement. He wondered if the occupants of the Jeep were as cool as their comrade.

He knew he was not. Although he did not show it the same way as Njo Finn, he was afraid. Not for himself but for the cause. At the same time, he had a thought that was also new to him. It was not so much a whisper of hope but a challenge.

If the Vodun gods existed, this would be a very good time for them to make themselves known.

FIFTY-THREE

Washington, D.C.
Friday, 3:10 P.M.

"Chief, we've got some weird stuff going on."

The call from Bob Herbert came while Paul Hood was checking in with the rest of the staff. There were other divisions of Op-Center that functioned independent of the core crisis management group. There was a small budget office, a human resources center, and a communications group that worked directly under Bob Herbert.

They monitored fax transmissions, cell phone calls, and satellite activities in regions where Op-Center personnel were working. Hood was lucky to have a great group of young go-getters and veterans working under him. Each learned from the others. Their briefings were always reassuring. As Bob Herbert had once put it, half joking, "They're the bedrock on which us big ol' titans do our striding." Hood was just happy to have a group that really supported him. That had been a big change from being mayor of Los Angeles. Unlike the city council and various departments in the city, everyone here was on the same page.

"What's happening?" Hood asked.

"There has been an unusual amount of radio traffic at the Air Wing of the Botswana Defense Forces," Herbert said.

"Define unusual," Hood said.

"An across-the-system jump from ten to fifteen communications an hour to more than three hundred," Herbert replied.

In the United States, that kind of increase would signify a Defcon One state of readiness.

"We've picked it up here, and the CIA noted it, too," Herbert went on. "Their frequency scanners at the embassies don't react unless there's a spike of at least one hundred percent."

"Do we know what the increased traffic is about?" Hood asked.

"Not yet," Herbert said. "The signals are all encrypted. We're collecting it and breaking it down here. Viens is trying to get us some satellite visuals of the bases. He's scraping together all the satellite time he can for us. The thing is, Jody Cameron at NAVSEA intelligence just told me they're also starting to get radar blips. One of their destroyers is picking them up from the Mozambique Channel."

NAVSEA was the Naval Sea Systems Command. The intelligence division was comprised of a worldwide deployment of cutters and destroyers. These ships were responsible for monitoring land and sea activities inaccessible by U.S. or allied bases. The intelligence collected by these ships determined whether vessels of the Maritime Preposition Force needed to be sent to a region. These were ships that provided military support prior to the arrival of main expeditionary warfare ships. The ships that patrolled the Mozambique Channel were responsible for covering the region from South Africa to Somalia.

"What did the blips suggest?" Hood asked.

"Chopper traffic," Herbert replied. "More than they've ever seen in the region."

"Are they doing search grids or heading somewhere?" Hood asked.

"The helicopters are heading north from the airfield outside Gaborone," Herbert said. "NAVSEA is saying this is either an action or a drill."

"We've got to assume it's not a drill," Hood said.

"Of course," Herbert said. "Hold on—Matt Stoll's shooting me some of the data from the encrypted transmissions."

There was a short silence that felt very, very long.

"Shit," Herbert said. "Son of a bitch."

"What is it?" Hood demanded.

"They've got a destination," Herbert said. "Okavango Swamp."

"Damn," Hood said.

"They also say it was Edgar Kline who gave them that destination," Herbert added.

"How the hell could Kline have given them a target?" Hood asked. "We didn't know it ourselves."

"I don't know," Herbert admitted.

It had been more than an hour since Hood had called Kline on his cell phone and given him the location for the rendezvous between Op-Center's teams and the soldiers from the *Unidad Especial del Despliegue*. And there was no way the Vatican Security Office could have extrapolated Dhamballa's location from what Hood told him. Op-Center did not even know for sure where the Vodunists were based.

"Get him on the phone," Hood said.

"With pleasure," Herbert said angrily.

Hood was uncharacteristically impatient as he called Mike Rodgers. He brought the general up to date, then conferenced him into the discussion. The two men waited as Kline's voice mail picked up on the cell phone.

"Goddamn him!" Herbert said. "He's ducking us."

Hood was frustrated, too, and angry, but he forced himself to stay cool and on target.

"Bob, do we think Kline's still at the Mission of the Holy See in New York?" Hood asked.

"That's the only secure place Kline could use to monitor a military action," Herbert told him. "Kline definitely would not have left if something is brewing." Before Hood could suggest it, the intelligence chief added, "I'm calling over there now. I'll find him."

"If you do, I'll do the talking," Hood said.

"You got it," Herbert said. "Only if I get to break his freakin' nose when this is all over. Screening calls," the intelligence chief went on. "That's so frigging low rent. You want to impede someone, do it like a man. Use diplomatic double-speak. Face-to-face, toe-to-toe."

Hood did not interrupt or comment. Bob Herbert frequently raged at something. It was in his hot Mississippi blood to do so. This time, though, Hood had to agree that Herbert had a good reason to boil.

Herbert reached an automated switchboard. The intelligence chief had no idea whose office Kline was using. He waited for an operator. The operator did not know anyone by the name of Edgar Kline. Exasperated, Herbert hung up and redialed the main number. When the voice menu came up, he punched the extention of the Path to Peace Foundation Bookstore.

"Can I help you?" asked the youthful-sounding man who answered the telephone.

"Yes," Herbert said. "What's your name?"

"Mr. Hotchkiss," said the clerk. "Can I help you?"

"Yes, Mr. Hotchkiss," Herbert told him. "Do you carry a copy of the last rites?"

"We do," replied the clerk. "It's in several books. The most popular is the *Concordance of Catholic Liturgy*—"

"I'll take it," Herbert said. "And I want a bookmark placed on that page."

"Any particular style of bookmark?"

"No," Herbert replied. "I'll need the book delivered to someone in your building."

"In our building?" the man said.

"That's right," Herbert replied. "Mr. Hotchkiss, is there anyone else working in your shop?"

"Yes—"

"Please ask him to deliver the book while I give you the credit card information," Herbert said. "Oh, and I want an inscription on the title page."

"Certainly, sir."

"It should read, 'Answer your cell phone, or you'll need this,' " Herbert told him. "Sign it Bob H."

"Excuse me?" the young man said.

"Just do it," Herbert said. "Lives depend on you."

Hood was impressed by the concern and conviction Herbert put in that one statement. The man was the best.

"I'll do it right away, sir," the clerk replied. "To whom is the concordance being delivered?"

"Man named Edgar Kline," Herbert said. "Ask around in the diplomatic corridors. Someone will know him."

"*I* know him," the man said.

"You do?" Herbert asked.

"He was in here before, buying a travel guide," the man said.

"To southern Africa?" Herbert asked.

"That's right," replied the clerk.

"Did he want to see maps?" Herbert asked.

"He did!" Hotchkiss replied. "How did you know?"

"Lucky guess," Herbert told him. "Mr. Hotchkiss, can I count on you to do this?"

"You can," Hotchkiss said. "Since I know what he looks like, I'll deliver it myself."

"Thanks," Herbert replied.

The clerk turned the phone over to his associate, and Herbert gave him the credit card information. While he did, Hood hung up. He consulted a computer map of northern Botswana. The rendezvous point for Maria, Aideen, and Battat was thirty miles from the swamp. He did not give Kline any information that could have led the Botswanan military to that region. The target had to have come to him some other way. But who would have known to contact him? The VSO was a highly secretive organization. They did not maintain ties with very many international intelligence groups. Only the Spanish, the Americans—and then it hit him. The intelligence did not come from the outside. They had missed the obvious source.

Mike Rodgers walked in. "What do you think, Paul?" the general asked Hood.

"I think it was Father Bradbury," he said.

Rodgers was puzzled. "What about him?"

"He's the only one who knows exactly where Dhamballa is," Hood said. "Either the VSO pinpointed the last call he made or, maybe more likely, he found a way to signal them."

"Radio equipment or a phone," Rodgers said. "Dhamballa has to have them. It's possible."

"Gentlemen, this is not good," Hood said. "We have to stop our people from going in."

"You're getting ahead of me," Rodgers said.

"The Botswana government thinks that Dhamballa's people killed our bishop," Hood said. "They have to move against him. The Air Force is going to clean the lot of them out."

"But not before the Spanish get in and save Bradbury," Rodgers said.

"Maybe no," Hood said. "If they think the Vodunists killed once, they can always be blamed for killing twice. Who will be able to prove that they did not kill Father Bradbury?"

"No one," Herbert said.

"We have to give Gaborone the photo Maria took," Rodgers said.

"That may not stop them," Herbert replied. "The photo will tell them they have a larger problem. Other enemies on the inside. They will still want to clean up this one first, as quickly as possible."

"I still don't think the Vatican will offer Father Bradbury up as an altar sacrifice," Rodgers insisted. "I do not want to believe that. Not while they have an option."

"Maybe not," Hood agreed. "What options do they have?"

"The *Unidad Especial del Despliegue*," Rodgers said. "They can get one of the air force choppers to airlift the Spaniards close to Okavanga Swamp. The soldiers go in and get Father Bradbury out."

"Eliminating the need for them to rendezvous with our people," Herbert pointed out.

"That's not the bad part," Rodgers said. "Our guys will still be heading for the swamp with Seronga. I've got a map of Botswana in front of me. If my calculations are even roughly correct, they should get there just about the time the Botswana Air Force arrives."

Rodgers grabbed the phone on Hood's desk. He called the embassy in Gaborone and asked to be patched through to Aideen Marley.

At once.

FIFTY-FOUR

Maun, Botswana
Friday, 10:31 P.M.

Aideen Marley and David Battat had decided to remain hidden for now. They would let Maria handle the approach. She was the most experienced of the three. She was the one on the inside.

Battat and Aideen had left the Jeep when they saw the approaching headlights. They were lying belly down on a three- or four-yard-high dirt rise several dozen yards beyond it. They could not rule out the possibility that Seronga would strafe the vehicle with gunfire before approaching. Of course, the two knew they would probably not be much safer lost in the wilderness, at night, without transportation. They had no idea what predators might be about. Still, not knowing Seronga's state of mind, this seemed like a reasonable precaution.

Aideen and Battat lay side by side as Maria and two men left the cab of the truck. Cautiously, the three approached the Jeep. They were silhouetted by the headlights, so Aideen could not see many details, but it looked as though one of the men had a gun. He appeared to be pointing it at Maria, who was walking several yards ahead. Aideen tried to read Maria's body language. The woman was striding as she had in Spain. As though nothing intimidated her. If she were in immediate danger, she did not show it.

"Hello!" Maria said at last. "Are you there?"

Aideen could not see David. The two had worked out a series of taps to communicate. She felt him rub the back of her hand. That meant he thought they should stay where they were. She agreed and rubbed him back.

The trio came closer.

"I am here with Leon Seronga and Mr. Finn," Maria said in a strong, steady voice. "There is another man in the back of the truck. No one will harm you. We all need to talk."

Aideen knew Maria's voice. The tone in the woman's voice put Aideen at ease. She believed the woman was telling the truth. Aideen tapped the back of Battat's hand. That meant she wanted to speak. Battat hesitated. Then he tapped the back of her hand in agreement. Slowly, Aideen rose.

"I'm here," Aideen said. She extended her hands to the side as she walked forward. "I'm not armed."

"Do you have any news for us?" Maria asked.

"Yes," Aideen said. "There are Spanish soldiers at least an hour behind you, possibly more. We need to split into two groups. One group will lead them away from Dhamballa's camp. The other will head toward it."

"Why?" a man shouted from the distance.

Aideen assumed this was Leon Seronga.

"We believe that the only way to prevent a shooting war is for the Vodunists to release Father Bradbury," Aideen said. She rounded the Jeep. The three were less than fifty yards from her.

"Who are 'we'?" Seronga asked.

"I've already explained to Mr. Seronga that we are not going to discuss our identities," Maria said.

Aideen had no intention of doing so. But she was glad Maria took the initiative. That gave her a little room to play good cop.

"There is no reason to discuss who we are, only what we want to do," Aideen said. "And that is to save lives."

"I believe you," Seronga said. "But I can't afford to trust you. You won't even tell me who you are."

"If something were to happen to you, we would not want that information to get out," Aideen said.

"You mean, if I were caught and tortured," Seronga said.

"Yes," Aideen said.

"What do you think this is, some primitive, degenerate society?" he asked.

"No. But these are dangerous times," she replied bluntly. "People do excessive things."

"They even kidnap people," Battat said as he came up behind her. "I will say this, though. The chances of something happening are greater the longer we stand here talking."

Seronga's group stopped a few yards from the Jeep. The leader of the Brush Vipers regarded Aideen and Battat.

Suddenly, there was a faint beeping.

"What's that?" Seronga asked.

"My cell phone," Aideen replied. She was surprised. Only the embassy could reach her out here. "I'm going to answer it," she said. She removed it from the pouch on her belt.

"Give it to me," Seronga said. He held out his left hand.

"I have to answer it first," she replied. "If I don't give them the code, they'll hang up." That was a lie, but Aideen did not want to hand over the phone. Not until she found out who was calling and why. She flipped it open. "This is Barley," she said. She chose a word that sounded enough like Marley so that the caller would simply think it was a glitch in the connection.

"Aideen?" said the caller.

"Yes."

"This is Mike Rodgers," said the caller. "Can you hear me?"

"Yes."

"Are you free to speak?" he asked.

"Not really," she replied.

Seronga strode over. He motioned for the phone as he approached.

"I am giving you over to Leon Seronga," Aideen said.

"No!" Rodgers said. "Are Maria and David with you?"

"Yes," Aideen said. She backed away and motioned Seronga back.

The Brush Viper pointed the gun at her. She did not stop moving. The woman was driven by purpose, not personal security.

Battat came between them. "Let the lady talk," he said. "We're here to help you."

Seronga did not lower the gun. But he did not fire nor did he advance.

Aideen continued her conversation. "Do you need them for something?" she asked.

"No," Rodgers told her. "What I need is for the three of you to abort this mission now."

"Why?" Aideen asked.

Seronga must have caught the concern in her tone. He stepped forward.

"We believe the Botswana Air Force is en route to the Vodun camp in the Okavanga Swamp," Rodgers told her. "You are to stay away from there. Do you copy?"

"Yes," Aideen replied.

"What is going on?" Seronga demanded.

Aideen did not answer.

"The Botswana military is probably monitoring the airwaves, so I'm signing off before this call can be traced," Rodgers said. "I don't want this order questioned or second-guessed. Get out. Now."

Seronga pushed Battat aside and walked toward her. "I asked you a question!" he snapped.

Battat grabbed the Brush Viper's arm as he moved past. A shot kicked up dirt and pebbles near Battat's feet. It came from the truck.

"If there is a next shot it will be through your heart!" a voice warned from that direction.

Battat released Seronga and stepped back. Seronga grabbed the phone from Aideen. He put it to his ear.

"Hello," Seronga said. "Hello!" After a moment he glared at Aideen. "No one is there."

"No," Aideen said. "My superior did not want the Botswana Air Force tracing the call."

"The air force? Why would they?" Seronga asked.

"Apparently, they found your camp in the Okavanga Swamp and are on their way," she said.

Seronga stood very still for a moment. Then he turned and yelled to the man in the truck. "Get the radio from the dashboard and call the camp," Seronga said. "Find out what the situation is."

The man in the truck acknowledged the order. Seronga turned back to the others.

"What else do you know?" Seronga demanded.

"Just that," Aideen replied.

Seronga waved his pistol at Aideen, Battat, and Maria. "Get in your Jeep, all of you."

"Why?" Battat asked.

"We are going to the camp," Seronga said.

"To do what?" Battat asked.

"If there is some kind of attack, we must make certain it is stopped," Seronga replied.

"How?" Battat asked.

"You two are Americans, I think," Seronga said. "We will contact the Botswana military and let them know you are there. They will be less inclined to attack if you are at risk."

"We cannot tell anyone we are here," Battat said.

"Why?" Seronga asked.

"Because officially, we are not here," Battat said.

"But you *are* here, and lives are at risk," Seronga said. "Your legal status is a ridiculous point."

"Not when it comes to Gaborone stopping Dhamballa," Battat said.

"But this woman knows we did not kill the bishop—" Seronga said.

"That will be irrelevant, unless you release the priest," Battat warned him. "I have a feeling that if the army attacks, they'll find him dead in the rubble of your camp."

Just hearing that gave Aideen chills. It was conceivable. It truly was.

"I have raised the camp!" the man in the truck shouted. "They see no sign of an aircraft!"

"Where are they now?" Seronga asked.

"They are out of the swamp and moving toward the diamond mine," the man in the truck answered. His voice sounded flat and mute by the echoless expanse of plain.

"Tell them they must change their course and come toward

us," Seronga said. "I will give them the coordinates in a minute."

"What if they won't listen?" the man in the truck asked.

"Then they will die!" Seronga said. "This is no longer about a rally but about survival. Tell them that!"

"I will!" the man shouted.

Seronga turned back to Aideen. As he did, his eyes caught a gleam of the truck headlights. They glinted bright, narrow, ferocious.

"You don't know when the attack is due?" Seronga pressed.

"I do not," she answered.

"Do you swear this?" Seronga demanded.

"I don't want any deaths on my conscience," Aideen replied flatly.

Seronga seemed to accept that. He looked around as if he were searching for answers, for inspiration.

"They must be using helicopters," he said after a moment. "Jets would have trouble spotting them through the trees."

"Can't they land?" Aideen asked.

"Not if they think we are still in the swamp," Battat said. "There's nowhere to set down."

"What if they know Dhamballa has left?" Aideen asked.

"We can still scatter and hide if we have to," Seronga told her. "And we can fire back. My soldiers are accustomed to working in small groups as well as independently."

"Something just occurred to me," Maria said. "What if the Spaniards are going in first?"

Seronga looked at her. So did Aideen.

"Explain yourself," Seronga said.

"We have to assume the Spanish soldiers were also given this information," Maria said. "In that case, they may not be coming here. They might have been picked up at the Maun airfield."

"You're right. The Spaniards could have leapfrogged over us," Aideen said. "By now they might have reached the camp, infiltrated it, and rescued Father Bradbury."

"Wouldn't Mike have told us if something like that were going on?" Battat asked.

"Probably, if he knew," Aideen said.

"The Spanish are not very open about the conducting of military maneuvers," Maria told him. "In Spain, separatist factions could use that information to plan acts of terror."

Seronga came toward Maria with the gun. "Get in the Jeep, all of you," he said urgently.

"Why?" Battat asked.

"We are going to join my group," Seronga said.

"Like hell—" Battat said.

"Now!" Seronga yelled. "I don't care whether you three are here officially or not. You are now my hostages. Your government will be informed. That will buy us time."

"I have a better idea," Aideen said.

"I don't have time to debate!" Seronga said.

"You're doing all the talking," Aideen yelled back. "Mr. Seronga, I need my phone."

"What are you going to do?" the Brush Viper asked.

"I'm going to call my people and ask them to put out fake intel," Aideen replied. "Something that will stall the Botswanans."

"What kind of information?" Seronga asked.

"I don't know," Aideen told him. "I'll figure it out. Look, you're wasting time. Whatever I do cannot be worse than what's already happening," the woman pointed out.

Seronga hesitated, but only for a moment. He handed her the phone. "Make your call from the Jeep. I'm returning to the truck. I want to be with my people as soon as possible."

Aideen looked at Battat. She could not see him well. But she could see him shifting his weight slightly from foot to foot. She could not decide if he were going to go along with this or try to disarm Seronga.

But there was one decision Aideen could make. She turned and strode toward the Jeep. "I'm going to join the Vodunists," she announced.

Battat hesitated.

So did Maria, but only for a moment. She followed Aideen. She stopped as she passed Battat.

"Aideen is right," Maria said. "If Op-Center can delay the

attack, we might find a way to stop this. If we leave, many will die." She cocked her head toward the sniper on the truck. "Including us, perhaps."

Maria continued toward the Jeep. She grabbed the roll bar, hopped over the door, and sat in the backseat. "Are you coming?" she asked Battat.

Battat glared at the truck.

Aideen had already reached the Jeep. She punched in the number of the embassy in Gaborone and was looking back. She saw Seronga lower his pistol and walk toward the truck. It was a gesture, nothing more, since the man in the truck still probably had his rifle trained on them. But it was a smart move.

Battat finally turned and walked toward the Jeep. Maria sat on the back passenger's-side seat, her head on the roll bar support. Her eyes were shut. Aideen was holding the phone to her ear. The night operator at the embassy had answered. Aideen had asked to be put through to Terminal 82401. While the woman waited to be connected, Battat climbed behind the wheel.

"It needed to be said," Battat told her defensively.

"You needed to say it," Aideen replied.

"All right. I needed it," Battat said in a harsh whisper. "I don't know if I agree with what you're doing. If we do stay with Seronga, we cannot afford to be identified. You understand that."

"I do," Aideen told him.

"Then why don't you stay out here?" Maria asked. "We'll send someone to get you."

"Because it isn't a question of my own security," Battat snapped. "We're in this deeper than we were ever supposed to be. We don't have the approval of the Congressional Intelligence Oversight Committee. Or the president. We're completely exposed, and the repercussions for Op-Center could be disastrous. Especially if we're caught helping rebels."

"You are right," Maria replied. "But this work, *our* work, is about risk. I don't mean just physical danger but political fallout. The United States will survive whatever we do. My

primary concern is about the people who may not survive if
we abandon them."

"That's why I'm going with you," Battat said. "If I'm going
to do the wrong thing, I want to do it for the right reasons."

Aideen was not sure she agreed this was wrong. But she did
not have time to think about it.

A moment later, Mike Rodgers was on the line.

FIFTY-FIVE

Washington, D.C.
Friday, 3:13 P.M.

Not long after Bob Herbert got off the phone with Hotchkiss at the Vatican mission bookstore, Edgar Kline called Paul Hood. Kline did so not because Bob Herbert had effectively threatened to kill him. He did it, he said, because he did not want to do what Hood and Herbert had done. Edgar Kline said that he wanted to tell the truth.

Mike Rodgers, Bob Herbert, and Paul Hood had remained in Hood's office after contacting the Vatican mission. They were seated around the desk when the call came through. The Op-Center director put Kline on speakerphone.

"Edgar—it's Paul," Hood said. "Bob and Mike are here as well."

"I got your message, Bob," Kline said.

"Good, you prick."

"Edgar, we all seem to be pressed for time," Hood said. "What's going on?"

"I'm sorry, but I was not at liberty to reveal what was happening," he said. "We did not want it to get back to Seronga. Someone there might have told one of your field personnel—"

"My feelings aren't hurt, and explanations don't matter now," Hood said. "Just tell me where we are."

"Father Bradbury managed to get a cell phone and call the archdiocese in Cape Town," he said. "During the brief call, Bradbury described the general direction and duration of their trip, as well as descriptions of the site itself. There was enough detail to give the Botswana military a good idea where Dhamballa is located. He was afraid to stay on the phone any longer for fear that Dhamballa would notice the phone was missing or see the *on* light on the console. The decision to go in after him was that of the Botswanans, not ours," Kline added.

"What if Dhamballa was not responsible for the death of the bishop?" Hood asked.

"Dhamballa cannot prove he wasn't involved in that," Kline said.

"Buy us the time to check," Hood suggested.

"Paul, I wish I could," Kline said. "If it were up to us, we would let the *Unidad Especial* handle this. All we want from this is the safe return of Father Bradbury and a restoration of order in Botswana."

"Edgar," Herbert interjected, "while you're busy coming clean, where are the Spanish soldiers?"

"I can't tell you that," Kline said.

"So much for trust," Herbert said.

"I'm being truthful," Kline said. "But that doesn't mean I'm at liberty to reveal everything."

"Do you know where they are?" Hood pressed.

"Yes," Kline replied. "But under the circumstances, I cannot share that information. In fact, that is part of why I did not call to tell you about Father Bradbury's message. I did not want information reaching Leon Seronga, either by accident or design."

"That would not have happened," Hood said. "We have had the same goal from the start. We sent our people in there to help you."

"Well, things change quickly in our world," Kline said.

"Not loyalties," Rodgers said. "Not ours."

"The only thing that changed is our agents went from being spies to being targets in the middle of a shit storm," Herbert said.

"Then withdraw them," Kline said.

"We may," Herbert said.

"Gentlemen, let's stay on issue," Hood said. "The point of this conversation is that we all want to rescue the priest and get our people out safely. We also should be trying to save lives. Is there some way we can keep the air force from hammering the Brush Vipers?"

"At this point, I very much doubt it," Kline said. "They are going to make an object lesson of the Vodunists."

"But what if that isn't necessary?" Hood said. "What if we can help get the priest out without any violence?"

"How?" Kline asked.

"Let me talk to my people over there. You talk to Gaborone," Hood said. "Ask for a delay."

"And what happens if the Brush Vipers use a period of détente to get away or to attack another compound?" Kline asked. "What happens if people die this time, Paul? What happens if the Brush Vipers decide to take hostages? Or kill other priests and deacons?"

"I can't guarantee they won't," Hood admitted. "But it isn't likely. Especially if they know what's being sent against them."

"All we're saying is give our people a shot," Herbert said. "Damnit, Edgar, forget all the shit that's gone on between us. Try to delay the attack. That's just basic statesmanship and something else the Church stands for."

"Which is?"

"Humanitarianism," Herbert said.

Kline sighed. "I wish it were that simple."

"It can be," Hood said.

"What happened to turning the other cheek?" Herbert asked.

"It went out when slaps became gunshots," Kline said. "Besides, we're not talking about bearing an insult. We're talking about the abduction and killing of priests. Never mind by whom. The survival of the Church in Botswana, in Africa, is being challenged. It has to take a stand. And the Botswanans have to show that they are in power. Don't forget, my friends. We did not ask for this war. The Vodunists chose this course."

"Perhaps," Hood said. "But someone else killed Bishop Max to escalate the situation. By doing the same thing, by escalating the war against the Vodunists, you are abetting the ones who attacked you."

"That will come out in time," Kline said. "First things first. We deal with the Vodunists and the kidnapping of Father

Bradbury. Then we find out who attacked the Church and Botswana."

Just then, Rodgers's cell phone beeped. He checked the number. It was the embassy in Gaborone. That meant the clock was running. There was no time to leave the room. If the call were being relayed from Aideen, it could be pinpointed within two minutes. Rodgers looked at Hood and dragged a finger across his own throat to kill the speaker. Hood did more than that. He asked Kline if he could hold the line for a few minutes.

Kline agreed. Hood hit the Mute button.

"I'm surprised he agreed, the bastard SOB," Herbert said.

"It's worth the wait for him," Hood said. "I might decide to share whatever information is incoming."

Meanwhile, Mike Rodgers accepted the patch-through. Hood and Herbert fell silent.

"Yes?" Rodgers said. He did not use his name in case Aideen had dropped the phone and someone had discovered it.

"We need help," the caller said.

It was Aideen. Her words were urgent, but her voice was calm.

"Go ahead," Rodgers said.

"We've linked up with Seronga and are headed toward a rendezvous with Dhamballa," she informed him.

"You're staying?" Hood said.

"We have to," Aideen said. "The Vodunists are changing their destination to meet us. Father Bradbury will be with them. We will try to obtain his release. We should be with them in about two hours. Do you know where the Spanish soldiers are?"

"No," Rodgers said. "But we believe they are trying to reach Father Bradbury."

"That was our conclusion," Aideen said. "General, we need time. Seronga seems inclined to support us. We believe it's possible to end this peaceably. Can you sell Gaborone on that idea?"

"I don't know," Rodgers said. "They appear set on ending this situation in a very public way."

"What if you tell them that we have already obtained the release of the priest?" Aideen asked.

"That would make things worse," Rodgers said. "The air force would still go in to mop things up."

"Then we have to find another way to delay them," Aideen said.

"Look, I'll talk this over with Bob and Paul," Rodgers said. "We'll try to work out something."

"Thank you," Aideen replied.

"I understand," Rodgers told her. "Proceed under the assumption that you're a go for a peaceful resolution. If there's a problem, I'll let you know. You've done very good work."

Aideen thanked him. Rodgers clicked off. The call had taken just over one minute.

"What have we got?" Hood asked. "Hold on," he added. He clicked on the speakerphone. "Edgar? Are you still there?"

"I am."

"Mike Rodgers just got a call from one of our agents who is with Seronga," Hood informed him. "You will be hearing the briefing from Mike the same time we do."

"Thanks, but I don't see what good this will do," Kline said.

"Can you be any *less* goddamn hopeful, you South African misery?" Herbert snapped.

"Enough, Bob," Hood snapped. "Edgar, if nothing else, it will renew the partnership we were supposed to have in this operation," Hood said.

"Fair enough," Kline replied.

"Mike?" Hood said.

Rodgers liked what Hood had done. It was a no-lose situation for Op-Center. It accomplished three things. It neutralized Kline's charges that Hood had not been forthcoming. It reinvigorated the idea of an alliance between Op-Center and the Vatican Security Office. And most importantly, it put the next move on the shoulders of Edgar Kline.

"Gentlemen, our three operatives are with Leon Seronga," Rodgers said. "The word is that Seronga seems tired. From the sound of it, this whole movement is suddenly tired, or at the very least scared. Our group is meeting with Dhamballa and the Brush Vipers in under two hours. Our people believe they can obtain freedom for Father Bradbury and perhaps even get the Brush Vipers to disband. They have asked us to find a way to give them that opportunity. They have asked us to buy them those two hours."

Hood waited a moment. Then he looked at the speaker-phone. "Edgar? Any thoughts?"

Kline was silent.

"I've said it before, and I'll say it now. We started this as a mission to save lives," Hood said. "We can't sit here and do nothing, just say this is out of our control."

"And I've told you, the Brush Vipers chose their own path," Kline said. "We are not responsible for what happens to them."

"Edgar, we are," Hood insisted. "This information just *made* us responsible. We have options. We have a duty. Our job is to manage crises, not sit on the bench and watch them explode. Your job, if I may, is to restore normalcy. We can do that. It's not impossible."

"The crime of kidnapping Father Bradbury does not call for a response of mass murder," Rodgers said. "It was wrong, it was illegal, but let's deal with it in those terms."

"And there's something else that just occurred to me," Hood said. "Edgar, we don't know who is traveling with Dhamballa. What if there are children at the camp who had nothing to do with any of this? Should they be punished, too?"

Hood let that thought soak in before continuing.

"Edgar, we don't have enough information to allow an air strike to take place," Hood concluded. "At least—at the *very* least—give our people the time to finish what they were sent to do."

"Paul, I don't know," Kline said. "Even if I wanted to, I don't know if I can make that happen."

"Try," Herbert said.

"Your say-so will get the Spanish soldiers to delay entering the camp," Hood said. "If they don't go in, the Botswana chop-pers won't strike for fear of killing Father Bradbury."

"You can tell them the camp is moving," Rodgers said. "It's true. They might miss it altogether."

"Paul, they may be in there already, with the Brush Vipers," Kline said.

"Then, Edgar, we can't afford to waste any more time," Hood pressed.

The silence that followed was tense, exaggerated. The hum of the computer fan sounded like a turbine.

Finally, Kline spoke. "I will do what I can. I'll ask them to hold," he said. "But I cannot answer for the Botswana military."

"They may not attack without knowing that Father Bradbury is out of danger," Rodgers said.

"I pray you're right," Kline replied.

The Vatican officer hung up.

"Well. All it took was three of us beating him with morality to get him to budge," Herbert said.

"I've had to use more than that to get you to move sometimes," Hood said.

"Yeah, but I'm usually right," Herbert said.

Calmer now, Herbert left the office to see what Darrell McCaskey might have discovered about the Japanese connection. Rodgers looked at Hood.

"I pray we're right, too," Hood said.

"Yeah," Rodgers said. "You want to make that official?"

Hood smiled. "Are you serious?"

Rodgers nodded.

"It's been a long time," Hood said.

"Then I'll lead," Rodgers replied.

The general slid off his chair and lowered himself to one knee. Hood did the same. Rodgers said something about God looking after the people in the field, especially those who were risking themselves for others. Rodgers knew from countless missions that the words themselves did not matter as much as the sentiment. His heart and soul were definitely in this. Not just because he felt they were right but because he understood the political crisis Botswana was facing. And he believed that only divine intervention could save Dhamballa and the Brush Vipers from being slaughtered.

FIFTY-SIX

Okavango Swamp, Botswana
Friday, 11:19 P.M.

These were the hours that made life worthwhile. They were the challenges for which Captain Antonio Abreo had been trained. They were a chance to pit himself against an unfamiliar environment and a new enemy.

They were an opportunity to savor life by risking it.

His nonmilitary friends and relatives told him it was a crazy way to make a living. They were all farmers and fishermen and tour guides. They had comfortable lives. They would probably have long lives. Eighty years of boredom did not appeal to Abreo.

Risk, and planning for that risk, did.

Captain Abreo had felt there was a better chance of getting to the priest with two men rather than an entire unit. Dressed in camouflage greens, Abreo and Sergeant Vicente Diamante had decided to jump to the site described by Father Bradbury.

The two men had taken off from Maun. They flew on a twin-turboprop EMB-110 that had been flown in from Gaborone. The Brazilian-made aircraft belonged to the Botswana Meteorological Research Department. The government had loaned it to the *Unidad Especial del Despliegue* to make the incursion. Though Gaborone was not happy to have foreign soldiers operating on their soil, their involvement would remain a secret. It was more important to restore order absolutely. At the same time, the remaining members of the team were making their way to the swamp in the company of the Botswana military.

The BMRD had detailed maps of the region. Captain Abreo had used them to pinpoint the likely location where Father

Bradbury was being kept. Then he and Sergeant Diamante had
parachuted to the nearest small island, which was about a quarter mile away. There, Diamante deployed a small rubber raft.
The men carried that plus a pair of night-vision goggles, a
radio, two M-82s, and a pair of nine-inch hunting knives.

While the sergeant inflated the raft, Captain Abreo hid the
parachutes behind a clump of vines. Then he scanned the darkness for signs of a camp. He found it with no problem. Lights,
sounds, activity. He did not even need the night-vision glasses
to see them. After dabbing mud on their faces and hands, the
Spanish officers put the raft in the water. Then they made their
way swiftly and silently toward the deserted northern side of
the small island. All of the activity seemed to be centered in
the south. It was clear that the Vodunists were breaking camp.
There were several small huts on the island. Abreo spotted one
where there was no activity. Where the windows were closed,
despite the heat. That was probably the shack where Father
Bradbury was incarcerated. Once the two soldiers had recov-
ered the priest, the plan was for them to head north. When
they were a half mile from the island, they were to radio the
commander of the Botswana strike force. The attack would
commence soon thereafter. When it was finished, one of the
helicopters would retrieve the two soldiers and the priest.

The sergeant was crouched in the rear, rowing. First on one
side, then the other. The dark water rippled gently around the
raft. The captain peered ahead. He ignored the few gnats that
clouded around his ears and cheek. Swatting them away would
accomplish nothing except to distract him. It was surprisingly
quiet out here. The only croaking and clicking they heard had
been around the island. The officer was aware of all of it. The
sounds, the smells, the gentle current under the raft. Once a
mission had begun, Captain Abreo became a part of his environment. Alert, patient, defensive rather than offensive.
Growing up on a sheep farm in the Basque country, he had
learned a very simple lesson from foxes. The ones who got
away were the ones you never saw coming.

As the elite soldiers neared the target, the radio blinked. It
was a dull brown pinpoint flash that would not be visible more

than a few feet away. Abreo picked up the headset. He attached the subvocal microphone to an elastic band he wore around his throat. Then he plugged the small disk-shaped microphone into the band. The tiny receiver plucked vibrations directly from his voice box. It would enable him to whisper and still be heard.

"Abreo," he said.

"Captain, this is CHQ," said the caller. That was the code name for Corporal Enrique Infiesta, the group's radio operator. Infiesta spoke fluent English and was liaison with the Botswana military.

"Go ahead," Abreo replied.

"Sir, the VSO liaison has asked us to postpone the operation," Infiesta informed him.

"For how long?" Abreo asked. The order had killed the captain's internal engines. He had to start them up again. They were still in a danger zone.

"Two hours," the caller replied.

"What's the reason?" Abreo asked.

"There is a simultaneous operation. That one has been given priority," Infiesta replied.

"Priority? By whom?"

"I don't know, sir," the caller told him.

"There is no one around but cult members," Abreo replied. "Do you know if this other party infiltrated the Brush Vipers?"

"I do not know, sir," Infiesta told him.

"Are they Spanish or Botswanan?" Infiesta asked.

"I don't know that either, sir," the radioman replied. "Do you want me to call and ask?"

"No. That won't change anything," Abreo replied.

Abreo looked out at the island. The cultists were running around loading the boats. They were so intent on leaving, they were not watching their flank. That was the problem with young movements. Leon Seronga was obviously the chief strategist. He was not here. Whoever was the number-two officer did not have the experience to mount a successful retreat. Or perhaps they felt they were not going to be attacked here.

Or perhaps they had learned that they were, Abreo thought.

If they had that information, that would explain the haste.

"Do the orders cover reconnaissance?" the captain asked.

"No, sir," said Infiesta. "Only what I told you."

"Very well," said Abreo.

"Will there be a return message, sir?" the caller asked.

"Tell the VSO liaison that the order was received, nothing more," Abreo replied.

"Yes, sir," Infiesta replied.

The captain signed off. He removed the headset and microphone and turned to the sergeant.

"There is another team engaged in the rescue," Abreo whispered. "VSO wants us to postpone."

"Are they Botswanans?" Diamante asked.

"I don't know," the captain told him.

"But we're just minutes away from possibly finding and rescuing the priest—" Diamante said.

"I know," Abreo replied. There was a trace of irritation in his voice. He got rid of it. The men were still on a mission, and annoyance was a distraction. "We have our orders, and we will follow them. However, we have no instructions other than to postpone. We are going to continue to the island and conduct on-site reconnaissance. If we happen to encounter the priest and he asks for our help, we will not refuse it."

"That would be wrong, Captain," Diamante agreed.

"Very much so," said Abreo.

The soldiers continued toward the island. Abreo continued to study the island.

The more he examined the hut through the night-vision goggles, the more convinced he became that it was a prison. Vines hung thickly in front of the window. They had never been cleared, which suggested that it was never opened. As they came closer, he also saw a dead bolt. On the outside.

When they were just one hundred yards from the northern shore, the men allowed the raft to drift with the forward momentum they had created. Even though there was shouting on the island, they could not chance that the rippling water would be heard.

A few minutes later, they were ashore. While Diamante tied

the raft to an exposed banyan tree, Abreo crept ahead. The shack was about two hundred feet to the southeast. Abreo used the night-vision glasses to sweep the area. Everyone was engaged in getting off the island. It looked as if they were nearly ready to depart. There would not be a lot of time to pull this off.

There was no one watching the hut outside. There might be a guard inside. Or perhaps the priest was not there. Or maybe they simply were not expecting a rescue attempt out here in the swamp. Captain Abreo would have to explore each of those possibilities in turn.

There was definitely someone in there. Slivers of light came through the shutters and from cracks in the walls. They seemed brilliant in the night-vision glasses. He put the goggles back in the case hooked to his belt. He motioned for Sergeant Diamante to proceed. Both men drew their knives and unbuttoned the flaps of their holsters. If they encountered any Brush Vipers, they would kill them silently and move on. Crouching low, they began moving forward.

Their boots sank deep in the mud of the island. Each step was accompanied by a soft *pop* as they fought the suction. Geckos ran over and around their feet. But Abreo never took his eyes from the shack.

It took four minutes for the men to reach the back wall. The captain and the sergeant separated. They went around the sides and checked the front. No one was there. They came back to the rear window where Captain Abreo looked around for a small rock. He found one and tossed it up to the roof. Standard operating procedure for an incursion like this was to cause a sudden noise and see what sounds came from inside.

The stone clattered on the tin roof and rolled off the far side. Abreo heard nothing from inside. A captive might not react to the sound. However, sentries tended to be tense or at least curious. There were no footsteps from inside. No one went to the door and looked out. If the priest was inside, chances were good he was there alone.

The next move was a little trickier. Abreo stood. Standing well to the side of the window, he used the hilt of his knife to rap on the shutter. He knocked twice. He heard distinctive muffled sounds. A man with a gag.

Diamante and Abreo exchanged glances. Someone was in there, probably the priest. Abreo moved toward the window. Diamante sheathed his knife and removed his pistol.

The captain regarded the window. It had the kind of shutter that lifted straight up. The dead bolt was at the center bottom. He indicated to Diamante that he would raise the shutter. The sergeant would then scan the room from behind his pistol. If the shack were clean, they would go inside and get the prisoner.

Slowly, Abreo raised the dead bolt. Squatting to the side, he picked up a fallen branch. He used it to lift the shutter. If anyone shot at him, he would be out of the line of fire.

Abreo and Diamante waited. The muffled cries returned. Diamante looked at Abreo. The captain nodded for him to investigate. Diamante nodded back. He rose slowly behind his pistol.

Abreo unholstered his own weapon. If anything happened to the sergeant, he wanted to be ready to return fire.

Diamante stuck his head inside. He looked quickly to the left, then the right. After a moment, the sergeant ducked back down. Abreo lowered the shutter and crouched beside him.

"There's a man in there, masked and tied to the bed," the sergeant whispered. "The room is empty."

"He's masked?" Abreo said. "Then why is the lantern on?"

"Probably because they will be coming back for him soon," Diamante suggested.

Abreo nodded. That made sense. In the haste of breaking camp, that would be one less thing to think about.

Now came the difficult part: the commit. If they could escape silently, they would. If not, they would escape any way possible. If that proved impossible, they would have to execute an exit plan that neither man wanted to use.

The soldiers had seen an old picture of Father Bradbury. They knew his age, that he was Caucasian, and that he spoke both English and Bantu. Still, the man in the bed was thinner, dirty, unkempt. He could be a decoy. The soldiers would not know until they went in and Diamante talked with him.

"Are you ready?" Abreo asked.

Diamante nodded.

Abreo dropped the stick and went to the shutter. He raised it. The priest was inside. He was gagged and bound spread-eagle on a cot. He was facing the window. He was just lying there. The captain climbed into the low window. Sergeant Diamante followed his commander in. The sergeant ran directly to the door and placed his ear against it.

Abreo took a quick look around in the light of the single lantern. There was no one else in the shack. He hurried to the cot.

The priest was facing away from him. He had a black hood over his head. His hands were tied behind his back. His clothes were filthy and torn. Abreo pulled off the hood. A gaunt, pale face looked up at him. He removed the cloth gag from the man's mouth.

"Padre Bradbury?" Abreo asked.

"Yes," said the man.

The captain studied him for a moment. He looked like a man who had been through hell. His eyes were soft. So were his hands. He was not a warrior or a laborer.

Abreo tossed the hood aside. Still holding his pistol in his right hand, he took out his knife and began cutting the bonds. First he freed the priest's left hand, then his right. The priest sat up.

And then Captain Abreo heard it. A low, dull hiss coming from under the bed. Diamante heard it, too.

It was then that the captain noticed a wire attached to the priest's right hand. It had been run down the headboard of the cot. Smoke began to pour from under the bed. That was why the priest had been hooded. So he could not tell them what had been done.

And Abreo realized, suddenly, why the lantern was still lit. When the tear gas was triggered, the African soldiers who came to investigate would be able to see just where the Spaniards were.

There was no time to finish freeing the priest. Already, yellow orange smoke obscured the window. Diamante was still at the door. They would have to go out that way.

Abreo yelled for the sergeant to open the door and get out. Gagging, Diamante pulled open the door. The captain ran out after him, feeling for the wall and the jamb. He found the door and ran out.

There were shouts. They were being ordered to stand down. Abreo did not have to understand the language to interpret the tone.

Abreo rubbed his eyes, trying desperately to clear the gas-induced blur. He turned to his left. He saw the edge of the shack. He had an instant to decide what course of action to pursue.

There appeared to be just one left.

The most important part of this mission was not simply to rescue the priest. It was to deprive the Vodunists of immunity from attack. As long as the Brush Vipers held Father Bradbury, the Botswanan military would not want to move against them. Vatican charities fed many Botswana villages. Gaborone would not want to risk that unless they had no choice. Not moving against them, they would be able to regroup somewhere else. They would continue to rebel against the government, to try and overthrow the Church. Above all, Abreo could not allow that to happen. It was a long shot, but they had to try. They had not become special forces soldiers to have things easy. The captain felt more completely alive in this moment than he had ever felt. He was almost giddy from the personal danger.

"Cover me!" Abreo yelled.

Diamante understood. He obeyed without question. The sergeant opened fire into the oncoming Brush Vipers. Abreo heard the fire fade to the west. The sergeant was trying to make his way around the shack. He would use the tear gas as cover to return to the water.

The captain also fired, then turned back toward the shack. Since he could not see, he would fire in the direction of the cot.

He never made it. A bullet tore through his right thigh. He

screamed from the pain and exhilaration. He had risked everything. The moment had come, and he had not run from it.

The bullet punched him forward, through the doorway. Abreo landed facedown and lost his pistol. To his left, he heard a scream. That had to have been Diamante. Mentally, Abreo saluted his loyal ally.

As bullets slashed the air above him, Abreo blinked hard. He tried to clear his vision and find his pistol. He spotted it a few feet ahead. The soldier attempted to crawl toward it, but his right leg refused to cooperate. It felt cold. To hell with it. He began pulling himself forward on his elbows.

The soldier moved ahead, but only for another foot or so. A fusillade from the doorway tore into the captain's back and shoulder blades.

Abreo did not feel the punch of the hot bullets as they tore through flesh and muscle, shattered plates of bone. The young captain was dead before the impulses reached his brain, before his chin struck the floor.

A moment later, the gunfire stopped. All was still.

FIFTY-SEVEN

Makgadikgadi Pan, Botswana
Friday, 11:40 P.M.

Leon Seronga was tired. He was tired in body and also in spirit. What he had just heard took even more out of him.

The Brush Viper was riding in the truck alongside Njo Finn. They were following the Jeep through the dark plain. Seronga put them less than an hour from the rendezvous with Dhamballa. That was when the call came from the original camp in the Okavanga Swamp. Seronga's hands were unsteady as he answered the radio. He did not want bad news.

As it turned out, the radio message from the decoy elements of Dhamballa's camp was both welcome and disturbing.

The Brush Vipers who had remained behind to keep the Spaniards from following Dhamballa had been successful. The Botswanans had let the Spanish soldiers reach the island. They had allowed the Spaniards to get into the shack. They had rigged a canister of tear gas to a Caucasian Brush Viper standing in for Father Bradbury. The Brush Vipers would have taken the intruders prisoner if they had surrendered. Instead, the Spaniards chose to fight. Two Brush Vipers died in the exchange. Both Spaniards were also killed.

Leon Seronga welcomed the news. It was becoming increasingly clear to Seronga that Father Bradbury could be the key to their survival. Not as a hostage but as an advocate. Someone who had spoken with Dhamballa and knew that he was not a killer.

The news also disturbed Seronga because two of his men had fallen. Seronga had lost very few soldiers over the years. He did not know the individuals well, and he was troubled that he would not get to do so. One of the men had children and grandchildren. The other was just eighteen years old.

The priest and the Vodunists had moved out to join Dhamballa and the rest of his party. It would be up to the Americans to communicate that information to their superiors without providing his specific location. And their superiors would have to notify the Botswana military that Father Bradbury was still a hostage. Gaborone would have to negotiate rather than attack.

Seronga told Finn to catch up to the Jeep. They pulled alongside, and Seronga motioned for them to stop. He opened the door and told Aideen to get in. It would be easier to talk to her than to the others. All the while, Pavant kept his rifle trained on the occupants. As soon as she was inside, Seronga told the Jeep to drive on. Finn continued following them.

"You don't look happy," Aideen said.

"There has been a firefight," Seronga told her.

"Between who?"

"My Brush Vipers encountered members of the elite Spanish force," Seronga told her.

"Where?" she asked.

"Does it matter?" he replied with resignation.

The woman glared at Seronga for a moment. Then she swore. "You did it, didn't you?"

Again, Seronga did not have to respond.

"You warned your camp that the soldiers were out there," she yelled. "Why? That was *not* part of our arrangement."

"My people had to be prepared," Seronga replied.

"What your people had to do was move from the target area!" Aideen said. "They had to get away from the Botswanan helicopters. That was why we gave you the intel."

"Dhamballa might have encountered the Spaniards en route," Seronga pointed out. "The two soldiers who invaded our camp were traveling independent of the others."

"That's possible," Aideen agreed. "At the very least, we should have been consulted about your plans."

"If the Spaniards had not engaged us, you would never have known about this," Seronga pointed out.

"If you had not kidnapped Father Bradbury, none of us would be in this situation!" Aideen snapped.

"That kind of lashing out is not going to help!" Seronga snapped back.

"You're right," Aideen admitted. "Let's deal with this. Were there any injuries?"

"There were four fatalities," Seronga told her. "Two of theirs and two of ours," he said.

Seronga could see Aideen regarding him in the green glow of the dashboard. Her expression was cold.

"Stop the truck," the woman said to Finn.

"What are you doing?" Seronga asked.

"I want *out!*" Aideen yelled. The woman turned in the cramped space of the cabin. She reached for the door handle. She reached out the window to open it from the outside.

Seronga reached across and grabbed her wrist.

"Let me go!" Aideen yelled. "I'm getting myself and my people out of here now."

"Wait! Listen to me!" Seronga said angrily.

"You treat people like bugs," she declared. "They bother you, you swat them. I won't listen to you. We won't be a party to that."

"It wasn't like that," he said. "The Spaniards came into our camp, armed for a fight. They tried to get away with Father Bradbury."

Aideen turned back to him. "What?"

"They broke into the shack where he was staying," Seronga said. "We cornered them with tear gas and attempted to apprehend them. We wanted to take them alive. If the Spaniards had surrendered, no one would have been hurt. They would have been held until it was feasible to set them free. Instead, they tried to shoot their way out."

"You're saying the Spaniards went ahead with a rescue attempt, even after we asked them to fall back?" she asked.

Seronga nodded.

"I can't believe that," she said.

"If you wish, you can speak to Father Bradbury yourself. He will tell you that he was removed and another was put in his place." Seronga held the radio toward her.

"I wouldn't know if it were really Father Bradbury or not," she said.

"I anticipated that," Seronga said. He took a scrap of paper from his shirt pocket. "I had my men provide me with the serial numbers of the Star 30PK pistols carried by the Spanish soldiers. You can relay those to your superiors. Have them check the numbers against the weapons that were issued to the soldiers. You will see I am telling the truth."

Aideen accepted the paper. "I will. It still won't prove your soldiers didn't hunt the men down."

"What did we have to gain?" Seronga asked. "We already had the priest. We did not need more hostages. We certainly did not need another reason for the Botswana military to move against us."

"I don't know about that," Aideen said. "Maybe you and your leader are developing martyr complexes."

"That is far from the case," Seronga replied. "For me, it's too late in life. And for Dhamballa, it is too early. He's only just begun his ministry. Maybe that is why I'm being so protective. He does not yet have the kind of following that will afford him protection from retribution."

"You might have told us all of this," Aideen said. "You could have taken us into your confidence."

"Sometimes people listen better after a thing is done," Seronga told her. "What is most important now is not what happened. What matters is what happens next. Dhamballa has left the swamp. That will leave the air patrol searching, but not for very long."

"We must convince them you still have the priest and will not harm him," Aideen said. "Will you turn him over, though?"

"That is for Dhamballa to say," Seronga told her. "But if you can hold them off, I will do as *I* promised. I will find a peaceable solution to this crisis. But neither the Botswana military nor the Spanish must attack my people."

"You were a soldier. Don't you know any people in the military?" Aideen asked.

"Some," he admitted.

"Can't you talk to them?"

Seronga smiled sadly. "Dhamballa represents change. Even if I could talk to my old friends, they stand to lose a great deal under a new government. They are not idealists. They are policemen."

"I understand," Aideen said.

Seronga apologized again for having acted without consulting Aideen. Then he had Finn catch up to the Jeep. Aideen rejoined her team. The two vehicles continued toward the rendezvous point.

The Brush Viper did not know if a nonviolent resolution were possible. The Botswanans clearly had an agenda. Perhaps the Vatican did as well. That was the elimination of possible insurgents.

There was only one way they could succeed, and Seronga would not allow that to happen.

For that, he would gladly give up his life. Not as a martyr, as Aideen had suggested, but as what he had always been: a soldier.

FIFTY-EIGHT

Washington, D.C.
Friday, 4:41 P.M.

Paul Hood, Bob Herbert, and Mike Rodgers were still in Hood's office, waiting for word from the field. Rodgers had spent the time studying computer files on the Botswana military. In case his people needed the information, Rodgers wanted to know the range, weapons configuration, and maneuvering capabilities of the helicopters. He also wanted to know how many men were on board each chopper. The answers were not encouraging. The Air Wing of the Botswana Defense Forces flew French Aerospatiale AS 332 Super Puma helicopters. They carried up to twenty-five troops each and could be configured to carry a variety of weapons. The choppers had a range of four hundred miles. That was enough to reach the swamp and then set out on a new search. If the squadron was traveling with a tanker ship, they could set off in another direction almost immediately.

Hood was on the phone with the president's national security adviser. Now that Americans were in a potential war zone, it was time to brief the White House.

"Where are the helicopters now?" Hood asked after giving the president an overview of the situation.

Herbert was looking at a radar feed into his wheelchair computer. "The choppers are holding their position at the edge of the swamp," he replied. "I'm guessing they were surprised by Dhamballa's change of plans."

"Mike, does that mean they'll have to turn back?" Hood asked.

"Not necessarily," Rodgers replied.

The general told him about the strengths and limitations of

the aircraft the Botswanans were using. Hood passed the information to the president. Hood told the commander in chief he would report back as soon as he had any news. Then he hung up and exhaled loudly.

"How did he take it?" Herbert asked.

"He does not want any of our people firing a shot," Hood said. "If for some reason they get snagged by the Botswanans, they're to go quietly."

"Go quietly and stay in prison so the Botswanans don't lose face," Herbert said. "Then, if we're lucky, Gaborone will believe they were tourists who got off track somehow."

"That's pretty much it," Hood said.

"Are you going to tell Aideen that?" Rodgers asked.

"What would you do?" Hood asked. "It's your operation."

"I'd tell them to do whatever is necessary to survive and exit," Rodgers replied. "I certainly wouldn't leave them defenseless."

"I agree," Hood said. "Aideen won't use violence unless it's absolutely necessary. And if that becomes necessary, the U.S. will have to deal with whatever happens."

"We all agree," Herbert said. " 'Out of chaos does come order.' "

"Or worse chaos," Rodgers said. "That's something Nietzsche and I never agreed on."

Herbert's mouth twisted, and he pondered that as Darrell McCaskey joined them.

"What's new on the Japanese front?" Hood asked him.

"Something that may or may not have any bearing on what's going on in Botswana," McCaskey said.

McCaskey appeared to have regained some of the old G-man steel. Rodgers was glad to see it.

"A group of Japanese tourists was stopped at customs in Gaborone three days ago," McCaskey said. "They were bringing all kinds of electronics into the country. The Botswanans let them in. According to the hotel records, two of the tourists never checked in. I tried to run them down but could not find them. However, two Japanese tourists did show up, renting a car in Maun. There was no record of those two having entered the country."

"You think they're the same people?" Hood asked.

"The timing works if they took the afternoon bus from Gaborone to Maun," McCaskey said.

McCaskey fell silent as Rodgers's phone beeped. The general answered immediately.

"Yes?" Rodgers said.

"It's Aideen," said the caller. "Two Spanish soldiers tried to rescue someone they thought was Father Bradbury. They were killed."

"Oh Jesus," Rodgers said.

The other men looked at him.

"The Vodunists lost two men," Aideen added. "The priest is still with Dhamballa."

"When did this happen?" Rodgers asked.

He noticed a crack in McCaskey's tough expression. Rodgers felt bad for him, but he could explain that nothing had happened to his wife. Not yet.

"The attack came at about eleven-thirty, local time," Aideen replied.

"After we called Kline," Rodgers said.

"That's right," Aideen said. "Seronga had left the priest and several men behind as decoys. The Spaniards went for it. I have serial numbers for the weapons they were carrying as proof."

Aideen gave Rodgers the serial numbers. He wrote them down. Rodgers immediately recognized the PK prefix as belonging to the Star pistols carried by the Spanish military. He confirmed to Aideen that, apparently, they had gone in. Rodgers covered the mouthpiece. He asked Hood to get Edgar Kline on the line.

"What is it?" Herbert pressed.

Hood held up a finger as Aideen continued.

"The Vodunists will allow the Botswana military or the VSO to talk to Father Bradbury, to prove that they have him," Aideen went on. "We are very much trying to find a nonviolent way out of this."

"Do you need to be involved in that?" Rodgers asked.

"I don't think Seronga can do it alone," Aideen said. "If the Botswana military shows up, my sense is that they'll shoot first and justify it later. But if they know that Father Bradbury is here and we are here—"

"Understood. How much time do you need?" Rodgers asked.

"About two hours," Aideen replied.

"I'll try to get that for you," Rodgers assured her.

"We should be linking up with Dhamballa in less than an hour," Aideen said. "Father Bradbury will arrive shortly after that. We will call you on this phone. You'll have to put him through to the authorities, convince them that he is well. If we can delay the attack, we can also prove that the Brush Vipers had nothing to do with the death of Bishop Max."

"I like it," Rodgers said. "What we don't know is whether that will satisfy Gaborone's needs."

"I'm hoping we can also get the Brush Vipers to disband," Aideen said. "I spoke with Seronga. I think they've had enough."

"All right," Rodgers said. "We'll work it on this end. Meanwhile, is everyone all right?"

"So far," she replied.

"Good," Rodgers said. "Hang in. I'll get word to Kline. And Aideen?"

"Yes?"

"If we can't pull this off and it gets hairy, you bail," Rodgers said. "All of you."

"We will," she promised.

Rodgers clicked off. He looked at McCaskey. "They're all right," Rodgers told him.

The former FBI agent eased visibly.

Rodgers looked at Hood. "Have you got him on the line?"

"He's coming," Hood said.

Rodgers asked Hood to put the phone on speaker. Rodgers briefed the others while he waited. He was just finishing when Kline picked up.

"What is it, Paul?" Kline said.

"No, this is Mike Rodgers. Mr. Kline, about forty-five minutes ago, two members of the *Unidad Especial* tried to take Father Bradbury by force," Rodgers told him.

"Are you sure?" Kline asked.

"Yes," Rodgers replied. "They were killed. So were two Brush Vipers."

"Bloody hell," Kline said.

"It must have been," Rodgers agreed.

"General Rodgers, you must believe me; I had no knowledge about the Spanish soldiers," Kline said. "They were ordered to stand down. The message we sent was received and acknowledged. I don't know what happened in the field. Perhaps the Brush Vipers were the aggressors."

"That isn't the story I was told, but it is not important at this moment," Rodgers said. "What I need you to do is keep the Spanish and the Botswana military away. You know we have people on site. They need two hours. They think the Brush Vipers can be persuaded to disband."

"General, I obviously didn't have a lot of pull with our people. I certainly don't have a lot of sway with Gaborone," Kline said. "None of us does. That was why we had to go to Spain in the first place. I also don't know if the Botswana government will accept a delay or even the surrender of Dhamballa. This isn't only about justice anymore. It's about seeming to appear weak. They can't afford that, especially if the Brush Vipers did in fact kill those Spanish soldiers."

"I understand," Rodgers said. "Which is why you have to convince Gaborone that if they attack, Father Bradbury will die. So will my people. Maybe it will help if you tell them that they are three American tourists who were picked up by the Brush Vipers."

Herbert shook his head vigorously. "Gaborone could use that kind of standoff for publicity," the intelligence chief said. "They may want to show off their hostage negotiating skills."

"At least it will hold off the attack," McCaskey said, "give our people a chance to get out."

"Maybe," Herbert said. "I agree with Edgar. At this point, I think the Botswana government feels it needs a show of force. A hostage situation will also cause questions to be asked about who the Americans are and how they got in. We can't risk that."

"Then call our team and tell them to cut loose," McCaskey said. "What else is there to do?"

"Running through the wilderness while Botswana pilots are looking for people running through the wilderness may not be the best course of action," Rodgers said.

"That is probably true," Kline said, "though I don't think they'll shoot at people who don't fit the profile of Brush Vipers."

"Aideen will concoct some story about being out on safari," Herbert said.

"They'll have a Jeep to prove it."

"Gentlemen, without saying anything about your people, I'll do what I can to settle the situation," Kline said. "I'll call you as soon as I have an answer."

"And try to make *this* order stick," Herbert said.

Hood had moved to kill the call as soon as Kline finished. He obviously expected Herbert to say something. Rodgers did not think the VSO officer heard. Not that he cared one way or the other. Kline had not proved to be a particularly effective partner.

"So this is where we've ended up," McCaskey said. He was not so much angry now as resigned. "They go forward, whatever the price."

"For now," Rodgers said. "Just for now."

"We just have to acknowledge that at this moment there are risks in flight," Herbert said.

"Darrell, you know what my orders are to Aideen," Rodgers said quietly. "If anything goes wrong, they *will* pull out. I'm sure they can find a place to hole up until the crisis passes."

"Maybe," McCaskey said. "And maybe Aideen and Battat will do that. I'm not so sure about Maria."

"They all will," Rodgers said. "If it comes to that, I will order it."

"More forcefully than you did before?" McCaskey asked.

"Yes," Rodgers replied. "I deferred to the judgment of the

individual running the mission in the field. The situation is different now. Anyway, you're forgetting something important, Darrell."

"What's that?"

"Maria loves you," Rodgers said. "She's committed to you. She wants to come back to you. If this thing goes south, she's not going to stay there just for the hell of it."

"No," McCaskey admitted. "She's not suicidal."

"She hasn't been married to you long enough," Herbert said.

Hood made a face. Herbert shrugged it off. But Darrell smiled for the first time in two days.

"I'll tell you what I'm afraid of," McCaskey went on. "We don't know what they're thinking in Gaborone. Father Bradbury may mean more to the Botswanans dead than alive. The air force can say they struck after he was killed. And Gaborone will use his death as an excuse to come down hard on any dissent in the future. If that's the case, they won't care who is with Dhamballa. The air force will go in and wipe them all out."

"I'll let Aideen know your concerns," Rodgers said. "We can prepare for that. Maybe put some distance between our group and Seronga."

"Mike, I'd like to do something else," McCaskey said.

"What's that?" Rodgers asked.

"I'd like to talk to Maria," he said.

"I don't think you should," Rodgers said. "Every time we speak with them, there's a chance we can be traced. We don't want to give the Botswana Air Force a map to where our people are."

"I'll keep it short," McCaskey promised. "Unless there's some other reason you're against it?"

"Frankly, there is," Rodgers admitted. "I don't want Maria getting upset or distracted. Not now."

"How about encouragement?" he said. "Maybe she can use some of that."

"Talking to you won't be a neutral event," Hood said. "You know that. Let's see how this plays out, okay? Maybe we can revisit it later."

McCaskey looked as if he wanted to argue. He thought better of it. Instead, he got up to go.

"Darrell, about those Japanese who went to Botswana," Hood said. "Any chance we can find out who they really are?"

"We're talking to a guy in Tokyo who deals in fake passports for the entire Pacific Rim," McCaskey said. "He wouldn't have actually made these, but he thinks he can find out who did. We'll get someone to talk to whoever that is, convince him to cooperate."

"I can save you the trouble," Herbert said. "My gut tells me these guys are working with Fujima."

"That could be true," Hood said. "Which brings us to the next obvious question. Why the hell are the Japanese so interested in Botswana?"

"I don't know," Herbert said. "But I am convinced of one thing."

"Which is?" Hood asked.

Herbert replied, "That a bunch of people are keeping some very big secrets from us."

FIFTY-NINE

Makgadikgadi Pan, Botswana
Saturday, 12:30 A.M.

Maria Corneja knew that she should not think when she was tired. At those times, her thoughts were cynical, pessimistic. And that was not what she needed now.

But she could not help herself. She was what she was.

The woman was still perched on the back of the Jeep. The wind was keeping her alert as she looked out at the extraordinary blackness. As vivid as the stars were, their indifference bothered her. They were the same as they had been when apes with no ambition crossed the salt pan. They would be the same when the earth was a dead ball.

So what are we all doing this for? she wondered. The stars will burn, the world will turn, and life will go on, whether we succeed or not. *If I were to leave now, nothing would change.*

Except for one thing. However impassive the universe was, Maria still had to face herself in the morning. And she wanted to be able to do so with a sense that she had been true to herself. Unfortunately, she was not quite sure what that meant in this case. She did not believe that Leon Seronga was a bad man. As far as she could tell, his tactics had not been excessive. And his ambitions seemed to be moral. Unfortunately, they were also illegal.

Still, she wondered what she would do when it came time. Even though she had worked for Interpol, she had never been a company player. It had always been a question of right versus wrong. Fortunately, Interpol had usually been on the side of right.

Then there was Darrell. He was probably insane with anger, worry, and resentment. Maybe he was even a little proud of

her, though that was probably buried deep. She refused to
think about any of that. If she let herself be influenced by his
emotions, her own would get fired up. This situation did not
need more passion. It needed as much calm reason as she could
summon.

As Maria's mind probed the blackness, her eyes did the
same. She was watching for the arrival of Dhamballa and the
Brush Vipers. It was not announced by lights on the horizon
but by Seronga's truck speeding up. Within moments, he had
pulled alongside the Jeep.

"My group is close by!" Seronga shouted. "They are less
than four miles from here, at Lake Septone. We will meet them
there."

"Have all the Brush Vipers arrived?" Aideen asked.

"Yes!" Seronga told her. "They are deploying themselves
among the rocks around the lake. You might want to pass that
along to your superiors. They can inform Gaborone."

"I wouldn't advise that," Battat said. "They might think it
was provocative rather than defensive."

Maria knew that it was both. Even if the Brush Vipers did
not intend to challenge the choppers, their action suggested
they were ready to do so. In Seronga's position, she would
have done exactly the same.

The truck pulled in front, and the Jeep followed. Obviously,
Seronga was no longer concerned about the Op-Center team
leaving. Perhaps he had decided to trust them. Decisions were
easy when there were no options.

They reached the lake in less than ten minutes. It was not
quite the fortress Maria had pictured. In the glow of the headlights she saw less than a dozen boulders the size of desk
chairs. They were clumped here and there where some ancient
flood must have deposited them. The lake itself was less than
a square mile. It did not appear to be very deep. Maria thought
she could see reeds jutting out from the center of the water.

As they neared the lake, the truck driver killed his headlights. Only the parking lights remained on. Aideen did like-
wise. It was a strange sensation to be moving through near-

absolute darkness. Yet the vastness of the land did not go away. The sounds from the vehicles seemed to travel forever. It was different than a sound that echoed from a group of trees or a canyon wall. It just rolled out and diminished slowly.

The truck stopped. So did the Jeep. Several lanterns were turned on along the lake. People were approaching. Seronga switched on his own flashlight and walked toward them.

Battat sidled up to Maria. Aideen joined them.

"How do you want to handle this?" Battat asked.

"I think that's up to Seronga," Aideen said.

"Shouldn't we be involved in the discussions?" Battat pressed.

"Yes," Maria agreed. "Before they become carved in stone."

She started forward briskly. The other two came after her. As they walked, it occurred to Maria that this was how warring tribes must have approached each other five thousand years before. She could not decide whether it was exciting to be a part of that history or whether it was sad because we had not advanced very much in all those centuries.

As they approached, Maria felt something in the air. It was an extremely low vibration, like the rumble from a subwoofer. It felt as if it were coming from the ground, but that was not the case. The ground was trembling slightly from whatever was causing her to shake.

What was just a hint of motion became more pronounced over the next few seconds. Maria stopped and looked up.

"Do you feel that?" she asked.

Aideen and Battat also stopped.

"I do now," Battat said. "Feels like a tank."

"Not a tank," Maria said.

They heard a low hum. She looked among the stars. Finally, she saw one that was moving.

"A scout," she said. "They sent out scout choppers."

She started running toward the lake.

"Seronga!" Maria shouted.

"I see it!" he shouted back.

"No lights!" he cried even louder. "Everyone shut their lanterns!"

Along the lake, the lanterns snapped off. But as the light in the sky grew larger and the sound became louder, Maria had a feeling they were too late.

SIXTY

Makgadikgadi Pan, Botswana
Saturday, 12:45 A.M.

Seronga knew what had to be done. He had one job, one goal. To save Dhamballa. And there was really just one way to achieve it.

The Brush Viper trotted toward the caravan. He shouted now and then to get his bearings. The other Brush Vipers would shout back. The roar of the rotors was not yet strong enough to drown them out. Their voices told him where he should be headed.

Seronga's one job was to protect the future of Vodunism. That was the only place the pure heart and soul of Botswana still survived. It had to be kept alive. To do that, Seronga needed to make certain that Dhamballa was not captured or killed. That meant holding off the assault and getting Dhamballa out of here. What Seronga did not know was whether Dhamballa would agree.

Seronga reached the nearest of the boulders. Pavant and Finn arrived a few moments later.

"There are three others coming behind us," he said as he moved past the guards. "Let them pass."

The men said they would.

A dozen yards beyond them, he saw the flickering of a shielded cigarette lighter. The face of Nicholas Arrons was behind it. He was the driver of the van in which Dhamballa was traveling. Seronga ran toward him. When he was a few feet away, the light flicked off. Breathing heavily from the short run, Seronga stopped by the front of the van.

"Do you hear that?" Seronga asked.

"Of course," Arrons replied. "A scout?"

"Very likely," Seronga said. "Where is the decoy group?"

"They left the swamp double-time and caught up to us about a mile back," Arrons replied. "They're resting by the lake. At least, they were. I'm sure they heard the helicopter."

"We'll have to deploy them in case we're strafed," Seronga said.

"I ordered the rocket launchers deployed," Arrons told him.

"No one fires unless we're fired upon," Seronga said.

"Those were my orders," Arrons replied.

"Where is the priest?"

"He is in the other van," Arrons said.

"Have Terrence bring him over," Seronga said.

"The ordeal in the swamp was difficult for him," Arrons said. "So was the drive here. He has not slept or eaten very much."

"There will be time enough for that soon," Seronga said. "Bring him to me now."

"Yes sir," Arrons said.

The soldier left, and Seronga stepped to the side of the van. Though they had been speaking by radio since Dhamballa broke camp, there was something different in Arrons's voice now. It was as though he were hiding something.

Seronga knocked on the door, then pulled it open. Dhamballa was sitting cross-legged on a mat. The interior lights had been covered with duct tape. Only a faint, muddy light illuminated the inside.

Seronga bowed his head slightly. There was no formal way to greet a *houngan*, but Seronga felt he needed something to show his respect. He had settled upon this.

"I'm glad you are safe, Dhamballa," Seronga said.

"What happened at the airport?" Dhamballa asked.

The beating of the rotor was getting louder. Seronga glanced back at the sky. The light was three times more brilliant than any of the stars.

"Sir, we can discuss this later," Seronga said.

"I must know," Dhamballa said.

The helicopter was now a steady drone. It seemed increasingly likely that the chopper had spotted them.

"I don't know," Seronga said. "Pavant and I were waiting for the bishop, when someone shot him. We don't know who that was."

Dhamballa stepped closer. He looked into Seronga's face, at his forehead, at the edges of his mouth.

"The bones told me that someone close will betray me, so I must ask again," Dhamballa said. "Either by action or by design, were you responsible for the death of the American bishop?"

"Neither I nor my soldiers had anything to do with the assassination," Seronga said. "We have not always agreed on policy, *houngan.* I would tell you if it were otherwise."

The Vodun leader regarded him for several seconds longer. "I believe you," he said.

"Thank you," Seronga said. He was glad, since he had no intention of adding to his answer. "Perhaps the betrayal came from the outside. From the men who were helping you to power."

"If so, I will find that out," Dhamballa said.

Maria, Aideen, and Battat walked up behind Seronga. Pavant and Njo Finn joined them.

"Mr. Seronga, we need to make some decisions," Aideen said.

"Yes," he agreed. He gestured behind him. "*Houngan,* during the past few hours, these people have helped us with information and planning. Maria was at the airport with me. She saw the killing and has evidence that will help authorities find the assassin."

"Arrons told me about these people and what they've done," Dhamballa said. "Thank you all."

"Sir, you can thank us by breaking up this party and moving out as soon as possible," Battat said.

"And what would we do?" Dhamballa asked.

They heard footsteps in the dark. Arrons was approaching from behind the car. He was bringing Father Bradbury.

"We believe there is a way to save the movement," Seronga said. "But to do so, we must have time. There are two ways to get that time. First, we must turn the priest over to these people. We must let the government know that we have released him. Second, you must go."

"Go where?" Dhamballa asked. He seemed genuinely surprised by the suggestion.

"Away from this area," Seronga said. "And quickly, sir. We are soon to have company."

"We have a rally scheduled," Dhamballa replied. "We cannot disappoint our people, show them cowardice. Now that we are together, I think we should turn around and trust in the gods to protect us."

"You will never *get* to the rally," Maria insisted. "The gods may protect your spirit, but I wouldn't bet on them against a 2.75-inch rocket."

"Seronga and his men will be with me," Dhamballa remarked. "They have arms. And I believe the government will not want a massacre. If those are not deterrent enough, we still have the priest."

"Holding Father Bradbury may not help you," Maria warned. "Not any longer. The outside world will perceive the incident at the airport as the onset of chaos. And your movement will be blamed."

"We are not responsible," Dhamballa said.

"Unfortunately, you won't have the opportunity to make that case," Battat told him. "Gaborone needs this situation to go away."

"Situation?" Dhamballa said. "Is that how the oldest religion on earth is perceived?"

"Not the faith," Battat told him. "The actions of the practitioners. Whether or not you killed the bishop doesn't really matter now. You kidnapped Father Bradbury. You precipitated this crisis. I know something about how blame works, and trust me. You will be blamed."

"We're wasting time," Maria cut in. "If that helicopter has seen you, it will signal the others. They will be here within an hour. You will all be arrested or cut down. There will be no rally."

Dhamballa turned to Seronga. "What do you say?"

"I believe these risks are very real, *houngan,*" he replied.

"If we are all dead, no one will be in a position to dispute what the government says. We must not give them the opportunity to take us down."

Arrons and the priest arrived.

"You're asking me to run," Dhamballa said to Seronga.

"Not run. Walk with dignity. Leave with these people," the Brush Viper said. "You and Father Bradbury. Maria knows we did not kill the bishop. Just by emerging from the salt pan, Father Bradbury will attest to the fact that while his stay may not have been pleasant, he is alive and well."

Father Bradbury had been looking at the others. His eyes stopped on Seronga.

"Those clothes," the priest said suddenly. "Where did you get them?"

Seronga did not answer.

"Where did you *get* them?" the priest demanded. "No, you don't have to tell me. I know. You got them from my deacons. You had to. If they had left Botswana, they would have taken their clothes with them. What did you do to them? Are they all right?"

Maria looked at the Brush Viper. "Seronga, *were* the deacons still at the church when you arrived?"

"Yes," Seronga replied.

"Where are they now?" she asked him.

Seronga wished there were time to explain what he had done. How this was a war and that lives are lost in war. How he needed information about Bishop Max and there was only one way to get it. How compassion would have cost them everything they had struggled to achieve.

He wished, most of all, that Dhamballa did not have to hear this.

"The missionaries are with their god," Seronga replied.

"By your hand?" Dhamballa asked. His voice was a whisper. If disbelief had a sound, this was it.

"Yes," Seronga said. "We killed them. We had no choice."

Dhamballa sat absolutely still. It was the posture of disbelief.

"Jesus wept," Father Bradbury said. He made the sign of

the cross, then tightly folded his bony fingers. "How many more people have to die for this insane crusade?" he asked. His hands began to shake. He glared at Dhamballa. "How can you call yourself a holy man when you *allow* things like this?"

"All religions kill!" Seronga yelled angrily. "When oppression cannot be stopped with reason, what other course is there?"

"Patience," Father Bradbury replied.

"For far too many years we were patient, priest," Dhamballa said. "But I did not want to advance our cause with the breath of the dying."

"No! Yet you knew it could happen when you surrounded yourself with soldiers," Seronga said. "There is not one person here, not one faith or government represented, who has not advanced an idea by killing."

The helicopter came lower, then hovered. A searchlight was turned on. They would spot the men in the boulders.

"Dhamballa, we must get you out of here," Maria said urgently. "You and the priest."

"Yes, you must go," Seronga agreed.

Dhamballa regarded his lieutenant. "What will you do? Fight?"

"No," he vowed. "I will lead the helicopters away."

"How?" Dhamballa asked.

"I don't have time to answer," Seronga said. "Maria, will you take them from here?"

"Yes," she said.

The Brush Viper regarded Dhamballa. "Sir, maybe we could have done things differently. All of us. Perhaps we took on too big a challenge. Or perhaps the faith was meant to stay underground. I don't know. But I *do* know one thing. You must continue what was very nearly begun here. You must carry it to others. You must live to speak of it."

"And pray for us, sir," Pavant added, his eyes on the sky. "Please do that as well."

Dhamballa nodded silently, sadly. "I will do all of those things." He looked at Seronga. "In the end, we must consider the future, not the past."

Maria stepped around Seronga. She reached into the van, her hand extended toward Dhamballa. He hesitated. Then he accepted her hand and stepped into the night.

"I'll bring the Jeep around," Battat said.

A gentle wind stirred from Seronga's left, from the west. It did not come from the rotor of the chopper. Dhamballa turned his face toward it. There was something poignant about the moment. The Vodun leader seemed to be saying good-bye and looking ahead at the same time.

Aideen took Father Bradbury by the arm and led him toward the Jeep. Pavant and Arrons left to join the other men. Only Maria was left. She turned her back on the men but did not leave.

Dhamballa kissed Seronga lightly on both cheeks. Then he pressed his left index and middle fingers to the Brush Viper's forehead. He drew the finger down along the bridge of Seronga's nose to his nostrils.

"May the gods look down and preserve you," Dhamballa said. He put a palm over his own eyes. "May they also forgive you."

"Thank you," Seronga said.

Dhamballa lowered his hand. He held it out, palm up, and exchanged a knowing look with Seronga. Then he turned and left with Maria. Seronga walked after Pavant. He stopped and turned back.

"Maria!" he shouted.

"Here!" she called back.

"Get home safely," he said. "All of you. And thank you."

"We will meet again, I hope," she replied.

The Brush Viper continued after Pavant. He did not believe that he would ever see Dhamballa or the others again. The helicopter spotlight was playing across the terrain, picking out the rock formations and studying them. The crew had to have seen the Brush Vipers.

Seronga would lead them away in a few minutes. Part of him hoped the helicopter followed. He did believe in Dhamballa and his work. He believed in it because he believed in Botswana. In Africa. In the people among whom he had lived and fought and laughed. He could not have asked for a more fulfilling life. Or, if it came to that, a more fulfilling death.

Prince Leon Seronga moved from one small group to the next. He told the men to get back into the vehicles and head north. He told them to move in different directions to make pursuit more difficult.

"What do we do if we are fired upon?" Arrons asked.

"I would prefer that you stay hidden and escape when you can," Seronga replied. "If necessary, fight back. If it is absolutely necessary, surrender."

"What will you do?" Pavant asked.

Seronga thought before answering. "I must clean the black magic from Dhamballa's hand," he replied.

"The killings?" Pavant asked.

"Yes."

"How can that be done?" Pavant asked.

Seronga smiled. "By me, and me alone. I want you to join the others before the helicopters arrive."

Pavant lingered for a moment. He saluted his commander with a sharp, clean snap. It was the first time that Seronga could remember Pavant saluting. Then he turned and ran into the darkness. Soon, all Seronga heard was the beat of the helicopter rotor and the growl of the engines as the trucks and vans slipped away.

He hunkered down beside one of the boulders. But he did not pick up any of the weapons. He simply watched the helicopter. And he made sure it saw him for a moment. Soon, other lights appeared in the distance. The squadron was coming. One of the helicopters would have to land to make sure this area was cleared of Brush Vipers.

It would be, very nearly.

Seronga unholstered his pistol and thought about the land. He thought about the night and about his life.

Seronga had no regrets. In fact, he felt surprisingly at peace. When all of this was done, his body would still be a part of this great continent. His spirit would be part of an eternal collective.

In the end, that was the most anyone could ask for.

After a few minutes, the scout helicopter landed. Troops emerged. They were fast-moving silhouettes in the bright searchlights mounted to the side of the chopper.

Seronga counted ten of them. The men went from rock to rock, securing each position. They were good, these kids. They moved well. He wondered how he would have fared if he were their age, competing with them.

Then the soldiers noticed the tracks of the vans. The men pointed to the north and northwest.

Eventually, the soldiers headed toward his position.

Seronga fired at the nearest soldiers. Not to kill. Not to wound. Simply to delay. They hit the ground, rolled behind the boulders, took shelter while they covered one another. These kids were very good. They belly-crawled to new positions so they could triangulate fire on the rock.

After a few minutes, it became clear that Seronga could delay no longer. He did not know if they would take him alive. He did know they would probably beat him for information. Or perhaps drug him. Only the latter scared him. He also knew what his fate would be for murdering the two deacons.

With gratitude for the life he had lived, Prince Leon Seronga put the barrel of the pistol to his temple.

He fired.

SIXTY-ONE

Washington, D.C.
Friday, 6:19 P.M.

The tension in the office was not like anything Paul Hood had ever experienced. Hood, Rodgers, Herbert, and McCaskey sat in their chairs, waiting. Lowell Coffey had joined them. No one was talking because there was nothing to talk about. There had been no further word about the Japanese or the Europeans. Everyone was focused on the situation in Botswana.

Hood could tell that Herbert was not comfortable with the silence. It was not in the man's gregarious nature to be silent among friends. After shifting in his wheelchair several times, Herbert finally spoke.

"When I was a kid, I saw a movie called *Sink the Bismarck*," the intelligence chief said. "I don't remember whether the movie was accurate or not, but there was this one scene that really stuck in my mind. The commander of the British naval forces was running the search-and-destroy operation from his underground HQ in London. After he gets word that the *Bismarck* has gone down, he looks at his watch. It's six o'clock. He's been working for days straight. He goes out for dinner and realizes it's actually six A.M. Time got totally screwed up for him down in the bunker."

Everyone was silent for a long moment.

"Are you saying that you're totally screwed up, Bob?" Lowell Coffey finally asked.

"No," Herbert said. "What I'm saying is that perceptions get warped when you're in a crisis situation. We're sitting here, cut off from other stimuli. No windows. No news about the world. No phone calls from friends or family. I don't know if that's a good thing."

"Whether it is or isn't, what choice do we have?" Coffey asked.

"I don't know, but we should talk to Liz about that," Herbert replied. "She should come up with some sort of activity or music or some feng shui decor that helps us keep perspective."

"Like floral pattern wallpaper," Hood said.

"I wouldn't go that far," Herbert cautioned.

"I tried taking my mind off things once by playing blackjack against the computer," Hood said. "I lost. It didn't make me feel any better."

"Losing at anything is not supposed to make a person feel good," Herbert pointed out.

"You did have one consolation, though," Rodgers said.

"What was that?" Hood asked.

"There was a Reset button on the game," Rodgers said. There was a whisper of bitterness in his voice.

"I don't think any of this is relevant," McCaskey said. "We have perspective, and we have direction and resources. What we don't have is a goddamn resolution. That's what makes a person nuts."

While McCaskey was speaking, Rodgers's cell phone beeped. He punched it on and simultaneously glanced at his watch. As he did so, Rodgers carefully noted the time.

"Yes?" Rodgers said.

"Good news," Aideen said. "we've got the priest, and we're on our way back to Maun. Dhamballa is also with us."

"That's great!" Rodgers said. "How is the team?"

The general saw McCaskey lean forward intently. McCaskey briefly put his forehead against his folded hands. Then he leaned back and looked over at Mike Rodgers.

"Everyone is fine here," Aideen told him.

Rodgers felt his chest grow lighter. He gave McCaskey a thumbs-up. The FBI liaison shut his eyes, threw back his head, and laughed.

"We just heard shots," Aideen went on. "We can only assume it's Leon Seronga. He stayed behind to cover our retreat."

"What about Father Bradbury?" Rodgers asked.

"He's a little shaky and says he could use a bath, but we think he's okay," Aideen replied.

"Did Dhamballa come willingly?" Rodgers asked.

That brought a surprised look from the others.

"He's *with* them?" Herbert muttered.

Rodgers nodded.

"Seronga convinced him that he had to leave," Aideen said. "I don't know what Dhamballa's plans are, though."

"Do you think Dhamballa will seek immunity?" Rodgers asked. He snapped his fingers at Coffey.

"I think he wants to stay here and try to relaunch his crusade," the woman replied.

"Just in case, I'll put Lowell on it," Rodgers said. "We'll have the process in motion."

Coffey nodded. He got out his cell phone.

"What is the status of the Brush Vipers?" Rodgers asked.

"When we left, they intended to go deeper into the salt pan," Aideen told him. "The idea was to lead the helicopters away from us."

Rodgers glanced over at NRO image on the computer. "Radar still has them moving north," he said.

"I'm glad to hear that," Aideen said. "We'll reach Maun well before the sun is up. Once we do that, we'll be in the clear."

"Aideen," Rodgers said, "we're all pulling for you. You've all done an amazing job over there, all of you. Thanks."

"We're kind of happy right now," she admitted.

"Tell Maria I love her," McCaskey said softly.

"Aideen? Is Maria available?" Rodgers asked.

"Yes, she is."

"Tell Maria her husband would like to speak with her," Rodgers said. He looked at his watch. He and Aideen had been on the phone just over a minute. Rodgers shot McCaskey a look. "He would like to speak with her for thirty seconds, tops," Rodgers added.

McCaskey got up quickly, and Rodgers tossed him the cell phone. McCaskey took it into the hall.

"That was nice," Hood said. "Thanks."

Herbert was visibly impatient. He was not usually sentimental. He was less so during a crisis. "Mike, what's happening out there?"

As Rodgers briefed the others, McCaskey returned. He lay a hand on Rodgers's shoulder and gently squeezed as he walked past. For a moment, all seemed right with the world.

Suddenly, Herbert glanced at the computer screen.

"Shit. They're changing course," the intelligence chief said.

The others gathered around Herbert's computer.

"See these two?" Herbert said. He pointed at a pair of blips. "They're moving southwest. That's the direction our people are headed."

"It could be just an exploratory thing," Coffey said.

"We could also have had the line open a little too long," Herbert said. "They may have triangulated the call."

It was possible. They had gotten sloppy and complacent. McCaskey might have stayed on just a few seconds too long.

"There aren't a lot of vehicles out there at night," Herbert said. "And our guys don't have a big head start."

Rodgers took the phone from McCaskey.

"Ideas, anyone?" Hood asked.

"If the military catches our people with Dhamballa, they're going to be screwed," Coffey said. "Abetting a revolutionary is not going to play well in a Botswana court."

"They can't be caught," McCaskey said.

"They won't be," Rodgers said. He called Aideen.

"What are you thinking?" Hood asked.

"I'm thinking we can get this to work in our favor," Rodgers replied.

SIXTY-TWO

Makgadikgadi Pan, Botswana
Saturday, 1:56 A.M.

Aideen Marley was sitting between Father Bradbury and
Dhamballa in the backseat of the Jeep. Battat was behind the
wheel, and Maria was beside him. They were thumping across
the terrain at a rapid pace. They had stopped just once, briefly,
to fill the tank from the gas can in the back.

The fog lamps threw wide, bright circles of light across the
immediate landscape to the front and forward sides. The brilliant lights blanched the dirt and shrubs. They looked almost
like black-and-white photographs.

Aideen was surprised when the cell phone beeped again.
She prayed that nothing was wrong. The last call had run a
little longer than the others. Not long enough for it to be triangulated, she hoped.

"Hello!" she said.

"We think you've been spotted," Mike Rodgers said.

Aideen covered her open ear with her palm. The Jeep was
making a lot of noise as it slammed across the uneven terrain.
She wanted to make sure she heard that correctly.

"Repeat?" she said.

"Several choppers are headed in your direction," Rodgers
said.

"Intent?" she asked.

"Unknown but unlikely to be moderate," Rodgers replied.
"I think I have a solution."

"Go ahead!" Aideen shouted.

"Your team and Dhamballa *must* exit the Jeep," Rodgers
told her. "Let Father Bradbury have it. Do you understand?"

"Yes," she said.

"When the Botswana army finds him, he must tell them he escaped," Rodgers went on. "He cannot say anything about you or Dhamballa. The rented Jeep won't be traceable. Elements of the Spanish army will probably get the credit."

"They can have it," Aideen said. She looked behind her. She thought she saw three stars moving slightly. They might be satellites. Or small planes.

Or they could be helicopters.

"You'll have to find some other way out of the salt pan," Rodgers said. "We'll see what we can do from this end."

"We'll figure something out," Aideen said. "I'll let you know what we're doing."

"Good luck," Rodgers said.

Aideen hung up. She tapped Battat on the shoulder and told him to stop at once. He did. He also killed the engine and the lights. The world grew dark. The sound of the nocturnal insects was strangely threatening. Aideen looked behind her. The movement of the lights were the same as the single helicopter had been earlier. She listened.

"What's wrong?" Battat asked.

"Do you hear that?" Aideen asked.

"Cicadas," Battat said.

"No, from the sky," Aideen said.

The woman heard a faint drumming sound droning far, far away. It had to be coming from the lights. They had to be helicopters. They were about twenty minutes away.

Quickly, Aideen explained the situation to the others. When she was done, she looked at Father Bradbury.

"Will you do it?" she pressed. "Will you leave us and take the Jeep?"

The priest looked at Dhamballa. "Will you swear to me on your gods that you had nothing to do with the death of my deacons?" Father Bradbury asked.

"Killing is against my beliefs. It is contrary to the white arts," Dhamballa replied. "I would never authorize such a thing."

"Then I will do what you ask," Father Bradbury said, looking at Aideen.

Aideen thanked him and got out of the Jeep. Dhamballa followed the woman out.

"How are we going to make sure we aren't killed ourselves?" Battat asked. "I was looking around as I drove. There were big eyes glowing behind foliage. A lot of them."

"I'll make sure you are all right," Dhamballa said.

"How?" Battat asked.

"Do you have a flashlight?" Dhamballa asked.

"Yes," Battat said.

He pulled one from the glove compartment, switched it on, and handed it to Dhamballa.

"We will use petrol," the Vodun leader said.

"For what?" Battat asked.

While the others climbed from the Jeep, Dhamballa went to the back. He reached into the open storage compartment behind the full-size spare tire. He removed the three-gallon tank of gasoline and unscrewed the top.

"Predators do not like the scent," Dhamballa informed him. "It resembles rotting meat. If you put some under your arms and along the front of your thighs, all but the carrion feeders will move on. And they are cowardly. You will be able to scare them off."

Aideen came over. "By shouting and that sort of thing?" she asked.

"Just so," Dhamballa said. He went over to Battat. "You will only need a little under the arms and inside the thighs."

Battat pulled a handkerchief from his pocket. He wadded it then allowed Dhamballa to splash on gasoline. He dabbed some where the Vodun leader had instructed. Aideen was next. She looked over at Maria, who was standing at the side of the Jeep.

"Maria?" Aideen said.

"I've been thinking," Maria said. "We may not have to stay out here for very long. Dhamballa, what is the best-known landmark in this area? A village, a mountain, a river. Anything."

"We are about two miles from Wraith's Point," he told her.

"It's a dried geyser that whistles when the sun and temperature go down."

Maria asked for the phone, and Aideen gave it to her. While the Spanish woman placed a call, Father Bradbury moved behind the wheel of the Jeep. He made sure he knew where all the controls were located.

Aideen stood behind the vehicle, watching the sky. The smell of the gasoline made Aideen dizzy. She breathed through her mouth to minimize the impact. The lights she had noticed before had doubled in size. The patting sound had grown louder. Aideen looked anxiously at Maria. She could not imagine what the woman was planning. Whatever it was, she hoped it happened very soon.

Suddenly, Maria shut the phone and strode over. She took the can of gasoline from Dhamballa and poured fuel onto her palm.

"We'd better get going," Maria said as she rubbed the gas on. "Those are definitely helicopters."

"Who did you call?" Aideen asked.

"The cavalry," she replied. "Let's go."

In Spain, Aideen had learned that it did not pay to try to pull information from Maria. Aideen would go along with this because they had no choice. Battat seemed too tired to argue. Nor was there time. They had to get away from the Jeep.

Aideen turned to Dhamballa. "Which way do we go?" she asked.

"To the southwest," the Vodun leader said. "I will leave you with this," he added and handed her the flashlight.

"Leave us?" Aideen said. "Aren't you coming?"

"No," he replied. "I go a different way."

"Where?" Maria asked.

"To a new beginning," he replied.

"You need not do this," Maria said. "I will tell them you did not kill the bishop."

"The bones have told me that someone betrayed us," Dhamballa said. "I must find out who that is. And *you* must go!"

"We will," Maria said. "Be careful."

Dhamballa thanked her. Then he walked over to Father

Bradbury. Aideen listened to the exchange as she, Maria, and Battat walked off.

"I am sorry for all that has happened," Dhamballa said.

"The truly repentant are forgiven," Father Bradbury replied.

"I do not require forgiveness from you or anyone," Dhamballa answered confidently. "But I *will* do things differently the next time."

"I hope you will," the priest replied. "There is room for your faith and mine to coexist."

"Not here," Dhamballa replied. "Not in Africa."

That was the last thing Dhamballa said before walking off in the blackness.

Aideen heard the Jeep as Father Bradbury started the engine. She turned back as the headlights came on and the priest sped into the night. Soon, the Jeep engine was a faint buzz, its lights lost in the distance.

The choppers sounded louder. They were nearly as loud as the locusts. Battat was looking toward the east as they walked.

"We may have dodged a bullet," Battat said. "The helicopters seem to be veering off."

Aideen looked over. Battat was right. She took a long, slow breath. Aideen had not realized how tense she was. Not until she felt the relief of seeing the helicopters following the Jeep.

It was strange. The three of them had accomplished far more than they set out to do. Yet Aideen could not help but feel a sense of defeat.

It was not just the blood that had been spilled. She could not shake the idea that something pure and fragile had been corrupted during these past few days. A vision. An idea. An *ideal*. Perhaps it was too old or too young to bear the weight that had been placed upon it. Maybe it had been polluted by politics and finance and having an army.

She did not know. All she knew was that this was not a victory.

For anyone.

SIXTY-THREE

Makgadikgadi Pan, Botswana
Saturday, 3:19 A.M.

Light.

Throughout this long and troubling night, the danger had all been about light. The searchlights of the helicopters in the sky. The hungry eyes of predators behind the scrub. Finally, after a long trek, Maria and her group were endangered by the failure of light.

The flashlight died nearly a half hour before Maria and the others reached the extinct geyser. Fortunately, Wraith's Point was appropriately named. The group was still able to locate it. The site howled deep and hollow. It reminded Maria of a strong canyon wind in the Pyrenees. The sound came intermittently, every minute or so. It was caused as gases baked underground throughout the day rose through the channels just below the surface. The group simply followed the sound. With nothing to create an echo, it was relatively easy to track the howling. They stumbled here and there over rocks and into gullies. But if there were any predators, Dhamballa's solution kept them away.

Aideen had asked Maria why they were going to the geyser. Maria told her. Aideen accepted the information without comment. Maria did not know whether the woman believed her. She did not know whether she believed it herself. Over the years, she had grown extremely skeptical about people and their promises. But cynicism did not mean having no hope. She had that.

When the three reached the mound, they stepped around it single file. They moved carefully, feeling their way as they went. They determined that the geyser mound was approximately twenty feet around and three feet tall. Up close, the howling sounded like someone was blowing into a giant bottle. Maria was surprised to find that there was very little outgassing from the geyser. It was primarily an acoustic phenomenon.

After rounding the geyser, the group sat. There was nothing else to do. Father Bradbury had been given the cell phone. By now, he was probably safe aboard the helicopter. Maria felt a great sense of accomplishment about that. But she also felt sadness for Dhamballa. He was a young man with a vision. Maybe he was too young to have carried this through. If his beliefs were as important to him as he said, he would be back.

Maria also felt bad for Leon Seronga. She did not imagine that he had survived the night. Someone had to take the fall for the deaths of the deacons and the killing of the *Unidad Especial del Despliegue*. He would not want the Brush Vipers to take that hit. They were protecting their leader. Presumably, the soldiers would all return to the lives they were living before the Vodun movement began. She did not know whether that was a good thing or a bad thing. Sometimes nations benefited from a good shaking. Maria came from a country that had its own active, separatist movement. As long as the challenge did not degenerate into anarchy, she found the process, the questioning, to be a healthy one.

But Maria felt good about what she and her colleagues had done. She enjoyed being in action, in a new environment. Yet there was also something disturbing about it. A familiar loneliness. A familiar weight. The responsibility of leadership, of getting friends and adversaries to do what you needed them to do. Maria wondered the same thing she had wondered when Darrell proposed this second time. Whether it was a good idea to continue carrying that load. The challenge was invigorating, exciting. Yet when that responsibility became too much, and it was time to put it down, she did not want to be alone.

That puts you right where you were when you said yes to Darrell, she realized.

They sat there in silence for forty minutes. There were no sounds other than the blasts from the geyser. There were no more lights moving in the sky. Their eyes were accustomed to the dark, and the stars were breathtaking. It was good to have this short stretch of peace.

And then there were two lights on the horizon. They were far away, moving toward them on the ground. If Maria was correct, they were lights that signified help, not danger. A few minutes later, there was sound.

"I don't believe it," Aideen said. She started to rise.

"Stay down," Battat said. "We don't know who it is."

"David is right," Maria said. But she rose anyway. She brushed off the dirt of the mound as she walked slowly toward the oncoming lights. Maria did not think it was a military vehicle. They would most likely be traveling in pairs for protection. It could be a ranger on patrol for poachers. Or it could be a tour group out on a real safari, not one of those luxury trips. They might be heading for a site to watch the sunrise.

But it was none of those. It was a taxicab.

It was Paris Lebbard.

The taxi bounced forward and pulled to a stop near the geyser. Maria walked over as Lebbard rolled down the window. She could see his face in the wide glow of the headlights. He was smiling broadly.

"Thank you," she said.

"You are very welcome." Lebbard beamed. "This is going to cost you a great deal."

"Doesn't it fall under the day rate I paid you?" she asked.

The Botswanan shook his head. "This is a new day, my friend."

"True enough," Maria replied. "I will pay, and I thank you anyway, Paris. You saved our lives."

"Several times today," Lebbard pointed out. It was a proud statement not a boast.

The others had walked over. Maria introduced them by first name. Lebbard invited them to get in the back.

"You smell of petrol," Lebbard said as Maria got in beside him.

"Animal repellant," she replied. "It's probably a good thing I gave up smoking."

Lebbard swung the taxi around, and Maria slumped in her

seat. She was spent. Her mind immediately lost the focus to which it had clung for so many hours. She found herself feeling detached from the others. They were not the familiar faces from Interpol. And what was this place? The salt pan, even Maun, were not the well-known streets of Madrid or the outlying cities and towns and mountain roads. And she had never smelled like this.

It was all very disorienting. Maria had never worked set hours. It was always on a case-by-case basis. But maybe she needed structure more than she had ever imagined.

There will be time enough to consider all that, Maria told herself. To think about the past and the future. Right now, she needed to rest.

She did not close her eyes, but she closed her mind. And for the moment, that was enough.

SIXTY-FOUR

Gaborone, Botswana
Saturday, 6:09 A.M.

Henry Genet watched the sun rise.

The Belgian diamond merchant was sitting in a comfortable armchair in his room at the Gaborone Sun Hotel and Casino on Julius Nyerere Drive. He was drinking coffee he had made in the in-room coffeemaker. His chair was angled so that he could see both the sun and the imposing National Stadium, which was located to the southeast.

There were no swarming or biting insects. There were no birds or amphibians vocalizing. Just the hum of the air conditioner, which was turned on high. This was far, far better than the hut and canvas cot he had been forced to endure in the swamp.

If only things had worked out differently.

Genet had flown back to the city in his small plane. Then he had come here to wait for a flight to London on Monday. He had left the camp harboring doubts about whether Dhamballa would be able to reach the mine for his rally. Upon reaching the hotel, he turned on the radio. There was news about a showdown on the salt pan. It claimed that the abducted Catholic priest had been rescued. The report also quoted the military commander in Gaborone as declaring that the Brush Vipers had been dispersed and their leader slain. He concluded by saying that the "minor cult leader" Dhamballa had disappeared. Officials presumed that he was in hiding and would probably attempt to flee the country. The government wanted to reassure everyone that order had been restored.

Of course they did, Genet thought.

But they were wrong.

Genet took a sip of coffee from the white ceramic cup. He contemplated the things that he and his partners would be doing over the next few months. These things would have been quicker and easier with a revolution in Botswana. A revolt that would have spread to South Africa and the rest of the African nations. A war that would have required countless weapons and ammunition provided to both sides by Albert Beaudin. A war that would have given Genet and his partners the diamond mines as well as access to countless ore-producing sites.

A war that would have given them the money to ramp up for the bigger war they hoped would come. That war would have left them poised to become one of the most powerful military-industrial consortiums in world history.

Now Beaudin and his people would have to settle for something else or find another way.

Genet was tired, but he could not go to sleep. He had to call his partners in Paris. They had to be informed, before they heard it on the news, that they had failed to put a puppet in a place of power. Genet was bracing himself to make that call. This operation was under his direct supervision. Beaudin and the others would not be pleased.

Beyond the failure to elevate Dhamballa, what bothered Genet most was what *did* happen here. The Brush Vipers had not assassinated the American bishop. His own people had not killed him. Theoretically, the Vatican could have shot him to rally support. But apart from being against God's law, a move like that would be politically insane. If it were ever revealed that the Church had acted, they would be crippled for decades. Perhaps the Chinese had some idea who had done it. Beaudin would have to ask his contacts there. If they would speak with him. For they, too, lost with the failure of the Vodun movement. They were going to share in the growth of Beaudin's industries. Many of the new factories would have been located in China. Beijing would not only have earned profits, they would have benefited from the development of new weapons.

Genet looked at the clock on the nightstand. It was nearly six-thirty. He would place the call at seven. Beaudin would just be waking up then to check the stock markets in Asia.

The diamond merchant took another swallow of coffee. He glanced at the package he had made it from. Ironically, it was a French blend.

Henry Genet's world seemed strangely inverted. He had no idea how the Group would proceed. Yet he still knew one thing.

He knew how the matter would end.

SIXTY-FIVE

Washington, D.C.
Saturday, 12:52 A.M.

After Rodgers had placed the call to Aideen, the ventilator died in Hood's office.

"Overworked from all that musk and testosterone we've been pumping out," Herbert deadpanned.

More likely it was something that hadn't been updated when the former Cold War command center was renovated for Op-Center. Hood, Rodgers, Herbert, McCaskey, and Coffey moved into the Tank. The conference room had more space and more phones. Also, it had been renovated. Hood should have shifted there in the first place. But they had all been too caught up in the moment to move. They grabbed sandwiches from the vending machine down the hall and talked about anything else while they waited to hear from one of the three members of the group. Some of them checked E-mail. Knowing that Aideen no longer had the cell phone made it worse. At best, they would hear nothing until the operatives reached Maun. With luck, that would happen around two-thirty.

Hood had received E-mails from his son Alexander. That was how the boy communicated when his father was tied up. They had a separate life together on-line. Different topics and a different language. Even a different relationship than they had when they were together physically. Alexander was more serious on-line, and Hood more flip. It was strange. Hood knocked out some quick responses so the boy would have them in the morning.

The first call that came through to the Tank was from Edgar Kline. Hood put the VSO officer on speakerphone. The Vatican Security officer was calling to inform them that Father

Bradbury was located by a Botswana military helicopter. He was safe.

"I wanted to thank you all," Kline said. "Especially you, Bob and Paul. I know we had some disagreements along the way, but I hope that won't stand in the way of future cooperation."

"Every family has its disputes," Hood replied. "The point is, we are still family."

Herbert made a face. He moved both of his fists up and down. He was right. But this was how the game was played, and Herbert knew it. And in the end, the results were what mattered.

"Against the odds, your people secured Powys Bradbury's freedom," Kline went on. "You probably saved his life."

"Thank you, but we don't know that Father Bradbury's life was in danger," Hood cautioned.

"Perhaps he would not have been murdered as the bishop was," Kline acknowledged. "But I am informed that he had been tortured and looked deathlike. We cannot be certain he would have died without you. But we are certain, now, that he will live."

"I'll grant you that," Hood said. "I'll also pass your thanks along to the others."

"I also want you to know that a Botswana patrol has found Leon Seronga," Kline reported. "He is dead."

"By whose hand?" Hood asked.

"He took his own life."

"Are they sure?" Herbert asked.

"They're very certain," Kline replied. "He took a single gunshot wound to the temple. He must have known it was over. Or maybe he was trying to keep the government from interrogating and trying him."

Hood looked at Herbert and Rodgers. Obviously, they were all thinking the same thing. Leon Seronga did that and more. He fell on his sword for Dhamballa. He had given the government of Botswana a fall guy. They could blame this on him and present his death as the end of the threat. There could be an immediate return to normalcy.

Kline had nothing else to say. He asked to speak with the three field operatives as soon as possible. The Vatican wanted to convey their thanks to them personally. He was sure Father Bradbury would like to do that as well. Hood promised to make that happen.

"What about you?" Kline asked. "Do you have any further information on the murder of Bishop Max or about Dhamballa?"

"No," Hood replied. "Not a thing."

There was a short silence. Hood had learned to read the silences of foreign officials. It meant that they did not believe the last thing you had said, but they were too diplomatic to tell you so.

Having made his point, Kline thanked them all again and hung up.

"Yeah, friend. We're gonna tell you that we let Dhamballa walk off into the sunset," Herbert muttered.

"To tell you the truth, I'm not sure we did the right thing there," McCaskey said.

"We established our mission parameters, and we stuck to them. Our people are safe, and they're coming home. We did the right thing," Rodgers declared with finality.

"We also lost an opportunity to establish close ties with the Botswana government," McCaskey pointed out. "In the end, that kind of relationship can prove extremely useful."

"Especially if it turns out that something else is going on in that region," Herbert said.

"Then we would have had to tell them why we were there and how we got in," Hood reminded them.

"That would not be a basis for establishing trust," Rodgers said.

"Trust is not a factor in this, Mike," McCaskey said. "*Need* is a factor. If they need us, the rest is irrelevant."

"We can go to the Botswanans when this done, make fresh overtures," Hood said. He winked at McCaskey. Things had gotten tense again between the former G-man and Rodgers. Hood wanted to take the edge off. "You can do that when you go to collect Maria. Make it a belated honeymoon."

"That would be nice," McCaskey admitted.

"What would be nice is figuring out where the Japanese fit in all this," Herbert said.

"We also have to get that information out somehow," Coffey said. "Let people know that the Brush Vipers did not kill the bishop. I don't know if I sympathize with Dhamballa and Leon Seronga. I certainly don't like what they did. But they should not take the rap for something they did not do."

"I agree with you one hundred percent," Hood said. "We have to try to clear them and at the same time gather evidence about how and why the Japanese are tied to this."

"What a time to not have a press department," Herbert remarked. "Ann would have come up with some good ways to leak this."

"My staff can handle whatever needs to be presented to the media," Coffey remarked.

"Yeah, but Ann Farris had panache," Herbert said. "She presented things to the media from ten different directions. From here, through the newspapers, on radio talk shows. It was a coordinated assault."

"Bob, we'll figure out how to do it," Hood said.

"Maybe Ann will consult," Herbert suggested.

"We'll get it done," Hood assured him. He looked away. He did not want to think about Ann Farris. That was both a personal and a professional issue. He had no time for it right now.

The phone beeped. Hood grabbed it. "This is Hood," he said.

"Paul, it's Aideen."

"Talk to me, Aideen!" Hood said.

"We made it," she told him. "We are in Maun."

Hood did not realize how tense his shoulders were until they relaxed. The others in the room cheered.

"Did you hear that?" Hood asked.

"I did," she said.

"How are you?" Hood asked. "*Where* are you?"

"Paris dropped us at a hotel—the Sun and Casino. There are rooms. We're taking one."

"Be our guest," Hood said.

"We will be," Aideen replied.

"Everyone come through all right?" Hood asked.

"We're tired, but that's it," she said. "Hold on. Maria would like to talk to her husband."

Hood punched off the speaker. He transferred the call to McCaskey's station. The other men rose. They left the Tank to give McCaskey some privacy.

Coffey and Herbert left to go home. Rodgers turned to go. Hood lay an arm on his shoulder.

"You did a great job, Mike," Hood said. "Thank you."

"They did it," he said, pointing to the Tank. "The people overseas."

"You picked them, you sold them on it, you ran it," Hood said. "You did a helluva job. This is going to work. The human intelligence team is going to knock some heads together out there."

"I believe you're right about that, anyway," Rodgers replied.

"Go home," Hood told him. "Get some rest. We'll need it for the wrap-up tomorrow."

Rodgers nodded and left. Hood noticed that, tired as Rodgers was, his shoulders were strong and straight, just as they must have been when he was a recruit at the age of nineteen.

As Hood was about to leave, McCaskey emerged. He looked like a kid on the night before Christmas.

"Good talk?" Hood asked.

"Yeah," McCaskey said. "Real good. Maria sounds absolutely drained but satisfied."

"She should be," Hood said. "They did an amazing job over there."

"She wants to come home as soon as possible," McCaskey went on. "I'm going to fly to London and collect my wife."

"Great," Hood said. He felt a stab of sadness. He was going to go home to an empty apartment.

McCaskey's eyes became wistful. "Listen, I'm sorry about the way I've been acting since this started. It hit a primo sore spot—"

"Don't apologize," Hood said. "I've got 'em, too. We all

do." He smiled. "The important thing, Darrell, is that we learned something very important."

"What's that?" McCaskey asked.

"How *not* to engage HUMINT operatives in the future," Hood replied.

McCaskey smiled and left. Hood went back to his warm office. He took an old fan from the closet, set it on the floor beside his chair, angled it up, and turned it on. It felt good. If he shut his eyes, he could imagine he was on the beach in Carlsbad, California, where he used to go with young Harleigh and Alexander. They would stroll along the miles-long concrete seawall, occasionally going down to the beach to sit, drink, or watch for dolphins.

Where did those breezy, innocent days go? How did he end up alone? How did he land in the windowless basement of an old military building, leading a team of military officials, diplomats, and intelligence officers, trying to put out fires around the world?

You wanted to get out of politics but still do something important, he reminded himself.

Well, Paul Hood got that. He also got the pressures and demands that came with that challenge.

Yet there is also deep, deep satisfaction, he had to admit. And this moment was one of them.

But now it was time to get back to work. Before Hood left for the night, he wanted to send Emmy Feroche an E-mail to thank her for her help and tell her not to worry about Stiele, for now. Then, after a long night's sleep, there was a conversation he had to try to have. A chat with the man who probably knew much more about this situation than he had let on: Shigeo Fujima. Hood suspected that, at best, the conversation would go something like the talk with Edgar Kline. On topic without being particularly illuminating.

Only this time, it would be Paul Hood generating those carefully measured pauses.

SIXTY-SIX

Tokyo, Japan
Monday, 3:18 P.M.

The red telephone beeped in Shigeo Fujima's office at the Ministry of Foreign Affairs.

The head of the Intelligence and Analysis Bureau had no intention of answering it. Not unless the call came in on his private black line. Fujima was waiting to hear some very specific information. Without that information, other conversations were not relevant. Nor were they of any interest at the moment. Fujima's deputies could handle those.

The young, clean-cut intelligence officer was smoking an unfiltered cigarette. He sat with the phone headset resting on his head as he looked at a map of Botswana on his computer. The map was marked with symbols signifying copper, coal, nickel, and diamond mines. China produced a great deal of coal. But those other assets would have been useful to them. The map was also marked with red flags. Those were targets he had hit. One at the airport in Maun. The other, a psy-ops strike, at Dhamballa's camp in the Okavango Swamp. His people had used a laptop to re-create Seronga's voice, using taped radio communiqués. Communiqués that also enabled them to pick up the password. Then they had broadcast their own message to Dhamballa, that Seronga had been the one who killed the American bishop.

That had put doubt in Dhamballa's mind about the loyalty of Leon Seronga. If the Botswanans had not brought Dhamballa down, Fujima had to make certain that the cult itself was unstable. The Vodunists could not have been allowed to succeed with what they were planning.

Now, just two things remained:

First was to make sure that both the Europeans failed. That was an easier task.

Then there were the Chinese. That would take more time, but it must be done. Beijing and Taipei were an even greater threat.

The outside line kept beeping. Fujima used one cigarette to light another. He looked at his watch. It was about eight A.M. in Botswana. The operatives should have reached the target by now. They tracked him from the swamp, first by boat and then by air. They should have found him.

And then the call came. Fujima continued to smoke as he punched the button to answer. He inhaled quickly, then blew out smoke to relax.

"Mach two," Fujima said, using the code word that was changed daily. "Go ahead."

"I would recognize that exhaling of cigarette smoke even if you did not use the code word," the caller remarked. "So might an enemy, if he were using my secure phone."

"Point taken," Fujima said. That was the trouble with so many field agents. They had to be invisible and silent most of the time. When they got a chance to speak their mind, they did. Agent Kaiju was no exception.

"We found him," Kaiju went on.

"Where?" Fujima asked. As the intelligence director spoke, he accessed a drop-down menu of the cities in Botswana.

"City one, sector seven," the caller reported.

"I'm there," Fujima replied. The Belgian was in Gaborone near the athletic stadium. He dragged silently on his cigarette. Then he exhaled from the side of his mouth.

"He is in a hotel," Kaiju informed him. "The sign is in English. I cannot read it."

"The Sun and Casino," Fujima told him, consulting the map. "That's the only one in the area."

"Very good," the caller said. "What do we do?"

Fujima thought for a moment. "Debrief and neutralize," he replied.

Kaiju repeated the instructions. Fujima acknowledged them.

He hung up and promised to call back when he and his partner had more information.

Fujima sucked hard on his cigarette. He blew out angrily. He did not like to authorize killings. But surgical eliminations were sometimes necessary to prevent greater loss of life in the future. It was made easier by the fact that the target was someone who had helped to create the current chaos.

But even with that accomplished, Fujima did not imagine that the looming crisis would go away. All the interrogation would give them was more information, more time to plan a response.

His telephone continued to beep. Fujima continued to ignore it. He had not slept in over a day, and he was tired. He did not want to slip and say something he would regret.

Instead, the intelligence director punched out his cigarette. He sat back in his high leather chair, closed his eyes, and waited. He waited to hear that this part of the mission was at last concluded. Though the respite, he suspected, would be a short one.